KNIGHT ERRANT

THE NOBLE KNIGHTS of Bretonnia are bound by duty and honour to fight for their king, and defend their lands from invaders.

With their father, the Lord of Bastonne, grievously ill, his two sons Calard and Bertelis are left to uphold the glory and honour of their line. When a horde of goblins swarms out of the Forest of Châlons, the knights are summoned to Bordeleaux to gather their forces and repel the foul beasts. Little do they realise, though, that the true enemy has yet to reveal itself. Deep in the arboreal gloom, something is stirring: a deadly foe that will bring the land of Bordeleaux to its knees and reveal a terrifying secret from Calard's past.

D0911372

By the same author

WARHAMMER

MARK OF CHAOS
EMPIRE IN CHAOS

WARHAMMER 40,000

DARK APOSTLE

A WARHAMMER NOVEL

KNIGHT ERRANT

ANTHONY REYNOLDS

To the beautiful and talented Serena, for your boundless love and for helping me battle through the Realm of Chaos...

A BLACK LIBRARY PUBLICATION

First published in Great Britain in 2008 by
BL Publishing,
Games Workshop Ltd.,
Willow Road, Nottingham,
NG7 2WS, UK

10 9 8 7 6 5 4 3 2 1

Cover illustration by Alex Boyd
Map by Nuala Kinrade.

A CIP record for this book is available from the British Library.

ISBN 13: 978 1 84416 551 3
ISBN 10: 1 84416 551 5

Distributed in the US by Simon & Schuster
1230 Avenue of the Americas, New York, NY 10020.

See the Black Library on the Internet at
www.blacklibrary.com

Find out more about Games Workshop
and the world of Warhammer at
www.games-workshop.com

THIS IS A dark age, a bloody age, an age of daemons and of sorcery. It is an age of battle and death, and of the world's ending. Amidst all of the fire, flame and fury it is a time, too, of mighty heroes, of bold deeds and great courage.

IN THE WEST of the Old World lies Bretonnia, a fabled land of magic and chivalry. It is also a land of honour and virtue, where noble knights of the realm keep their domains safe as their peasants till the fields, where knights errant strive to win their spurs in battle and where questing knights venture in search of the most holy of artefacts – the grail. For it is said to sup from this most holy chalice a knight will become more than just a hero, he will become a saint.

UPON HIS THRONE in the city of Couronne sits King Louen Leoncoeur, just ruler of Bretonnia and its greatest champion. By the will of the Lady of the Lake, beneficent deity of all Bretonnia, by lance and sword, are the lands of the king kept safe from greenskins and the mutant beastmen of the darkling forests, from malicious daemons and the walking dead.

AS THE TIME of battle draws ever nearer, Bretonnia will need its heroes like never before.

Bretonnia

The Battles of Gilles the Uniter

City-port or Walled Town

Major Castles

PROLOGUE

A CLAMOUR OF rooks erupted from the branches, filling the air with raucous cries. Unnerved, the destrier tossed its head, snorting.

The knight calmed the warhorse with a word and guided it deeper into the forest. Twigs like talons scratched against his heavy plate armour, and an icy breeze made the skeletal limbs of the trees shiver.

A second horse whinnied, stamping its hooves. The knight turned in the saddle to regard his hooded companion. With a sharp jerk on the reins, the man brought his steed back under control.

'I'm sorry, my lord,' the hooded figure breathed.

Without a word, the knight turned and continued on. He cast his eyes heavenward, peering through the thick mass of branches overhead. Darkness was falling swiftly, and the first stars could be seen flickering in the deepening colour of the sky. There were scuffling noises in the undergrowth from unseen creatures, and a fox, startled, turned its sharp features towards the knight. It froze for a moment, its nose twitching, before it disappeared into a thick tangle of brambles. Wolves howled in the distance as, somewhere, a new hunt began.

The eyes of small, scurrying creatures glinted in the dim light as the riders guided their horses ever deeper into the forest. This was not a place where men were common, and the trees groaned and creaked as they leant over these intruders into their ancient realm. The knight stared resolutely forward, one gauntleted hand resting upon the pommel of his sword.

As the last colour in the obscured sky succumbed to darkness, the pair entered a small clearing. The rotting, swollen bole of a tree lay uprooted on the soil, exposed roots hanging heavy with dirt. The fallen tree had created a small glade, and an abundance of new plant life strained up towards the gap in the canopy.

'This should be far enough, my lord,' said the hooded figure, eyeing their back trail, ensuring that they had not been followed.

The knight nodded curtly, and lowered his armoured weight from the saddle. He crushed a tiny sapling underfoot as he stepped down onto the wet earth. The plaintive cry of a newborn came from the swaddled shape bundled against his breastplate.

His face grim, the knight stepped towards the bole of the fallen tree. Its bark was rotten, and clusters of mushrooms clung to its moist sides like limpets. Insects rustled through the rotting leaf-litter, and worms writhed in the rich soil.

As his hooded companion looked on from horse-back, the knight unhooked the sling from around his shoulder and lifted the newborn away from his chest. His expression hard, he placed the swaddled babe upon the ground before the fallen tree. It was tightly wrapped in linen, its round face all that was exposed to the chill air.

In one swift motion, he drew his sword.

The newborn cried out once more, and the knight closed his eyes tightly against the sound.

'Lady, give me strength,' he whispered, his voice hoarse and strained. He lifted his sword before him, gripping the hilt with both hands, and placed a kiss against the cold metal blade.

Reversing his grip, he stepped towards the newborn. Holding the sword downwards like a dagger, he placed the tip of the blade against the babe's swaddled breast. His armoured fingers flexed on the hilt, and he looked down into the face of his son.

The babe gurgled up at him, and he felt his heart wrench. Steeling himself, he lifted the blade up, ready to plunge it down in the killing blow. There the sword hung poised, trembling slightly. A tear ran down the knight's cheek, and he clenched his teeth.

'Do it,' urged his hooded companion.

With a violent surge, the knight plunged the blade down.

He sank to his knees, shoulders slumped. The sword was embedded deep in the earth, the babe unharmed.

'My lord, you must finish it,' snapped his hooded companion. 'It must die, you know this.'

Opening his eyes, the knight looked into the angelic face of his child.

'No,' said the knight forcefully.

'But…' began his companion, but the knight turned and silenced him with a glare.

'Forgive me, Lady,' the knight whispered, standing and pulling his sword from the ground.

All semblance of purity was sloughed off as the babe's face twisted into a sudden snarl. Its lips parted, exposing an array of tiny, barbed teeth, and it hissed up at its father like a feral wolf cub.

The knight turned away from the newborn, full of revulsion. Walking to his warhorse, he remounted. Without a backward glance, he rode away, his hooded companion behind him.

In the darkness of the trees, hateful eyes watched the departing figures. Only when they were long gone, leaving just a lingering scent on the air, did the eyes flick towards the tiny, abandoned newborn.

Then the beasts of the forests crept from the darkness and moved towards the infant.

CHAPTER ONE

CHLOD BLINKED THE sleep out of his eyes and sat up. He was beneath a rotting wagon, his companions sprawled around him, clustered together for warmth under the damp blanket they shared.

He looked around the small clearing, seeing it in daylight for the first time, for they had hauled the wagon here the previous evening. A low fog hugged the ground, and long stems of grass glistened with the heavy morning dew.

Chlod grinned as he pulled a small, squirming shape from within a deep pocket. Lifting it to his misshapen face, he smiled as the whiskers of the scrawny black rat twitched in the cold air.

Producing a small piece of stale biscuit from his pocket, Chlod took a bite before offering the crumbling remains to the rat. It eagerly grabbed the food in its paws, and began gnawing at it frantically. Chlod grinned again.

'You feeding that damn rat again?' said a muffled voice from beneath the blanket.

Chlod held the half-starved creature protectively to his chest.

'He's mine,' he grunted, too loudly. 'There is enough food.'

Muffled protests came from under the blankets as Chlod's harsh voice disturbed the others' slumber.

He made a face in the direction of the voices, and turned his attention back to the rat. It had finished its meal and its head was lifted high, nose twitching as it sought more sustenance, making Chlod grin once again. He twitched his own nose in imitation, puckering his lips and showing his crooked, yellow teeth. He extended one stubby, dirty finger to the animal, and it gripped his short-bitten nail, sniffing. Finding nothing edible, it wriggled free of Chlod's grasp and leapt from his hands. He frowned, and snatched at it, but it was quick, and burrowed beneath the dank blanket. Chlod's pink, slug-like tongue emerged from the corner of his mouth as he struggled to grab it.

There was an irritated groan at the sudden movement, and an elbow jabbed into Chlod's ribs, making him scowl darkly. He balled his thick sausage-fingers into a fist and thudded a punch into the shape beside him in retaliation, which was met with more protests from the others as they woke. They shifted their positions, and pulled the blankets tightly around them against the cold.

Having regained his hold on the rat, Chlod shoved it roughly back into the deep pocket on his stained tunic front, and crawled awkwardly out from the tangle of bodies. Curses and groans emerged from under the blanket as he made his ungainly progress out from beneath the rotting wagon.

Blinking against the dull pre-dawn light, Chlod blew out a long breath that fogged the air in front of his face. He shoved a hand down the front of his patch-work trousers and scratched at the lice in his nether regions.

He stamped his feet against the icy cold. A thick mist surrounded him on all sides, so that he could see barely ten yards. Ghost-like trees loomed like wraiths through the wet fog, and Chlod limped over to check on Beatrice.

'How are you this fine morning, my beauty?' he grunted as he approached Beatrice. She lifted her heavy head in response, her beady eyes fixing on the approaching peasant. Seeing nothing that interested her, her head slumped back down into the wet earth.

Chlod bent down and scratched her between the ears. She endured his attention, studiously ignoring him. The swine wore the peasant group's best blanket over her back, and Chlod gave her one final, solid pat before rising once more.

He limped towards the still-smouldering fire pit, over which was spitted the remains of the previous night's feast. Chlod's belly was fuller than he could ever remember, and he patted it contentedly. Life was good, he decided.

He opened up the flap of his trousers and sighed contentedly as he emptied his bladder onto the smouldering ash. Steam rose from the thick yellow stream, and the fire pit hissed. Chlod hummed tunelessly and passed wind loudly.

He froze, the tune dying on his lips as he heard the jangle of a horse's bit behind him. He spun around, his uneven eyes bulging in their sockets as he focused on a pair of knights sitting astride massive warhorses. He swallowed heavily, his heart lurching, as his eyes flicked from one to the other, like a cornered animal.

Fully armoured in gleaming plate, the knights stared down at him disdainfully. Neither wore helmets, and a flash of envy and awe overcame him as he saw that their youthful faces were free of disfigurement and their shoulder-length hair was free of tangles or burrs. One, the taller of the pair, had hair the colour of dried wheat; the other had hair as dark as pitch, and wore a serious, grim expression. Neither looked as though they had seen more than twenty winters.

Both wore brightly coloured shields upon their left arms, proudly displaying their heraldry and colours. The caparisons of their steeds also bore their heraldic colours, and each of the knights held a lance upright in their gauntleted right hands.

Chlod saw that there was someone else with the pair of knights, a hunched peasant with a squint, who was trying to hide behind the nobles. Chlod focused on the man, who lowered his head, pulling his hood down low under the scrutiny. Chlod's eyes narrowed.

'Nastor, you squint-eyed bastard,' spat Chlod. 'You sold us out.'

'Silence, you,' snapped the fair-haired knight, who was bedecked in black and red. His voice was cultured and noble, each word clearly enunciated, and far from the crude accents of the lower classes. 'And make yourself presentable!'

Chlod glanced down and realised that his trousers were still undone. Hurriedly, he did himself up again.

The fair-haired knight nudged his steed, and the warhorse stepped obediently forward. Chlod flicked a glance towards the wagon where the remainder of the peasant band slumbered, unaware of the danger they were all in.

The knight moved his warhorse towards Chlod, and he instinctively edged backwards. The beast was massive, powerful muscles rippling up its legs and chest, and he flinched as it snorted loudly. He had never been so close to a noble mount, and he kept his arms stiffly at his side. For a lowborn to touch a knight's warhorse unbidden was a punishable offence, and he wanted to keep his hands.

'Lower your gaze, wretch,' snarled the knight. Chlod dropped his eyes, feeling the hot breath of the immense horse on his face. 'Lower,' said the knight, and Chlod prostrated himself on the ground, pushing his face into the mud. This was the end, he thought.

The other knight then spoke, his voice loud enough to carry across the clearing.

'I am Calard of Garamont,' he said, 'first born son and heir of Lutheure of Garamont, Castellan of Bastonne.'

Chlod pushed his face deeper into the mud.

'And you, peasants, are trespassing on Garamont land.'

CALARD'S FACE WAS dark as he surveyed the effect of his words. Panicked voices rose from beneath the rotting wagon, accompanied by frantic scrabbling. A dull wooden thump was followed by a curse, as one of the peasants sat up too quickly and struck his head. A putrid, dank blanket was thrown aside, and Calard's nose wrinkled in disgust as he watched the wretched peasant outlaws begin to crawl out from beneath their crude shelter, their eyes wide with fear.

His brother, Bertelis, gave a snort of disbelief.

'By the Lady, look at the number of them,' he said, 'huddled together under there like vermin.'

Calard had to agree with his half-brother. The peasants must have been practically sleeping on top of each other to have all sheltered beneath the wagon. They stood up, glancing nervously at each other, scratching themselves.

They truly were a pathetic-looking bunch of individuals. Encrusted with filth, they were uniformly scrawny, malformed and wretched. Several had pronounced limps and twisted legs, while others had grotesque protruding foreheads, lazy eyes, and teeth that stuck out at all angles from lips blackened with dirt. As far as Calard could make out, at least one of their number was a woman, though she was no less filthy than the others. The peasants squinted around them with slack-jawed nervousness.

Calard's gaze swept around the makeshift encampment, and fell on the blackened, skeletal carcass spitted over the fire-pit. It was clearly the remains of a young deer, which it was illegal for a peasant to hunt and kill, let alone eat. He sighed, and turned back towards the peasant rabble.

'You are illegally encamped on Garamont lands, and are accused of poaching Castellan Garamont's stock. The proof of this claim is there in front of me. More than this, you are accused of avoiding taxes levied by the Marquis Carlemont, a vassal of lord Garamont. It is also claimed that one of your number killed a yeoman of the marquis in cold blood and stole his truffle swine. As such, you are outlawed, and will be accompanied to Castle Garamont, where you will face the penalty for such crimes.'

Several of the peasants broke into tears at the pronouncement, while others dropped to their knees. They all knew that the pronouncement was as good as a death sentence. Shouts of protest and despair erupted from coarse throats. A scuffle erupted, and two of the peasants fell on another, grabbing him forcefully.

'It was Benno, here, milord what done the yeoman in! It was him! We done nothin'!'

Bertelis, who had circled around behind the wagon, gave a derisive snort, and answered before Calard could respond.

'Did he force you to flee the service of your lord? Did he force you to poach, and eat of Lord Garamont's venison? No, I think not. You will all hang.'

'Have mercy, young lords!' one of the peasants cried, before collapsing, sobbing, into the mud.

'Warden! Take them into your custody,' Calard ordered.

A small regiment of peasant men-at-arms walked out of the mist, carrying tall shields painted in the red and yellow of the Castellan of Garamont, his father. They carried simple staves, topped with curved blades and hooks. One of them held an old sword proudly in his hand, and nodded his head at the young knight's command. The men-at-arms began trudging towards the peasants. Lowborn themselves, the men-at-arms were only a little less pathetic in appearance than the outlaws. They were peasants too, after all, thought Calard.

'You there!' shouted Bertelis, seeing movement beneath the wagon. His warhorse snorted and stamped its hooves, sensing the tension in its young rider. 'Come out now!'

Calard stood in the stirrups, trying to see what was happening. There was a flash of movement, and Bertelis's steed reared. A sharp crack resounded as the flailing hooves connected, and a body fell heavily to the ground. Shouting erupted anew from the peasants, and they broke into movement.

'Hold!' shouted Calard, his young voice full of authority. 'Any man that runs will be assumed guilty and cut down! Warden! Take them!'

The men-at-arms tried to restore order, pushing several of the peasants roughly to their knees with the butts of their polearms.

'They've killed Odulf!' shouted one filthy man, who had clumps of hair missing from his head. He slammed his fist into the face of one of the Garamont soldiers, and Calard cursed. Others cried out, either in protest or fear, and Calard could hear Bertelis swearing.

'Stupid whoreson!' shouted Bertelis. 'The vermin came at me!' His voice sounded incredulous.

A peasant outlaw grabbed one of the men-at-arms' weapons, struggling against him. At a barked order from their warden, the other soldiers began laying about them with impunity, knocking peasants down into the mud with fierce blows. Calard swore again, and muscled his massive warhorse into the fray. He slammed the butt of his lance onto the head of one struggling peasant, and the man collapsed unconscious into the mud. Benno, the man accused by his comrades of murdering the yeoman, broke free of the restraining grip on him and bolted for the trees.

Kicking his spurs into the side of his horse, Calard broke free of the scuffle in pursuit, forcing men to leap out of his way, lest they be trampled. Hooves pounded up the muddy ground as he closed quickly on Benno. Calard thundered past him and pulled his steed sharply into his path. Benno, breathing hard, halted, eyeing the knight warily, and holding his hands up in front of him.

'I warned you not to run,' Calard said, glowering with outrage, 'but I wish to see no more blood spilt here today. Get back with the others before I change my mind,' Calard said, indicating sharply with his beardless chin. The man's shoulders slumped, and he turned back to where the men-at-arms were finally restoring order.

A flicker of movement attracted Calard's attention, and he saw a roughly clothed shape clamber atop the rotting wagon, a bow in his hands.

''Ware the wagon!' he shouted, even as the man drew back the bowstring, an arrow nocked. Calard could not believe what he was seeing; for a peasant to draw arms against a noble or one of his retainers was almost beyond comprehension.

Calard kicked his horse forward, shouting. The bowman spun around at Calard's cry, his bow swinging in the young knight's direction, and loosed his arrow.

It slammed into Calard's shoulder, and he reeled in his saddle. It felt like he had been kicked by a stallion, but he did not fall. He felt no pain, merely the shock of the impact, and he looked down incredulously at the shaft of the arrow protruding from the hole it had punched in his armour.

The bowman lowered his weapon, his mouth gaping wide as he registered the foolish, hasty act that had certainly doomed him. There was a shout of outrage and disbelief from Bertelis and the men-at-arms. The bowman half-jumped, half-fell from his position on the wagon, and began racing away towards the mist shrouded trees, panic lending him speed.

CHLOD LIFTED HIS face out of the mud, and his eyes widened as he saw the arrow protruding from the knight's shoulder. They had done it now. A peasant attacking a knight! Now, they were certain to hang.

Slowly, so as not to draw attention to himself, he began to crawl away through the wet earth, elbow over elbow. He glanced behind him, expecting someone to see him escaping at any moment, and shout out.

Once at a distance he judged safe, he rose to his feet and began running low, as fast as his clubfoot would allow him, loping off into the trees, his heart pounding.

He shoved a hand into the deep pocket on his jerkin, hoping that he had not crushed his rat. It bit him hard, and he jerked his hand back out, wincing.

With a final glance behind him, Chlod disappeared into the mist.

CALARD TOUCHED A hand to the arrow, still in shock at the peasant's action. Bertelis pounded across the ground, quickly closing the gap with the fleeing bowman, his lance lowering expertly before him. Several men-at-arms also broke into a run in pursuit of the fleeing man. The lance took the peasant in the lower back, punching through his body, and he fell with a cry. Bertelis rode past him and pulled his steed around sharply.

The man's piteous cries were ended as the men-at-arms reached him and slammed their polearms down onto his head, smashing his skull.

'My lord, are you hurt?' asked a voice at Calard's side. He looked down into the concerned, coarse face of the warden at his side.

'I have an arrow in my shoulder, Guido,' he said dryly. The man reddened, but Calard waved him away. 'I'm fine.'

Swinging his shield over his back, he gripped the shaft of the arrow tightly. It had punched under his pauldron, breaking several of the chainmail links beneath, before sinking into the thick padding he wore beneath his armour, though it had not reached his skin. Thankfully, the shot had been taken in haste; a fully-drawn Bretonnian longbow fired at such close range could easily have killed him. He pulled the arrow free, tossing it to the ground.

The other peasants had ceased their struggles, and knelt compliantly in the mud while the men-at-arms stood over them grimly. Several of them were whimpering, and all looked blankly around, their faces pale, shocked by the actions of their comrade.

Bertelis, his face thunderous, rode back to the peasants, his steed stamping and snorting. He reversed the grip on his lance, and thrust its point forcefully into the ground before sliding from the saddle. He drew his sword from its scabbard with a metallic hiss, and advanced on the closest of the kneeling peasants, who stared up at him in numb horror. The men-at-arms flicked glances between them, but none of them would dare to step in the path of the enraged young noble.

'Brother,' said Calard, a warning tone in his voice. The younger man ignored him, striding purposefully towards the group of peasants, the sword held firmly in his hand.

'Bertelis!' he said more forcefully, finally giving his brother pause. The younger knight swung his head towards Calard, his wavy fair hair flicking. 'Hold your arm. I will not see these people killed in cold blood.'

Bertelis gaped at Calard in bewildered astonishment, as if he had suddenly sprouted horns.

'Brother,' he gasped, 'you have been struck by a cowardly arrow fired by one of their number, you, a noble son of Bastonne! An example must be made of these wretches.'

'Just punishment has been meted out to the offender. Sheath your sword.'

'But–' began Bertelis.

'Sheath your sword, brother,' said Calard forcefully, cutting him off. Reluctantly, Bertelis did so. He stormed away from the peasants, glaring at Calard, and remounted. He pulled his lance free from the earth.

'Are you all right?' he asked, his scowl fading. 'My heart skipped a beat when I saw the peasant loose that shaft.'

'It is nothing,' replied Calard. 'It didn't even scratch the skin.' He smiled broadly and shook his head, exhaling slowly. The years slipped away as his strong face relaxed, and, for the first time that morning, he looked his twenty-one years of age. 'The Lady was looking over me. I thought Morr was going to claim me, for a moment.'

Bertelis grinned back at him, his dark mood forgotten.

'He wouldn't want you. Too ugly by far.'

Calard snorted, and turned towards the peasant men-at-arms, a serious expression falling across his face like a mask.

'Warden,' he said, 'we are done here. My brother and I will return to Castle Garamont.'

The peasant touched the brim of his helmet respectfully. 'I will bind 'em, lord, just in case any of 'em try to make a run for it.'

'Do as you must,' Calard replied, waving a hand dismissively. He turned his steed away, his heart still racing.

A wretched, squinting peasant stood before him, clutching a cloth cap in his hands. It was the man who had guided Calard to the outlaws. He was a weasel, but at least he knew his place. The young knight raised an eyebrow.

'Well?' he asked.

'Young lord,' the peasant began, 'since I led you here faithfully, I was hoping that, if it is not too much of an inconvenience, that perhaps I could… My family is poor, lord, and I have no food for my little ones. That is to say, I…'

The greed of the lower classes was without bounds, thought Calard. They tilled the lands of their lord faithfully, and in return were allowed to keep up to a tenth-share of their produce, and were protected from harm.

'You will be recompensed for this duty, peasant,' Calard cut in.

The man dropped to his knees in the mud, bowing and scraping.

'You are too kind, young master,' said the peasant, though Calard found it almost impossible to understand his words, spoken out of the side of the mouth and thickly accented.

'Warden,' said Calard, 'see that this man is recompensed. I think a half-copper would be more than generous.'

'Far more than generous,' said Bertelis darkly.

'Thank you, lord! Thank you,' said the peasant, lowering his head to the ground once again.

'I am sorry to detain you, my lord,' said the warden, 'but the truffle swine? Shall I have it returned to the marquis?'

'Have it given to this man here,' said Calard, feeling generous, 'in lieu of his payment. If that suits you, peasant?'

'Oh yes, lord! You are most generous indeed!' said the kneeling man.

'Fine. See it done,' said the young knight, before wheeling his horse around and exchanging a glance with Bertelis.

'Come now Gringolet,' he whispered, leaning forward in the saddle and patting his steed's dappled grey neck. 'You can beat him this time.'

With one final grin towards his brother, he shouted and kicked his destrier into a gallop.

Giving their powerful steeds their heads, the pair of young knights raced through the mist-shrouded trees, rejoicing in the feeling of freedom and power. The icy wind pulled at their hair, and they urged their steeds on, faster.

They rode well, completely at ease in the saddle. Indeed, they had been placed in the saddle even before they had learnt to walk, and it was as natural to them as breathing, as if the horses were merely extensions of their own bodies. The brothers were evenly matched in horsemanship, and their steeds too were close in strength, power and endurance. Nevertheless, Bertelis's chestnut steed was fierier in nature, and the tenacity of the beast would more often than not mean that he was the victor of their races.

Gringolet leapt a fallen stump, and Calard laughed out loud as he pulled briefly into the lead. He heard Bertelis urging his palomino steed on, and he grinned. They pounded up the earth as they galloped towards the edge of the trees marking the northern extent of the grand forest of Chalons.

No steed of the Empire, nor of Estalia or Tilea, could match the strength and power of a pure-bred Bretonnian horse. None of them were the equal in sheer speed, and the Bretonnians were rightly proud of them. Protected in thick layers of plate barding beneath their flowing cloth caparisons, and carrying the weight of a fully armoured knight, the noble steeds could outpace any horse in the Old World.

Sighting the edge of the trees, Calard kicked Gringolet forward, riding hard. He flicked a glance sideways, and saw that Bertelis was alongside him, the two horses neck and neck. With a last burst of power, Bertelis pulled ahead, and he shouted in victory as they broke from the tree line.

Laughing, the pair reined their steeds in. Their warhorses were lathered in sweat, and their massive chests heaved in great gulps of air. Calard patted Gringolet's neck fondly. He had raised the destrier from a foal, and he was a fine, strong and noble beast.

They were on a rise, overlooking verdant rolling hills of grassland. Sheep were clustered in fluffy white clumps across the hills, accompanied by hunched peasant shepherds, and the sun was just starting to break free of the clouds, making the whole region glow with early morning light.

A mess of small, rude hovels in the dip of a small valley marked a peasant settlement, and they could see dozens of dirty men and women shuffling about their duties. As far as they could see, from horizon to horizon, and beyond, was Garamont land, a fiefdom that had been in the family for nine generations, bequeathed from son to son. The Duke of Bastonne had gifted the land to Gundehar, the first lord of Garamont for acts of chivalry and honour on the field of battle.

Calard and Bertelis had grown up on the land, and they knew it as well as anybody could claim to. As boys, they had ridden and played from one end of their father's lands to the other. It took almost a full day to ride from Castle Garamont to the eastern border of his lands and back, and as youngsters these lands seemed impossibly vast and filled with adventure.

They would often purposefully lose their chaperones, much to the distress of those bidden to see them safe, and embark on quests and crusades against imaginary foes. How many fair damsels had been rescued from the maws of monstrous beasts, and evil knights bested in those childhood years? Certainly the number of punishments they suffered at the hands of the old chamberlain, Folcard, was legendary, as was the number of witless peasants who sported bruises and bumps when set upon by the wooden swords wielded by the pair.

Those days were long gone, however, and the lands of Garamont no longer seemed vast. The pair of young knights had insisted they would ride out to find the peasant outlaws, merely for something to do. Calard's usual, serious expression fell back into place over his features as the thrill of the race wore off.

'You know that the taxes levied on that peasant for becoming the owner of that hog will make him poorer than he is now,' said Bertelis finally, breaking the silence.

'I know, but he deserves no more. He's a treacherous swine. He and the pig will be good together.'

Bertelis grinned in response. His skin was a healthy bronze from the sun, his body tall and strong from years of weapons practice and riding. His eyes were dark, his face lean and handsome, and his hair the colour of the sand that was said to lie upon the beaches on the coast. He looked every inch the epitome of Bretonnian knighthood.

'Come, brother,' said Calard, 'let us go home.'

CHAPTER TWO

THE SUN WAS shining brightly as the pair of knights rode towards Castle Garamont. Pennants flying Castellan Lutheure's colours whipped in the wind from atop the parapets. It was a fine, strong fortress, built in the time of the first ruler of Garamont, nine generations earlier. Constructed from locally-quarried pale stone, the castle glowed a warm rose colour in the rising, morning sun.

Perched atop a rocky bluff, the castle was the highest visible structure for miles around. The location of the fortress had been carefully chosen, both for its defensive value and for the dominating aspect it held over the surrounding countryside. The approach from the south was gently sloping, though the northern side of the castle dropped away sharply, falling hundreds of feet down to the sprawling village of peasant hovels clustered in the shadows beneath it. To those lowborn

and living within the squalid abodes, the castle looming over them was an ever-present reminder of the
strength and power of the lord of Garamont.

The walls of the castle were tall and thick, and scores
of men-at-arms stood sentry upon the battlements,
day and night. Seven tall towers were interspersed
along the crenellated walls, three of them topped by
sharply tapered spires. An eighth tower, grimly dubbed
Morr's Rest, had been part of the original construction,
but its upper section had collapsed some five generations past. Though the repair of the tower had been
started on separate occasions by two successive lords
of Garamont, fatal accidents among the work crews
had postponed the work indefinitely, and now it was
part of the local superstitions of those too simple to
know better. The fact that for five generations the
ruined tower had been the roost of countless ravens
merely added to the superstitions, and it was perhaps
for these creatures that the tower was named.

The powerful gatehouse that led into the castle faced
to the south, looking out towards the Forest of
Chalons in the distance, and it was from this direction
that Calard and Bertelis approached. Peasant militia-
men doffed their caps and iron-rimmed helmets as the
young nobles cantered past, ignoring them. Other
peasants, bearing goods and produce on their
hunched backs, scurried off the muddy roadway leading to the castle, bobbing their heads respectfully.
Mangy dogs, emaciated and gaunt, trotted behind
them, sniffing around the cuts of meat that were being
delivered to the castle kitchens.

The brothers cantered across the thick wooden drawbridge spanning the deep ditch below. At the base of

the ditch was a muddy mire of reeds, and pools of stagnant water. A decade earlier, Calard and Bertelis had played there, catching tadpoles and frogs, ambushing and challenging startled wayfarers attempting to cross the bridge and enter the castle.

Cantering beneath the mighty portcullis, they passed through the arched gateway and into the dimly-lit passage leading through the gatehouse. Murder holes and arrow slits eyed their progress. The gatehouse was probably the most defensible part of the castle, and it doubled as the barracks for those peasants given the honour of becoming Garamont's men-at-arms.

Passing back into the light on the far side of the gatehouse, the knights errant angled their steeds across the muddy expanse towards the stables. The area was teeming with activity, hundreds of peasants rubbing shoulders with each other, and bustling about with livestock and carts piled high with freshly harvested crops. The air was filled with their crude shouts, mixing with the din of braying animals. The stink of the peasants and the animals was strong.

Men caked in mud and other more offensive substances pulled their donkeys and bovine charges out of the way of the young knights. Dirty children laughed and chased a group of piglets through the crowd, followed by a red-faced man who was swearing loudly. He apologised profusely when he saw Calard and his brother, bowing his head, before resuming the chase.

'I loathe harvest-tide,' said Bertelis, his noble face twisted in a grimace as the sounds and smells of the unwashed peasants surged over them. 'Get out of the way, peasants!' he shouted impatiently.

The pair entered the stables, and young stable
hands rushed to take their reins. The lads were
peasant-born, but their faces were at least
marginally cleaner than those outside, and their
backs were straight; only the best were chosen to
tend to the horses of Garamont. The knights handed
their lances to waiting servants and dismounted.
Before the armoured horses were led away, Calard
removed his right gauntlet and walked around the
back of Gringolet, running his hand down the
destrier's right, hind leg. The horse obediently lifted
the long limb, and Calard poked at its hoof.

'Have the farrier come up and see to this shoe,' he
ordered, stepping away from the horse. One of the
peasants nodded his head in response and sent a stable boy running out to the blacksmith's with a curt
command.

Calard found Bertelis smiling slightly when he
turned around.

'What?' he asked. Bertelis shook his head.

'You, dirtying your own hands. That's what these are
for,' he said, indicating the stable hands with a wave.
Calard slapped his brother across the shoulders.

'A knight of Bretonnia must know how to take care
of his steed,' he said.

'I know how to take care of a horse: tell a peasant to
do it,' countered Bertelis.

Calard's face was serious as they stepped back into
the sunshine, and looked up at the high walls of the
eight-sided keep that functioned as the family living
quarters.

'Come. We must see how father fares.'

* * *

LORD LUTHEURE OF Garamont, Castellan of Bastonne, coughed heavily. Fluid rattled deep in his chest, and his whole frame was rocked by the hacking cough, his expression pained. A serving maid held a silk handkerchief to his lips, and when it was removed there were flecks of blood upon it.

'You should be in bed,' scolded Lady Calisse gently, placing her hand upon her husband's shoulders. 'The drafts down here do you no good.'

Lutheure pushed away his breakfast plates, his meal unfinished. Hovering servants instantly cleared them away.

'I am the lord of Garamont. I will not huddle under the covers in my bedchambers during the daylight hours being spoon-fed by servants,' he said darkly.

His wife sat quietly, her delicate hands folded on her lap, but he could feel her eyes boring into him. A pretty young serving girl entered the room bearing a steaming goblet upon a silver tray, and Lutheure winced as an acrid, foul stench reached his nostrils.

Without a word, she placed the tray upon the table.

'Thank you Annabelle,' said Lady Garamont, and the girl curtseyed in response before making her exit.

Lady Calisse stared at Lutheure frankly for a moment, her face immaculate and pale. She was a handsome woman, despite her years. 'Drink your remedy,' she said finally.

Lutheure sighed, eyeing the goblet filled with the stinking concoction with distaste and resignation. Under the stern, watchful gaze of his wife, he lifted it, staring at the swirling cluster of bark, herbs, and the Lady knew what else, within the muddy, stinking concoction. His wife raised one perfectly plucked eyebrow, and Lutheure sighed. He raised the goblet to his lips and gulped down a mouthful of the foul brew.

He choked it down, his eyes watering.

'She is a good servant, that one,' said Lady Calisse, rising from her plush seat.

'Aye, a fine gift she was,' said Lutheure. The girl had entered his service the previous summer, a gift from one of his vassals, the ageing Lord Carlemont.

'If you will not rest, just promise me that you will do nothing to exert yourself today,' said Lady Calisse.

'For you, anything, my love,' said Lutheure, closing his eyes in contentment as his wife began to toy with his hair.

'Thank you,' she said, and planted a kiss upon his sunken cheek.

Goblet in hand, Lutheure got up from the table and moved to the window. The last six months had seen a dramatic change in the castellan. Though he was still tall and broad shouldered, the sickness had robbed him of his muscle. His barrel chest had been reduced to a frail cage of ribs, and his arms and legs, once so strong from years of riding, sword practice and war, were wasted and thin.

It was in his face, however, that the most dramatic transformation had taken place. It was as if he had aged two decades in the space of two seasons. Last summer his face had been strong, broad and noble, and, though he was in his middling years, he had radiated a powerful aura of strength, virility and command. Now his face was pale, and his eyes flashed with a feverish light. His fair hair was streaked with silver, as was the long moustache that hung down past gaunt cheeks. His cheeks were sunken, his cheekbones protruding sharply, and his eyes were set deep in hollow sockets.

He knew how he looked, but steadfastly refused to accept his deteriorating health. To please his wife, he had allowed himself to be poked, prodded and bled by a stuttering chirurgeon with a strange penchant for leeches, after the rotund priestess of Shallya had thrown up her hands, unable to determine the cause of the sickness. The chirurgeon had consulted with the castle's apothecary, and, together, they had concocted the foul remedy that he was to drink twice daily, morning and night. Nevertheless, his health continued to decline, much to the grief of his family and his loyal knights.

Lutheure stared out through the tall, north facing, arched window, revelling in the feeling of warmth as the sun touched his lined skin. For a moment, he felt like his old self, but a hacking cough suddenly rose in his chest, and he winced as he clutched his chest, the pain fierce. His wife's cool hands took the goblet from him lest he spill it, and she looked up at him with eyes full of concern.

'I'm fine,' he wheezed, giving her a weak smile.

The doors to the private dining chamber were slammed open, and Lutheure turned to see his sons enter the room, the tall, smiling Bertelis in the lead.

'Breakfast!' declared the young, sandy-haired knight, sending servants scuttling out of the room.

Lady Calisse moved across the room, her long flowing dress trailing behind her.

'My son,' she said warmly. She drew him down to her height and kissed him on each cheek. Calard stood somewhat stiffly behind.

'Mother,' said Bertelis, before extricating himself from her grasp and moving to his father. He dropped to one knee before the lord of Garamont, bowing his head low. Lutheure smiled warmly at his son, who was the spitting image of himself, some twenty-five years earlier, and lifted him to his feet, a hand on each of his thickly armoured shoulders.

Calard bowed to Lady Calisse, who studiously ignored him, and the young knight moved to his father. He too lowered himself to one knee, and bowed his head. Lutheure slapped Bertelis on the shoulder, sending him towards the table as servants entered bearing fresh bread and wine. Lutheure turned to regard his firstborn son and heir, his eyes hardening.

'Did you find them?' he asked.

'We did, my lord,' said Calard, rising to his feet and standing to attention, one hand resting on the pommel of his sword. 'They resisted, and two were killed before order was restored. The remainder are being led here for trial.'

Lutheure nodded his head, and turned away from his dark-haired son. Calard bowed again, and moved to join his brother at the table. Lutheure took his seat at the head of the table. His wife sat opposite him, doting on Bertelis, who was digging into the food with gusto.

Calard took his place opposite his brother, and broke a loaf in two. More food was brought in, game birds and venison, delivered by the pretty serving girl, Annabelle. She blushed as Bertelis gave her a solicitous wink. The young knight's eyes followed the retreating figure of the girl as he sipped from his wine goblet, and Lutheure chuckled. *Another serving girl deflowered by the lad*, he thought.

'How are you faring this day, my lord?' asked Calard stiffly.

'I am well,' he replied, barely registering the question. 'Bertelis,' he said, smiling at his other son, 'Gunthar tells me that you could be the best he has ever taught, *if* you dedicated yourself more to your training. You are missing too many of his classes.'

Bertelis sighed. 'I would make more of an effort to attend the old man's classes if he could make them more interesting, father,' he said.

'Old man,' scoffed Lutheure. 'Watch your tongue, Gunthar is not much older than I am.'

'Calard is more suited to his classes than I, anyway' said Bertelis. 'He has a mind like a sponge. He learns much faster than I, and is far more dedicated.'

'I have to train hard. I have not your natural talent,' said Calard humbly.

'Nonsense. You are clearly the better swordsman, though I am certainly far superior in the saddle,' said Bertelis, flashing a smile at his brother.

'And it is in the saddle where a knight is rightly judged,' said Lutheure.

THAT NIGHT, AS the castle slept, Calard dreamt. He had fallen asleep quickly, his body exhausted after spending much of the day in the saddle, practising his jousting technique under the watchful gaze of the weapon master, Gunthar. Time and again, he had kicked Gringolet into a gallop and struck the stationary training target, bracing himself for the impact as his lance-tip made contact. The heavy wooden target would teeter and fall to the ground only against the finest of knocks, whereupon peasant servants would scramble to right it, ready for his next pass.

For hour after hour he had charged the heavy target, until his shoulder and arm were bruised a dark purple from the lance. Over and over, he heard his father's words as he slept.

And it is in the saddle where a knight is rightly judged.

In his dream, he was astride his powerful destrier once more, charging the practice target. He struck his lance against it, but it was as unyielding as stone, and his arm was jarred as his lance shattered against it. He turned his steed, another lance having appeared in his hands, and charged again. As he closed on the wooden target, he saw it change shape, turning into a towering, dark figure with massive horns curling from its shadowy head.

He struck a mighty blow, but again it was like striking stone, and his lance splintered and broke. The monstrous dark creature turned towards him, and he threw the broken lance to the ground in desperation, drawing his sword. As his hands closed on the hilt, however, his blade changed into a hissing serpent that turned and struck towards his face, fangs bared in its overextended mouth.

He felt the prick of its teeth against his cheek and cried out, pulling his head away sharply. Instantly, the snake was gone, and there was nothing in his hand but his sword.

His surroundings had changed again, and a child walked through the mist that now surrounded him.

'Who goes there?' he shouted, his voice muffled by the sudden fog.

He gasped as he made out the face of the child. He had not dreamt of his sister for many years, though she was often in his thoughts. As dark-haired as him, they had been inseparable as children, and it was as a child that she appeared to him now, for that is how he remembered her, before she was taken.

His twin looked at him with deep, soulful eyes that spoke of mysteries and secrets. She looked at him sadly, and he wanted to go to comfort her, but then she turned away. She began to fade, and he found that he could see through her body, as if she were as insubstantial as a spirit. He cried out, but in an instant she was gone, swallowed by the mist. He tried to follow her, kicking Gringolet forwards, and they plunged blindly into the fog. He found his way barred by branches and twigs that snagged at him, scratching his face, and he hacked wildly at them with his sword.

He heard a roar, a deep rumbling bestial sound that filled his ears and made his head spin with its power. Then something struck him solidly across the chest, and he was thrown from the saddle. He hit the ground hard, and came awake instantly, his heart pounding, and his bedclothes saturated with sweat.

CALARD GRITTED HIS teeth as he attacked, his blade swinging in hard towards his opponent's head. It was parried with ease, as he had expected, and he swiftly whipped a second attack lower, into the body. His blade was knocked aside, and he took the return blow on his shield. His riposte was quick and strong as he saw an opening, forcing the weapon master back a step.

'Good,' said Gunthar, putting up his sword. The ageing knight's skill with blade and lance was unparalleled in all of Garamont, indeed, in all of eastern Bastonne.

The weapon master was armoured in simple, old-fashioned, functional armour. It was battered and dull with age, though it was meticulously cared for, and was as strong as it had ever been. Still, it looked ancient to Calard's eyes, a relic from a time long past. Fashion changed quickly in Bretonnia, and he and his brother wore gleaming fluted armour in the modern fashion.

'Now you,' said Gunthar, nodding his head towards Bertelis, who was reclining on a nearby bench. Bertelis lifted himself languidly to his feet, a bored look on his face, and drew his own blade.

The sandy-haired youth rolled his armoured shoulders, and advanced on the weapon master, who stood waiting for him. Calard moved to the side to watch.

The training session was taking place on one of the many terraces on the north face of the Garamont keep. It was ringed in low shrubs, and the sun was shining on them weakly.

He had spoken the truth the previous morning. Bertelis *was* more talented than him, as he was in most of their physical contests. He was taller and swifter, and he had a relaxed suppleness to his movements that Calard would never be able to emulate.

Gunthar and Bertelis raised their blades up to the sky in honour to the Lady, the protective goddess of Bretonnia. Then they bent their arms, bringing their swords down before their faces, and kissed the flats of the blades. Then, in one swift movement, they sliced the air before them, completing their salute, and took up a ready stance.

Calard watched with open admiration as his brother began to trade blows with Gunthar, his every movement balanced, poised and controlled. If he applied himself fully, Calard was of no doubt that Bertelis would become one of the finest swordsmen in Bastonne. He himself was good with the blade, better than Bertelis, but he had to work hard at it, and he found it both galling and irritating that his brother took to it with so little effort.

Nevertheless, as he watched his brother and the weapons master begin to spar, he could see that his brother's technique had room for improvement. He relied on his natural ability too much, and though this alone made him superior to most, he would be undone against a more talented opponent, and he would certainly lose against a knight of similar ability who had a more rigorous attitude to his training.

Bertelis sliced left and right with powerful swift blows, but Gunthar turned them aside with barely any effort. Getting frustrated, Bertelis began to attack more wildly, putting more strength than necessary into his attacks. He feinted high and whipped his sword down to strike low, but his effort was deftly turned aside, and he found himself with the weapon master's blade at his throat.

Bertelis threw his sword down in frustration and disgust.

'I'm not getting anywhere with this,' he said. 'Give me a horse and a lance any day. I am just more suited to them!'

'No, you are not,' said Gunthar evenly. 'You are as gifted a swordsman as I have seen. How many hours have you spent practising your jousting technique this past week?'

Bertelis shrugged in response.

'Take a guess,' said Gunthar.

'Maybe two hours a day?'

'And with the sword?'

'You know the answer,' said Bertelis.

'I do,' agreed Gunthar. 'An hour, perhaps, over the last week.'

'A knight's place is in the saddle! Why must I practise fighting on foot like a peasant? I do not plan on trudging through the mud to war like a commoner.'

'A knight does not always have the luxury of choosing the circumstances he fights in. What happens if your horse is slain beneath you?'

Bertelis rolled his eyes in response. 'I'll get a new horse!' he shot back, making Calard smirk.

'What if the battle takes place upon a muddy mire, and your lord orders you to fight on foot?'

'Then my lord would be a damn fool for choosing such a ridiculous battlefield!' snapped Bertelis.

Gunthar stared at the young man with cold, humourless, grey eyes. His moustache twitched in irritation.

'Pick up your sword,' he ordered, his voice cold.

'I am done with training today,' said Bertelis arrogantly.

'You are done with your training when I say you are done,' growled the grizzled veteran.

'I will not be ordered around like a servant,' said Bertelis haughtily.

'In my training area, I am lord and master,' said Gunthar. 'You may be the son of my lord castellan, but here you are nothing more than an arrogant, undisciplined child. Pick up your sword.'

'I will not be spoken to like that,' said Bertelis hotly, snatching up his blade once more.

'What are you going to do about it?' asked the weapon master. Calard saw Bertelis's face darken.

With a snarl, Bertelis attacked, his blade a blur through the air. The clash of steel on steel rang out, and the pair moved around each other, blades flashing. They parried and blocked each other's attacks, and Bertelis let his anger flow down his arm, powering each blow. He was clearly stronger than the ageing weapon master, and each of his blows was fuelled with rage, driving the older man back.

Bertelis overextended on one of his attacks, too eager to land a blow on the older knight, and he found himself off-balance. Gunthar stepped in close, slamming his shield into the taller youth. The young knight reeled backwards, losing his footing on the flagstones, and fell with a crash to the ground.

Gunthar sheathed his sword, and with a smile, offered his hand to Bertelis. With a dark look, Bertelis took the proffered hand, and allowed himself to be hauled to his feet.

'Why did I win?' asked the weapon master.

'You are more skilled,' Bertelis replied.

'Yes, I am, but that is not why I won.'

'You made him angry,' said Calard. Gunthar nodded.

'Exactly. I deliberately baited you, to explain this lesson.'

'I don't understand,' said Bertelis.

'He made you angry,' said Calard. 'Your anger gave you strength, but it also made your attacks more wild, less controlled.'

'A knight must always be in control of his actions,' said the weapon master. 'Once controlled, anger can be used to your benefit. It will give you strength, as Calard rightly points out, but if that anger is controlled, you do not lose your focus.'

Bertelis glowered, still angry. Gunthar smiled in response, and slapped the young knight on the shoulder.

'It is not easy,' he said, his voice softening. 'It comes with age, and with practice. I was young too once, as impetuous and quick to anger as you.'

Bertelis grinned impishly, his foul mood evaporating.

'I find it hard to imagine that you were ever a young man,' he said. Gunthar snorted.

'Now you are trying to make *me* angry. It's not going to work.'

'Are you never angry then, Gunthar?'

'Of course I am, but I keep that anger controlled. I do not let it control *me*. Enough, today's lesson is over. Now get away with you both.'

They heard a sudden blaring of horns, and Calard's head shot up. He exchanged a look with Bertelis, and the pair were off and moving as one, racing from the training terrace, their armour clanking.

Gunthar chuckled, watching them go. On the cusp of manhood, they appeared so like the boys he had grown to love as his own at that moment, racing through the castle as they had done when they were children, terrorising the servants and disrupting the serene calm. The smile faded from his face.

They would not have the luxury of being boys for long, and they would have far harsher lessons to learn than he could teach.

* * *

CALARD AND BERTELIS burst into their father's audience chamber, slamming the door wide open before them. Folcard, the household's fierce chamberlain, shot a look of dark reproach in their direction, and they instantly composed themselves. Standing tall and regal, they walked with stately calm to join him in awaiting the lord castellan.

Calard bristled with impatience. The grand double doors that were the main entrance into the audience chamber were sealed. The portal was guarded by a pair of men-at-arms, who stood motionless with their long pole arms crossed in front of the massive doors. They would not open until the lord of Garamont was seated in his tall throne carved of dark wood.

The seat had always fascinated Calard, and, as a child, he had occasionally sneaked into the room to test it, his legs dangling above the ground. It was a beautiful, ancient piece of furniture, its high back carved with miniature scenes that recreated the twelve great battles of the founder of Bretonnia, Gilles the Uniter. It was a source of pride that Gilles had been borne of Bastonne, just as his own family was, though his step-mother, Lady Calisse, held closer ties to his direct lineage than had Calard's own mother. A feeling of melancholy descended on Calard as he looked at the throne, wondering how long it would be before he would sit there as the lord of Garamont. He knew he was not ready for such a heavy burden of responsibility, and he whispered a silent prayer to the Lady for his father's good health.

Courtiers, advisors and knights were slowly filtering into the chamber through side doors and partitions. The chamberlain sent servants scurrying in all directions, and the room was filled with a gentle murmur of speculation.

'Who do you think it is?' whispered Bertelis. Calard shrugged in response. 'Please let it be an emissary from the king announcing a new errant war,' said Bertelis.

The room hushed, as the black and gold door in the back wall of the audience chamber was opened and a rotund, bearded man, dressed in the red and yellow of Lutheure's livery stepped forth.

A blare of horns echoed deafeningly through the chamber, causing the doves roosting in the upper beams of the lofty expanse above to take flight.

'The Lord and Lady Garamont,' bellowed the rotund crier.

As one, the gathered knights and nobles dropped to one knee, their heads bowed, and the ladies of the court dipped low in delicate curtsies.

Lord Lutheure, resplendent in a fashionable tunic and robe that would have cost more than a peasant could hope to see in a lifetime, walked across the dais with his wife on his arm. Lutheure wore his coat of arms embroidered upon his chest, but he was far out-shone by his wife, wearing a velvet dress of deepest crimson that trailed behind her. Her fair hair was hidden beneath her velvet headdress, over which she wore a glittering circlet of silver. Lutheure led his wife to her luxuriously padded chair, before taking his own seat upon his massive throne. He did well to hide his illness, though, to Calard's eyes, it was obvious that his gaunt frame no longer filled the throne as once it had.

The lord of Garamont nodded regally to his chamberlain, who signalled the men-at-arms at the door.

They stepped back, uncrossing their long ceremonial weapons, and the doors were thrown open.

Having hurried across the room to the doors, his face red with the exertion, the rotund court crier announced the newcomer.

'Sigibold of Bordeleaux, Knight of the Realm and Equerry of Duke Alberic of Bordeleaux,' he thundered.

'Not from the king then,' muttered Bertelis, for which he received a sharp glare from the chamberlain, Folcard.

There was muttering as the knight entered the court, striding purposefully towards the seated lord of Garamont. He was fully armoured, and his cloak was tattered and worn. He carried his helm beneath his left arm, and his hair was wet with sweat and plastered across his head. He tracked mud and dirt into the audience chamber, and there was tutting amongst the gathered nobles.

Reaching the dais, the knight dropped to one knee and bowed his head.

'The Duke of Bordeleaux sends his warmest regards,' replied the knight. Lutheure bowed his head, accepting the courtesy.

'You honour my household with your presence, sir knight. Can I have a room readied for you? You have the look of one who has travelled far, and you may, if you wish, refresh yourself before we address the purpose of your visit.'

'Alas no,' replied the knight with a bow, 'time does not permit me to accept your noble offer.'

'No? Speak then,' said Lutheure.

'My lord, I bring grim news. The south-eastern lands of Bordeleaux are overrun. I come to seek your aid in its retaking.'

The court erupted in gasps and muttering. Calard flashed a glance at his brother, his eyes lighting up. A slight smile touched Bertelis's lips. Lutheure lifted a hand for silence, his rings of office gleaming, and the hubbub died away.

'This is grim news indeed,' agreed Lutheure. 'What enemy besieges his fair lands?'

'Greenskins,' replied the knight bitterly. This was met with curses and dark mutterings, which Lutheure allowed to continue for a moment before he lifted a hand again for silence. The castellan thought on this for a moment, a deep frown upon his face.

His eyes turned skywards, as if seeking divine communion, staring up towards the high arched windows replete with stained glass, where images of his ancestors stared down at him. The courtiers looked expectantly to their lord. There was no particular love between the people of Bastonne and Bordeleaux, but in times of strife they had always united against a mutual foe. At last, he lowered his gaze, and looked again at the knight awaiting his answer.

'You have already sought the aid of other knights of Bastonne?' he asked.

'I have, my lord. I have received pledges of more than two thousand knights of your most esteemed land.'

'You have already spoken to the lord of Sangasse, a days ride to the west?' asked the castellan, his eyes glittering. At mention of the name, Calard stiffened. The Sangasses had been the mortal rivals of Garamont for nine generations.

'I have, my lord,' said the knight, oblivious to the tension in the room. 'The noble lord of Sangasse has pledged his knights. They are to be led by Maloric, his son, the young Earl of Sangasse.'

Calard scowled.

The castellan's expression was unreadable as he digested this information. At last, he turned his eyes in Calard's direction, and there was a silent communication between them.

'Bertelis, Calard,' said the lord of Garamont, 'come forward.'

Bertelis ascended the steps of the dais, his head held high. Calard followed, his heart hammering. They took up positions on either side of their father, standing alongside his throne.

'Sir Sigibold, these are my sons and my rightful heirs. They will ride for Bordeleaux, to aid your duke's knights against the hated enemy. The knights of my household will ride at their side.'

Calard could not help but let the joy he felt erupt in a broad smile that he saw was mirrored on Bertelis's face.

'The Duke of Bordeleaux will be honoured by their presence,' replied the knight, 'and I convey his thanks for your commitment to his cause.'

Lutheure rose from his throne, and Calard twitched as he saw his father wobble slightly. Still, he did not step forward to give his father support, knowing that to do so would be to emphasise his father's weakness in front of his court. Recovering, the lord castellan steadied himself and addressed the gathered nobles.

'Let the word be spread, that the sons of Garamont will ride for Bordeleaux on the morn. Tonight the lord of Garamont shall host a banquet, wishing them victory and glory on the fields of battle.'

A cheer rose from those gathered below the dais.

'Sigibold, will you do us the honour of dining with us this evening?' asked Lutheure.

'Alas, I cannot, noble lord,' replied the knight. 'I must be on my way to secure more knights for the duke's cause.'

Lutheure nodded.

'My lords and ladies,' he said, 'we prepare for war.'

CHAPTER THREE

'LET US DRINK to my sons! Let the Lady guide their lances, and let them return to my side in glory and triumph!'

There was a cheer around the assembled revellers, and Calard and Bertelis clinked their goblets heavily together. They each took a long swig of wine. Their cheeks were already glowing, and their bellies were full of food.

The detritus of the vanquished meal lay before the gathered nobles, strewn across the sprawling expanse of tables in the banquet room. Bones were thrown onto the straw-covered floor, where they were fought over by Lutheure's hunting dogs, and, when no one was looking, the peasant servers. Carcasses of roasted boar and deer, stuffed with herbs, garlic and sweetmeats lay stripped of flesh upon giant platters, and the bony remains of quail and hare lay discarded on plates of lead and silver, swimming in thick, creamy sauces of mushroom and cheese. Extravagant dishes, upon which had lain the grilled forms of the large carnivorous fish that swam the River Grismerie to the north, lay cast aside. Only the luminous white bones and massive gaping jaws of the creatures were left, with the remnants of white wine sauce swilling around them.

The wine was flowing freely, for the lord castellan had opened up his cellar, wishing to toast his sons off to war in style. The nobles supped at the exquisite fare of Bordeleaux and Aquitaine, extolling their various virtues as they swirled them around their goblets and sniffed at their aromas. Calard and his brother, knowing little of fine wine, swigged exorbitantly expensive, hundred-year-old vintages as if they were water.

Bertelis grinned, feeling content, full of food and well on the way to drunkenness. He looked across the tables to his father, who was smiling proudly at him, and he raised his goblet in response, smiling. Folcard stood behind Lutheure, looking for all the world like a fierce bird of prey. His thin shoulders were slightly hunched, though he stood taller than any knight present, and his hooked nose protruded sharply from his gaunt face. As if feeling Bertelis's gaze, the chamberlain turned his cold, dark eyes towards his lord's younger son. Even after all these years, the chamberlain still made him feel like a naughty child, and Bertelis quickly looked away.

His eyes darted to his mother, who sat deep in conversation with Tanebourc, a tall, ginger-haired knight who was one of his mother's favourites. He saw the light touch that his mother laid upon the knight's forearm, and frowned, but was instantly distracted as an army of servants descended on the banquet room at a clap from the castle's chamberlain. He leant politely out of the way as a serving girl bent over him to collect his plate, exposing a not inconsiderable amount of her bosom as she did so.

'Sir Bertelis, I think you might be dribbling,' someone teased, and he turned sheepishly to face Lady Elisabet of Carlemont. An attractive young noblewoman with a delightfully devilish gleam in her eye, she sat beside a doting Calard. She wore a stunning dress of deepest purple, and a shimmering, diaphanous shawl was wrapped around her pale shoulders. The eye was drawn to her cleavage by a large, star-shaped pendant that hung low around her neck. Calard was beaming at her side, no doubt at least partly due to that cleavage. They made a good couple, Bertelis thought, and he was certain that one day they would wed, for their affection for one another was well known and easy to see. His brother was distressingly loyal to her, refusing to lie with any of the servants, claiming that Elisabet was the only one for him. She was certainly a desirable woman, but sometimes he just did not understand his brother.

'I fear you may be correct, my lady,' he replied, theatrically wiping at his chin and flicking his hand towards the ground. 'I am but a knight of weak morals, easily won over by a pretty face and a bounteous bosom. Not like noble Calard at your side. He is girded of firmer stuff.'

'I should hope so,' said Elisabet, turning her seductive dark eyes towards the older of the brothers, giving him a playful pout. Calard blushed, making both Elisabet and Bertelis laugh.

'Brother,' declared Bertelis, indicating to a servant for more wine, 'a toast.'

With their goblets filled, the brothers raised them.

'To glory and honour!' said Bertelis.

'To glory and honour,' said Calard, and the pair clinked their goblets together once more.

'And to conquests in the bedroom as well as on the field of battle!' added Bertelis as Calard went to drink. The older sibling snorted, the ruby-coloured wine spilling from his nose and mouth.

Elisabet burst into very unseemly and unladylike laughter. The dour-faced wife of one of Lutheure's knights shushed her, as the lord castellan lifted his goblet high. Calard held his hand to Elisabet's mouth, as she looked fit to explode into further giggles.

'To Bertelis,' their father declared, 'who I am sure is destined to become one of the finest knights of Bastonne.' This was met with cheers, and the sound of Elisabet's contagious giggling made Bertelis smile. The lord castellan's face turned serious. 'Bertelis, you are the finest son a knight could wish for. Come back alive.'

People were unsure if that was a toast or not, and continued to hold their glasses in the air.

'Honour and glory!' shouted Bertelis to break the unease, lifting his goblet high. His words were echoed around the room, and everyone drank and went back to their conversations. He noticed vaguely that Elisabet was no longer laughing, and that his brother's face was dark.

Regardless, Bertelis clinked goblets with his brother, and again they drank, tension evaporating. Jesters came out to entertain the crowd, tall gangly jugglers and capering dwarfs, and Bertelis laughed loudly at their somersaults and antics.

Castellan Lutheure took his leave, retiring to his bed-chamber with his wife and, with the official duties concluded, the real drinking began.

CHAMBERLAIN FOLCARD STOOD motionless in the shadows beneath the archway, hawk-like eyes glinting fiercely. He receded further back into the darkness as he spied a hooded figure turn into the corridor, a shuttered lantern in hand. The figure moved softly down the cold hallway, casting a conspiratorial glance behind it. In that moment, the light caught on the figure's face, and Folcard saw the Lady Calisse's proud features.

The lady slipped through the doorway opposite the chamberlain's concealment, closing the door softly behind her. Folcard ignored the discomfort in his arthritic joints as he felt the cold seeping into his body. He did not have to wait long.

Less than two minutes after the lady of the household's appearance, a second figure entered the hallway, striding purposefully down the corridor. He made no attempt to conceal his appearance, and Folcard felt his anger rise at the man's arrogance.

Tanebourc smiled as he paused briefly outside the door through which Lady Calisse had entered, and then he knocked softly. A moment later, he pushed the door lightly open and slipped within.

Folcard shifted position, his anger simmering.

He loved Garamont fiercely, and he chafed at the shame being done to his noble lord.

He knew the castle better than anyone, and his eyes and his ears saw and heard all that occurred within its walls. He alone knew of all the secret passages that riddled the fastness, ones that even the Lord Garamont and his sons were unaware of.

He waited no more than five minutes before the door opened and the Lady Calisse slipped out into the corridor once more, pulling her hood up over her head. At least she had enough respect to conceal her appearance. After she had been gone for some minutes, the door opened again, and Tanebourc emerged. He was flushed, and Folcard saw frustration and impatience etched on his face. Good, he thought. His carnal urges had clearly been unsatisfied. That would work to his advantage.

'Tanebourc,' said the chamberlain, slipping out of the concealing darkness. He took perverse pleasure in the way the knight paled at his sudden appearance.

'Lady above!' gasped Tanebourc, his eyes wide and fearful. 'I thought you were an apparition!'

'I bear a message from the lady of the house,' said the chamberlain, his voice deep and sepulchral.

Recovering, Tanebourc's gaze flashed down the hallway, though Calisse was long gone. 'Oh?' he said, feigning disinterest.

'She wants you to know that she would be best pleased if the boy did not return to Garamont from this endeavour. You know of whom I speak.'

Tanebourc's eyes widened as he absorbed what the chamberlain was saying.

'What? She never said–'

'The lady would favour any who achieved this task. She would freely give him that which he desired, if he but did this small thing for her,' said Folcard, his eyes boring into the ginger-haired knight.

'It is no small thing—' began Tanebourc, but Folcard interrupted him again.

'Such are the lady's terms,' said the chamberlain. He saw the lust in the man's eyes, and knew that he had him.

'Think on it,' he added, before turning away.

CALARD WOKE WITH a groan. The pounding on the door of his chamber was incessant, and he rolled over, trying to ignore it. It felt like someone was smashing a hammer into his head, over and over, and his mouth felt like some foul creature had crawled in there and died while he slept. The pounding on his door continued unabated, giving him no peace.

'I'm awake!' he shouted. 'Go away!'

He closed his eyes in relief as he heard whoever it was move away, though he heard the banging begin anew further down the corridor. His brother's door, he realised.

With a moan, he rolled over on his pallet, and lifted himself to a sitting position. Swinging his legs to the flagstones, he realised that he was still wearing his high leather boots. Indeed, he was wearing the entire outfit he had worn the previous night. He had no memory of getting to bed, though he had a vague recollection of being helped up the twisting stone stairs to the eastern wing of the castle to his chambers. He groaned again and rose unsteadily to his feet, moving to the window. He poured a jug of ice cold water into the stone basin there, and washed his face. He drank deeply.

Looking out of the window, blinking against the painful light, it took him a moment to register that the sun was high in the sky. He swore colourfully, his language more fit for ribald commoners than for the son of a noble castellan. He tore his shirt from his muscled body and pulled on a freshly laundered tunic.

Swearing never to drink again, he pulled open his door and stepped into the corridor. He saw a flustered servant banging on Bertelis's door. With another self-pitying groan, he began staggering down the hallway. The man tried to say something to him, but he waved him away as if he was an irritating insect.

Without ceremony, Calard pushed Bertelis's door open. It caught on something on the floor, and he looked down. It was a woman's dress, a simple piece of clothing with little ornamentation. He gave the door a more solid push and walked into the room. The stink of sweat, wine and sex assailed him, and he blinked in the dim light.

Bertelis was sprawled naked on the bed, the nubile form of a young woman nestled against his chest. She turned as the door opened, pulling the sheets up over her body, modestly, her eyes filled with the wild fear of a rabbit caught in the open.

'Wake up,' said Calard. 'It's late.'

Bertelis squinted up at him, opening and closing his mouth as if tasting something foul upon his tongue. He dropped his head back down onto the goose feather stuffed pillow.

'Come on, get up,' said Calard more insistently. Bertelis sighed in resignation, and stood, stretching, without a thought for modesty.

'Get out,' he said casually to the girl. She stared at him blankly for a second, and he turned towards her. 'I said get out.'

The girl, the sheet wrapped around her, retrieved the clothing that was scattered all over the room, doing her best not to catch Calard's eye. She fled the room, and Calard could hear her soft steps as she ran up the hallway.

'Who was that?' he asked.

'Who?' asked Bertelis as he took a long swig from a water jug.

'That girl?'

'Oh, I don't know. Just some…' said Bertelis vaguely, one hand flapping as he sought the word. 'Some… girl.'

Calard snorted, shaking his head, and immediately regretting it as his vision spun.

'That was quite a night,' said Bertelis, dressing quickly.

'My memories of it are somewhat… vague,' said Calard. Bertelis snorted.

'After the speeches, the dining and the dancing, after father and mother had retired, you spent most of it declaring how you would slay a hundred orcs, and drooling into the cleavage of the young Lady Elisabet of Carlemont.'

Calard groaned and slapped a hand to his head. It was starting to come back to him.

'Oh, Lady protector, tell me I did nothing to embarrass myself in front of her,' he said.

'Well, the last thing I saw was her and that young serving girl, Annabel, helping you to your room. What happened after that, I know not,' said Bertelis with a lascivious grin. He dunked his head into a basin of water and flicked it back, spraying water across the room behind him. Wet, his golden hair seemed darker, and hung in long strands down his back.

'Come on then, we'd better get going,' said Bertelis brightly, stepping out into the corridor. Calard could have strangled his brother. Somehow, he always seemed to avoid the after-effects of overindulgence, which was perhaps why he indulged so often. In the light streaming through the arched windows, Bertelis looked over at him with a critical, pitying expression.

'You look twice as bad as I feel,' he said, eliciting another groan from Calard. 'Let's go armour up. Father will skin us alive if we keep him waiting.'

THE KNIGHTS OF Bastonne sat astride their warhorses on the grassland beyond the towering walls of Castle Garamont, their armour shined to perfection and colourful banners whipping in the stiff breeze. Each proudly bore his colours and heraldry, and each carried his helm in the crook of his left arm, his lance held vertical in his right, and his shield thrown over his back. Their number had been carefully chosen so as to outdo the Sangasse contribution, and only a handful of knights would remain at Garamont.

Hundreds of men-at-arms stood in the mud behind them, straining to see and hear the goings on, wearing tabards of red and gold, the lord castellan's colours, and holding polearms and tall shields in their muddy fists. A further contingent of peasants stood alongside the men-at-arms, a muster of bowmen drafted into service from amongst the populace, each holding a longbow of yew in his labourer's hands.

Fully armoured and wearing flowing cloaks that mirrored the colours of their livery, Lutheure's sons knelt before their father, the lord castellan of Garamont. Calard could still smell the delicate scent of Elisabet's perfume in his nostrils, and he breathed in deeply. Moments before, he had shared a delicate farewell with her, and he had almost been overwhelmed by his love for her as he saw tears well in her soulful eyes.

'I shall return in glory, and then we shall be wed.' He realised that he had spoken without thought, and his face reddened. 'If you will have me, I mean,' he added.

Despite her tears, Elisabet had laughed, her pale cheeks blushing the delicate colour of roses. In answer, she had loosened a violet silk scarf from around her head and tied it around the steel rarebrace that protected his left upper arm. He had been speechless, drinking in the sight and scent of her closeness.

'Be safe, Calard,' she had said, and the young couple embraced. Too soon, she pulled away from him. Turning as her tears threatened to flow anew, she fled into the protective arms of her father, who was smiling broadly at Calard. He had watched her go, feeling exultantly happy, but sad at the same time. He dragged his mind forcefully back to the present.

His heart pounded with barely restrained excitement as he knelt before his father, though he felt a tinge of unease. On one hand, this was his chance, at last, to prove himself on the field of battle, and he was full of noble confidence in his own abilities and those of his brother. He could not deny, however, that his father's health was worsening, despite the façade that he presented to the court. He knew that just to be standing outside, fully decked in his gleaming armour, wishing his knights well, would tax him dearly, and that he would most likely spend the rest of the day abed, exhausted. He prayed to the Lady to see his father safe, but he had a sickening feeling in his stomach that he would not see him again.

He pushed these morbid thoughts from his mind as he lowered his head to accept his father's blessing.

'Lady, may your wisdom and care protect these noble knights from harm, and inspire in them the strength and courage necessary to return home in triumph. Embolden them with your divine light, and in your name, let them cleanse the lands of Bordeleaux of its evil taint, and do Garamont and Bastonne proud. Lady, bless them that they may uphold your name with virtue. Honour is all. Chivalry is all.'

The two kneeling knights repeated these last two sentences, intoning them quietly.

'Rise, my sons,' Lutheure said, and the two young knights errant rose up to their full heights to look down upon their lord and father. Lady Calisse swept past the castellan in a wave of flowing silk and scented perfumes to embrace Bertelis, leaving Calard standing awkwardly before his father. The older knight's expression was distant.

'I will make you proud, my lord,' he said softly.

'Your mother was from Bordeleaux,' said the castellan softly, ignoring his son's words. Calard's eyes widened. In all the long years since his mother's death, his father had spoken of her perhaps twice. As if realising he had spoken aloud, the castellan frowned, and his usual, cold mask dropped over his face once more.

'Keep your brother safe,' Lutheure said brusquely. Calard swallowed, and bowed his head.

Lutheure embraced Bertelis, and Calard bowed graciously to his stepmother, though the Lady Calisse turned her head away from him, and spoke to a handmaiden.

With a cheer, the two young knights mounted their massive destriers. Squires passed them their weapons and shields, and Calard felt trembling excitement at the prospect of war. They joined the ranks of knights, drawing their steeds alongside their grim weapon master, Gunthar, who was to accompany them to battle.

'How are you feeling?' Bertelis asked in a low voice, throwing his brother a sideways glance.

'Like a horse is kicking me repeatedly in the head,' said Calard, though he maintained his smile. His brother smirked.

The lord castellan's ancient sword was brought forth, borne upon a cushion by his chamberlain, and Lutheure lifted it into his trembling hands. The sword of Garamont had been handed down to each of the successive rulers of Garamont, and it was an heirloom of priceless value, said to have been blessed by the kiss of the Lady of the Lake. Its scabbard was inlaid with spiralling designs picked out in gold, and the pommel of the sword was shining blue steel forged in the shape of a fleur-de-lys, the symbol of the blessed Lady. The lord castellan pulled the blade free, the sound of the blade ringing out over the gathered knights.

For a moment, as he lifted the sword high into the air, its blade shimmering with silver, fey light, Lutheure resembled the powerful knight that he had once been, strong, fearless and full of implacable courage.

'To victory!' he shouted, his voice deep and strong. This was met with another cheer, and the host of Garamont lifted their lances high in salute to their lord. Calard caught Elisabet's tearful eyes through the crowd of well-wishers, and he kissed the silk scarf wound around his arm while he maintained eye contact. She blew him a kiss in return, her eyes welling with tears. Then his eyes flicked to his father once more, settling on the powerful, distant man that he knew not at all.

'I will make you proud of me, father,' promised Calard. Then he wheeled his horse and joined the column of knights as they turned to the west, towards the distant sea and the lands of Bordeleaux. Blushing ladies threw flowers before the resplendent knights, and peasant children and dogs ran alongside them. Trumpets blared as they rode away from Castle Garamont, and Calard gave the castle that had been his home these last decades a final look, before kicking his spurs into Gringolet's flanks. Bertelis whooped in excitement, and Calard laughed at his brother's exuberance as he felt his own excitement rise.

CHLOD SQUINTED AS he surveyed the distant castle and the parade of knights that rode from it. He felt his pet, nestling against his scabrous neck, squirm and wriggle.

'Do you see them, my beauty?' he asked the mangy rat. It twitched its nose, unimpressed.

Chlod had laid low these last days, keeping to the forest. In the distance he could see the limp forms of his former comrades, hanging from the gallows erected alongside the approach to the castle, testament to the justice of the Bastonnian lord.

His stomach growled loudly, and he thought wistfully of the roasted venison that he had enjoyed some four days earlier. It had been so tender that it had almost melted on his tongue. Just thinking of it made his mouth begin to water, and he wiped a long string of drool from his chin with the back of his hand.

He was sure that there was abundant food all around him, but he was no huntsman, and had not the knowledge or means to catch any of the swift hares that he glimpsed sometimes at dawn and dusk. He had picked a handful of mushrooms from the base of a tree the day before, praying that they were not poisonous, but had not yet plucked up the courage to eat them.

No, foraging in the wilderness was not for him. A shepherd by birth, he had been kicked out of his home by his mother for his laziness, and had made his way in the world by scavenging on the outskirts of villages and towns, taking what he could lay his hands on when he could. He had received countless beatings from irate farmers over the years, but he never complained. Better to be beaten than to be hanged.

His small, piggy eyes watched the departing army intently. He knew that an army on the march would have countless hangers-on, and that there would be an abundance of food and game needed to supply the knights and their peasant militia. His stomach rumbled again, and his mind was made up.

'We will have food aplenty soon enough, my beauty,' he said, and he set off in the direction of the departing army, limping unsteadily through the fields.

CHAPTER FOUR

CALARD'S EARLY ELATION to be bound for glorious battle was soon replaced with mind-numbing boredom as the monotony of the journey ground home. He didn't know why he had expected anything different, for Bordeleaux was hundreds of miles to the west, but this did nothing to improve his foul mood.

The first day had seemed like the dawn of some grand adventure, and as soon as he had thrown off the worst effects of his hangover, Calard had felt his spirits soar. The sun was shining, he was wearing a token of his love's affection on his arm, he had his brother at his side and he was riding to war with a grand company of seasoned knights.

The lands of Bretonnia were not without peril, for, despite the rigour with which the realms were protected, it was well known that all manner of foul beasts dwelt within the great tracts of forest and within the high mountains. Outlaws preyed upon travellers, and even this far from the cursed lands of Mousillon, commoners barred their doors at night against the horrors of the night. Nevertheless, the knights of Garamont were unconcerned. Travelling in such force, few enemies would dare to strike against them.

The first night had been fine indeed, the knights swapping exaggerated stories of their heroics in battle as they ate, drank and made merry. Calard and Bertelis listened intently, hanging on every word spoken by the veterans. The night was glorious, unseasonably warm and clear as autumn deepened, and the brothers had felt a thrill to be encamped in the wilderness, their minds filled with tales of heroism and glory.

Even the next day, which was overcast, and with a sullen wind whipping at them, Calard's spirits had been high. It was only that afternoon, as the rains had begun, that his elated mood began to evaporate. It seemed somehow appropriate that, as they passed into Sangasse lands, the weather was turning. Knights of Garamont had rarely entered these lands peacefully, and the gathering black clouds mirrored Calard's darkening mood.

For generations, Garamont and the Sangasse had been fierce rivals, and though it had been nearly half a century since blood had been spilt between the families, Calard was uneasy travelling through their realm. He knew that his brother felt likewise, as did all the knights of Garamont, but it was necessary, for it would have taken them hundreds of miles out of their way to circumvent Sangasse's borders.

The contingent from Garamont had linked with the knights and foot soldiers of neighbouring Montcadas, travelling to Bordeleaux beneath the shining white banner of Baron Montcadas, emblazoned with its fiery red heraldic sword. The baron led his knights, himself. He was a squat, broad-shouldered warrior with a booming voice and a massive beard. Calard had met the man on several occasions. Indeed, the baron had briefly hoped to marry his plain, big-boned daughter into the Garamont line, and for a few months the previous year Calard had been terrified that his father would accept the offer on his behalf. Thankfully, nothing had come of the pairing, and the girl was married off to some other unlucky noble's son to the north.

As was the Bretonnian way, the knights of Garamont allowed Baron Montcadas command without question, for he was the most highly ranked noble present.

A strange figure accompanied the Baron of Montcadas, a man dressed outlandishly in the strange fashion of the Empire, far across the Grey Mountains that marked the border of the two mighty lands. He wore silk stockings beneath his knee-high riding boots, and bizarre slashed, puffy sleeves billowed around his arms. A black lacquered breastplate protected his body, in the centre of which was the gold emblem of a twin-tailed comet. Calard dimly recalled from his schooling that the insignia represented the barbarian Sigmar, who had founded the Empire, and who had, in time, been deified by his followers. The Cult of Sigmar was apparently the official religion of the lands of the Empire, which Calard found unfathomable. Sigmar had certainly been a mighty warrior, but to worship him, a mere mortal, as a god seemed ridiculous.

A black lacquered sallet helmet sat upon the man's head, a long red feather bobbing from its rim, and he rode a horse of Empire stock, neither as powerful nor as regal as one of the pure Bretonnian bloodline. Calard was intrigued by this strange man and the strange land he hailed from, and he stared in fascination at him as he was introduced.

The Empire soldier, for it was clear that he was a soldier, despite his bizarre and faintly ridiculous dress, was young, perhaps no more than five years Calard's senior. His cheeks were shaved smooth, as was his chin, but upon his upper lip he sported a prodigious moustache, the points of which were tweaked and waxed into tight curls. The effect was humorous to Bretonnian eyes, though it was clear that the man took his appearance very seriously. Indeed, he seemed to be fastidious to a fault, brushing off any speck of dust from his clothes, and ensuring that his every buckle and bootstrap was shined and untwisted, and that everything was placed correctly about his person.

His name was Dieter Weschler, and Calard had spoken the name awkwardly, trying and failing to pronounce it correctly. The man had corrected his attempt, his voice guttural and clipped to Calard's ears. He spoke Breton better than Calard had expected, though his accent was strange. He had strength in him, Calard had decided as he had gripped forearms with the man and looked into his eyes.

Bertelis had appraised the Empire man with a critical eye, sizing him up, and he was clearly unimpressed. There was no doubting that he was wealthy, for his outlandish clothes were richly made, and he wore rings and earrings of gold, but, to a Bretonnian eye, he appeared more like a lowborn peasant merchant that had come into money than one born to it through noble bloodline.

He had a sword strapped at his side, but it was his other weapons that were making Bertelis wrinkle his nose in disgust. A long-barrelled handgun was strapped over Dieter's shoulder, and a brace of three pistols hung loosely at his side. In Bretonnia, weapons that caused death from afar were regarded as cowardly, and no knight would dream of sullying himself by making use of a bow or crossbow, outside of the hunt. To use such missile weapons on the field of battle marked one as a peasant, for there was no glory to be had in defeating one's enemy from a distance. A noble warrior's weapons were the lance and the sword, the mace and the morning star. It was only those who lacked honour, bravery and self-respect that resorted to the use of such weapons as the bow.

Black powder weapons were all but unheard of in Bretonnia, but Dieter explained with dignified pride that they were commonplace in the wealthier Empire states, apparently oblivious to the less than enthusiastic response of his audience.

It was with some shock that Calard learned that Dieter was a blood relative of the ruler of the Empire, and thus of the noblest stock of the land. He could tell that Bertelis too was stunned by this revelation. The Baron of Montcadas said that Dieter was a guest in his household, come to Bastonne to learn more of Bretonnia and strengthen the bonds between the two great lands. His own son, he proclaimed proudly, was currently a guest of the Empire, living in a far off city called Altdorf, housed within the Emperor's palace.

'I don't like him,' declared Bertelis when they were out of earshot. 'The people of the Empire must be weak indeed if their nobles dress in the manner of merchants and carry peasant weapons to war.'

'Perhaps,' said Calard noncommittally. 'I would like to speak to him more though,' he added after a moment of silence. His brother raised an eyebrow.

'Why?' he asked.

Calard shrugged.

'To learn of his lands, their customs, their way of doing things. It interests me.'

Bertelis snorted, shaking his head.

The rains had increased in intensity, turning the trail into a quagmire of clinging mud. Water ran uncomfortably down the inside of Calard's armour. The horses plodded on through the worsening weather until a halt was finally called. The knights sat astride their horses in silence as peasants scrambled through the mud to erect their tents and get cooking fires burning.

Sitting beneath a canvas awning, Calard and Bertelis watched as the rains redoubled in strength, and it was not long before booming peals of thunder echoed across the heavens, making the picketed horses whinny in fear. A table had been set up before the pair of young knights, and upon it were scattered the remains of their meal. Calard fingered his goblet thoughtfully, watching the peasants scurrying back and forth through the downpour on errands and duties.

Lightning flashed across the sky in a stunning display, followed seconds later by thunderous crashes that resounded across the bleak landscape. Bertelis wore a sour expression on his noble face as he watched the rain come down. He was gnawing on a bone, and hurled it out into the downpour in frustration at being held up.

Calard watched dispassionately as a pair of peasants scrambled through the mud towards the discarded bone. One of them was hunchbacked, and had a pronounced limp, while the other was smaller and weasel-like.

'A gold crown says the small one gets it,' said Bertelis.

'You're on,' replied Calard. The hunchback was closer, but he stumbled, and fell heavily in the mud as he closed on the prize. Bertelis laughed in victory as the smaller peasant swooped in and grabbed the scrap of food, and he held out his hand to receive his gold crown from his brother.

'Wait,' said Calard, as the hunchback picked himself up off the ground and dived on the smaller figure, tackling him into the mud. Bertelis guffawed and yelled encouragement as the pair rolled over and over in the mud, fighting for possession of the food scrap. He threw his hands up into the air in disappointment, as the hunchback rolled on top of the smaller figure and began pounding his fists into its face. At last, he stepped away from the body, picking up his prize.

'You there! Peasant!' shouted Bertelis, standing up. The hunchback froze. 'Yes, you!' Bertelis hollered over the downpour, 'Come here!'

The hunchback glanced around furtively, shoving his prize into a deep pocket on his tunic. For a moment, it looked like he was going to run, but he clearly thought better of it, and began to approach the knights errant.

He limped heavily towards them, pulling his hood down low over his face. Behind him, the beaten figure of his rival pushed itself groggily to its feet and staggered off though the rain. With shock, Calard realised that it was a woman, and he shook his head in disbelief.

The hunchback stopped just outside the canvas awning that protected the knights, standing in the rain, his head low.

'Yes, my lord?' said the man humbly.

'Take off your hood,' ordered Bertelis. Somewhat reluctantly, the man did so. He was an ugly brute, thought Calard, thick jawed and caked in mud, and his lowered eyes were uneven.

'You just lost me a gold crown, peasant,' said Bertelis imperiously. The man glanced up fearfully at the young knight towering above him, before his gaze flicked down to the ground once more.

'I'm sorry, lord,' he mumbled, clearly having no idea what was going on.

'Well, what are you going to do about it?'

'Um,' stuttered the man, shifting his weight nervously. 'I… ah.'

Calard narrowed his eyes as he looked at the man. There was something familiar about him, but he couldn't put his finger on it.

'I'll tell you what you can do. My brother and I are in need of entertainment, and you certainly have the look of a clown about you. Dance.'

The man blanched, opening and closing his mouth soundlessly. He threw a glance towards Calard, who was still regarding him closely, and quickly turned his gaze away.

'I... I don't know how, my lord,' he stammered.

'Well, just give it a try, hmm? Dance for us.'

'Oh, leave him alone,' said Calard.

'No, brother,' replied Bertelis. 'I would have him dance for us. Well, come on then! Dance!'

The hunchback began to hop from foot to foot, and Bertelis howled in laughter, clapping his hands. Apparently encouraged by this, the man began to hop more energetically from foot to foot, and began to lift his arms up and down.

'That's the way! You've got it now!' laughed Bertelis, and Calard found himself snorting in pitying amusement. The wretched peasant grinned stupidly, and turned an ungainly pirouette on the spot, which was greeted with more laughter. Calard was well used to the tortures his brother inflicted on the lowborn at every opportunity, but he had to admit that the sight of this wretched creature capering in the pouring rain was funny. A rat poked its black furred head out of the peasant's tunic, which elicited further laughter from the brothers.

Tears streaming from his eyes, Bertelis waved for the peasant to stop, his body still shuddering with amusement. He picked up another discarded bone from his plate, and held it out to the peasant. The man eagerly reached for it, his crooked eyes lighting up, but Bertelis retracted it just before the peasant could close his grubby hand on it. He extended it once more, again pulling it back just before the peasant could grasp it. The peasant grinned stupidly at Bertelis's jest, and the third time the young knight offered it and retracted it, he slapped his leg and laughed out loud.

Finally, Bertelis hurled the bone away from him. The man followed its arc carefully, but did not chase after it immediately.

'Well, go,' said Bertelis finally.

'Thank you, young lord,' said the man, turning away from them. The stupid grin dropped from his face, replaced with a scowl of anger and humiliation, and he loped towards the discarded tidbit, shouting and waving his arms as other peasants moved towards it.

Still chuckling, Bertelis watched him go.

'Did you recognise that man from somewhere?' asked Calard, still troubled that he could not place the man.

'Who, the hunchback? I don't know. Maybe. They all look the same to me.' Calard grunted and pushed the thought from his mind.

'How far is it to Bordeleaux?' asked Bertelis.

'Five days' ride, Gunthar says,' replied Calard.

'We had better pray to the Lady that the battle is not over before we get there,' said Bertelis. A flutter of concern passed through Calard at the thought.

That night, with the rain lashing down on the tent he shared with his brother, Calard lit fourteen candles, each one representing one of the Dukedoms of Bretonnia. He carefully unfolded the hinged wooden triptych that served as his shrine to the Lady. Humbly, he touched his fingertips to the centre of his forehead, his lips and his heart in turn, before kneeling.

The central, arched panel held a portrait of the Lady painted in oils and protected with thick lacquer. It was a delicate image that seemed to glow from within, showing the Lady holding her holy, golden grail before her.

In the left-hand panel was a finely detailed painting of Gilles the Uniter, the founder of Bretonnia. He knelt humbly with his head bowed, his famous dragon-skin cloak thrown over his shoulders. Gilles had slain the malevolent great wyrm, Smearghus, when he was little more than a boy, and had cut the cloak from its flesh. The revered artefact hung in the duke of Bastonne's castle, and every year thousands of knights made the pilgrimage to stand beneath it in awe.

The right-hand panel showed the fabled Green Knight, the unearthly guardian of Bretonnia's sacred places. Pictured as a fey spirit of awesome power and majesty, the Green Knight wore ancient armour, and was surrounded by coiling mist and ivy.

It was the central image, that of the Lady of Lake, that Calard focused on. Her deep eyes that the unknown artist had captured so skilfully, full of motherly love, but also with profound strength and mystery, captivated him, and he stared longingly at the golden chalice clasped in her delicate hands.

To be visited by the image of the Lady, and to sup from the grail was the ultimate aim of every knight of Bretonnia, and only the most determined, pure and worthy knights would ever achieve this goal. It was said that only the truly pure of heart survived drinking from this hallowed chalice, and any that had even the smallest hint of corruption or flaw would be instantly killed. Calard longed for the day when he would be able to take up the quest and go out into the world in search of the Lady. She would only appear to one who had travelled far, embarking on a great journey, and who had fought against all manner of beast and injustice. Such an event was many years off, and Calard sighed in impatience, longing for that time when he attained the honour and glory needed to take up the questing vow.

Pushing such thoughts from his mind, he focused on the image of the Lady before him. She wore a garland of flowers and ivy around her head, and her long hair flowed freely around her. She was the very epitome of noble beauty and chastity.

In a soft, humble voice, he prayed firstly for the king, Louen Leoncouer, the Lionhearted, that he may reign long and true. Then he prayed for the health of his father, and for his sister, Anara, long lost, asking that the Lady look over her wherever she might be. He prayed for his brother Bertelis, that he might gain much honour and renown in the battles to come, and that he would live a long, fulfilling life. Lastly, he prayed for himself, though he felt a twinge of guilt to pray for selfish means. Still, he pushed these thoughts aside, and prayed fervently.

'Lady of Chivalry let the battles in Bordeleaux be glorious and noble, and let the forces of the king prove victorious against the evil that defiles your realm. Lend me strength, Lady, and let my faith in you be the armour of my soul. Let me prove my honour before all on the field of battle, and let me return to Garamont victorious. Lady of the Fair Isle, I swear it, I shall not rest until I have proven myself worthy in your eyes,' said Calard, taking a deep breath before he continued. 'And I shall not rest until I have proven myself worthy in the eyes of my father.'

In the darkness, Bertelis lay awake in the darkness, listening to his brother's solemn and puritanical words.

At last, the fourteen candles were snuffed out, and the tent was plunged into darkness.

CHAPTER FIVE

CALARD RODE AT the head of the column of knights snaking across the verdant landscape, savouring the feeling of the sun on his back. It had seemed that the entire host had been galvanised by the same concern that plagued Calard: that they would arrive in Bordeleaux too late to make a meaningful contribution in the war against the greenskins, and so the nobles had pushed on with renewed vigour. They awoke before dawn, peasants quickly striking the tents, and the entire force was moving before the first rays of the sun speared over the horizon from the east.

They pushed on at a formidable pace, eating up the miles as they crossed farmland, keeping the forest of Chalons always within eyesight to the south, following the curve of the great expanse of trees. They passed through countless peasant villages and by a dozen fortified stately homes and castles, and, at last, the plains of southern Bastonne rose into the undulating hills of Bordeleaux.

They maintained their relentless pace into the night, leaving the footslogging men-at-arms and the rabble of bowmen commoners far behind, before camp was made. The colourful tents of the nobles were hastily erected by yeomen, and the knights' horses were brushed down, fed and watered. It was long after midnight, after all but a handful of nobles had eaten their fill and retired for the night, when the peasant soldiers arrived in camp. They collapsed to the ground exhausted, choosing to cluster together under filthy blankets rather than expend the energy needed to erect the crude mass awnings that served as their shelters.

They kept up the mile-eating pace for five days. The rains had passed, but the days remained dull and grey. Miserable, cold peasants in the fields leant on their hoes, wiping hands across their brows as they watched the parade of knights pass. Some of them waved, but not a single knight so much as acknowledged their existence. Only the taciturn Empire noble, Dieter, gave the workers a response, nodding curtly to them as they stared at him in curiosity.

'What crops are being tended?' Dieter asked, gesturing to the endless rows of tall, gangly plants, his voice clipped and heavily accented. Stakes connected with twine had been driven into the ground along the perfectly straight lines of cultivated plants to keep them upright, and fruit hung in dense bunches from the spindly limbs.

Calard laughed out loud, looking at the Empire envoy to see if he was making some joke that did not translate. Seeing nothing that would suggest humour in the man's

serious face, he shook his head slightly at Dieter's igno-
rance. He seemed so learned in some areas, but, in
others, his lack of knowledge was astounding.

'This area is renowned throughout the Old World for
its vineyards,' said Calard. 'These are grape vines you
see stretched out before you.'

'Ah!' said Dieter, wagging a finger in the air in pleasure and excitement, as if he had uncovered some great
hidden knowledge. 'This is where your wine is made!'

'Well, it is where the grapes that make wine is cultivated, yes,' said Calard, amused at the usually reserved
man's obvious excitement. 'Do you not have vineyards
within the Empire?"

'Oh yes, some, but not in Reikland.'

Calard frowned. 'So, what do you drink?'

'Beer, predominantly, strong, full flavoured and
invigorating. Some of the wealthy drink wine, but it is
not common.'

'In Bretonnia, even the lowliest peasant drinks wine,'
said Calard proudly, 'and none more so than those of
Bordeleaux, hence the expression, "the sober man of
Bordeleaux".'

Dieter frowned. 'I do not understand,' he said.

'If something is unusual, or unexpected, it is said to
be as rare as the sober man of Bordeleaux.'

Dieter repeated the phrase quietly, committing it to
memory as if it were of great import.

'It's a jest,' prompted Calard. 'In Bordeleaux, there is
such an abundance of readily accessible and cheap
wine that the inhabitants are jokingly regarded to be
constantly inebriated.'

'Yes, I understand the humour. It is most amusing,'
said Dieter seriously. Calard rolled his eyes as the

Imperial envoy turned away. If all the people of the Empire were as humourless as Dieter, it must be a grim place indeed.

There was a shout of alarm, and Calard turned in the direction that some of the knights were pointing, seeing wafts of dark smoke rising into the sky in the distance.

'It's probably just peasants burning off refuse,' said a knight, but there was little conviction in his voice.

'Men are riding towards us,' said Dieter suddenly. His accent made his pronunciation amusing to the ears of the Bretonnians, and Bertelis, riding just behind the pair, sniggered.

'Zey are peasant scouts,' said Bertelis, imitating Dieter's accent. Calard smirked, and flicked a sidelong glance at the Imperial noble. His face was impassive. If he realised that he was being made fun of, he made no acknowledgement of the fact.

Four outriders rode towards the column of knights, crude spears in their hands. They rode draught horses more generally used to pull hoes and wagons. It was a rare honour for any peasant to be allowed to ride a horse, and a great sign of status among the unruly commoners, though the heavy steeds were utterly outshone by the noble warhorses ridden by the nobility.

Gunthar pulled his steed up alongside Calard, and addressed the dirty peasants as they drew their horses to a halt alongside the column.

'What news, yeoman?'

The leader of the motley horsemen, a stinking man with a vicious scar running across his face, nodded his head in deference to Gunthar. He wore a tabard of iron-studded leather over his body, and, bizarrely, had a dead pigeon strapped to his steel-rimmed helmet. His luncheon meal, most probably, thought Calard in disgust.

'A village, m'lord, under attack up ahead.'

'Under attack? Greenskins?' asked Gunthar curtly.

'Aye, m'lord.' Calard and Bertelis exchanged excited glances.

'How far?' cut in Calard eagerly.

'Not far, m'lord, maybe five miles? Up yonder, in the dip past that hill,' said the scarred yeoman, gesturing with his spear towards a rise up ahead.

Calard and Bertelis instantly kicked their steeds forward, though they wheeled them sharply around when they realised that the other knights were not following their lead.

'Well, what are you waiting for?' asked Bertelis.

'Have some patience, young lord,' said Gunthar darkly. 'It is foolish indeed to rush off to battle without knowing first what one faces.'

'What one faces?' asked Bertelis. 'The peasant said it himself: greenskins.'

'But how many, and from which direction? These are questions that a knight must ask before he charges off to battle.'

Calard huffed in impatience. His steed, sensing its rider's excitement, was snorting and stamping its hooves as it turned on the spot.

'Ah, the lads are just eager to whet their blades,' said the deep booming voice of the Baron of Montcadas as he rode to the front of the column. 'I can't say I blame them, either,' he added. 'The last week has been a drain on my patience.' Calard gave the broad shouldered knight a grin.

The baron's bushy beard parted in a broad, toothy smile, and he pulled his morning star from his side, the heavy spiked ball falling to hang alongside his horse as the chain was released from its leather binding.

'Let's go get 'em, eh lads?' said the baron, winking towards Calard.

The young knights errant whooped in anticipation, and the baron swung his bulk around in the saddle to address the knights behind him.

'Knights of Bastonne!' he roared with the thunder of an angry bear. 'We ride to battle! Form up!'

With that, the baron kicked his steed forward into a trot.

'Stay close to me lads,' he rumbled to Calard and Bertelis, and they fell in alongside the stocky knight of Montcadas. Gunthar pulled his steed alongside them, his moustache twitching in irritation.

'Don't tense up, and don't break formation when the charge is launched,' he said. 'Keep tight, and don't lose your momentum.'

'We know how to fight, old man,' retorted Bertelis, but the veteran knight ignored him.

'Follow the lead of the baron. He will be the point of the lance, and you must ride close. We must be as one, for if we become splintered we will lose our advantage.'

Bertelis groaned in exasperation, and Calard too felt his frustration and embarrassment rise.

'We are not children,' Calard snapped, feeling a blush on his cheeks to be spoken to in this manner within earshot of the more senior knights.

'That will be determined shortly,' said Gunthar. 'Just remember what I have taught you.'

* * *

CALARD'S HANDS WERE sweating within his gauntlets and his throat was dry, as the knights crested the hill.

The buildings of the village were crude dwellings, constructed from a latticework of sticks, and covered in a thick gruel of straw, mud and manure. Such wattle and daub lodgings were common in Bretonnia, for it was illegal for a peasant to make use of stone in the construction of their own dwellings. The streets were filled with screaming peasants, who ran in all directions.

Several of the hovels were ablaze, and black smoke rose, in billowing clouds above them.

Calard's eyes, however, were drawn to the enemy. He had never seen a live greenskin before, though he had stared for hours on end at the massive stuffed head of one of the brutes, mounted in the castle banquet hall, marvelling at its savage, thick features and gaping, tusk-filled maw. That severed orc head had always made him shiver, but it was as nothing compared to witnessing the brutal creatures in the flesh.

Each of them was as tall as a man, though they were hulking monsters of muscle, far broader and heavier than the peasants they were slaughtering. The air was filled with their savage roars, and they hacked around them with heavy cleavers and cudgels, butchering everything in their path.

The ground reverberated with the pounding of hooves as the knights of Bastonne galloped towards the beleaguered villagers, and Calard felt his breath catch in his throat. He saw one roaring greenskin slam its crude weapon into the shoulder of a screaming peasant, blood spurting from the mortal blow as it drove deep into the man's body. An axe slammed into the neck of another, nigh on severing the peasant's head, and the greenskin monster roared its pleasure as hot blood sprayed into its face.

Scores of peasants had already been massacred, and the few that tried to fight their attackers with pitchforks and hoes were cut down mercilessly. Calard saw a man's head rupture as it was slammed violently into the doorframe of a barn, and heard the cries of peasants that had chosen to die in the flames consuming their homes rather than be torn apart by the animal ferocity of the greenskins.

The village was a scene of nightmarish brutality and horror, with screaming peasants running in every direction, seeking escape, and dozens of hulking, green-skinned creatures revelling in the panic and slaughter. Calard saw a child impaled upon a spear hurled through the maelstrom of battle, and, as he watched, he saw a woman hurl herself from the upper storey of a barn, desperate to escape the flames threatening to burn her alive, only to be leapt upon and ripped apart by a pair of massive green-fleshed brutes.

'For Bastonne and the King!' bellowed Baron Montcadas, swinging his spiked morning star over his head, and the knights kicked their steeds into a gallop. The baron formed the apex of the charge, pulling ahead of the line of knights, and the other nobles of Bastonne formed a tight wedge behind him. Calard guided his steed expertly with his thighs and spurs, and lowered his lance before him as he had been trained, and the knights of Bretonnia thundered into the main street of the village.

A greenskin raised its thick head from the struggling peasant it had just clubbed to the ground, its small eyes glinting with savagery. The spiked metal ball of the baron's morning star swung into its head with brutal force, and the creature was sent flying backwards, its skull a shattered ruin, before it was trampled beneath the hooves of the knights' steeds.

Everything was happening in a blur. The riot of noise was overwhelming, as screams of pain and anger mingled with animalistic roars and bellows above the pounding of horses' hooves and the clanking of plate armour. The heat of the flames washed over Calard like a wave, the hot air scalding his lungs with each breath. Burning buildings flashed past as the knights pounded into the village, and peasants dived out of the way, frantic to escape being trampled to death. The stink of blood, death and burning human flesh filled Calard's nostrils. His heart was pounding and his breath was coming in short, sharp gasps.

'Keep tight!' shouted Gunthar, and Calard snapped back into focus. His whole existence seemed to become suddenly centred on the tip of his lance, and he levelled it at the barrelling chest of a greenskin brute that roared its defiance as he bore down upon it.

The creature leapt forward to meet the knights head-on, and Calard followed its every move with the tip of his lance. He took in every detail of the barbarous creature: its foul hide, which was the colour of rotting vegetation; the assortment of rusted armour plates that covered its broad shoulders; its malicious red eyes filled with bloodlust and bestial hatred. Gore dripped from the heavy bladed cleavers clasped in its massive fists, and thick tusks extended from its lower jaw. Its heavily scarred arms were immense, easily as thick as his thighs.

The lance tip smashed into the orc's chest with a shuddering impact, and Calard tensed his muscles as he drove the lance through the creature's ribcage, as he had been taught on the practice fields of Garamont. The power of the blow shuddered up Calard's arm and into his body, as the vamplate of his lance was driven back into his breastplate, and his body rocked backwards in the saddle. The lance drove clear through the creature's body, impaling it, and the weapon was ripped from Calard's hands.

The fallen orc was trampled beneath Gringolet's hooves, its bones crushed as it was kicked and stamped by the knights close behind. Then Calard was past the orc, his sword hissing from his scabbard in a flash of silver. In what seemed like a fraction of a second, he had been blooded in battle, and had made his first kill with the lance.

Calard's blade flashed out, glancing off the skull of an orc as he surged past, and other greenskins were lifted into the air as they were impaled on the lances of the other knights.

Calard's earlier nervousness was replaced by an empowering surge of adrenaline, and he whooped savagely, voicing his enthusiasm and excitement as the formation of knights thundered through the village, running down and slaughtering the greenskins. Nothing could stand against them, and the feeling of power and speed was intoxicating.

CALARD'S HANDS WERE shaking as he dismounted, and he took a deep racking breath, exhausted and exhilarated. His body was tense, and it felt like he had been fighting for hours rather than the scant minutes that had actually passed.

Kneeling, he wiped the dark blood from his sword on the tunic of a peasant lying face down and unmoving in the mud. The image of the orc as his lance had impaled it kept flashing into his mind, and he clenched his fist, feeling again the killing blow.

Bertelis whooped as he dropped from the saddle alongside him, and Calard beamed at him as the brothers clasped forearms.

'Our first battle a noble victory!' said Bertelis. 'I saw your strike, brother, a fine blow it was.'

'As was yours,' said Calard. Bertelis's lance had taken an orc in the throat, ripping its jugular free in a spurt of blood.

'And the baron!' exclaimed Bertelis. 'He was like the spirit of Gilles reborn! He must have killed, what, five of them?'

'It was truly a sight to behold,' he said, nodding in agreement, awed by the prowess of the knight.

'You did well, young lords,' said Gunthar gruffly, pulling his horse alongside the pair of knights errant. 'You remembered your training in the chaos of battle. More than a few knights have stumbled in their first engagement, freezing up or becoming overwhelmed by their fear. I am proud of you both.'

Calard beamed up at Gunthar, feeling a surge of pride at the rare praise.

Peasant women wailed over the mutilated corpses of fathers, husbands and sons, while others struggled to contain the fires that still raged, but Calard was oblivious to their suffering, focused completely on his own victory. He had been tested in the forge of battle and had proven himself worthy.

'This was but a skirmish,' said Gunthar. 'The enemy was unprepared for our attack, intent on the slaughter of the defenceless, but it is good that your blades have been whetted in blood. Remember this day, for things will never be the same again. Today, you have become men.'

With a curt nod, the weapon master wheeled his horse around, and began barking orders at the men-at-arms bearing the colours of Garamont, who were just now arriving in the village, organising them into work teams. A pit was dug on the outskirts of the village, and the corpses of slain peasants were hurled unceremoniously into the shallow grave. The bodies of the greenskins were dragged onto the smouldering remnants of a hovel gutted by fire, and the air was soon filled with a nauseating stink as their flesh was consumed in the flames. More than half the village had been levelled by fire, and peasants poked through the ruins to salvage anything of value.

'Knights of Bastonne! The armies of Bordeleaux are near!' bellowed Baron Montcadas. 'We push on!'

Calard pulled himself into the saddle once more, feeling older and more self-assured than he had only an hour earlier. He accepted a new lance offered to him by a soldier, bearing the colours of his father, and at the sound of a horn blown by one of the knights the nobles of Bastonne rode from the devastated village. The men-at-arms and bowmen trudged along in their wake, stomping and slipping through the mud.

The peasant villagers watched them go, their faces pale, and streaked with blood and filth as they stood despondent amid the scene of destruction all around them.

The warriors of Bastonne did not look back.

CALARD'S JAW DROPPED as he drew to a halt atop the rise and looked down upon the seething battle underway below.

They had ridden for half a day before encountering the scouts of Bordeleaux.

Clarion horns sounded, and thousands of knights churned up the earth as they thundered across the field, lances lowering as they smashed into the massed ranks of the enemy. The greenskins surged like an overwhelming tide, their numbers inconceivable. Dim roars and screams carried up to the knights of Bordeleaux, and barbarous drums echoed across the battlefield. The greenskins pounded weapons against their shields, creating a resounding din, like the beating heart of some infernal god of war.

The earth was littered with the dead and dying, hundreds of broken figures that twitched and moaned in pain. Horses with legs broken beneath them screamed in inhuman agony. Dark clouds of arrows descended through the air, killing hundreds with each volley.

'Ah, what I would give to have a handful of cannons from Nuln here, now,' said Dieter, to no one in particular. Bertelis flashed a look of disgust at the Empire soldier.

Thousands of men-at-arms and greenskins were locked in brutal combat, and Calard could see the line of the Bretonnian forces begin to buckle against the strength and ferocity of the foe. Even as he watched, he saw a heraldic black and white banner fall amidst the mayhem, and a few men-at-arms broke ranks, fleeing away from the foe. These men were like the first rocks that started an avalanche, and soon hundreds of men-at-arms were streaming back towards their own battle lines. Scores of them were cut down by the enemy that surged forwards as they fled, and hundreds more would have been slaughtered were it not for the knights that powered into the greenskins, stemming the gap in the line. They ploughed through the undisciplined enemy ranks, felling dozens with lance and sword, and scattering the survivors before them.

The greenskin lines parted, and rattling chariots of crude design were dragged through the breach by giant war boars, murderous scythes spinning from their axles. Calard cried out as he saw a trio of these machines of war smash into a phalanx of knights. Nobles fell heavily as their steed's legs were cut from beneath them, while other knights were lifted from their saddles by the thick spears thrust by the orcs riding upon the backs of these wheeled constructs. The gigantic war boars, bristling with blood lust, gored and ripped with thick tusks capped with iron, and noble warriors of Bordeleaux were crushed beneath the metal studded rims of chariot wheels.

The carnage was breathtaking. This was war, with thousands of men and beasts clashing in mortal combat.

A formation of knights, its momentum lost, became mired in combat, deep within an enemy formation. Their horn blower sounded his instrument frantically, as the greenskins surrounded them on all sides and began dragging them from the saddle, cleavers hacking at the knights savagely.

A lance of knights, hearing the distress call, wheeled their steeds around to aid their comrades, and it was then that Calard saw a fresh line of orcs erupt from the tree line, riding upon the backs of hulking boars. The powerful beasts hurtled across the ground, angling towards the flank of the knights who were oblivious to the threat. The knights of Bordeleaux overlooked the field from a vantage point, and only they could see the danger. The boar riders would slam into the flank of the knights, and more proud Bretonnians would be slaughtered.

'Ride!' shouted Baron Montcadas, kicking his steed onwards, and the knights of Bastonne powered down the grassy hill to intercept the threat. Calard, his face flushed with anger, shouted a wordless war cry, which was lost amongst the cacophony of war, as he urged Gringolet on, willing the stallion to gallop faster.

Too late, the boar riders realised this new danger, and tried to haul their bulky steeds around to face the knights' charge. The creatures were stubborn, obstinate beasts, and they snarled and slavered as their riders pulled brutally at them. Several of them threw their riders, bucking and spinning, and the massive tuskers gored each other in the confusion. The scent of blood drove them to madness, and they ripped at each other, as their riders tried frantically to control the wild beasts. Then the knights of Bastonne slammed into them.

Calard's lance glanced off the armoured shoulder of an orc, throwing it off balance, and Gringolet's armoured bulk smashed the creature aside. It lost its precarious balance upon the ridged back of its mount, and fell beneath the flashing hooves of the warhorses, even as the boar was impaled upon the lance of another knight, spitting and snarling as it fell.

There was a sharp crack from nearby, followed by an unfamiliar, acrid smell, and an orc was felled as a lead shot punched through its thick, bony forehead. Calard glanced to his side to see the Empire soldier, Dieter, with one of his long, ornate pistols extended, smoke spilling from the barrel.

A knight alongside Calard was thrown from the saddle as a spear struck his breastplate, and he saw his brother's lance break as it sank deep into the body of another boar. Tucking his own lance tightly under his arm, he drove its point into the face of a savagely painted greenskin, feeling the satisfying impact as the long weapon drove through its eye socket and brain, before punching through the back of its skull.

Then the knights were free, having smashed through the flank of the boar riders, splitting them.

'Wheel right!' roared Baron Montcadas, swinging his gore splattered morning star above his head, spraying blood all around him. In perfect unison, the knights of Bastonne pulled their steeds around to the right in a wide arc, wheeling to face the remnants of the boar riders.

'For the glory of Bastonne!' roared the baron, echoed by the shouts of the knights riding behind him, and charged into the confused enemy.

Calard screamed in savage fury as he killed. His lance was wrenched from his hand, so he drew his glittering sword and split the helmet and head of another greenskin.

Within the hour, the field had been won, and the remnants of the greenskin army was fleeing back into the trees, pursued by small regiments of knights and mounted yeomen.

Calard reined his steed in, breathing heavily. His immaculate blue and red tabard was splattered with blood, and ripped where a cowardly arrow, fired by the enemy, had glanced across his chest. His shield, bearing his white dragon rampant upon a blue and red field was battered and scratched.

In one hand, he held the delicate material of the scarf given to him by Elisabet, and he lifted it to his nose, inhaling the perfume that clung to it, feeling comfort in the familiar scent. He tucked the silk cloth beneath his breastplate, and bent forwards in the saddle to pat Gringolet heavily on the shoulder, whispering to the powerful destrier.

'You did well, boy. You did well.'

CHAPTER SIX

THE BLARING OF horns and the roar of cheering greeted
the victorious knights as they rode into Duke Alberic
of Bordeleaux's camp. The smell of roasting meat all
but concealed the stink of bodies, sweat, horses and
the open pit latrines. Heralds shouted the names and
deeds of nobles as they approached, and groups of
young knights, flushed with victory, were already cele-
brating loudly, toasting their success and boasting of
their exploits.

The camp was like a grand city, with thousands of
tents arrayed in orderly rows upon the grass, each one
proudly displaying the colours of its owner, and flying
pennants and banners. Deer and pigs were roasting on
spits, over cooking fires tended by peasants, and the
heady scents of herbs and garlic rose tantalisingly from
heavy pots stirred by dutiful servants.

A mock duel was underway, performed by gaudily costumed players, and a rowdy crowd cheered as a black-clad knight, bearing the heraldry of cursed Mousillon, was cut down, bladders of pigs' blood spilling from the 'mortal' wound inflicted by the dashing hero. This noble knight grabbed a comely wench around the waist and delivered a dramatic kiss upon her lips, dipping her backwards theatrically, as jesters capered around, waving rats and frogs on sticks and making obscene gestures behind the couple, accompanied by laughter from those gathered around them.

Livestock screamed as they were slaughtered, and peasants led carts laden with fresh produce through the crowd. Wagons piled high with wooden casks of wine bearing the stamp of Bordeleaux were pushed through the mass of people.

The duke's massive blue pavilion took pride of place in the centre of the camp, positioned atop a knoll that dominated the area. It was rimmed with gold, and each of its sprawling wings was topped with sky-blue streamers and pennants, edged in gold thread. The duke's standard was held aloft atop the hill, proudly showing the golden trident upon a field of blue that was his personal heraldry.

The tents of those nobles and knights closest to the duke through birth and favour were positioned around this massive pavilion, and it was clearly a show of status: the closer one's tent was to the duke's the more respect one was due.

Calard smarted that, due to their late arrival, his peasants were forced to erect his tent on the lee side of the hill, towards its base. Positioned lower still, in the muddy dip that fell away into marshland, was the vast peasant camp, where the nobles' militias and men-at-arms conglomerated. Here too, a form of hierarchy was displayed, for the peasant soldiers of the duke had taken the highest ground, furthest from the mud and reeds.

Scanning the thousands of heraldic designs and colours on display, Calard saw that knights had gathered here from all across Bretonnia. He saw a silver unicorn upon a field of black that must have been the heraldry of a knight from Quenelles, and the black image of a squat fortress upon a halved field of white and yellow that was clearly the heraldry of a knight from distant Montfort.

By far the majority of the knights were from Bordeleaux, as was to be expected, and the vast majority of these sported variations of the duke's heraldry. Everywhere was the tri-forked image of Manann's trident, and Calard was amazed at the sheer amount of variety in that simple image. Here was a pair of crossed, long-hafted white tridents upon a quartered field of blue and black, there an image of three trident heads, the tips of each resembling the fleur-de-lys, upon a field of red. Other shield designs were more unique, representing long held family traditions and honours. Calard saw a silver stylised bull's head upon a black background, and a sinuous golden beast that must have been a cockatrice upon a shield divided into countless diamonds of blue and red.

'Every knight bears heraldry that is utterly unique to him, yes?' asked Dieter, staring around him in what Calard took as awe.

'That's right,' he replied. 'The image may relate to some heroic deed done by an ancestor or the knight himself, or it might be passed down to him through family tradition. The colours used are generally taken from one's parents.'

Calard gestured to his own shield.

'The dragon is a traditional emblem of Bastonne,' he said, pointing to the white image of the fire-breathing dragon rampant. 'Many knights of Bastonne bear such an image, for it harks back to the time of Gilles the Uniter, who hailed from Bastonne. It was he who first took the dragon as his symbol, after he slew the great wyrm Smearghus that had plagued the realm for centuries.'

'And the colours?' asked Dieter. He seemed fascinated by details, and this was a subject that Calard warmed to.

'The red,' he said, indicating the field on the left of his shield, 'is taken from my father's shield, in honour of him. The blue is taken from my mother.'

Dieter frowned.

'Bertelis is your brother, yes?' asked the Empire noble, indicating the other knight errant riding ahead. Calard nodded in response.

'His colours are red and black. Why are his colours not red and blue, as yours are?'

'Bertelis and I are born of the same father, but my mother died when I was young, and our father remarried. Bertelis bears the black from *his* mother's side. He is my half-brother.'

'Ah!' said Dieter in triumph. 'Now I see! And he has a yellow dragon's head upon his shield, which marks him as coming from Bastonne.'

'Correct, more or less. Not all knights who bear the symbol of a dragon are from Bastonne, but the vast majority are.'

'The other knights,' said Dieter, gesturing towards the hundreds of pennants all around them, 'are from Bordeleaux, for they bear a trident?' Calard nodded. 'Why do they bear this symbol?'

'Duke Alberic's realm is bordered to the west by the sea, and his lands have long maintained a close link with the god of the ocean depths, Manann. You know this deity?'

'I do. He is worshipped within my Empire as well.'

'It is said that the first duke of Bordeleaux, the great lord Marcus, who fought alongside Gilles, had a special bond with Manann. In the Canticles of Battle, it is said that Manann and Marcus fought side by side against their enemies, and that Marcus took his heraldry in honour of this relationship.'

'I see,' said Dieter. He frowned. 'Why is it that there is no green on any of the heraldry?'

'Green?' asked Calard, incredulous. 'The colour has two connotations, neither of which a knight would choose to associate himself with.'

'Oh,' said Dieter, 'I am quite partial to the hue.' Calard realised that the soldier wore a sash of green around his waist, but he ploughed on regardless.

'For one, green is a simple colour to achieve. Green dye is common, easily affordable, cheap. Green is a peasant colour, and as such, no knight would deign to wear it.'

'I see,' said Dieter, fingering his sash, 'and the other reason?'

'Green is also the colour of the fey.'

'The *fey*? I do not recognise this word.'

'The fey are the spirits of the woods; unpredictable and capricious, they are as likely to aid a knight lost in their realm as they are to lead him to his doom.'

'They sound dangerous.'

Calard smiled. 'Well, yes, they are dangerous for the unwary and anyone who knows not the charms spoken to divert their attentions. Do you not have similar creatures in your Empire?'

'Perhaps,' said Dieter vaguely. 'Many strange and dangerous beings dwell within the mighty Drakwald, and the east of our realm was once plagued by vengeful creatures that roamed the nights.' He smiled. 'Ghosts and night terrors, perhaps, nothing more than stories told to frighten children.'

'The fey are very real,' said Calard seriously. His eyes widened as they passed a knight in deep conversation with another man. The noble's cheeks were unshaven, and his battle gear was worn and bloodied, his cloak and tabard tattered. A massive two-handed sword was strapped across his back, and his steed was laden with rolls of blankets and equipment. Scraps of parchment, holy writings and prayers, hung from the horse's caparison. The knight felt Calard's eyes upon him, and inclined his head in acknowledgement of the young warrior, though he did not break from his conversation.

When they had passed, Bertelis drew alongside his brother.

'Did you see?' he asked in a low voice.

'I did,' exclaimed Calard. 'That was Gundehar of Raisol, was it not?'

'He is a famous knight?' ventured Dieter. Bertelis scoffed, throwing a scathing glance at the Empire soldier.

'He is the victor of Albermale Fields, and the slayer of the Beast of Rachard!' Bertelis said. Dieter looked blank. Bertelis turned away in disgust.

'Gundehar of Raisol,' said Calard, 'is a knight of Bordeleaux, who is engaged upon the noble quest. He seeks the grail of the Lady, and until he achieves his goal, he may not rest. His deeds are renowned all across Bretonnia.'

Dieter raised an eyebrow.

'Does he think your goddess is to be found here?'

'She is everywhere,' said Calard, 'but she will only appear to one who has proven his devotion to her, who has defeated many enemies of Bretonnia in his quest to find her.'

'He did not look as… impressive as many of the other knights.'

'A knight engaged on the holy quest must forsake earthly comforts,' said Calard, 'and he must never spend two nights under the same roof, for to do so displays a lack of conviction to his cause, which the Lady would frown upon.'

'But for us, tonight, earthly comforts are what we seek!' declared Bertelis loudly. 'For we have been victorious in battle, and we will drink to our success! Wine and women, we shall have our fill of both!'

THE TWIN MOONS were high in the sky, just beginning their descent towards the horizon, and the night was still filled with the sounds of celebration. Flaming torches and lanterns lit the encampment, and the sounds of revelry were all around.

Duke Alberic had given a speech earlier in the evening, but Calard could only dimly remember what he had said. It was something about the war not being over, that they had achieved a great victory, but that the war was not yet won. He pushed the thoughts from his mind, as his brother raised his goblet for another toast.

'To our glorious victory!' shouted Bertelis, and the brothers drank. Calard spilled his wine as he tried to set it down, and it spread out across the table before him, much to the hilarity of those lounging around it.

'My dress!' screeched a young woman, rising unsteadily from the table as the wine splashed over her lap. She overbalanced, and fell backwards, tripping over her stool.

Calard stood up unsteadily, chivalrously going to the woman's aid. Wine stained her front, and Calard thought she might be about to break out in tears at the sight of her ruined clothes. Instead, she erupted into throaty laughter, and the others joined in, pounding the table in their mirth, sending plates of discarded food and goblets jumping.

Calard helped the girl to her feet, and she leant against him as she fought for balance.

'You're handsome,' she slurred at him as he set her atop her righted stool, and he grinned foolishly at her. He dabbed at her bosom with a cloth, his eyes goggling at the impressive display, while his brother reclined, smiling, and was fed sweetmeats from the hand of a woman languidly stretched upon a lounge, like a cat.

'The lady that gave you this is very lucky,' said the girl, touching the silk scarf wrapped around his arm.

'I am the lucky one, in truth,' said Calard, gazing numbly at the girl's soft, pale hand upon his arm. She lifted her head, staring up at him with unfocused eyes, her pupils dilated.

'She is far away though, is she not?' asked the girl in a husky voice, moving closer. He saw the thick layer of make-up that the girl had applied to her face, and the scent of cheap, cloying fragrance enveloped him.

Calard blinked and pulled back, reaching for his goblet.

'She is with me always,' he said, his voice wistful. 'She is my muse, a paragon of earthly beauty and sweetness, and I dedicate my victory today to her.'

The girl pouted, flicking her blonde hair. She turned unsteadily, and practically fell into the arms of another young and clearly intoxicated knight.

'Such a romantic, brother,' said Bertelis, sipping from his goblet as the pair of girls on either side of him cast venomous glances at each other, both clearly vying for his attention. One had a hand draped over Bertelis's shoulder, playing with his sandy-coloured hair, while the other was stroking his thigh.

Only a lowborn peasant woman would behave so, thought Calard. Women of class were far more refined than any of these desperate hangers on.

Calard unwrapped the pale scarf from his arm, closing his eyes as he held it to his face, breathing in deeply. Tucking it back into his tunic, he drained the last of the bottle of Bordeleaux wine. He stared blankly at the empty bottle before tossing it over his shoulder.

'More drink!' he declared, lifting himself to his feet.

'Let us take a moment of fresh air,' said Bertelis, untangling himself from the arms of the two women who flashed each other dark looks, as if it were the other's fault that the handsome young knight was leaving. He swung around and took the hand of the first, and she fluttered her eyelashes at him as he kissed it delicately. Breaking away, he leant over the other girl and kissed her lingeringly on her neck, her eyes closing in pleasure.

'Adieu, adieu, fair ladies,' said Bertelis theatrically as he rose to his feet. 'We shall return anon, and every moment not in your presence shall pain us greatly.' Bowing to them both, he backed away and joined his brother. Together, they walked out into the warm night air, their balance unsteady.

'Wenches,' said Bertelis disparagingly.

'I thought you liked them,' said Calard.

'Too clinging,' said Bertelis, dismissing the girls with a wave of the hand. 'This is *our* night, my brother. Let us drink and be merry!' Bertelis raised his arms into the air dramatically, but stumbled as his foot slipped in the mud. He fell against a tent, almost pulling it to the ground.

Calard laughed, as his brother righted himself with some difficulty. Bertelis gave the tent a dark look, pointing an accusing finger at it.

'I think we might already be rather merry, brother,' Calard remarked.

'You might be right,' admitted Bertelis, and the pair began staggering along the line of tents, arms thrown over each other's shoulders.

'Do you have any idea where we are?' asked Bertelis.

'I was hoping that you did,' Calard said, laughing, and they stopped, swaying from side to side. They turned left and right, brows lined in drunken thought, and broke into laughter once more.

'Well, look at this, my friends,' said a snide voice, 'a pair of young lovers, arm in arm. How touching.'

The brothers straightened, pulling their arms from around each other's shoulders, and Calard's face flushed an angry red. It took him a moment to focus on the speaker, a slim man slightly older than Calard, standing with his hands on his hips. His finely cut clothes were spotless white and edged in silver, and a red dragon in flight was emblazoned on his chest.

'Maloric,' he snarled as he glared into the face of the youngest member of the Sangasse family. 'I thought I smelt something foul upon the air.'

Maloric was a rakishly handsome man, some three years older than Calard, and were it not for the long-standing feud between their houses they might have been friends. However, the bitter enmity between the two noble families ensured that they would never be anything but rivals. Both came from renowned noble bloodlines, and though Garamont had won more accolades from past battlefield victories, the Sangasses held a stronger political position within Bastonne, due largely to their close marital ties to the royal households of Bretonnia.

'Ouch,' said Maloric, feigning hurt as he stepped closer to the Garamont brothers, touching a hand to his breast. 'You wound me, dear neighbour.'

One of the heavyset men behind Maloric smirked.

'So you finally made it to Bordeleaux, did you, Garamont? I thought you were cowering at home, too scared to take to the field. Or were you hoping to arrive once the battle was done?'

'Sangasse dog,' snapped Bertelis, and he spat into the ground. The men behind Maloric bristled, and the slim young knight turned towards Bertelis.

'What's this? Is it Bertelis, Garamont's brat? You two look nothing alike, you know,' he said, his finger passing back and forth between the brothers. 'But then you were born from different mothers, weren't you. How old must you be, Bertelis? Eighteen summers? But wait!' he said putting a hand to his cheek in mock outrage. 'That would mean that you were born well within a year of *your* mother dying,' Maloric continued, pointing a finger at Calard, his voice mocking. 'Scandalous! Dear me, that raises all kinds of questions, does it not?'

Bertelis took a step towards Maloric, his hands clenching into fists. Calard stepped in front of him, turning his back on Maloric, and placed a hand upon Bertelis's chest. The younger brother paused at the touch, his chest rising and falling heavily as he stared hatefully at the Sangasse noble.

'This is not the time, brother,' said Calard through clenched teeth. His brother gave a slight nod of the head, and Calard turned to face Maloric once more. The slim noble stared at Bertelis with cold, dangerous eyes, the hint of a mocking smile playing on his lips.

Calard saw that Maloric wore a silk scarf wrapped around his upper arm, clearly a token of affection.

'What sort of poisonous viper would see fit to give you her token?' he snapped, seeing a satisfying anger in Maloric's eyes. It was there for less than a second, and was replaced with mocking humour.

'Poisonous viper? A bit harsh, methinks. This was given to me by none other than the fair Lady Elisabet of Carlemont. Her family was the guest of Sangasse for the equinox. I believe you know her?'

Calard felt the colour drain from his face.

'You lie,' he said.

'Why would I bother? The truth is much more amusing,' said Maloric, and now it was Calard's hands that clenched into fists.

'Not the time, remember? He speaks naught but poison,' said Bertelis in his ear, and Calard glared at Maloric before answering.

'You are right brother. Let's leave this place. It reeks of offal and filth, all of a sudden.'

'That's right, dogs, run. I think you will find that your tents are down the hill, away from your betters.'

Calard turned away from the smirking Maloric, chuckling humourlessly. Then he swung around violently and slammed his fist into the slim noble's face. There was a satisfying crack, and blood spurted from the knight's nose. He fell to his back in the mud, as Bertelis guffawed in shocked amusement.

He stepped forward and delivered a brutal punch to the jaw of the first of Maloric's men to react, knocking him senseless.

Then the area was suddenly filled with drunken revellers, who threw aside a tent flap and emerged into the thoroughfare, laughing and singing.

Calard saw Bertelis double over as a fist slammed into his midsection, and he pushed people out of the way to get to his brother. He slammed into the heavyset thug standing over his brother, knocking him into a tent that collapsed as his weight brought down its uprights. There was an angry shout from within and a woman's scream. Heart pounding, Calard pulled his brother upright, and the two of them pushed their way through the crowd away from the fracas.

'What I wouldn't give to see that punch of yours again,' said Bertelis. He laughed, and then winced in pain. 'It certainly wiped that smug look off the bastard's face.'

Calard grinned. It certainly had felt satisfying.

Their heads still buzzing with adrenaline and alcohol, the pair wended their way through the tents, having no clear idea of the direction of their tent lay in.

'Well, would you look at this!' said Bertelis as they stopped to paused for a moment to get their bearings.

'What?'

Bertelis gestured, and Calard laughed out loud as he saw that they were standing next to a tent of pure white with a red dragon emblazoned on its tent flaps.

'I was just thinking I needed to relieve myself,' remarked Calard, loosening his trousers.

'My thoughts exactly,' said his brother, and the two of them stood side by side as they pissed on Maloric's tent.

'We are over here,' said Calard as he retied his belt, catching a glimpse of familiar heraldry in the distance. Bertelis grunted in response, and the pair made their way towards their tents.

'A good night!' declared Bertelis. 'Booze, women and seeing you break Maloric of Sangasse's nose! What more could a man want?'

Calard laughed, and when his head hit his pallet, he was asleep instantly, dreaming of Elisabet and victory. He thought he heard his sister's voice calling to him, but he could not find her, and soon it faded, replaced with darkness.

CHAPTER SEVEN

CALARD AWOKE WITH a start as he felt a hand on his shoulder. His dagger was in his hand instantly, and the young squire backed away, his face paling, before he fled the tent.

'Calard of Garamont,' someone shouted, and he recognised the voice as Gunthar's. Calard winced as he felt the throbbing pain in his fist, and he looked down at his bloodied knuckles, remembering dimly the events of the previous night. The weapon master shouted again, and Calard rose to his feet, his head pounding. Bordeleaux wine was indeed fine, but it was no less painful the next day than any other.

'What?' he grunted irritably as he stepped out into the overcast morning light. He squinted up at Gunthar, who was fully armoured and astride his warhorse, glaring down at him.

'Get your armour on,' said the weapon master, his voice icy. 'Battle awaits. I will see you in ten minutes in the field west of here. Your brother is there already.'

Gunthar kicked his steed into a trot, leaving Calard standing alone in his bedraggled clothes from the night before. The words of the veteran knight made him come fully awake in an instant, and he curtly ordered for his horse to be brought to him. Swinging around, he re-entered his tent, shouting for his servants.

He ripped off his clothes and hurriedly pulled on the thick padding that protected him from the bruises, cuts and chafing that the joints and edges of his armour would otherwise inflict. He bent forwards and lifted his arms as his chain mail hauberk was pulled over his head, and he stood up, letting the long-sleeved chain shirt settle.

'Quickly now,' Calard snapped, and with practised ease his breastplate was fitted in place, its leather ties fastened. The rest of his armour was fitted gradually into position, the heavy plates overlapping each other and tightened. While the squire affixed his greaves and cuisses to his legs, Calard pulled on his soft leather gloves, and strapped his rarebraces and vambraces to his arms, before his cowters and pauldrons were fitted over the top. As the last buckles and ties were fastened, Calard pulled on his steel gauntlets, and his sword was strapped at his waist. His red and blue tabard was pulled over his armour and, fully garbed for war, he knelt before the small triptych shrine of the Lady. Bowing his head, he spoke a quick prayer, asking for strength and valour, before he stood and strode from his tent.

The sun was vainly trying to break through the clouds overhead, and his hangover was forgotten as his heart raced in expectation of the coming battle. He did not stop to consider why no other knights were rushing to make themselves ready for the forthcoming engagement.

Gringolet was led towards him, the mighty dappled grey steed saddled and bedecked in its fine red and blue caparison. The destrier's head was protected by its spiked, steel chanfron, and the warhorse stamped its hooves eagerly.

Lifting one armoured foot into the stirrup, Calard pulled himself into the saddle smoothly. He accepted his shield and lance as they were handed to him, and urged Gringolet on. Why had his brother gone without him, he wondered angrily?

He pushed through the crowd, the massive destrier muscling peasants out of the way, and cursed at his slow progress. At last, he broke free from the press of bodies and tents, and kicked Gringolet into a gallop, heading away from the duke's camp. He turned his steed to the west, and rose in the saddle as the destrier leapt a dry-stone wall, and thundered towards the group of knights and mounted peasants in the field beyond.

He slowed as he approached the gathering of mounted warriors, his brow furrowing. He saw Bertelis with a foul expression on his face, and brought Gringolet to a halt before Gunthar, who was glowering at him.

'You took your time,' the veteran said.

'What's going on?' asked Calard. He saw that all the knights, apart from Gunthar, around twenty in total, were young, and yet to earn their full knighthood. The peasants were yeomen, mounted upon unarmoured workhorses, and armed with spears and bows. The Empire envoy, Dieter, was there too, though Calard noted that he no longer wore his green sash. The Empire soldier looked bright and cheerful, which irritated Calard, whose headache was returning with a vengeance.

'We are on scouting duty,' said Bertelis sourly.

'What?' asked Calard.

'Ducal orders,' snapped Gunthar. 'There are still a large number of greenskins within the western fold of the forest, and such are their numbers that they remain a considerable threat. Along with dozens of other parties, we are to scour the forests and drive them into the open. '

'So, no battle then?' asked Calard darkly.

'Not just yet. It got you ready quickly though, didn't it?' said Gunthar, giving him a humourless smile.

'Isn't this duty more fit for peasants? Where is the honour to be earned in chasing shadows?'

'The peasants have enough trouble scaring pigs from the trees, let alone an army,' said Gunthar lightly, and several of the young knights laughed. 'No, this duty requires strong, brave young knights. What enemy would not flee before such noble warriors?'

'There is no honour in it,' snapped Calard.

The smile slipped from Gunthar's face.

'This is a necessary duty,' he said, 'and the order comes from the Duke of Bordeleaux, or did you think that a knight's duty was merely to sleep, drink and womanise inbetween battles?'

Calard bit back an angry retort, and Gunthar drew closer to him, out of earshot of the other young knights.

'You are not ingratiating yourself in front of your peers, Calard,' hissed the knight. 'You sound like a spoilt noble's son, unwilling to sully his hands with duties he sees as beneath him.'

'This duty *is* beneath me. And how dare–' began Calard but his words were cut short.

'How dare I speak to you like a child? Act like a knight and I shall treat you as one. Even your libertine brother managed to rouse himself and make it here on time. I expected much more of you, Calard.'

Calard felt the colour in his cheeks rise in shame and anger.

'You are not the lord of Garamont yet, Calard, and I am responsible for you while we are engaged in Bordeleaux. You will do as I order, or I will have you shamed in front of all these knights.'

Calard clenched his teeth, and looked down, quivering with rage.

'Do your father proud, Calard,' said Gunthar, more softly, and Calard nodded his head. Satisfied, Gunthar pulled his steed around sharply.

'We ride! Now!' he shouted, and kicked his steed forwards, angling it towards the south. The other knights fell in behind him, and the peasant yeoman kicked their steeds hard, ranging out in front.

'Why didn't you wake me?' asked Calard darkly, pulling alongside Bertelis.

'Sorry,' his brother replied casually. 'I was up early. I thought you would wake in time. I didn't think–'

'No, you didn't,' said Calard.

BORDELEAUX, IT SEEMED to Calard, was a land blessed by the Lady. Its soil was rich, and he could imagine what it would be like in the height of spring. The rolling hills would be awash with life, and the air would be rich with the promise of summer.

The dukedom was a coastal one, and even this far inland there was a freshness to the air that carried hints of the wide blue seas. Calard longed to travel to the coast, to see the mighty cliffs and witness with his own eyes the crashing of the waves. One day, he said to himself.

Less than a mile from the duke's camp, there came a shout from one of the yeoman outriders.

Bertelis stood in the stirrups, straining to see further ahead.

'What is it?' snapped Calard, not bothering to look.

'I'm not sure,' said Bertelis. 'Wait... there is a big group of peasants, fifty or more, I'd say... and I can see a banner,' he said, straining. 'It is blue, and is emblazoned with... with a silver horse, standing side on, with a foreleg raised. No, not a horse, a unicorn.'

That got Calard's attention.

'Anything else?'

'I think so... Yes!' said Bertelis in rising excitement. 'Beneath the unicorn is a silver grail, with a blue fleur-de-lys upon it!'

'Reolus!' breathed Calard, standing in the stirrups to see with his own eyes. 'Are you sure?'

'Yes! It *is* him!'

The other young knights around them were exclaiming in wonder and amazement as they too strained to catch a glimpse of the famous knight.

'Is this another knight who quests for your Lady's grail?' asked Dieter.

'No,' said Calard in awe, 'this is one who has drunk from it.'

* * *

THREE PEASANTS WERE running ahead of the entourage. One of them blew several long tuneless notes on a rusted horn as he ran, his cheeks puffing out like inflated bladders. The peasant in the lead was a portly, balding individual, who held aloft a shield, cloven in two by some mighty blow. Despite the damage done to it, the heraldry upon its face was clear: a silver unicorn upon a field of blue, above an image of the holy grail.

'The shattered shield of Reolus,' remarked Bertelis in amazement, staring at the holy artefact. There was not a man in all of Bretonnia who did not know the names, deeds and heraldry of every hallowed grail knight, for they were veritable avatars of holy power, and their every action was recorded and spread the length and breadth of the land. Fathers regaled their sons with tales of these mighty paladins, and noble courts listened attentively as the actions of the most famous grail knights were portrayed in verse, song and performance. The arrival of a grail knight at the fortified gates of a town or city resulted in parades and feasts, and a day of rest for all workers as the streets quickly filled with those hoping to catch a glance of the holy warrior.

Gunthar called the knights errant to a halt, urging their horses off the muddy road so as to allow the grail knight Reolus free progress. They dismounted, to show proper respect, and Calard saw that even Gunthar seemed agitated and nervous, straightening his tabard and smoothing his flowing moustache. The heroic figure could still not be seen, surrounded as he was by a surging mass of pilgrims.

'Hearken ye! Hearken ye!' bellowed the balding peasant as he reached the knights, panting and sweating from the exertion. He hefted the shattered shield high above his head. 'Witness the coming of a living saint, beloved of Quenelles, one who has supped from the grail! Bear witness to his holy shield, shattered by the mighty devil troll of Carcassonne, before he spitted the foul beast upon his lance and did cleave its head from its shoulders with one mighty blow!'

'You are blessed, sons of Bretonnia!' yelled one of the peasant's companions, draped in what must once have been a cloak discarded by the grail knight, though it was now tattered and ripped. 'You are blessed for you shall bear testament to the coming of Lord Reolus of Quenelles, favoured of the Lady, as he answers the Duke of Bordeleaux's call to war!' This pilgrim had clearly seen battle himself, for he had a brutal scar across his face and wore a rusted sword upon his hip. 'Enemies will wither beneath his shining gaze, and friends will become emboldened by his presence,' he yelled, spittle flying from his toothless mouth.

'See the ruin that comes to those who face his holy wrath!' bellowed the third of the pilgrims, an ugly brute with a lopsided face and the crown of his head shaved bare of hair. He pulled a severed head from a bloody sack, holding the grisly trophy up in the air before him, his face a mask of feverish devotion. The head was rotting and flyblown, and the stink was atrocious, making the knights grimace in revulsion. 'This was the cursed necromancer Merogant of Mousillon, cut down by Saint Reolus on the fields of Bodkin Moor!'

Several of the knights errant hissed, and spoke silent prayers of protection to the Lady, and Calard saw

Dieter touch a hand to the twin-tailed comet emblem on his chest.

'Blessed are ye!' shouted the third pilgrim, moving his hands in the air in some form of awkward benediction, before the three peasants continued on their way, clumping awkwardly through the mud towards the duke's camp in the distance.

Then the main troupe of pilgrims arrived, the bizarre panoply of the procession dizzying in its strangeness and fervour. There were lowborn men and women of all ages in the motley entourage, and they held aloft pieces of rusted armour, broken shoes, shreds of blue cloth and chunks of half-eaten food: all items discarded or cast aside by the grail knight. These pilgrims, who worshipped the knight as a living saint, saw each of the cast-offs as an artefact of holy significance, and they treasured them as if they might impart a small fraction of the holy knight's favour.

Most were armed for war, with cudgels, daggers and maces hanging from rope belts, though more than a few sported rusted or shattered swords that they had scavenged from fallen warriors. One wore a dented, ill-fitting knight's helmet on his head, while another proudly wore a breastplate with several crossbow holes through it, the bolts having, most likely, slain its previous owner. Many carried wooden shields that had been daubed with blue paint, and onto these had been nailed all manner of further devotional items: arrows, scraps of vellum torn from holy texts, and the bones of those slain by their unwilling benefactor.

'There he is!' breathed one of the knights in awe, and Calard stood tall as the revered grail knight approached.

He seemed like an immortal, divine paladin, a fault-less living legend, and strength, majesty and faith radiated from him like the heat from an inferno. Calard's breath was taken away, his mouth gaping open as he was overcome by awe. Grail knights were the epitome of knightly perfection, the ideal that every knight of Bretonnia aspired to, and to merely be in the presence of one of these esteemed paragons was over-whelming.

Riding upon the back of the biggest warhorse that Calard had ever seen, the grail knight towered above his pilgrims, and the young knight errant felt suddenly like a child. The midnight-black stallion must have been nigh on twenty hands tall at the shoulder, and it was bedecked in a regal blue caparison, its edges stitched with shimmering silver thread. The venerated grail knight rode tall and proud, his presence awesome and terrifying in equal measures.

Whether it was coincidence or divine favour, the clouds parted as the grail knight drew near, bathing him in warm, golden beams of light. His armour shone like the sun, and Calard squinted against its brightness. The knight's armour was a work of inspired artistry, every inch of it covered in intricate detailing, engravings, and inlaid with finely worked silver. A shimmering cloak of blue, lined with soft mink fur, fluttered behind him, held in place by a heavy golden brooch in the shape of the Lady's grail. The knight was adorned with countless devotional tokens and sacred icons, from holy beads to miniature pendants carved from the finger bones of saints into the likeness of the Lady.

He rode slowly along the muddy roadway, stoically ignoring the pilgrims that capered and proclaimed his noble deeds in loud voices. His shield was a master-piece of craftsmanship, clearly made by the same genius who had forged his armour, and his lance was the finest example of its kind that Calard had ever borne witness to. Its silver vamplate was worked into the visage of a snarling dragon, and Calard thought he saw, for a brief second, a shimmering light coruscate up the length of the lance. It was named Arandyal, and it was one of the most hallowed artefacts of Quenelles. Blessed by the Lady, Reolus had wielded it against innumerable foes, and it was the weapon that the grail knight was said to have used to slay the dragon Grel-malarch, a beast that had terrorised the people of Carcassonne for centuries.

The grail knight's full-faced helm was topped by a majestic heraldic unicorn of silver, which was sur-rounded by a host of candles. The Lady's fleur-de-lys was cut into the right side of the helmet as a breathing grill, and Calard felt his heart lurch as the grail knight turned his head in his direction.

The grail knight's eyes glinted from within the dark-ness of his helmet, and Calard felt a surge of primal terror beneath the gaze, as if his soul was stripped bare. As one, the knights errant dropped to one knee before the grail knight Reolus, lowering their heads, and Calard, sweating profusely, was glad to no longer be locking eyes with the awesome knight. Never in his life had he encountered anything with such a powerful presence.

Raising his gaze and standing once more, Calard felt exhilaration fill him, as the grail knight dipped his lance in salute to the knights, bowing his head ever so slightly. Then he was past them, and the world seemed to grow a little dimmer. The clouds closed ranks once more overhead, and the radiant brilliance that had bathed the grail knight faded.

'The grail knight Reolus,' whispered Bertelis, shaking his head in wonder. 'Did you see the size of him? I had thought that the legends of his exploits may have been exaggerated, but seeing him here, I doubt them not at all.'

'We have been blessed indeed to have stood in the presence of such greatness,' said Gunthar as he pulled himself back into the saddle. Minutes later, distant cheering and the blaring of trumpets announced Reolus's entrance into the duke's camp. 'Remember this moment, knights of Bretonnia. Through courage, devotion and duty, you too may one day achieve such lofty heights.'

Calard's eyes misted over as he imagined people cheering his name, proclaiming his deeds and being awed in his presence. Gunthar's voice cut through his daydream.

'That isn't going to happen standing around like a bunch of dullards. To become a grail knight, one must display utter devotion to one's lord and the Lady, and perform all one's duties, however mundane, with pride and honour. Right now, our duty is to enter the forest and scare out the enemy. So let's not linger here any longer.'

Calard swung into the saddle, still amazed and honoured by having been so close to a grail knight: the mighty Reolus, no less. Faced against such a warrior, the enemy had no chance. The mere possibility of seeing the knight riding into battle was a thrilling thought.

The forest loomed like a malevolent beast in the distance. He shivered, scanning the tree line for movement. Gringolet snorted uneasily, and Calard gave the destrier a comforting pat, staring darkly towards the looming trees. It felt as though hateful eyes watched their progress.

Pushing such childish thoughts from his mind, he concentrated on envisaging his triumphant elevation to the heady ranks of the grail knights, and smiled.

CALARD'S UNEASE RETURNED as they pushed into the forest of Chalons. The outskirts had been open and filled with light, the coppiced trees young and widely spread, allowing the knight easy progress. Late-blooming bluebells spread beneath the shadows of the trees, creating an otherworldly vision of remarkable beauty. Bones and the occasional grinning skull, the remains of some long-forgotten battle, peeked from beneath the softly lilting, purple-blue flowers.

Sparse woodland had slowly given way to denser, darker tracts, where the trees were older and more tightly clumped, and the knights' progress slowed. The ground was thick with fallen, rotting leaves. The light that pierced the thick canopy of twisted branches diminished, and the shadows deepened, becoming more menacing. Calard's eyes darted around, jumping from shadow to shadow, feeling eyes upon him and glimpsing flickers of movement out of the corners of his eyes.

After hours of travel, they were pushing into the dark, old forest, untouched by human hand. Thick oaks, gnarled like twisted old men, leant over the knights as they progressed, creaking and groaning.

Moss and lichen clung to the trunks, and toadstools and fungus grew in abundance. Mighty trees of ash and beech grew thick and tall, and small creatures rustled through the leaf litter and danced through the branches overhead. Leaves and sticks fell upon the knights, and they eyed their surroundings warily. The paths worn through the trees by boars or deer were twisting and convoluting, and the branches of trees pressed in on all sides, making the knights duck and shield their eyes against twigs that clawed at their exposed faces.

This was not a place for a knight of Bretonnia, and Calard imagined that the ancient forest was resisting their presence, resentful of the intrusion into its dark heart. Again, he felt eyes boring into him, and he swung in the saddle, casting his gaze around, trying to pierce the gloom, but seeing nothing untoward.

There were dozens of other groups pushing into the wilds, spread wide like a net, scouring for signs of the enemy, and driving the greenskins ever closer to the forest's edge. Most were young knights errant, like Calard, and he still chafed at what he saw as a task better suited to peasants.

A shout from up ahead pulled him from his morose thoughts, and, as he pushed through a mass of twisted bracken, he saw one of the yeoman scouts kneeling over several corpses sprawled upon the dark earth.

'There are more of them over there,' said the yeoman to Gunthar, gesturing vaguely to the east.

The knights errant crowded in, and Calard caught a glimpse of green flesh. The dead creatures were small, no more than four feet in height, and their skin was covered in barbaric piercings, raven feathers and black tattoos.

'More goblins,' said Gunthar. The veteran had dismounted, and pushed one of the corpses onto its back with his foot. The creature's face was frozen in a leering rictus that might have been terror, though it was hard to discern. The goblin's lips were drawn back, exposing an array of sharp, yellow teeth, and its beady eyes were wide and surrounded by smudges of coal. A large black tattoo dominated the creature's face, a barbaric and crude depiction of a spider, its barbed legs spreading out over each side of the goblin's face, and its bulbous body on his forehead. The image had been tattooed in such a way that the goblin's eyes filled in for the eyes of the arachnid, and its oversized fangs framed the greenskin's mouth. Bones and fraying, black feathers had been pushed through the flesh of its drooping ears. It was a feral, loathsome creature, and Calard found it morbidly fascinating and repulsive at the same time.

Dark blood leaked from a large gash in its head, where the skull had been caved in. The other diminutive, vicious creatures had been just as brutally slain, and bore deep wounds caused by strong, savage blows.

This was the second group of slaughtered greenskins that they had encountered in the last hours.

'Infighting?' Calard had suggested when they had come across the first corpses. Gunthar had shrugged.

'Possibly. Perhaps a power struggle between rival tribes in the aftermath of battle. Who knows.'

'Gunthar,' said Calard. The weapon master grunted in response, probing at the goblin's wound with the tip of his sword. 'If this wasn't the result of infighting, then what killed these things? A scouting party like ours?'

'No, these are not blows caused by Bretonnian hands,' said Gunthar. 'None of these creatures was slain by lance or arrow, and, as far as I can determine, no other scouting party has come this way.'

Occasional distant blasts from horns sounded through the trees as other scouting groups sighted the enemy.

'At least we know we are behind them,' said Gunthar. 'They are moving before us towards the edge of the forest, as we had hoped. Either they keep moving and break from the forest, or they turn to face us.'

'Or whatever else it is that hunts them,' said Dieter thoughtfully. 'Could we perhaps be between *two* enemies?'

'Nonsense,' said Bertelis dismissively. 'The greenskins are little more than animals. Their pack leader was probably killed in battle, and they are now fighting each other to claim dominance. They hear us closing in on them, and run like deer before us.'

Gunthar shrugged his shoulders.

'You could be right,' he said.

'Listen,' said Calard, and the knights fell silent. The only sound was the dry wind rustling through the trees and the occasional whinny from a horse.

'I don't hear anything,' said Bertelis.

'Exactly,' said Calard, 'not even the cry of a bird, or the scuffling of a wood mouse.'

'You're right,' said Gunthar. 'There is something unnatural in the air. Come, let us push on. The sooner we are out of this forest, the better. It feels like we are being watched.'

The other knights muttered in agreement, staring around with wide eyes. Only Bertelis seemed unconcerned.

Calard started as he heard a shout from deeper in, his heart lurching. Bertelis smirked, and Calard reddened.

'Lord Gunthar, you'd better come and see this,' called a yeoman.

THE TREE WAS immense, an ancient and contorted oak that must have been old when Gilles the Uniter walked the earth, over a thousand years earlier. It would have measured more than fifty feet around its massive trunk, and twisted roots spread around it. The thick roots had grown over a stand of giant boulders, and, in places, had cracked the stone after centuries of relentless pressure.

Immense branches like the powerful arms of a wrestler reached up into the air, and from these ancient limbs hung dozens of bodies.

'Lady, lend me strength,' whispered Calard as he gaped in horror up into the canopy overhead.

The corpses swung gently from the boughs, hanging from ropes and chains. Others had been nailed into the trunk of the tree, their blood mingling with the sap that leaked from the wounds. Heads impaled on wooden stakes protruded from the ground, and dozens of corpses, many little more than crumbling skeletons, were piled up around the base of the mighty oak, along with rusting weapons, scraps of armour and shields. Calard was shocked to see more than one Bretonnian helmet and shield amongst the pile, and many of the skeletons were clearly of human origin.

The bodies of recently slain goblins and orcs hung alongside withered skeletons, and fresh blood dripped from the horrendous wounds that many of them bore.

Hundreds of black carrion birds were perched in the branches of the horrendous, deathly oak tree, and they stared accusingly down upon the intruders. Many of them paused mid-feast to glare at the knights, while others continued to gulp down eyes, like peeled grapes that had been plucked from sockets, and tear strips of flesh from bones with wickedly sharp beaks.

A yeoman hurled a rock at one of the bloated birds, and it fluttered its heavy black wings, issuing a harsh, hateful, accusatory cry.

Bertelis dismounted and began approaching the base of the tree warily, drawing his sword.

'Bertelis,' hissed Calard, eyes darting around nervously. His brother ignored him, advancing slowly forward.

'Let us not tarry here,' said Gunthar, his voice strained.

Still, the younger Garamont brother walked towards the grisly oak tree. He pushed aside a goblin corpse with his foot, and bent down, peering at shapes almost completely hidden beneath the tangle of roots.

'Bertelis,' hissed Calard again.

The sandy-haired knight flashed an irritated look at his brother, and reached a hand between the dark roots of the tree, biting his lip. He couldn't quite reach whatever it was that glinted in the darkness, and he bent lower, straining, and groping deeper beneath. It looked like the tree would come to life and swallow the young knight at any moment. Calard knew such a notion was foolish, but he felt anxious and uneasy nonetheless.

'Come on, brother!' he snapped.

He saw Bertelis stand, hefting something from beneath the twisted roots. He turned it over in his hands, and Calard saw that it was a helmet, old and rusted. A skull slipped from within it, falling at Bertelis's feet, and the young knight jumped, and then laughed out loud at his own foolishness.

'This helm bears the heraldry of Walden of Lyonesse,' Bertelis called out. Walden had been a knight engaged on the holy quest for the grail, and rumour had it that he had suffered a mortal blow from a dark knight of cursed Mousillon. His retainers had claimed that the Lady had appeared upon a ghostly ship, powered by neither sail nor oar, and had borne him to her immortal realm. 'It would appear that he did not join the Lady on her misty isle after all.'

Bertelis shook his head sadly and dropped the helmet to the ground. Somewhat reluctantly it seemed to Calard, he walked away from the tree and mounted his horse.

'Let us be away from this cursed place,' said Gunthar.

Dieter stared long at the grisly tree, his brow furrowed, his expression serious. He had heard of such things before, deep in the darkest reaches of the sprawling Drakwald forest, in the realm of his homeland. He shook his head, dismissing the notion. No, it was surely as the young knight had said: the greenskins were probably leaderless and barbarically preying on each other. He could not, however, fully shake the notion that there was something else within the forest, something hateful and jealous, something that watched them even now.

He glanced around once more, swallowing heavily, his mouth suddenly dry.

CHAPTER EIGHT

WITH THE SOUND of straining timbers and the sharp snap of leather and rope, the massive trebuchets fired. Leather slings, filled with great chunks of masonry, were whipped through the air behind the long rotating arms, as the massive counterweights descended. As the groaning long arms were flung past the vertical position, the masonry was hurled high into the air, spinning end over end.

The massive blocks of stone and mortar seemed to hang in the sky for a moment of weightlessness as they reached the apex of their trajectory, before plummeting towards the ground.

With pounding thuds that rocked the earth, the colossal missiles slammed down into the massed ranks of the greenskins, embedding themselves deep into the ground and crushing scores of the enemy.

Other blocks skidded and bounced before coming to rest, crushing and killing dozens more.

The Bretonnians had scoured Chalons for two weeks, driving the greenkins before them. Hundreds of knights and peasants had worked in concert to push the greenskins out into the open, so that a decisive battle could be won against them.

This was that battle. The sheer number of greenskins that Chalons had harboured was staggering. A victory would be had, here, that would clear the area of the greenskin menace for decades, or the armies of Bordeleaux would fail, and the dukedom would burn.

At a shouted command, hundreds of bows were raised to the heavens, arrows nocked to strings. At another command, the bowmen loosed, and the air was filled with a dense cloud of deadly arrows that hissed as they sliced through the air. High into the sky they arced, and, as they began to fall towards the earth, a second volley was fired.

It was ducal law that every able Bretonnian peasant boy learnt to fire the longbow, though in truth the law was rarely upheld. Few peasants had the means or skill to purchase or craft a bow, and fewer still had the strength needed to draw one. Still, those peasant families that were blessed enough to own a longbow, which was often passed down from father to son, pushed their sons to practise with it, building their strength, for the coin earned through going to war, though so miniscule as to be nigh-on ridiculous, was, to most peasant families, a princely wage.

Calard hissed in frustration and shook his head, bristling with impatience as he watched the enemy being mercilessly cut down by the missile weapons of the duke's peasant militias. Scores of peasants strained as they rotated the powerful winches that lowered the arms of the trebuchets, readying the powerful weapons for another shot. Further volleys of arrows descended into the enemy massing on the field before them, and Calard swore as hundreds were cut down.

'Where is the honour in this?' he snarled from his position within the massed line of knights arrayed against the foe. The nobles of Bastonne were gathered together, and knights who owed fealty to his father surrounded him. The intimidating bulk of Baron Montcadas and his knights were nearby, the bearded baron toying with his spiked morning star as he glared at the enemy.

A little way off, Calard could see Maloric and those warriors sworn to Sangasse. He was pleased to see the ugly bruising that marred the young knight's face, and, as if sensing Calard's gaze upon him, Maloric turned and glared hatefully across the line in his direction.

'I'd say you've improved his looks drastically,' said Bertelis. Calard chuckled as his brother made an obscene gesture at Maloric, who bristled in anger.

Casting his gaze further along the line of Bretonnians, Calard could see more than three thousand knights arrayed for battle. Banners and pennants, proudly displaying the heraldry of the most powerful nobles, whipped in the wind, and his eye was drawn to the duke's banner, held aloft in the centre of the knights. He could make out the vague figure of the grail knight Reolus in the distance, sitting tall in the saddle among the duke's entourage.

Some ten thousand men at arms stood in ragged lines behind the resplendent ranks of the nobility.

They were arranged in deep blocks of troops, bearing shields and pennants in the colours of their lords. Their number was prodigious, but Calard had little faith in their strength. The battle would be won or lost in the charge of the knights.

'How can we hope to prove ourselves when the enemy is cut down by mere peasants?' asked Bertelis.

'Compose yourself,' snapped Gunthar, his eyes alert and piercing. 'Your time will come. The duke wishes their lines to be thinned before we engage.'

'There will be nothing left alive *for* us to engage,' replied Calard sourly. 'This is not how battle is fought, to stand idly by while the enemy is slaughtered by bow and war machines.'

'Quiet, both of you!' snapped Gunthar. 'Have some patience, and learn from the duke's strategy. This battle *will* still be won by knightly charges, but the duke wishes to ensure a complete, resounding victory, with minimal losses. See how he has sent the knights of southern Bordeleaux out to the north to flank the enemy? He wants the enemy to charge straight towards his bowmen. When they are nearing, we will charge into their front, while the flanking knights charge their exposed side. At the same time, a force of some fifteen hundred men-at-arms is encircling the enemy through the forest to the south, cutting off their escape. If we charge ahead now, the duke's plan would be ruined.'

'Charging straight into the foe would be more honourable than hiding behind peasants with bows,' said Bertelis sourly. Gunthar sighed and gave him a long look.

'In the pages of legend? Yes, you are right, but this is reality, and the duke's strategy has merit. He will win a great victory here today, and *that* is what will be remembered. Have patience, young lords of Garamont. You will be in the thick of the fighting soon enough. There will be plenty of time for you to earn your honour this day.'

The knights had harried the enemy within the woods, engaging them in running battles and skirmishes, driving them always towards the west, towards the edge of the forest. Regiments of yeomen peppered their ranks with bow fire, galloping away from them when the enraged greenskins sought to engage them, drawing them slowly out into the open. Sorties and attacks from lances of knights had killed hundreds of the greenskins, retreating once more when the enemy gathered in strength. Like sheep being herded by dogs, the greenskins were bunched together in a mass, and driven beyond the reaches of the forest, out into the open fields, where the thunderous charge of the Bretonnian knights would dominate.

The enemy was a seething, roiling mass of bodies, and they roared as they surged across the open ground, uncaring of the terrible toll that was being inflicted upon them by wave after wave of arrows and hurled stones. Poles hung with skulls, bones and feathers were waved above heads, and the brutal creatures bellowed like animals as they ran, cleavers and axes in their crude hands.

Calard saw a miniscule goblin clamber atop a chunk of rock, embedded in the earth, that had been fired by one of the trebuchets, climbing above the surging sea of greenskins that broke around the chunk of masonry. Despite the distance, Calard could see that this creature had a crown of black feathers embedded in its scalp, and that it carried a staff that looked like a fused spine.

Its eyes rolled back in its head as the creature began to shudder and leap, froth bubbling from its mouth. Its bizarre capering seemed to fill the surging greenskins with fervour, for they began chanting a grunting, repetitive mantra, striking their weapons and shields against each other in time to it.

'Sorcery,' spat Bertelis.

Calard whispered a prayer to the Lady as the shaman continued to caper and scream.

Whatever foul magicks the diminutive creature was attempting to unleash were, however, forestalled. It paused midstream in its summoning of power, looking up into the sky. A massive block of masonry was hurtling towards it, spinning end over end as it dropped through the air.

It slammed into the shaman, crushing it to pulp. The chunk of masonry split into two as it slammed into the rocky outcrop the goblin had been perched upon, and the two halves bounced into the press of greenskinned bodies, crushing limbs and flattening bodies.

Bertelis gave a barking, short laugh in surprise.

The enemy was less than two hundred paces from the Bretonnian line, and closing fast. Calard could make out individual, savage faces, covered in black tattoos depicting spiders, skulls and geometric shapes. They were big brutes, the smaller greenskins being thrust out of the way and trampled underfoot, as the largest and strongest pushed their way to the front, roaring and bellowing.

'Hold!' roared Gunthar fiercely, eyeing the line of young knights, sensing their impatience and tense eagerness. He flicked a glance up the line of Bretonnians, watching for the duke's signal.

Calard licked his lips, and gripped his lance tightly, as the wall of greenskins surged towards them. A bugle sounded, and the first line of peasant bowmen turned and fled, running lightly back through the ranks of the knights, slipping between the formations, their arrows spent. Upon the slopes behind the knights other peasants continued to launch their deadly missiles, clouds of black arrows arcing overhead and falling amongst the packed enemy ranks.

Calard tensed, tightening his grip on his lance, as the horde of greenskins streamed forwards. He felt Gringolet's muscles bunching, the destrier's ears flat against its skull, eager to charge forwards.

Gunthar raised his lance high into the air, and Calard's heart was beating wildly in anticipation.

Finally, all along the line, trumpets and horns sounded.

'Charge!' roared Gunthar. As one, the knights errant rammed spurred stirrups into the flanks of their warhorses, and charged, forming a thick wedge behind the weapon master.

Hundreds of knights kicked their steeds forward, and the entire line surged into motion. They started slowly, and the ground began to thunder as their momentum picked up. The field was churned to mud in their wake, and lances began to lower as the pace of the warhorses increased. Less than fifty paces out from the enemy, the knights kicked their steeds into the charge.

Thousands of peasant men-at-arms took up the cry of battle, and they too surged forward like a living tide,

running at full pace towards the foe in the wake of
their mounted lords and masters.

'For Garamont!' roared Calard. The ground was a
blur beneath him as Gringolet leapt forwards, and he
shouted into the wind as the knights errant thundered
across the field towards the enemy. Bertelis was at his
side, a look of exhilaration on his face as he echoed
Calard's battle cry.

The sound of three thousand charging knights was
unlike anything that Calard had ever experienced.
The rumble of crashing hooves was deafening, and
the ground reverberated as if shook by an earth-
quake.

Three thousand couched lances were lowered, and it
seemed to take an age to cross the open space between
the two forces, though it must have only been mere
seconds. Then the forces collided with a colossal
impact, their lines blurring together as flesh smashed
against metal with bone-crushing force.

Calard's lance took a snarling orc in the throat, the
tip exploding through the back of the creature's neck,
and impaling another close behind, taking it in the
face. Others were smashed aside by the sheer weight
and power of the knights, limbs shattered and skulls
crushed beneath flashing hooves.

His lance gone, Calard's sword was instantly in his
hand, and he hacked at the blur of enemies as the
knights errant surged forwards.

The screams of pain and anger were deafening, but
the knights maintained their momentum, ploughing
deep into the enemy formation. Calard's blade cleaved
down, carving through flesh and bone. A spear glanced
off his breastplate, and he thrust the point of his sword

into the gaping mouth of another orc, blood gurgling from the fatal wound.

Kicking Gringolet fiercely, urging the powerful beast to continue its charge and not slow, Calard saw Bertelis deflect a blow on his shield, the force of the attack nearly knocking his brother from the saddle.

A hulking orc roared, and hacked the forelegs from beneath a warhorse nearby, and the steed screamed as it was felled, ploughing a furrow in the earth. The knight was hurled from the saddle, smashing into the rabble of orcs in front, and metal was bashed out of shape as spiked clubs and cleavers hammered into the fallen warrior. Then both the knight and his murderers were overrun and crushed into the mud, to be left bloody and broken in their wake.

Gringolet stumbled, and Calard struggled to keep his balance. A blade was thrust towards his chest, and he reeled back from it, deflecting it with a desperate sweep of his sword. Then his attacker was smashed to the ground by the bulk of Bertelis's warhorse, disappearing from view.

From the saddle, Calard had a good view over the sea of enemy warriors, and he could see formations of knights to the east charging across the ground, crushing enemies beneath them, before they too ploughed into the flanks of the main enemy battle line. All across the battlefield, the knights were riding through the enemy ranks, smashing aside all resistance.

'Pull to the east!' roared Gunthar, driving his warhorse with his thighs, and the knights errant maintained their formation close behind him, cutting and slicing with their swords. Calard winced as a blade struck his thigh, denting his armour, and sent a return blow that shattered the cheek of the snarling orc.

Then they were free of the engagement, breaking from the side of the enemy formation. Calard was shocked to see that less than half their number still rode at their side, and he could see pockets of the knights all across the battlefield still engaged in frantic combat, mired deep in the heart of the enemy formation. With a barked order, Gunthar had the knights wheel sharply, and they thundered back into the heavy press.

Before long, their momentum had been lost, and they found themselves surrounded on all sides. Men cried out as they were dragged to the ground and slaughtered, and all order to the battle became lost. Horses reared, screaming in inhuman pain as they were pierced by dozens of spears and blades.

A blow glanced off Calard's shield and grazed his temple, and he was thrown from the saddle. There was a moment of weightlessness as his arms and legs flailed uselessly in the air. The ground seemed to rise towards him with shocking speed, and he slammed into the muddy earth with jarring force.

He felt impossibly heavy, and blood was pumping from his head wound, flowing down his face, though he felt no pain. He lifted his head, and saw a knight no more than a metre away rising to his knees. Calard tried to shout a warning, but the din of battle swallowed his cry, and he watched in anguish as an orc smashed a heavy blade down into the knight's head, splitting it from crown to jaw.

Calard pushed groggily to his feet, and he thought he heard someone call his name. He barely had time to raise his shield as he saw a flash of movement coming at him, and he was driven to his knees by the force of an attack delivered by another orc.

Pain shot up his left arm and shoulder, and he struggled to find the strength to stand. The creature towered above him, a mountain of muscle and brutish strength, and it roared in bloodlust, spraying spittle from its gaping, tusked maw.

A sword sliced down and hacked into its neck, and dark blood pumped from the wound. The orc's head lolled to one side, hanging loosely by muscles and tendons, all but decapitated, and the creature slumped into the mire.

'Calard!' someone shouted again, and he looked up to see Gunthar looming above him, blood dripping from his sword. Calard nodded his head, and swung around to find Gringolet, praying that the noble steed had not fallen.

A blade flashed towards him, and he ducked beneath the blow, letting it slide off his shield. Then he lunged forward, driving the point of his sword into green, tattooed flesh. He stumbled as he lunged, and fell atop the orc, his armoured weight driving the blade home.

Even in death, the creature refused to back down, and it roared in his face and clubbed him aside with a meaty fist that was almost the size of his head. His vision swam, and he staggered to his feet to deliver the killing blow, but flashing hooves caved the creature's head in. Gringolet stood there, nostrils flared and chest heaving, and the destrier shook its head, stamping.

'Get in the saddle!' hissed Gunthar, as he and another knight moved their steeds to intercept a pair of greenskins that launched themselves towards Calard. Needing no prompting, Calard put his foot in the stirrups and hauled himself, with some difficulty, up onto the destrier's back.

The enemy was crushing in against them from all sides, and, every second, more knights were falling, dragged down into the mud and butchered. He saw a flash of white, and his anger rose as he saw the figure of Maloric through the press of bodies, cutting around him, his blade streaming with blood as he killed.

Refusing to be outdone by the Sangasse noble, Calard kicked Gringolet forward again, pushing into the enemy, his blade singing through the air.

How long the battle lasted, he could not later recall, but his arm was leaden, and he was splattered with blood when he heard trumpets blaring. He looked around to see fresh lances of knights smashing into the foe, their weight and momentum splintering the orc ranks and driving through their midst.

A wave of panic surged through the enemy ranks like a raging wildfire. Where, moments before, there was nothing but savagery and a lust for battle, now there was the shadow of doubt, and, as the first greenskins turned and fled, the enemy resolve was shattered.

With a shout, Calard felt his limbs invigorated with renewed strength, and he fell upon the panicked foe ruthlessly. The enemy retreat soon turned to a rout, and they streamed towards the forest. Contingents of knights and peasants that had been sent by the duke to outflank the enemy were already blocking the retreat, and thousands of greenskins were cut down as they became caught between the Bretonnian forces.

Calard felt a wild euphoria descend over him as he ran down the fleeing enemy. His sword hacked into the neck of one creature as it fled, and he saw Bertelis kill another with a powerful downward swing.

Pockets of resistance still held out, where the biggest and darkest-hued greenskins refused to abandon the field, and the men-at-arms were directed against them, while the knights ran down those fleeing towards the safety of the trees. Five or more peasants were hacked apart for each of the brutish creatures that fell, but slowly the enemy was enveloped and brought down, and the duke's banner was planted in the middle of the battlefield amid a great pile of the dead.

From somewhere behind, Calard heard Gunthar barking for the knights of Garamont to reform their ranks, but he ignored the weapon master, intent on cutting down the panicked enemy. He saw Maloric ahead of him, butchering the greenskins, and he kicked Gringolet forward to overtake him.

The field was strewn with the dead and dying, and men-at-arms moved across it, dispatching those not yet dead, and dragging back the bodies of injured knights. Horses with broken legs and shattered spines screamed as their throats were cut, and fallen banners were lifted free of the mud and blood, recovered to be reunited with their owners or sent back to their castles in mourning.

Knights thundered through the mud in front of the forest, running down fleeing greenskins, and splintered groups of the enemy cut left and right as they sought the safety of the trees. Calard smashed his sword onto the head of another enemy, and swung Gringolet around, seeking more enemies to kill.

The knights guarding the retreat of the foe were too few to contain the sheer number of the greenskins, and hundreds were swarming back into the safety of the trees.

Scores of knights, mostly young knights errant like himself, streamed towards the trees in pursuit, and he urged Gringolet on, eager not to miss out on the slaughter. Bertelis was at his side, and he saw Maloric kick his black charger forward, casting a hateful glance at the brothers.

'For Garamont!' yelled Bertelis, and the brothers thundered through the trees as they entered the forest of Chalons. Bodies of orcs and goblins lay sprawled on the ground.

Bertelis kicked his steed hard as he sighted a fleeing goblin, and Calard swung his sword around as he closed on a wounded orc that was clutching at its bleeding, limp arm as it tried to escape. The greenskin turned as the sound of pounding hooves drew near, and swung its cleaver blindly up at him.

Gringolet shied away from the attack, and Calard met the blow with one of his own, the two weapons clashing with the ring of steel. Then a sword sliced into the greenskins back, dropping it to the ground, and Calard swore as Maloric swept past. He kicked Gringolet into pursuit.

They pursued the last of the enemy deeper into the forest, ducking their heads beneath whipping branches, and leaping over fallen logs. Almost a hundred knights thundered down into a shallow natural gorge, galloping through the low ferns and passing swiftly by moss covered rocks.

There, they came upon a scene of slaughter.

Knights, horses and greenskins lay sprawled together, scores of them lying bloody and broken, their lifeblood leaking out onto the forest floor. Calard and the other knights dragged their horses to a halt, staring around with horrified, wide eyes, their hearts pounding.

Calard wheeled Gringolet in a tight circle, eyeing the surrounding trees fearfully. The destrier snorted, and its ears flattened against its head, nostrils flaring. Rocks covered in moss and fern ringed the gulley, and, as he scanned the undergrowth, Calard once again felt as if someone, or *something*, was watching.

There was no sound beneath the dark canopy far overhead, except for the clank of armour, and the whinny and stamp of horses.

'I don't like this,' hissed Calard softly. The silence beat down on him like a hammer, unnatural and oppressive.

Every pure-bred Bretonnian steed was reared to be accustomed to the din and chaos of battle, of weapons clashing and the screams of the dying. They were trained to be inured to the scent of blood, and to respond instantly to the directions of their rider. They were strong-willed and aggressive beasts, for a horse too sedate in nature would not have the necessary spirit in the heat of battle, and Bretonnian steeds were trained to kick and bite the enemy. Through long and extensive training regimes, Bretonnian warhorses were not easily panicked.

When the gentle wind changed direction, however, gusting into the gulley from the south-west, suddenly every horse went wild, rearing and whinnying in fear. Several knights were thrown to the ground, and Calard clung tightly to Gringolet's saddle as the destrier bucked and kicked, his panicked eyes showing as his orbs rolled in the sockets in abject terror.

The sudden blare of crude hunting horns echoed deafeningly close, and dark-furred shapes appeared atop the gorge, bursting from the undergrowth in a violent explosion of movement, roaring and braying for blood.

Calard caught a glimpse of bestial faces, mockeries of humanity twisted by hate, before the beasts hurled themselves from the moss-covered rocks, smashing into dozens of the knights, and tackling them from their saddles.

Most had curving horns spiralling from their fore-heads and temples, and their heavily muscled flesh was covered in fur. The fur was short upon their mas-sive, naked chests and stomachs, though it was thick, long and matted on their backs and shoulders, and down the backs of their powerful arms. Their legs were like those of a stag's, or a goat's, with powerful bunched muscles around the thighs and an additional joint that gave them an odd, backwards-jointed leg, ending in cloven hooves.

The attack was so sudden and so swift that the knights were able to form little defence against it, and they fought not only this deadly foe, but for control of their steeds, which were terrified by the sudden appearance of the predators.

There was a bestial roar to Calard's side, and he swung around to see one of the beastmen kick off from a rock towards him. Its strongly muscled arms were thrown back over its head, and it swung a mas-sive double-handed axe back for the killing blow as it hurtled through the air towards him, eyes filled with hate locked to his own.

Calard recoiled from the beast, lifting his shield before him, and the axe slammed into it, splitting it down to his arm. The blade wrenched his vambrace out of shape, and he was hurled from the saddle by the powerful blow, falling heavily.

Gringolet bolted, hooves flailing as he raced free of the gulley, and Calard dimly watched him go. His kite-shaped shield was useless, and he ripped it from his arm as he struggled to his feet, dazed from the fall.

The beast that had struck him was crouched low to the ground, and it snarled at him. It stank like rancid meat, rotting vegetation and faecal matter, and launched itself towards him, swinging its heavy axe in a lethal arc.

Calard stepped forwards quickly with a shout, and, with both hands, he rammed the point of his sword into the beast's gut before the blow could fall. The blade sank deep, and hot blood washed over Calard's gauntlets, even as the axe dropped from the creature's fingers. With a backhanded blow, it sent Calard sprawling backwards, his head ringing and sank to ground.

The beasts were butchering the knights, ripping into them with terrifying savagery. One knight was killed as his head was rammed repeatedly into a sharp rocky outcrop, and others were literally hacked apart by axes as they lay prostrate on the earth, having been tackled from their saddles.

From the ground, Calard saw his brother Bertelis struggling against a pair of beasts, the flashing hooves of his steed keeping them at bay. Calard lurched to his feet, and staggered forward to pull his sword from the body of the dead beastman.

'Bertelis!' he roared. 'Ride!'

One of the beastmen landed on the ground in front of him suddenly, having leapt from the rocks above. It rose up to its full height, muscles tensed, its thick chest rising and falling rhythmically. It towered over him, standing some six and a half feet in height, and its lips drew back to reveal the mass of yellowed, savage teeth of a predator. Its massive arms were ringed with twisted bronze torcs, and thick rings of dull metal pierced the flesh of its nipples and cheeks. A brand had been burnt into the centre of its broad head, the mark having seared away fur and skin. It was a crude, eight-pointed star, and the flesh around it was red and sore.

It surged towards him, a curved scimitar cutting though the air. Calard lifted his blade to defend himself, meeting the blow with a clash of steel. The strength of the attack drove him backwards, jarring his arm. The creature realised his weakness, and its eyes, like those of a goat, glinted with feral amusement. Behind the beast stalking towards him, Calard saw more knights being butchered, ruthlessly cut down and murdered. He glimpsed the white tabard of Maloric, who was battling with a pair of the powerful creatures. He prayed that the Lady would spare the young noble of Sangasse, so that *he* could cut the bastard whoreson down, in the future.

The beast attacked again, striking high for Calard's head, and the young knight lifted his sword to protect him. The blow drove him to his knees, and the beast, seeing him vulnerable, leapt forwards and slammed its knee into Calard's face.

He fell back against the rock face, struggling to get to his feet, lifting his sword weakly in his hand.

Another beast ran at him from the left. The creature was smaller and more sinewy than the first, and its face was perhaps more human, which made it seem all the more horrific. Its horns were short, stubby nubs that protruded from its brow, and it jabbed a spear towards him, but its progress was halted by a bark from the larger beast. The smaller creature turned away with a snarl to find another victim.

With a contemptuous kick, the powerful beast that had claimed him as its own sent Calard's blade flying from his hand, and placed the tip of its scimitar against his throat. He weakly pushed it away, but the creature merely placed it there again. Once more he pushed it away, but again it returned the sharp weapon tip to his throat, and a trickle of blood ran down the inside of his breastplate.

The creature was toying with him, and Calard felt rage swelling up within him. He screamed in anger and pain, and swatted the blade away from his throat with the flat of his hand, before launching himself at the beast, hands clutching for its throat.

It seemed to give a braying laugh, and made no move to step away. Rather, it moved into Calard's path and slammed its wide forehead into his face, felling him instantly.

His vision swimming before him, Calard was kicked onto his back, and he felt a cloven hoof press down upon his chest. He dimly registered the figure of the beast above him, and saw it draw back its scimitar for the killing blow.

Calard prayed that his brother had escaped the ambush as he waited for the blow to fall, but it never came.

There was the pounding of hooves, and Calard thought he felt warm light upon his skin. Then the beastman was sent spinning away from him, falling heavily to the ground. Calard stared numbly at the headless corpse as its hot lifeblood gushed out onto the forest floor, and then the head of the creature hit the ground, rolling end over end.

Calard tried to rise to his feet as the armoured shapes of knights charged by, but his strength abandoned him, and he slumped back to the ground. He saw a knight bedecked in blue and silver carve his way through the fray, surrounded by a hazy shimmering light.

Then Calard's vision swam before him, and he fell face down onto the ground.

REOLUS TORE THROUGH the fern gulley, smiting the enemy like the avenging paladin of the Lady he was. In his right hand, he wielded the silver lance, Arandyal, shining in the dimness of the forest with a glimmering light, and in his left, he held the lance's mate, the glowing sword Durendyal. Both holy weapons were said to have been blessed by tears shed by the Lady, and only one of pure heart was able to hold them. Blood slipped off the weapons like oil, and they struck with the speed and potency of enraged serpents.

Reolus tore through the beastmen, impaling them on Arandyal's length and cutting heads from shoulders with each swing of Durendyal. He lifted one struggling beastman high into the air, watching dispassionately as it slid down his lance, before he hurled the creature away from him with the flick of his wrist. It slammed into the rock face, broken and dying.

Fey light shone in the grail knight's eyes as he killed. Nothing could stand against this avatar of the Lady's fury. Horns blared, and the beastmen slipped like ghosts back into the deep forest, leaving a scene of destruction and violence in their wake. Defiant and burning with holy passion, Reolus watched them flee.

The grail knight lifted his gaze, and scanned the trees. His eyes locked onto a distant, motionless figure overlooking the carnage.

He sensed the burning hatred within the creature, and felt his pride and anger rise as he registered the power it wielded. Tall and filled with incredible strength, it held a twisted staff of gnarled heartwood, and three pairs of horns rose from its head. It bared countless sharp teeth at him as he began to advance cautiously towards it, guiding his pure white steed with his knees.

Pale eyes the colour of a frozen lake stared back at the advancing grail knight. Set within a different face, those eyes might have been considered noble, but in this inhuman, bestial face they were horrific and disturbing.

Its face was criss-crossed with stitches and scars, a mask of flesh that was pulled tight across its features. Thick ropes of matted hair and fur hung down its back, and it hissed a taunt as the knight approached.

The horrific beast slammed the base of its staff into the ground with a snarl. Tendrils of roots unfurled from the twisted wood, probing the earth like skeletal fingers. They burrowed into the ground, and Reolus felt a wrench within him as they began drawing power from the land. Ferns withered and turned black, all moisture drained from their leaves, and worms and beetles in the earth writhed and contorted as the life was sucked from them. The beast quivered ecstatically as black, pulsing veins appeared upon the surface of the staff.

With a movement both elegant and menacing, the creature lifted its other long arm, and planted its spider-like, taloned hand upon the trunk of the twisted oak tree.

A knot on the bole of the tree split open with a painful tearing sound, and dark fluid that stank of rotting meat ran from the wound. The rent gaped wider and wider, opening like a dripping, foul orifice, and the beast stepped within. Reolus urged his steed forward, asking the Lady for strength, but the rent was instantly sealed. He stared at the tree before him and swore.

Thirty miles away, a tree was ripped open, and the beast stepped forth.

CHAPTER NINE

ANNABELLE POURED THE boiling water into the goblet, wincing at the acrid stench that rose with the steam. Pieces of bark and herb floated around in circles within the steaming liquid. The serving girl looked around, ensuring that none of the kitchen staff of Castle Garamont were nearby. Then she drew a small pouch from within a fold in her dress, and carefully loosened its ties.

She withdrew a heaped amount of powder from within with a small wooden spoon, careful not to breathe in any of the potent mixture. The powder was the colour of congealed blood, and she tipped it into the steaming brew. It dissolved into the mix instantly, and she slipped the wooden spoon back into the pouch, fastened the ties and concealed it once more within the folds of her dress.

She lifted a wooden pot from a shelf, and opened its lid, breathing in deeply of the sweet scent within. Stealing a glance around her, she dipped her finger into the thick syrup, and closed her eyes in contentment as she sucked the honey from her fingertip.

As a pair of haggard old servants shuffled into the kitchens, carrying cane baskets filled with dirt covered vegetables, Annabelle busied herself, spooning out a generous portion of the fresh honey and mixing it into the steaming goblet, before putting the pot back on the shelf.

Moving to the basin, she washed her hands thoroughly and wiped them dry on her apron front. Then she removed the apron, and hung it from a wooden peg. With the flat of her hands, she smoothed back the simple cloth shawl that covered her head and straightened her clothing.

Satisfied with her appearance, she lifted the silver tray on which the steaming goblet stood, and began to make her way swiftly through the castle, heading towards the lord of Garamont's chambers.

Annabelle did not know what the powder was that she mixed into her lord's draught each day. The lady was insistent that she not be observed adding it to the hot water, which had made her uneasy and reluctant, but the lady had made her swear on her life that she would do as she was bidden and speak not a word of it to anyone.

In recompense for her silence and duty, the lady gave her a copper coin with each turning of the moon.

For Annabelle, who had two young children to care for in the hovel-town at the base of the castle, that coin meant the difference between them eating or going hungry, and the unspoken threat in the lady's eyes made her fear to refuse.

The side door reserved for servants was pushed open by a guard stationed there, and Annabelle nodded her thanks. The entrance room was stuffy and dim, the drapes drawn across the windows.

Lady Calisse of Garamont was there, bedecked in a flowing dress of deep purple, her hair held up in two coils inside her veiled, rich headdress. She talked in a hushed voice with a black-clad, elderly physician, who was a frequent visitor of late. They spoke out of earshot of the lord of Garamont, who was dozing in his bedchamber beyond, and, as Annabelle drew near, intending to scurry past them and leave the steaming goblet upon the side table beside her lord, she overheard their words.

'I fear Morr is calling him,' said Lady Calisse, her face drawn and pale, her eyes red-rimmed and filled with sorrow. 'Please, in the name of the blessed Lady, you must be able to do something.'

'I cannot understand it,' said the bent, elderly physician, shaking his head woefully. 'We should have seen improvements by now. This… this is beyond my skill, I regret to say, my lady. It is as if some unholy malady is eating away at him from within, and I am at a loss as to its cause.'

'He is drinking the draught you ordered to be prepared for him, every day,' said lady Calisse, her face drawn, pale and full of lamentation and despair. Annabelle lowered her head and made to scurry past the pair.

'You girl,' said the physician, and Annabelle froze, raising her eyes like a startled rabbit. 'Come here.'

Bending her knees in a slight curtsey, careful not to spill the steaming goblet, Annabelle approached the physician. The elderly man lifted the goblet from the silver tray with withered hands covered in liver spots, and held it under his nose. His sharp eyes seemed intense and cruel to Annabelle.

'What are you adding to this draught?' he asked, his voice tense. The lady Garamont looked at her sharply, her immaculate face and plucked eyebrows making her appear cold and unforgiving. Annabelle cringed beneath their withering gaze.

'My lord?' she stammered.

'It is a simple question, girl. What are you adding to this draught? You are putting something else in it.'

The lady Garamont leant forward and sniffed.

'Honey,' she said.

'Yes, my lady,' said Annabelle in a rush. 'I have been adding a spoon of honey to my lord's draught each morning. I had hoped that it might make it more palatable for my lord.' Her worried eyes flicked to the glowering physician. 'I hope that I have not done wrong.'

The physician's harsh glare softened, and he smiled, placing the goblet back upon the silver tray.

'No, you have not done wrong, girl. Lord Garamont is blessed indeed to have servants that clearly love him.'

Avoiding their gaze, Annabelle blushed deeply and curtseyed once more. She hastily backed away from the nobles, and entered the lord of Garamont's bedchamber.

Luc sighed into the darkness. He was unable to sleep. His mind was restless, thoughts of the wearisome duties and tasks of the day ahead intruding on him. Tomorrow was the start of the annual maintenance of the dry-stone walls of the southern hill, a dreary task that would take the better part of two weeks to complete. The southern hill, a mile from the village, yielded the sweetest grapes in the area, and it was of paramount importance that the fields were tended with diligent care. Though the hill had the best drainage and sunlight in the area, relentless winds battered the slopes, and so hundreds of low, curving walls were constructed around the precious plants, to protect them from having their soil stripped from their roots by the winds.

Those walls had been in existence for dozens of generations, yet after harvest time each year the entire village gathered to rebuild walls that had fallen, and to extend them further up the slopes. It had been this way for hundreds of years, and now the vineyard sprawled as far as the eye could see. It was a source of constant pride to the villagers that the grapes that made the region's finest wines were grown here, though of course none of them had ever been allowed to sample the fine vintages.

Their work had been deemed of such importance that the village had been exempt from sending any of its men to join Lord Sagremor's gathering army. Luc did not know why an army had been mustered, but word had come of a great victory in the north. There had been other mutterings since then, though, of villages burnt to the ground, their inhabitants slaughtered.

Such rumours made the villagers nervous, and some had even spoken of fleeing to the west. Luc had poured scorn on those who repeated such gossip. The lord of Sagremor had long been good to them, and he would certainly protect them if there were any threat. Luc's family had tilled the soil here for five generations, and he would not bring shame upon their memory by fleeing his responsibilities. The gossipmongers were most probably speaking falsehoods anyway, he had assured his frightened wife.

With another sigh, Luc carefully slipped from the rough pallet, careful not to disturb his wife. She moaned in her sleep and rolled over but did not wake, and, in a moment, her breathing had become deep and regular once more. Luc moved across the cramped, simple room that was his home, stepping over the sleeping forms of his wife's sister and husband, huddled together under a blanket. He crouched down beside the cot where his two children slept, curled up with their cousins. He listened to the sounds of their rhythmic breathing and smiled. I am truly blessed, he thought. I have a wonderful wife, a pair of beautiful children, and shelter over my head. He prayed to Shallya, goddess of mercy, that the twins would survive the coming winter, and brushed the yellow hair from his daughter's forehead.

Luc had fathered five children in his twenty years, but the twins were the only ones to have survived longer than three summers. His first child had been stillborn, and its mother had died during the difficult birth. Luc had remarried, and his new wife had borne him a daughter, who was sickly and had not lasted a week. Then, she had borne him a son. He had seemed strong and healthy, despite his malformed arm, but he had succumbed to the wasting cough, and died just days before his third birthday.

These two, his twins, were his pride and joy. With hair the colour of corn and eyes that sparkled with mischief, they were the sunshine of his life.

Standing carefully, so as not to disturb anyone, Luc moved to the single window in his home, and drew the wet-smelling blanket that served as a curtain aside. Peering out in the night, he glanced up at the moons. They were low in the sky. It was three hours until dawn.

Knowing that he had only an hour before he had to rise for the day's work, Luc was about to move away from the window back to bed, but a movement in the corner of his eye drew his attention. A shape was moving in the darkness, and he paused, waiting for the sliver of the white moon to come out from behind a cloud to light the figure.

He heard the clomp of hooves, and, as the clouds parted, he saw the shape of a man slumped in the saddle of a horse. As he watched, the man fell forwards, sliding from the saddle, and dropped heavily into the mud of the main thoroughfare through the village.

Luc dropped the blanket curtain back over the window, with quiet movements, and left his home, closing the swollen wooden door behind him. The air was chill, and he walked warily towards the horse and its fallen rider. One of the man's legs was caught in the stirrups, and he was being dragged through the mud. It was a commoner's draught horse, not a pure-bred, and yet to be allowed to ride a horse at all spoke of this man's exalted position. He was a yeoman, the highest status that a commoner could attain, and, as such, he was a wealthy and esteemed individual in Luc's eyes.

Raising his hand, Luc spoke soothingly to the horse, and it halted. It was lathered in sweat, and its eyes were wide with fright. Moving carefully, ensuring he made no swift movements, Luc drew closer, his eyes flicking down to the fallen rider.

The yeoman wore a tabard of yellow and red, and had a shield strapped to his arm. He had carved a furrow through the mud where he had been dragged, and his face was obscured. He wore a pot-helmet on his head, and Luc saw quivers of arrows and a bow strapped to the horse's saddle.

'Bertrand!' called Luc, shouting out for his brother-in-law, asleep in the family home. He stepped cautiously to the side of the large horse and unhooked the yeoman's foot from the stirrup. Kneeling, Luc rolled the man over. His tabard was awash with blood, and he saw a broken spear shaft imbedded in the yeoman's stomach.

'Bertrand!' he shouted again, more urgently, and he saw the glow of pig-fat fuelled lanterns being lit in nearby hovels as the village awoke to his cry. Pressing his thick, calloused fingers to the man's neck, he felt a weak pulse.

The yeoman's eyes flicked open, and he cried out in pain and fear.

'They are coming!' he whispered hoarsely.

'Hush,' said Luc, trying to calm the man as he struggled weakly to rise to his feet.

Villagers, woken from their slumber, crowded around, their voices fearful and questioning.

'Help me get him inside,' ordered Luc, and the yeoman was carried into his home and laid upon his pallet. His wife's face was full of concern and fear, and the twins began to cry.

'No!' cried the man, fighting against them. 'They will eat our flesh and grind our bones!'

The yeoman fell unconscious, suddenly going limp, his eyes rolling back in his head. The words he had spoken were lifted straight from a common children's tale of the terrible creatures dwelling in the dark depths of the wild woods, but to hear a soldier speak them with such conviction made the villagers whimper in fear.

'I told you we should have fled,' wailed a voice, and others voiced their agreement.

'Be silent!' thundered Luc. A well-respected man in the village, his commanding voice cut through the hysteria. 'He is delirious. We must tend his wounds.'

Luc was well aware that if the man died in his home he would be held accountable, and he had no intention of letting such a thing come to pass. He pulled the man's shield from his arm, and laid it to one side. His eyes lingered on the red and yellow design upon it, of a rearing dragon with flames spewing from its maw. He did not recognise the heraldry, and it was forgotten in an instant as his brother-in-law, Bertrand, cut open the man's tabard with a knife to expose the horrible wound.

The spearhead was embedded deep in the man's stomach, and blood covered the area. Even if he somehow survived the deadly injuring, a secondary infection would probably claim him.

That was when he heard the first horn.

Within minutes, every villager was dead.

THE WARGOR KNELT over the bodies, its nostrils twitching. Gore dripped from its scimitar, and it licked the blood from the fur around its mouth.

The slaughter had been brief and frenzied. None had escaped the wrath of the beastmen.

Rising up, the wargor was forced to duck its horned head to keep from hitting the ceiling of the hovel, which made a growl of anger rise from its chest. It hated such unnatural structures created by the hands of men, and its desire to destroy flared powerfully. The stink of humanity was strong, further fanning the fires of hatred.

It kicked out at a small wooden table, smashing one of the legs and sending it crashing to the hay-strewn floor. It stamped a cloven hoof down upon the wreckage, splintering the wood and smashing it to pieces. It moved around the room with sharp movements, smashing clay pots with its blade, spilling seed and grain, and it slashed at the pallets strewn across the floor. Steam rose in the cold air as it urinated on the blankets that were thick with the stench of humanity.

Discovering a leather flagon tucked in a corner, the wargor ripped the lid off it, sniffing. Lifting the flagon over its head, it poured the alcohol into its mouth, the fiery liquid sloshing over the fur of its chin and down its chest. Draining the flagon, the beastman hurled it away.

Feral black eyes spied a shield leaning against the wall, and it snarled, thick fingers tightening around the hilt of its scimitar. It stalked across the room, and lifted the shield up, gazing intently at the red and yellow design.

The wargor snarled again and defecated, its foul-smelling spoor thudding to the floor, before it stalked out of the hovel, roaring to its kin. Many of the buildings were ablaze, and the heat of the flames made the beast's heart race. The herd was busy slaughtering the last of the villagers and smashing down the hovels in which they lived, trampling them into the ground. They lived to tear down civilisation, and nothing fired their blood like wanton destruction and butchery. Nevertheless, in its brutal, violent mind, the wargor knew that the shield was important, and that the Gave would be pleased with its discovery. It roared again, and raised its bloody scimitar high in the air.

Within minutes, the bray herd was on the move once more, the beastmen running swiftly as a pack through the night towards the welcoming darkness of the forest.

THE KNIGHTS RODE in silence. They passed knocked-down, ancient dry-stone walls, and fields of dead sheep and cattle. Most of the butchered animals were clustered in the corners of their paddocks, where they had huddled in panic and been viciously hacked apart. Many had broken their legs in futile efforts to leap the fences, and countless others had been trampled beneath the hooves of the terrified flock, before brutal blows to skulls and through necks had killed them.

The cold light of predawn was grey and lifeless, and mournful trails of smoke rose from the burnt-out cottages in the dip below. Bodies lay strewn around the crude buildings. The carrion birds were already at work upon them, and their calls were harsh as they squabbled and burrowed their heads into the carcasses.

The stench of burnt flesh reached Calard's nostrils as the patrol entered the ravaged village. Men and women lay sprawled in the mud alongside children, dogs and livestock, all killed by savage blows, their flesh hacked apart and heads caved in.

It was the same all across the east of Bordeleaux: villagers and towns sacked, their occupants butchered. It was clear now that the greenskins had been driven out of Chalons by the beasts of the wild woods, and, though the knights had yet to sight the full force of the enemy, much less face it in open battle, an enemy that could force the brutish orcs and goblins from the forests was one surely to be respected.

It was only an hour past dawn, and the ground was still covered in dew. A low mist hugged the dips in the landscape, and there was an icy chill to the air.

The knights were all tired, having been out on patrol since midnight. They had just been returning to camp near the grail chapel of Theudric, the night having passed without major incident, when they had seen smoke rising in the distance.

'Dismount and look for survivors,' ordered Gunthar, his voice impassive.

'Survivors?' baulked Bertelis. 'They don't leave survivors.'

Gunthar gave the knight errant a hard look. With an exasperated sigh, Bertelis swung his leg over his saddle and slid to the ground. Calard and the other knights of Bastonne did likewise, and they began to search through the ruination wrought only hours earlier.

Two weeks had passed since the destruction of the greenskins and the night of butchery that had followed.

As if the ambush against the knights by the creatures of the forest had been a signal heralding the commencement of slaughter, thousands of corrupted beasts burst from the forest of Chalons, descending upon Bordeleaux with hatred and savagery.

As darkness fell across the hills and fields of Bordeleaux, hundreds of scattered bands and raiding war parties had emerged, intent on bloodshed and mayhem. They fell upon unprotected villages, towns and isolated castles, killing and burning. They slaughtered men, women and children, livestock and dogs. Those that were not butchered were dragged screaming and kicking back into the forest to face whatever vile fate awaited them before they too were killed.

They smashed down hovels, and tore down the walls of inns and homesteads. They had rampaged through the night in a fury of destruction, butchering and tearing down any vestige of civilisation they came upon. Windmills were toppled and crops trodden into the earth, sheep and cows slaughtered, and bales of hay and homes were put to the flame.

Terrified peasants blockaded doors and windows, but such meagre defences were useless against their hateful murderers. With violence almost beyond comprehension, the beasts smashed their way into homes and food-stores, and, though the lowborn inhabitants defended themselves with pitchforks and hoes, they were hacked down and butchered in front of their children and wives. Babes were slain without mercy, their heads dashed against walls, and the elderly and crippled were ripped apart in an orgy of death.

Hearing the blare of horns from all around, and seeing the flames of burning villages in every direction, the duke had ordered his knights and their indentured men-at-arms out into the night. Hundreds were killed

as the beasts ambushed them en route to the beleaguered villages, and a desperate night of bloodshed
had ensued.

The beasts displayed a low cunning, avoiding the
strength of Bordeleaux and striking only against the
weak and vulnerable. When they did strike at the
forces gathered by Duke Alberic, they targeted isolated
groups of knights, setting on them from all sides.
Nothing but corpses remained, testament to the sudden violence done to them.

Howls and braying roars had echoed through the
night. The beasts had chosen the time of their attack
well, for the silver moon of Mannslieb was new in
the sky and cast little light through the massed
clouds. The baleful eye of Morrslieb was fuller, an
insidious half crescent of glowing green, but it did
little to light the fields, even when the clouds parted
and it peered malevolently down upon the horror
being wrought.

When the sun at last rose, and the night of blood was
ended, Duke Alberic's knights found the countryside
in ruin. Black smoke rose in the distance to the north,
west and south.

Word had filtered into the camp of scores of other
massacres further afield, leagues to the north and
south. Outriders and yeoman rode in, bearing the
grim news, having seen with their own eyes the butchery meted out across the fair land.

As the tally of destruction grew, the duke reluctantly
ordered his forces to be split, to protect a wider area
from attack. With no knowledge of where the beasts
would strike next, he spread his forces wide in prepa-
ration for further incursions.

Calard and the other knights of Bastonne had ridden to the south. They were some thirty leagues from Duke Alberic's camp, and only half a day's ride from the broad river of Chalons, which formed the natural border between the lands of Bordeleaux and the dukedom of Aquitaine.

They had been patrolling the area for two weeks, and, in that time, they had seen more than a dozen villages razed to the ground, every inhabitant slaughtered or dragged into the wild woods. These, thought Calard darkly, looking at the dead peasants lying in the mud, had most probably been the lucky ones.

The knights fanned out and began to enter the burnt out peasant homes, sifting through the rubble and detritus, seeking any sign of life. The thatched roofs of many of the hovels were still smouldering.

'Why did these people not flee?' asked Dieter Weschler, his foreign accent clipped as he stared around at the brutality of the carnage. As ever, the Empire soldier's appearance was immaculate, his black breastplate highly glossed, and his moustache carefully oiled and upturned.

'And become outlaw?' asked Calard. He looked down in distaste at the corpse of a man lying face first in the mud, a sickle clutched in his pale, lifeless hand. The back of the man's head had been smashed open like a nut, and he sported a horrible wound in his back that had severed his spine. He had probably been trying to run, which would account for his wounds being on his back.

They do not understand honour, he thought in disdain and pity. He could not expect anything else of the lower classes, but he still found it galling that a man would rather flee in dishonour than face his enemies. Not that there is anything honourable about the enemy, he reminded himself.

'I do not understand,' said Dieter, frowning. He looked at his host, Baron Montcadas in confusion.

'The life of a commoner is forfeit if he leaves the lands he is bonded to work upon without the express permission of his lord,' said the baron, his broad, bearded face serious.

'I see,' said Dieter. 'A sad day this is. The Emperor would be grieved to hear of this tragedy. As an envoy of the Empire, I express my heartfelt condolences to the people of Bretonnia,' he said, bowing stiffly.

'Bretonnia thanks you for your gracious words,' the baron replied, inclining his head, 'and I am sorry that you have chosen such an ill time to journey to our fair lands. Now, please excuse me, Dieter.'

'They are only peasants, Empire,' said Bertelis scornfully, as the baron walked to speak with Gunthar, looking like a bear decked in armour.

'They are people, like you or I,' observed Dieter. He was a diplomat, and though his face was expressionless and his words carefully chosen so as not raise the ire of his hosts, Calard observed that he was irritated by Bertelis's words.

'They are not,' said Bertelis hotly. 'They are a breed apart, vermin born to serve.'

'Only by chance of birth are men like you and I born into privilege,' said Dieter.

'Bah!' snorted Bertelis. 'Sometimes I envy the simple lives of the peasants. They do not realise how good they have it.'

'Oh?' asked Dieter coldly. 'How so?'

'They have homes to live in and food on their tables. They can marry whomever they want without the concern of politics, and they live under the protection of their lord. They have not a worry in the world, and no responsibilities. They work, they eat, they sleep and they rut. It doesn't sound like a bad life to me.'

Dieter glanced down at the corpses around them. As one, they were gaunt to the point of starvation, and stunted by malnutrition and inbreeding.

'Indeed. They seem very lucky indeed.'

Calard snorted, and ducked his head to enter a hovel. Its door had been smashed down, and he blanched as the stink from inside assailed him. It smelt like the lair of some foetid, wet animal.

There were several corpses here, all very dead. He felt a twinge of remorse as he looked upon the bodies of two children that were so similar in appearance that they must have been twins.

He thought then of his own twin, Anara. He had not been much older than these two butchered children when last he had seen her.

Sickened, he moved back into the fresh air, and breathed deeply. A shout drew his attention. A ginger-haired knight of Garamont, whom Calard recognised as Tanebourc, waved to him. The man was good company. Quick to smile, witty, and always with a ribald tale to tell, he was popular amongst the knights of Garamont. Nevertheless, his face was uncharacteristically grim as he stood over a corpse. Looking down, Calard saw that the corpse was a man-at-arms, bearing the red and gold livery of Garamont.

'Who is he?' he asked, not that he knew any of the men-at-arms by name.

'He was assigned to a scouting party that never returned last night.'

'A deserter?'

'Perhaps,' said Tanebourc, 'but I wouldn't think so. A deserter would have discarded his tabard, but he might have been too stupid to think of that,' said Tanebourc with a grim smile. Then the smile dropped from his face. 'I would expect that we will find the rest of his scouting party somewhere around here, butchered by the beasts.'

Tanebourc had been correct in his evaluation. Fifteen Garamont yeomen were found some two miles distant, slaughtered along with their steeds. Calard sighed.

'Build a pyre,' he ordered his men-at-arms.

THE GAVE FELT the tentative approach of the wargor as it picked its way past the moss-covered rocks and skulls. He could feel the creature's animalistic, destructive urges, the primal savagery of its nature. Its heart burned hot with hatred, but it was cowed and fearful as it drew near the holy gibbet tree. Though it hated the Gave with all its being, as the Gave hated himself, it knew who was the master, and slunk forwards full of respect and fawning submission. He could sense the wargor's fear as its eyes flicked warily between the immense, sleeping forms of the giants, the twins of one flesh. Had they been awake, the wargor would already have been dead.

The Gave's blue eyes flicked open. All was darkness around him, and he felt the warm, rotting heart of the tree against his body, clutching him like a child to its bosom. Grubs and worms burrowed through the soft flesh of the tree, and they crawled over him as he breathed deeply the musty scent of rotting wood. He felt the blood of the sacrifices offered to the tree upon his skin.

The gibbet tree opened with a sickly, wet tearing sound like muscle being ripped apart. Like a ribcage being torn open, the rotting wood of the tree parted and the Gave stepped from within. His twisted staff was held in long, spider-like hands, the roots of the staff imbedding themselves into the earth every time the Gave slammed it into the ground.

He moved with a gangly intensity, each movement sharp and stilted. He looked upon the twins of Chaos, their titanic, fifty-foot frames reclining amongst the roots of the great tree. The bones of countless meals were piled around them, and their immense chests rose and fell in unison as they slumbered.

The wargor cowered before him, an object clasped to its chest. It inclined its neck, exposing its jugular in an act of utter subservience.

The Gave towered a full head and a half taller than the powerfully built beastman. He gazed with icy blue eyes at the wargor, and there was more than a hint of madness lurking within their pale, liquid veneer. They stared from within a grotesque mask of stitched together human skin. Only the Gave's mouth and chin could be seen beneath this mask of flesh. That mouth looked almost human, until the pink lips parted, exposing hundreds of tiny, razor-sharp teeth embedded in rows within blood-red gums. An eight-pointed star was cut into the skin-mask of the creature's forehead, and dark blood oozed from the incisions.

Matted clumps of dark hair hung in thick ropes from the Gave's head and shoulders, and three pairs of horns rose from his skull. One pair jutted from his forehead and was tall, straight and spiralling, rising several feet above its head; the second pair was thick and tightly curled like those of a mountain-ram, and protruded from the Gave's temples. The third pair emerged from the centre of the curled horns and swept down, jutting like tusks to either side of his chin.

The Gave was unclothed, and thick fur covered much of his body, though his chest and inner arms were bare. This exposed skin was smooth and translucent, as pale as the moonlight of Morrslieb, and the muscles were lean and taut. Runes of the dark gods pulsed beneath the flesh like angry welts, and veins and arteries could be seen pumping blood through the Gave's body in rhythmic surges.

Why do you disturb my sleep of ages, whelp? roared the Gave, though no sound issued from its throat.

The wargor staggered beneath the mental onslaught, and blood began to seep from its ears. Reeling, it fell to its knees, and threw off the fur that covered the shield clasped to its chest. As blood dribbled from its nostrils, the beastman pushed the red and yellow shield towards the cloven hooves of the Gave.

His pale blue eyes widened, and a hiss issued from his throat. He slammed his staff into the earth, and its roots burrowed into the moist soil. Then he knelt down and lifted the shield. Running his hand over the design on the shield, fingers lingering on the dragon heraldry, the Gave licked at his human lips and gave a barking laugh of triumph.

The wargor began to go into convulsions at its feet. It would be devoured as soon as the giants awoke.

The Gave placed the shield upon a twisted, bleeding root, and lifted his piercing eyes to the twisted branches of the great tree. Black carrion birds regarded him with hungry eyes.

Barking a savage word in the Dark Tongue, the birds erupted into flight, as one. Skeletal branches unfurled from the tip of the Gave's staff, sprouting outwards like the petals of a deathly flower, and the black birds landed among them, filling the air with their harsh, piercing cries.

Amid the raucous din, the Gave extended one hand and uncurled his long, spindly fingers, holding his palm upwards. With his other hand, he drew a long, cracked talon across the pale palm of his hand. Dark blood pumped from the wound, and he closed his hand into a fist.

The Gave plucked the first of the black birds from the branches grown from the staff, holding it in a crushing grip.

The bird cried out and struggled, clawing and biting, but it was held fast. Turning it on its side, the Gave lifted his wounded hand over the creature's face, and let a single drop of its dark blood fall into the raven's eye.

The effect was instantaneous. The bird's beady black eye blinked and turned blood red. A black sliver appeared in the orb, like the pupil of a serpent. The flesh around the eye began to throb and peel away, and the bird thrashed and struggled in agony, while the other ravens looked on impassively. The bird's orb swelled, wider and wider, weeping pus and foulness, until fully half the bird's head was nothing more than a pulsing, bulging red daemonic eye. It blinked, and as the Gave's eyes narrowed, so too the bulging red eye narrowed.

The bird was thrown into the air, and it flapped its way clumsily through the tangle of branches overhead, seeking the open sky. The Gave snatched another bird from its perch.

As the first red rays of dawn rose across the land, a dozen black birds were flying to the west. Once they cleared the forest they spread out in different directions, scouring the land below.

The Gave saw all that they saw, and licked his lips in anticipation.

WEARY AND GRIM, and with the stink of burning human flesh in his nostrils, Calard looked towards the dark shadow of the forest on the horizon. It crouched like a malignant beast, making ready to pounce. Chalons had become a looming spectre of dread in the Bretonnian camp: an impenetrable bosom from which the enemy erupted and wreaked havoc in the dark hours, before retreating as dawn surfaced. More, the forest itself *was* the enemy.

Each night it encroached further into Bordeleaux, creeping forwards like a giant, leafy beast, overtaking fields and swallowing villages close to its borders.

After that first night when the beastmen had revealed themselves, the duke's camp had awoken to find that the tree line had advanced some two hundred yards in the dark hours of night. Twisted briars and thorns had clawed across the earth in advance of the trees, which loomed dark and foreboding.

It was almost as if the trees had uprooted themselves in the night and crept across the ground. Like the questing tendrils of some monstrous, blind beast, the trees had pushed forth in uneven spurts, reaching out and reclaiming fields that had been tilled for generations, and though they were now once again inert, riding near them was eerie and disquieting. Ancient dry-stone walls had been engulfed by the trees, torn down by powerful roots and branches, as if a hundred years of wild growth had occurred overnight.

Nor were the trees in their prime of health; they were twisted, as if in pain, their roots contorted. Sap ran like blood from their limbs, and their branches were malformed, locked in crooked positions, reaching up to the sky as if in silent agony.

Corpses of greenskins, slain only the day before, were crushed beneath the thick roots of trees that should have taken decades to grow. Broken lances and shields had been swallowed by the grasping roots, and they stuck up between contorted limbs, like relics of ancient times, like tombstones marking the burial places of ancient warriors, not the debris of battle from the day before.

Even the fields of grass that had not yet been claimed by the forest were covered in tiny, twisted saplings, the smallest sticking no more than an inch from the churned up earth, but many reaching the height of a horse's shoulder. Twisted briars and thorns had clawed their way across the open ground, and hedges, dutifully trimmed and pruned for decades, had erupted in uncontrolled life.

The armaments and bodies of knights that had fallen in the night were pulled from this tangle of growth, as best they could, and prepared for return to their ancestral lands, though many were never recovered. Peasants strained to retrieve the bodies of their lords from beneath the strangling roots and limbs of trees that had taken root over them, but many had to content themselves with bearing merely a battered shield or helmet back to their lord's estates, the bodies of their masters forever trapped beneath the deathly grip of the trees.

No one could comprehend the sudden advance of the wild wood. On the duke's order, brush fires had been lit, and teams of loggers were brought in to force the woodland back to its earlier boundary. This, however, proved to be folly. The fires failed to take, and the loggers made laughably slow inroads. If anything, their shows of defiance merely seemed to encourage the forest, and at night it burst forth in wild growth wherever an axe had felled a tree. Halting the relentless advance of the forest was quickly deemed to be a hopeless endeavour, and the efforts were abandoned.

As the sun dipped below the horizon each night, branches and leaves began to rustle and shiver, even on nights when there was no wind. It was as if the forest was waking from slumber and stretching. Wary and tense, knights were posted to stand vigil against the forest each night, and men-at-arms whispered prayers and made signs to ward off evil spirits. As darkness, cold and hostile, descended, the forest sprouted forth, an unholy cancerous growth that pushed ever deeper into Bordeleaux lands.

Where would it end? thought Calard, staring with horror at the dark shape on the horizon. Each night it advanced a hundred, two hundred yards. How long would it take to claim all of Bretonnia? A few scant years? The thought was horrifying.

He saw a lone black bird circling high overhead.

Somewhere, wolves began to howl.

CHAPTER TEN

CALARD ROLLED OVER with an angry grunt. He pushed one ear into the stuffed, goose feather pillow, and threw an arm over the other, trying vainly to block out the sound of his brother's enthusiastic lovemaking. He didn't know who it was that Bertelis was coupling with, nor did he care. All he knew was that he was exhausted, and that sleep was eluding him.

Whoever the girl was, she seemed to be enjoying herself, for her gasps and moans were getting louder, joining Bertelis's animal grunting and the repetitive thumping of his pallet.

Unable to stand it any longer, Calard threw off the covers and got up. Quickly and with angry, sharp movements he dressed, throwing his blue and red tabard on over his underclothes. Hearing the movement, Bertelis, covered in a sheen of sweat, looked up from atop the panting form of a naked, dark-haired girl.

'What?' he said, pausing his action as Calard threw him a thunderous look. The girl was moaning like a banshee beneath Bertelis, and Calard swore under his breath, shaking his head, and stormed out of the tent.

The pair of men-at-arms stationed outside swiftly rose to attention from their bored slouches as Calard swept past them. He stamped away from his tent, not caring where he was going, just wanting to be away. His hands were clasped into fists at his sides, and peasants scurried out of his way as they saw the look on his face.

It was perhaps three hours past dawn, and he had only returned, tired and weary, from the patrol half an hour earlier. The revolting stink of burning human flesh still clung to him, but he had gone straight to bed, exhaustion driving him. Haunting images had rushed through his weary mind whenever sleep came close, and he was jerked back awake. He saw circling black birds and the menacing forest. The pale face of his long-lost twin sister emerged from the mists that encircled the trees, appearing as the child he remembered, though she would have been twenty years old by now. She spoke to him, though her lips did not move, and he could not understand her words. It was if she was whispering, just too faintly for him to hear, and he awoke, feeling frustrated and irritated. In truth he doubted that he would have been able to sleep even if Bertelis had not been rutting within earshot.

His brother could not understand why he had not taken any woman to his bed since he had begun courting Elisabet.

'You truly love her, then?' Bertelis had asked, somewhat bewildered.

'With every fibre of my being,' he had answered.

'I still don't see why that changes anything. It's not as if you are already wedded to the girl. Enjoy yourself while you still can!'

'That would bring dishonour on her, and me!' said Calard hotly.

Bertelis had shaken his head in bewilderment and wonder. Calard kicked at a scabby camp dog, and the creature yelped and ran from him, its crooked tail between its legs.

GUNTHAR SIGHED. HE was not as fast with the blade as he used to be, and he found himself exhausted when a decade ago he would have felt nothing. Of course, there were still few who could match his blade-work, but within a few years, perhaps half a decade at most, they too would fade.

Without a son to carry his name, he would be forgotten. For a moment, he regretted having never wed, and this brought back painful memories. He was haunted by the question of what might have come to pass if *he* had met her first, but she had already been betrothed to the dashing young Lutheure, Gunthar's closest brother-in-arms.

He had never spoken a word of his love for Yvette of Bordeleaux to any living soul, and it was a secret he would carry to his dying day. He would never have dishonoured himself, or them, by voicing his feelings. Instead, he had pushed them deep inside. It was a source of much rumour and gossip as to why he had never wedded, but only Gunthar knew the true reason.

He had been distraught when Yvette had died, no more than fifty miles from where Gunthar now stood.

He had wept for her, and it was out of love for her that he had stayed within the Garamont household to oversee Calard's training.

He pushed these thoughts away, as he saw Calard storm from his tent and stalk off through the camp, his every movement tense and angry.

He had tried to get the boy to talk through what it was that was frustrating him so much, about the raging anger that burnt within him, but it had ended badly. He realised that it was always going to. He had cursed himself for a fool afterwards. Young men always believed that they saw things so clearly. It was one of the quirks of being young. They always felt that the things they experienced had never been experienced by anyone before them, that the emotions they felt were more intense than those any other person had ever experienced.

Why was it, Gunthar mused, that it was only when the body began to ache and fail you, as old age began to creep up, that one started to gain some wisdom, some understanding of the world? He chuckled to himself. You really are getting old, he thought.

The boy had lost his mother at a tender age, and within the year his twin sister, his constant companion and shadow, was taken by the Enchantress. Thinking of her, Gunthar made a sign to ward off the fey. Gunthar loved Lutheure of Garamont like a brother, and knew that, in his heart, he was a good man, but when Yvette had died, something within him had died as well. All warmth towards the young Calard had been sucked away, and Lutheure had said barely a civil word to him in all the years since. Gunthar could understand it. Calard was the spitting image of his mother, and it must have caused Lutheure pain to look upon the boy.

Gunthar loathed the new lady of Garamont with a silent passion, seeing her as a cold, jealous woman. He was honest enough with himself to know that part of his dislike stemmed from the fact that she was, in his eyes, replacing Yvette in the household, but he believed that he would have disliked the woman even if circumstances had been different. She was cruel to servants and peasants to the point of maliciousness, a trait she seemed to have sadly passed on to her son Bertelis, and she had made life for Calard growing up in the castle a misery.

With a father who was cold and distant, and who had eyes only for his second son, and a vicious stepmother who derided him at every chance, it was no wonder that Calard struggled with issues of anger and self-doubt. He just wished that he could help somehow.

Trumpet horns sounded, and Gunthar craned his neck to see a troop of knights riding up the hill into camp, just back from a further patrol. Beastman heads were impaled on lances, and there was cheering as the knights rode through the camp displaying the grisly trophies proudly. They were the knights of Sangasse, he noticed.

At least someone had been successful in their hunt, thought Gunthar.

ANGRY AND TIRED, Calard walked blindly through the camp that the knights of Bastonne were using as a base for their patrols. It was a good defensive position, for the tents had been erected on a wide, flat-topped hill named Adhalind's Seat, and the land was clear for miles around. A small patch of verdant woodland hugged the base of the hill to the west, fed by a bubbling natural spring, and it was towards this patch of serenity that he now walked.

Hearing the blare of trumpets, he turned to see the victorious knights return. Jealousy stabbed at him.

His mood darkened as he saw Maloric riding with the group, holding a massive shaggy head aloft in one hand. Swearing, he swung around and stormed away from the victorious Sangasse knights. He knew that it was not honourable to give in to his anger, but at the moment, he just wanted to break something.

The camp was far less grand than the duke's in the north, consisting of no more than three hundred tents, and it took only a minute to reach its perimeter. Standing at the edge of the table-topped hill, he stared down at the small copse of woodland that hid the revered grail chapel. There were countless numbers of these holy shrines dotted around Bretonnia, and each was a site of pilgrimage and holy significance. This particular shrine was said to heal wounds of the heart, and hundreds of jilted and spurned lovers made the long journey to it each year to pray and make offerings.

It is said that Theudric, a questing knight from Carcassonne, was visited by a vision of the Lady here, and that it was in this location that he supped from her chalice and became a noble grail knight. In honour of this holy visitation, he had funded the construction of the small shrine built within the copse.

As he descended the hill and entered the trees, Calard felt his anger subside. The air was cool and fresh, and he passed his hand through the soft fern fronds that blanketed the earth. The trees were sparse and thin, far from the twisted, oppressive trees of Chalons. Breathing deeply, Calard wound his way through the ferns, the soft sunlight dappling the undergrowth.

The mausoleum that housed the body of Theudric was small and humble, made of pristine white marble that had been overgrown with ferns. Its sides were arched and open, and creepers had begun to claim the small structure.

Theudric had, if the stories were to be believed, been in love with a renowned beauty, Adhalind, a woman of unsurpassed grace and virtue. However, a hag, jealous of her beauty, had cursed Adhalind, so that if she were ever kissed, both she and the object of her affection would perish instantly. Fearing not for herself, but for the noble Theudric, she spurned his advances, but he was vociferous in his pursuit of her hand, for he knew that she loved him too. Determined to free her, Theudric set out to break the curse. Every day that he was away, Adhalind came to the shrine that he had built, seated atop the hilltop, watching and waiting for her love to return to her. For forty long years she waited for his return, and it was during this time that the hill was named Adhalind's Seat.

At long last, Theudric returned, kissing his love for the first time, now that the curse had been lifted from her. His life had been prolonged by the mystical properties of the Lady's grail, and he appeared as he had when he had left, but the years had been harsh to Adhalind, and she was an old woman, her face lined and her hair grey. Nevertheless, the couple were wed, and lived in joyous happiness until Adhalind passed away, a smile of contentment upon her face, a year later.

Theudric lived out the rest of his years as a hermit, tending the shrine, and only leaving it when the call to war came. He lived to one hundred and ninety years, and when he passed from the world, he was interred alongside his beloved Adhalind.

Calard stepped lightly up the mausoleum steps, looking in awe upon the stone sarcophagus that housed the body of the revered grail knight and his lady. It had been carved in the likeness of the knight and his beloved, lying side by side with their hands held clasped over their chests, as if in prayer. A marble sword lay by Theudric's side, and a carved marble shield acted as the couple's pillow. Theudric's feet rested upon a coiled dragon, while beneath Adhalind's carved feet was a resting unicorn. The white marble carving was perfect in every detail, even down to individual strands of hair, and Calard marvelled at the skill of the workmanship. The knight's face was strong and noble; his lady's young and virtuous. Calard stared into the carved likeness of Theudric's face, trying to perceive what it was that had made the man great.

Stepping down the steps on the other side of the mausoleum, Calard's breath caught in his throat as he glimpsed the glowing pale shape of a lady standing looking at him from the other side of a small pond. It took him a moment to realise that this was not a vision, but a statue, carved of the same clean marble as the mausoleum, and that the glowing intensity of the ghostly image was created by the sunlight dappling upon the stone.

He stepped towards it in awe, and dropped to his knees before the lily covered pond, gazing upon the pristine face of the Lady of the Lake. Divine hands must surely have guided the sculptor, for the representation was breathtaking in its detail and the incredible impression of life that had been attained.

The Lady was tall, slender and full of grace. One leg was slightly bent and her arms were held before her, as if she were stepping forward to embrace Calard. Her dress seemed diaphanous, flowing and almost translucent, as if it were delicate, impossibly fine silk, wafting in a slight breeze, rather than solid, cold stone. A jewelled grail hung from her waist upon a string of beads and entwined vines, and her flowing hair was filled with tiny, delicate flowers and leaves.

It was the Lady's facial expression, however, that was the sculptor's true work of artistic genius, and Calard felt tears on his cheeks as he gazed upon it. With beautifully carved, high cheekbones and lips that looked as soft as velvet, the Lady stared down at him with an expression of infinite compassion. The feeling of love and motherly devotion that exuded from the statue was almost palpable, and Calard swallowed heavily, enraptured by the divine vision that the sculptor had created.

Calard had only dim memories of his mother, for she had died when he was a young boy, but seeing this expression on the statue of the Lady brought those vague memories back into sharp focus.

Calard lowered his eyes, and looked down into the pond. Catfish with long, wafting whiskers swam too and fro beneath the mirror surface of the water, sifting through the leaves that had settled upon the bottom.

The reflection of the Lady shimmered like a holy apparition upon the pond, and Calard closed his eyes in prayer, feeling a great sense of calm and serenity descend over him.

He did not know how long he knelt before the statue, but when he at last opened his eyes, the sun had shifted. It was almost overhead, and no longer made the statue glow. He felt refreshed and cleansed, as if his act of prayer had washed away his ill mood.

He stood, whispered one final prayer, and made his way back into the camp, climbing the grassy slope of Adhalind's Seat. He felt calmer than he had done for weeks.

With some shame, he recalled the heated conversation he had had with Gunthar on the ride back to camp just hours earlier.

'You seem angry, frustrated,' the weapon master had said softly. 'Is it something that you would like to speak of?'

Calard had glared at the older knight. 'I'm not angry,' he said hotly. Gunthar raised an eyebrow.

'If you say so,' he said. They rode alongside each other in silence for a moment, each lost in his own thoughts.

'Are you still thinking of how you were unhorsed when ambushed by the beasts?' Gunthar asked at last.

Calard's face darkened. 'It was shaming,' he said, keeping his voice low so that none of the other knights heard his words. 'The beast could have killed me, but it was enjoying toying with me. I could see it in its hateful eyes. I would rather have been killed in battle than suffer being at the mercy of that creature.'

'And never see your fair Elisabet again?' asked Gunthar softly.

'I do not deserve her affection,' said Calard bitterly.

Gunthar laughed out loud, and Calard glared at him in outrage.

'Ah, the foolishness of youth,' said the weapons master. 'Do you have any idea the number of times that I have been unhorsed in battle? How many times I would have been slain, but for the intervention of another, or a lucky twist of fate? Don't dwell on it. You are alive, and your honour is untarnished.'

Calard had glared at the weapon master, and pulled his horse away from him. He had ridden the remainder of the journey back to camp in silent brooding. Only now did he see that he had been foolish. True, the shame of having been at the mercy of the creature stung him still, but far better men than him had died that day in battle. He felt like a foolish child.

Feeling calm and humbled, Calard walked back into the camp, smiling to himself as he thought of Elisabet, his earlier dark mood shaken off.

'Ah, Garamont!' said a snide voice. Calard looked up, the smile slipping from his face as he saw Maloric standing with his hands on his hips before his tent. The young knight was still armoured, and his white tabard was splashed with blood. Behind him, a peasant rammed a beastman's head onto a spear embedded in the ground, alongside half a dozen others. 'What do you think of my latest adornment?'

'It's quite charming,' said Calard mildly. 'A relative of yours?'

Maloric chortled, and smiled at him. 'Ah, so witty. I heard that you had another unsuccessful night's hunt.

It's almost as if you are *trying* to avoid the beasts. Is that it, Garamont? Have you found a local stable in which to cower each night, while real men go out to fight? Perhaps with a warm young stable boy to hold you tight?'

Calard felt the peace he had achieved in the grail shrine shred away. Other Sangasse knights stopped what they were doing, smirking, to see the young noble of Garamont's response. He saw one particular man, a slim young knight of the realm, perhaps in his mid-twenties, step close to Maloric, a hand resting lightly on his sword hilt, a half smile on his lips.

Calard sensed that this situation could rapidly deteriorate, but his pride was flaring. He thought of the cool, pale face of the Lady, and his anger subsided somewhat. He forced himself to smile.

'I congratulate you on your successful hunt. I shall take my leave of your presence now, for I would not wish to have to break your nose again. I fear your mother would be most displeased if your noble profile was permanently damaged,' said Calard amiably. He turned away, and under his breath he muttered, 'And I hear the wrath of the whore is impressive indeed.'

'What did you say?' asked Maloric.

'I said your mother is a fine woman,' said Calard loudly over his shoulder.

'And yours is dead and rotting in the ground,' snarled Maloric. 'Best place for her, mind. I heard tell that she was a witch.'

Calard froze in his tracks, the colour draining from his face.

'Wasn't your bitch twin sister a witch too?' continued Maloric. 'That *was* why she was taken away, wasn't it?'

Calard spun around and stormed towards the Sangasse noble, his face thunderous. Maloric smirked at him, and flashed a smile at the slim knight at his side.

Without ceremony, Calard slammed his fist into the noble's face, breaking his nose once more. He stood over him, his breathing heavy.

'Don't you ever speak of my mother or sister again, you whoreson,' spat Calard.

From the ground, Maloric held one hand to his bleeding nose, but he looked up at Calard, his eyes blazing in triumph.

'I accept,' he snarled.

'What?' snapped Calard.

'You have struck me down in front of all the knights gathered here. I accept your challenge, and I nominate Sir Ganelon here as my champion.'

The slim knight bowed his head, his half-smile mocking.

Calard swore.

He recognised the knight, now: Ganelon, champion of Sangasse; Ganelon the butcher.

A slim man of below average height, he looked more like a boyish libertine than the deadly warrior he was said to be. His hair was scented and brushed, and hung past his shoulders, and his fluted armour was ornate and highly shined. He wore a half-smile permanently affixed to his face, but his eyes were cold and dead, like those of a fish.

Ganelon was the victor of a score of duels, and it was said that he was more than a little unhinged in the head. If the rumours were true, he had a particular fondness for inflicting pain, be it on his opponent in a duel, or on a woman in the bedchamber.

'Fine,' he said at last. 'Name the time and place.'

'Noon,' said Ganelon, looking up into Calard's eyes. 'The west field beyond the camp.'

'I shall be there,' said Calard.

'I look forward to it,' said Ganelon. Beside him, Maloric did not even attempt to conceal his pleasure.

'No! I CAN fight my own battles!' said Calard.

'You cannot match him!' said Gunthar hotly, rounding on the young knight. Calard was being armoured by a servant, arms outstretched as the last pieces of his armour were fastened. 'The man is a cold-hearted murderer,' continued Gunthar, 'and his skill is beyond your own.'

'I will not let you fight for me!' protested Calard.

'I made a promise to see you safe,' the middle-aged knight said. Calard snorted in derision.

'To my father? He would not have asked to see me safe. The man hates me.'

'He does not hate you, Calard,' said Gunthar with a sigh, 'but it was not to him that I made the promise.'

'Oh? Then who was it to?'

'The Lady Yvette, your mother.'

Calard blinked in shock, the angry words he was about to speak frozen on his tongue. He dropped his arms to his sides, and ordered the servants to leave the tent.

'She made me promise that I would see you and your sister safe,' said Gunthar when the servants had departed, his voice soft and his eyes hazy as he recalled the conversation. 'She feared for you both. It was only a day before she… died. She was heavily pregnant, and wracked with pain, but her concern was only for you and your sister.'

'Pregnant?' asked Calard in confusion, his anger forgotten.

Gunthar realised he had said too much.

'Yes,' he said with resignation. 'The birth was difficult. It claimed both mother and child.'

Calard stared blankly into space.

'I never knew,' he said at last. 'No one ever told me how she had died.'

'I am sorry to have spoken of it. It was not my place to do so. Anyway,' said Gunthar, clearing his throat, 'within the year Anara was taken. I could do nothing, despite the promise I had made, but here and now, I can. To fail her with both her children… I could not live with that dishonour.'

'I do not wish to see you die on my account,' said Calard.

'I have no intention of dying, my boy,' said Gunthar. 'Let me do this. Let me honour your mother's wish.'

At that moment Bertelis entered the tent, his face grim. He looked upset and worried, biting his lip.

'It is time,' he said.

WORD HAD SPREAD, and all the knights in the camp were gathered to watch the contest. Men-at-arms and other peasants crowded around the roped off open area of the field, jockeying for position.

A murmur ran through the crowd as Calard approached, flanked by Bertelis and Gunthar, and a path was cleared for them.

The knights and peasants of Garamont cheered as he marched into the open area in the centre of the gathering, though there were shouts and jeers from the Sangasse camp. Maloric and Ganelon stood side by side in front of the Baron of Montcadas, who was to act as the official judge for the contest. Calard's face darkened as he saw them. He marched towards them, and halted a few steps away. Ganelon was still smiling his cold half-smile.

'I thought you might not have shown,' said Maloric. 'I am glad. At least you will die with some honour remaining.'

'*I* shall be fighting on behalf of Calard of Garamont,' said Gunthar firmly, before Calard could speak.

Maloric raised an eyebrow, smirking. Ganelon shifted his cold dead eyes to Gunthar, looking him up and down appraisingly.

'You would have an old man fight for you?' laughed Maloric. 'Ah, this is too good.'

'Calard of Garamont has named a champion!' boomed Baron Montcadas, his powerful baritone voice sounding out across the gathered crowd.

'Long have I yearned to cross blades with you,' said Ganelon mildly, locking eyes with Gunthar. 'It will be an honour to be the one to kill you.'

'In your dreams, boy,' said Gunthar.

'May the Lady bless you both,' said the baron.

'Oh, she does,' said Ganelon. Gunthar was silent.

The Baron Montcadas lifted up an ornate hourglass for all to see. 'The contest shall begin when the last grain of sand falls!' roared Baron Montcadas, turning on the spot as he spoke so all could hear his words. He turned the timer over and slammed it down onto a table draped with silk.

The two combatants turned away from each other, and strode to opposite ends of the roped out arena. A peasant brought Gunthar's horse forward, and others appeared bearing his shield and weapons.

'You do not have to do this,' Calard said, his voice thick with emotion.

'I do,' said Gunthar, 'if I am to honour the pledge that I made to your mother.' He smiled suddenly. 'Have courage, boy. I will not be killed by some Sangasse whelp.'

'Try to finish it from the saddle,' said Bertelis. 'He is better on foot than he is on horseback.'

Calard felt sick to his stomach, but he could not find the words to express his feelings. Bertelis was at his side, his face pale and tense. Gunthar knelt, bowing his head in prayer to the Lady.

Standing, he embraced both Calard and Bertelis, before pulling himself into the saddle of his powerful, armoured destrier. It snorted and tossed its head, and Gunthar slipped his shield over his arm. Lastly, he reached for his lance. Calard handed it to him.

'Fight well,' said Calard. Gunthar smiled in response. Then he lowered his visor, and turned towards the figure of Ganelon. The wait for the remaining sand in the hourglass to fall seemed to Calard to take an age, and he jumped when the horn was finally blown.

Without ceremony, the two knights kicked their steeds into a gallop, and thundered towards each other across the grassy field. This was no fancy tournament ground. There was no fence dividing the jousters, little fanfare and a distinct lack of the panoply that generally surrounded such an event: just two knights who would fight until one yielded, or one was unable to continue.

They thundered across the turf towards each other, and Calard found himself holding his breath. They came together with bone crushing force. Both knights took the blows on their shields, and they reeled in their saddles from the force of the impact. Neither man fell.

'Gunthar made the better strike,' said Bertelis. 'That will have weakened Ganelon. He can win this.' Calard did not answer. He felt ill.

The two knights trotted their steeds to opposite ends, shaken by the blows they had taken. They wheeled around sharply for another pass.

Spurring their warhorses on, the two slammed together once more. This time, Gunthar moved his lance tip just before it impacted with Ganelon's shield, and it took the younger man in the shoulder. A great cheer rose from the knights of Garamont, and Calard punched the air. Ganelon's lance shattered on Gunthar's shield.

Gunthar rode past his opponent, and wheeled his horse around for another pass. Ganelon hurled his shattered lance to the ground angrily and drew his sword. Seeing this, Gunthar dropped his lance to the grass, and slid his blade from its scabbard.

Then the pair were charging at each other once more. They came together hard, and the ringing of steel sounded as their swords clashed. They made another pass, this one slower, and traded blows at close quarters, guiding their steeds expertly with their knees. Ganelon's blade was fast, his sword darting in and out with astonishing swiftness. Gunthar defended himself with great skill, and his sword flashed back in deadly ripostes that the younger man turned away at the last second.

Ganelon slashed towards the older knight's chest, but at the last moment he pulled the blow, feinting, and the blade sliced towards Gunthar's head. The older knight anticipated the strike, and took it on his shield. His own sword stabbed out towards Ganelon's breast.

The younger knight swayed in the saddle and lifted his left arm slightly, opening his shield guard. The point of Gunthar's sword blade scraped across his breastplate before passing under the younger man's armpit. Clamping his arm down sharply, Ganelon trapped Gunthar's blade. Feeling his weapon trapped and useless, Gunthar slammed his shield hard into the smaller man, knocking him from the saddle.

Ganelon fell hard, but came swiftly to his feet. Gunthar's steed tossed its head, and the older knight stared down at his opponent. Then he swung one leg over his saddle, and dropped to the ground. He sent his horse running clear with a smack on its rump, and peasants ran forward to lead both horses away.

Ganelon lifted his helmet away from his head, and tossed it arrogantly to the side, confident in his abilities. 'A fine, if somewhat unconventional move,' he remarked.

Gunthar was silent as he circled, his sword and shield raised. Ganelon's stance was relaxed to the point of cockiness, his arms hanging loose at his sides. He jumped lightly from foot to foot, taunting his opponent.

'The arrogant bastard,' hissed Bertelis, at Calard's side.

Gunthar swung in with a powerful blow to the neck. Ganelon's blade flashed up from his side, sweeping the attack aside, before slicing back with a vicious riposte that Gunthar was hard pressed to deflect with his shield. Ganelon did not follow up the attack, but merely waited for Gunthar to attack again.

The weapon master stepped forwards and struck, a strong overhead slash that was taken on the shield. Ganelon's blade darted forward, but it was pushed away harmlessly by Gunthar's blade, and he stepped in close and bashed the smaller man with his shield. His sword followed the attack, and Ganelon was forced to back away from his opponent's blade as it slashed in, left and right. His cocky showmanship evaporated as he saw his opponent's skill, and what followed was the most dazzling display of swordsmanship that Calard had ever witnessed.

The two men fought toe to toe, each blow snapped with astonishing swiftness, each displaying remarkable skill. The swords crashed together time and time again, and the dance of blades as they thrust, struck, parried and riposted was dizzying to watch. The entire crowd was silent, enthralled by the contest playing out before them, aware that they were in the presence of two masters.

After minutes of frantic swordplay, the pair stepped away from each other, breathing heavily. Gunthar's helmet was dented in two places, and he had suffered a powerful blow upon his left rarebrace, which had sheared through the plate metal and the chain links beneath, and bitten into his arm. Ganelon's shield was bent out of shape from the heavy blows he had taken, and he bore a cut across his cheek that was bleeding profusely, though it was not deep.

Gunthar was the larger and stronger of the pair, and arguably more skilled, but Calard had never seen a man as fast with the blade as Ganelon. Added to this, the man was more than three decades younger than the ageing weapon master, and, as the fight wore on, Calard could see that Gunthar was tiring. His heart began to sink.

'He needs to end this quickly,' said Bertelis.

Ganelon too could see that his opponent was tiring, and his cocky strut was returning. Gunthar's attacks grew slower, until it was clear that exhaustion was getting the better of him.

With pained, helpless expressions on their faces, Calard and Bertelis watched as Ganelon stepped around their weapon master, leaping forward to strike a flurry of lightning blows, before leaping back once more. More blows struck Gunthar, denting his breastplate and helmet, and his left pauldron was hanging uselessly from his shoulder. Ganelon pulled the battered shield from his arm and hurled it away. Gunthar followed his every move with his shield held before him, his sword poised.

Calard had seen a similar battle played out once before. As a boy, he had watched from a distance as an ageing stag, still strong but past its prime, was harried by a pack of wolves. The wolves were respectful of the power of the stag, knowing they could be impaled on its antlers or crushed by its hooves, but they were also confident in their speed. Their jaws snapped each time they darted in, causing dozens of wounds on the noble beast, and it gradually began to tire. Growing bolder, the wolves darted in with growing confidence, until the stag was dead on its feet, exhausted beyond its ability to defend itself any longer. Then the wolves had leapt in, tearing out its throat, and the proud beast had died.

Another flurry of attacks, and Gunthar suffered a fierce blow to his head that wrenched his helmet half off. He pulled it free and dropped it to his side, blood flowing from his temple.

Darting forward again, his blade flashing dangerously, Gunthar defended himself with deft skill, despite his exhaustion. His sword flashed towards Ganelon's neck, but there was little power behind the blow, and it was swatted aside easily, leaving his body and throat horribly exposed. Calard held his breath, waiting for the fatal blow to fall.

Ganelon could have easily killed Gunthar then, but he did not. He stabbed his blade into Gunthar's thigh, the blade punching through his armour and sinking deep into the muscle. Gunthar roared in agony as the tip of the sword scraped his thighbone, and the leg collapsed beneath him.

The younger knight twisted the blade, before withdrawing it and stepping back, the half-smile still frozen on his face. He was toying with Gunthar now, drawing out his death before the gathered knights of Bastonne.

'Dear Lady above,' said Calard hoarsely. 'Let him die with dignity, you bastard.'

Somehow, Gunthar pushed himself back to his feet to face his opponent, grimacing in pain. His shield slipped from his arm, and he clutched his blade in both hands.

'I salute you,' said Ganelon. 'Never have I faced such a skilled opponent.'

'And you never will again,' said Gunthar, spitting blood.

'I think it is time for you to die, now. I am getting hungry,' said Ganelon demurely. 'Killing always gives me such an appetite.' He stepped towards Gunthar, his sword held poised.

Gunthar stumbled suddenly, and Ganelon surged forwards, his sword lancing for his enemy's throat. He realised, too late, that the slip was nothing more than a convincing feint, and he tried desperately to reverse his movement, but he was already committed, his whole body moving forwards. As his blade was turned aside by Gunthar's armoured forearm, the tip of the older knight's sword drove low into his body, slipping through the weak joints in his armour around his groin. The force of his momentum drove him further onto the blade, and he gasped in pain as the major artery in his groin was severed, and the blade sank deep into his flesh.

Ganelon stumbled backwards, and the blade slipped from his body. Blood spurted like a fountain from his fatal wound, the colour bright and vivid against the gleaming silver of his armour. He stared in disbelief at the gushing blood, and fell to the ground.

There was not a sound from the gathered onlookers. Ganelon looked around numbly, his expression one of shock, his mouth opening and closing like that of a fish stranded on land. The colour drained from his features as his lifeblood pumped from his body, pooling around him and soaking into the earth. In moments, he was dead, falling back against the ground, his eyes staring blankly at the grey sky.

Maloric turned away with a snarl, and began pushing his way through the frozen crowd. Gunthar fell face first to the ground, blood running freely from the deep wound in his thigh.

Shouting for aid, Calard ran to the wounded weapon master.

CHLOD'S EYES LIT up as he saw the coins. Half a copper crown! It was more money than he had seen for many moons, and far more than could be earned through honest work.

He reached across the table greedily, and snatched at the proffered coin. The solidly built warden pulled the coin back before he could grab it, and Chlod scowled darkly at him.

The last month had been tough. Twice he had been beaten: once by drunk, young knights merely for sport, and once by men-at-arms, who had caught him stealing from a knight's tent. He was lucky in the latter case that a beating had been all that he had received.

Just minutes ago, he had been sleeping, but had woken instantly as the first kicks slammed into his body. He guessed that at least one rib was broken.

Dragged through the mud like a swine being led to the slaughter, he had been brought before the warden, who was now leering at him. He knew the man by reputation: a black-hearted murderer and thief. He was clever, though. In front of the nobility he was all sunshine and roses, obliging and dutifully subservient. It was only amongst the peasantry that his brutality came to the fore.

The bastard charged a tax of his own, though of course the nobility were unaware of it. Safety tax, he called it. As in, if you pay it, you are safe, and if you do not, then you are beaten and punished for some fabricated crime. Being a yeoman warden, at the top of the pecking order of the peasantry, the bastard could torture and punish men and women as he saw fit without any intervention from the nobility. In fact, in Chlod's experience the nobility were pleased to see such acts, for it made them feel as if order was being kept.

He had seen men around the camp missing their hands, and he had learnt that this was the warning for failing to pay your safety tax. Your hand was hacked off with an axe and the stump shoved into burning coals to cauterise the wound. A second warning was never given, since few people asked questions about peasants that disappeared.

Chlod had heard that those who had in the past tried to bring his corruption to the awareness of the nobility were brutally murdered, along with every member of their family.

Not having had the coin with which to pay the warden the tax he demanded, Chlod was beaten with sticks, and kicked till he pissed blood before being dragged here.

Happily, though, things had not gone the way he had expected, and he still had both of his hands.

'You understand what it is I am telling you to do?' snarled the big warden.

'Yes,' said Chlod. 'You want me to help kill some knight.'

For a peasant, even to utter words of dissent against a noble was a punishable offence, usually resulting in the loss of fingers and ears, or a week in the stocks. For a peasant to lay hands on a noble, or even on his horse, accidental or not, was a far more serious offence, which often resulted in hanging. If a peasant physically *harmed* a noble, something that few would even comprehend, let alone premeditate, the punishments were of the utmost severity. On the rare occasion that such a thing came to pass, a peasant could expect agonising torture and slow dismemberment. His family would suffer a similar fate, and his friends and associates would be tortured and maimed. Such was the severity of the crime that the nobles made a brutal example of any who dared to assail them.

Chlod, however, had no family or friends. He had killed before, and had no qualms about doing so again, and the coin was enough to outweigh the dangers. He was no fool, and would do all that he could to make sure that no retribution would come his way, but he was well aware that things often turned out in ways that could not be foreseen. Plus, he was desperate.

'Kill some knight, that's the gist of it yeah,' said the warden, leering at him with his gapped teeth spread wide in a predatory smile. 'Two hours before dawn. The noble's on the early patrol, and is due back at midnight. Don't even think about making a run for it. My men will be watching over you from the moment you leave this tent. If you make any move to speak to anyone or leave the camp, you are dead, but not before you experience the most exquisite pain imaginable.'

Chlod believed he had a fairly vivid imagination, but he nodded and reached again for the coin. This time the warden allowed him to take it, and it disappeared instantly into a hidden pocket in Chlod's stinking clothes. He felt his scrawny, black-furred pet squirm against his skin, and he patted it roughly through his jerkin.

'Who's the knight, anyway?' he asked as he stood and made to leave.

'What?' asked the warden.

'The knight, who is he?'

'Why? Does it matter?' asked the warden.

'No,' said Chlod. The warden grunted.

'Garamont,' the warden said. 'Red and blue shield with a white dragon on it.'

Chlod's one good eye widened, and he grinned stupidly.

'Shame he didn't fight Ganelon today,' said the hunchbacked peasant. 'You could have saved yourself some coin.'

'Remember,' growled the warden, levelling a meaty finger at Chlod, 'the brother ain't to be hurt. Touch so much as a hair on his head, and we are all dead men. Now, piss off.' He inclined his head to a pair of brutes standing in the shadows, and Chlod was physically lifted and tossed into the mud outside.

Still grinning, he picked himself up and wiped the worst of the mud from his face. Then he moved off, a spring in his ungainly step.

CHAPTER ELEVEN

THE CAMP WAS sleeping, and there was no movement within it. The hour was late. The last patrol had come in hours earlier, and the next one was not due to return for some time.

On the outskirts of the camp, men-at-arms patrolled in groups of three. They fought off their tiredness, talking softly amongst themselves. The hours before dawn were the worst time, the time when sleep beckoned most strongly, but they knew that they would be whipped till their backs were bloody strips if they were caught resting while on guard. For men like them, such a beating was often a death sentence. The open wounds would likely fester and become infected, which was a slow and painful way to die.

There were fewer guards inside the camp, and they were less vigilant. No one expected an enemy within the camp, and their presence was more a reassurance than anything else. Most slept at their posts, enjoying what rest they could steal.

One guard, dressed in the red and yellow tabard of Garamont, walked between the dark, silent tents. He yawned and looked up at the silver moon. One more hour, and he would wake one of the others to take over, he thought.

His yawn was cut short as he spied a dark, hunched shape limping through the mud. Peering through the darkness, he tightened his grip on his polearm, and moved to intercept the figure. He stepped in front of it, and relaxed a little as he saw it was just some hunch-backed peasant, one of the scores of menial hangers-on that cooked and cleaned for the nobles.

'Cold night,' whispered the man, grinning inanely up at him. His eyes were uneven and he had clearly suffered a recent beating. He had probably failed to clean a spot of grease from his master's cloak, or some such minor offence.

'It is,' said the guard, his voice quiet. 'What's your business here?'

'Been sent by one of yer men,' whispered the hunch-back. 'He said you might like a drink.' He held up a half-empty wineskin.

The sentry's eyes widened, and he hurriedly leant his polearm against a wooden crate and took a long draught. He sighed in appreciation. The wine was bad, tasting like vinegar, but it was greatly welcome. His eyes flicked back to the hunchback.

'Who sent you?'

'Oh, I don't know his name, sir.'

'Was he a blond-haired young man? On the eastern perimeter?'

'Yeah, that was him.'

'My brother,' said the sentry. 'I owe him one.'

'Generous of him to think of you,' said the hunchback, his eyes flicking over the sentry's shoulder. A dark shape was moving through the shadows between the tents.

The sentry reached into his pocket and rummaged around. 'Here,' he said, producing half a small, bread roll from which weevils and moth-maggots hung. 'Have this for your troubles.'

'You are most generous, good sir,' said the hunchback, pocketing the bread in an instant and bobbing his head in gratitude.

The sentry lifted the wineskin over his head to drain it, and Chlod motioned with one hand. Shadowy forms slid out from between the tents, moving unseen past the distracted sentry.

'What's that over there?' asked Chlod suddenly, his voice low but filled with alarm. The sentry dropped the wineskin to the ground, and spun in the direction that Chlod was gesturing towards, turning his back on the hunchbacked peasant.

Chlod clamped one thick, hairy hand over the man's mouth and dragged his blade across the sentry's neck, severing the jugular. The man twitched in his arms, and Chlod felt hot blood gushing over his hands. He dragged him awkwardly back into the darkness, and pushed the man to the ground in the shadow of a tent. He held his hand clamped over his mouth until his twitching stopped, and then stood upright.

He grinned as he saw more shapes moving stealthily through the night. With sudden inspiration, Chlod bent down and roughly pulled the red and yellow tabard from the dead sentry's body. With awkward movements, he pulled it over his hunched frame, and planted the fallen man's iron-rimmed hat on his head. Lastly, he lifted the polearm from where it leant, and then he began to nonchalantly walk towards the tent that bore the red and yellow of the lord of Garamont.

This was going to be too easy, he thought.

CALARD WAS DREAMING of Elisabet, and he smiled in his sleep as he breathed in her intoxicating scent. They were lying together in the long grass overlooking Castle Garamont, enjoying the heat of summer, the sound of insects, and each other's body.

This was paradise, he thought, and Elisabet kissed his naked chest, nuzzling against him.

A voice was trying to intrude, but he pushed it away, not wishing the vision to break. It became more insistent, and in his dream he sat up, staring around him in confusion. Bees heavy with pollen flew ponderously from flower to flower, and tiny crickets clicked and leapt away from the sudden movement.

'What is it, my love?' asked Elisabet sleepily.

The voice was getting louder, more insistent.

'Anara?' he said, looking around in confusion.

Wake, said the voice, jolting him with its power.

He came awake instantly, and saw a flash of movement above him.

Throwing himself to the side, the knife stabbed down into his pillow, and Calard rolled from the pallet.

'Take him!' hissed an urgent voice, and dark shapes loomed towards him. His eyes flashed across the tent, and he saw his thrashing brother pinned down on his pallet by other shapes, a rough sack over his head.

A knife stabbed towards him, and he turned the blow aside as Gunthar had taught him, using his forearm to force the attacker's arm away. He thundered his elbow into the man's hooded face, and the attacker reeled backwards, falling heavily over the small chest that housed Calard's clothes.

Calard threw himself to his side as he sensed movement behind him, and he hissed as a blade that had been aimed at his neck slashed across his shoulder. Another attacker came at him, blade flashing, and Calard launched himself forwards, his hands reaching for the man's wrist.

His momentum made him slam into the attacker, who tripped backwards over the pallet with a curse. Going with him, Calard fell on the man heavily with his knee, driving the air from him. Sweeping up the attacker's knife, Calard rose swiftly to his feet, slashing around to keep the assassins at bay.

Three of them circled warily. He stole a quick glance towards his brother, who was still struggling against the men pinning him down. One of the men flicked a glance behind him, to see what was transpiring, and he swore. His accent was crude; a peasant's accent. Even had he not spoken, the stench of the assassins betrayed their lowborn status.

'Garamont!' roared Calard at the top of his lungs, and his brother began to fight anew, throwing off the men pinning him down.

The three attackers moved in on Calard. He swung to the right and grabbed one man's arm as it slashed towards him, knife gleaming. He pulled the attacker off balance and hurled him into one of the others, but cried out in pain as the third man's knife plunged into his side.

Dropping to one knee, he punched up, ramming his knife into the man's throat.

He stood upright, wincing at the pain in his side. Then he heard the hiss of a sword being drawn, followed by a horrible, pained scream, and Calard felt the presence of his brother at his back.

Faced with the two brothers, one armed with a sword, the assassins faltered.

'Garamont!' Calard bellowed once more.

CHLOD, STANDING WATCH outside the tent, flicked his glance left and right, biting his fleshy lip. Things were going horribly wrong, and the image of him hanging from the gallows flashed through his mind.

With a quick glance through the tent flaps, he saw the two nobles standing back to back, and he made up his mind. He could hear the approach of running men, and he stepped out into the thoroughfare.

'Over here! Our lord is attacked!' he shouted, as he saw several men-at-arms wearing the red and yellow of Garamont. 'Get in there!' he shouted as they raced past him. More people were appearing, knights emerging from tents in their bedclothes, roused from their slumber by the noise.

Glancing down, Chlod realised that the front of his stolen Garamont tabard was covered in blood from the murder of the sentry. Swearing, he ducked his head and shuffled quickly through the growing crowd.

There was more shouting inside the tent, and the sound of weapons clashing, but Chlod did not look back. There was a crash that sounded like a suit of armour being knocked over, and he heard one voice shout: 'Take them alive!'

He swore again. None of the others in the murderous group knew his name, but they could certainly describe him.

His misshapen face was covered in a sheen of sweat as he pushed his way frantically through the growing press of people gathering around. Pushing free of them, he broke into an awkward, loping run. He still clung to the polearm, and he almost tripped over it as he ducked between a pair of tents. He kicked something and tripped over it, falling to his hands and knees. The metal-brimmed helmet on his head fell forward to the ground and he dropped the awkward weight of the polearm. He struggled to push himself upright, and found his hands on a body.

He looked down into the face of the murdered sentry. He had not realised he had retraced his steps in his panic.

'You there! What are you doing?' someone shouted, and Chlod froze. He fought his instinct to run, and turned to face the speaker. It was a knight, standing half-dressed, a sword in his hand. Chlod licked his lips.

'Why were you running?' asked the man, stepping forwards and peering at him closely. Chlod gaped at him stupidly, his mind blank.

'Is that blood on you?' asked the knight.

Chlod nodded slowly. The knight furrowed his brow. 'Are you injured?'

'No,' stammered Chlod. Drawing closer, the knight's eyes widened as he saw the body on the ground. The peasant slipped a hand inside the tabard he wore, fingers closing on the knife at his hip.

'Did you kill this man?'

Chlod tensed, making ready to draw the knife. He nodded slowly, keeping his eyes locked on the knight.

'One of the assassins, was he?'

That gave Chlod pause, and he almost laughed out loud. Then he gave a demented, lopsided grin.

'Yes, my lord,' he said. 'I saw him run from the tent. I gave chase.'

'I see. Bring the body,' he ordered. 'It will need to be identified.'

With a nod, marvelling at his good fortune, Chlod bent down and began to drag the dead body out into the open.

'SANGASSE,' SPAT BERTELIS. 'It had to have been.'

Calard nodded, and then winced as the alcohol was poured onto the wound on his side. He screwed his eyes shut against the lancing pain.

'I'm sorry, my lord,' said the aged servant. Baron Montcadas had sent him to the Garamont tent.

'Glad to see you still alive, lad,' the baron had boomed, giving Calard a hefty pat on the shoulder that made him gasp in pain.

'The man might be a peasant, but he is the best damned healer of battle-wounds I've met.'

Calard waved away the old servant's apology.

The wound was dabbed dry, and Calard looked over his shoulder at the injury. It didn't look like much, but blood was leaking from the puncture wound, and it hurt like hell.

'Any more stitches, brother, and you will look like a scarecrow,' remarked Bertelis. Calard snorted. It was true, his body was criss-crossed with wounds and stitches.

The servant pressed a swaddling of cloth to the wound, and with the aid of another man, wrapped bindings of cloth around Calard's chest.

The man produced a clay jar, and placed it on the pallet next to Calard.

'This is honey, my lord,' said the man. 'Have a servant smear it on the wound twice a day, morning and night. As far as I can tell, the knife did no serious internal damage, though you will be sore for some time. The biggest risk is from infection, and the honey will help fight that. The wound must be dressed and cleaned daily. I will check on you tomorrow, my lord.'

Calard nodded, and the elderly man stood to leave, his knees creaking alarmingly.

'Give my thanks to the lord baron for your services,' said Calard. He turned to his brother as the servant left the tent, and he waved the other hovering servants to leave. They scooted out through the servants flap in the rear of the tent, passing through the press of men-at-arms stationed outside.

'Peasants!' spat Bertelis as he paced back and forth. 'Whoreson peasants sent to kill *us*! I wouldn't have thought even Maloric would stoop so low!'

'The man is a snake,' said Calard. 'It seems that nothing is beneath him.'

'I say we head to the Sangasse's now, and finish this once and for all.'

'No,' said Calard firmly. 'We need proof first.'

A serving boy pulled aside the main tent flap and stepped lightly inside, standing motionless and head bowed as was proper.

'What is it?' snapped Bertelis.

'Noble lords, Baron Montcadas and Lord Tanebourc wish to speak with you,' said the boy.

'Then don't leave them waiting outside like paupers!' snapped Bertelis. 'Stupid boy!'

The servant ducked back outside, and the broad figure of Montcadas entered, a deep frown on his bearded face. Such was his size that the interior of the tent seemed to shrink in his presence. Tanebourc was at his side, tall and lean, his face a mask of concern and controlled rage.

'You all right, Garamont?' asked Montcadas.

'I am,' said Calard.

'I thank the Lady that your injuries were not more serious,' said Tanebourc.

'Had I not woken, my throat would have been cut.'

'Then it must have been the Lady that stirred you,' murmured Tanebourc, and Calard thought again of the voice in his dream, his sister's voice.

'Two of the men were taken alive, yes?' asked Bertelis.

'They were,' replied Montcadas. 'Tanebourc here has offered to oversee their... questioning.'

'Good,' said Bertelis. 'Make sure they do not die easily.'

Tanebourc bowed his head to the younger of the brothers.

'Find out who sent them, Tanebourc,' ordered Calard, his words burning with anger.

'It will be done,' said the knight, giving a gracious bow, 'and, once again, may I say how relieved I am to see neither of you more seriously harmed from this despicable attempt on your lives.'

The tall ginger-haired knight bowed once more, and turned to leave.

'It was Maloric,' said Bertelis to Montcadas, his eyes burning with anger.

'I do not believe so,' said the baron softly.

'What?' asked Calard. 'Who else would it have been? Regardless, Maloric is cunning. Doubtless the attackers will not be traced back to him.'

'I have already spoken with him,' said the baron. 'He denies he had any involvement.'

'Well, of course he would deny it!' said Bertelis, outraged.

'Be quiet!' stormed Montcadas, his voice booming. Silence followed, and when the baron spoke again, his voice was softer. 'Maloric denied any involvement, and I believe him.'

Bertelis scoffed, but Calard was silent, thinking. 'One of his knights, then?'

'Perhaps,' said Montcadas noncommittally.

'I will challenge him,' said Bertelis suddenly.

'No,' said Calard firmly, thinking of Gunthar, lying wounded in his tent, half dead. 'Never again will I allow any man to fight my battles, never.'

'I was attacked as well, Calard! I would be within my rights to call him out!'

'*I* was the target,' said Calard. 'They had you pinned down. They could have killed you, but they did not. No, it was *me* they wanted dead. I shall challenge him myself.'

'No, you will not,' said the baron, his face stern. 'I will not allow it, and, as the most senior knight in the camp, my word is final.'

Calard gaped at the baron, and Bertelis's jaw dropped.

'This is outrageous!' the younger brother stormed.

'There will be no challenge!' bellowed the baron, his eyes glowering with anger. 'We are assailed by a devious foe that threatens the land, and this petty rivalry you have with the Sangasse family has gone far enough! One noble is already dead, and Gunthar, a finer knight than any us, is fighting for his life. Even if he survives, he may never ride again. No, there will be no more of your petty squabbles! Once this war is over, and you have returned to your lands, then you may do as you wish, but there are more important concerns here than a centuries-old feud.'

There was silence in the tent. Both Calard and Bertelis were looking at the floor, while Montcadas's furious gaze flicked from one to the other.

'I have spoken to Maloric of this as well, and I have made him swear on his honour that neither he nor any of knights will continue the feud until this war is over. I will have your word as well, brothers of Garamont.'

Calard glared at the floor and shook his head slightly. How had it come to this? he thought.

'Fine,' he said at last. 'On my honour, I swear it.' Bertelis mumbled his own oath.

'Good,' said Montcadas. 'Your attackers will be questioned, and if it comes to light that they were paid to carry out the deed, and they name their employer, then action will be taken. Now,' he said, 'get some rest. We have a long day tomorrow. There have been reports of the enemy moving in the daylight hours, some twenty miles to the south, and we are riding out to scour the area. I wish you good night, and may the Lady look over you.'

Unseen, Tanebourc stood in the shadows, having overheard the exchange. His face was thunderous.

* * *

As THE FIRST rays of dawn rose, another struggling peasant was wrenched into the air, his legs kicking uselessly beneath him as the rope tightened around his neck. Fourteen other bodies hung limply from the boughs of the trees.

Bertelis glared at the dying man, watching as he turned a deep shade of purple. With his hands tied behind his back, the would-be murderer kicked and struggled vainly, eyes bulging. A stink rose into the air as the man lost control of his bodily functions, and Bertelis shook his head in disgust.

The five surviving assassins had been questioned for hours. They had suffered all manner of pain before they had been brought here and strung up. Bertelis thought it too lenient. In his opinion, they should have been kept alive, to experience far more suffering before they journeyed on to Morr's eternal halls.

Tanebourc had been thorough, though. The man had extracted confessions and accusations from the men, hence the other bodies that were swinging in the breeze from the boughs. Bertelis stared at one of the corpses: a heavy set man, a yeoman warden no less. This was the man that the accusations had led back to. Tanebourc had interrogated the man; of course he had not sullied his own hands with the grisly task, for such a thing was beneath a knight of honour, but if the warden had been employed by one of the nobility, he had died with the secret.

He shook his head. You give peasants some responsibility, put some trust in them, and this is how they repay you, with treachery and attempted murder.

The warden gave a last shuddering kick of his legs, and hung limply, swaying slightly from the branch overhead.

THE RIDE TO the south was long and sombre. Calard rode much of the time in silence, lost in thought, thinking of the attack, and of Gunthar. He had spoken to Baron Montcadas's surgeon before they had left.

'He will live,' the small man had said, 'and he may yet keep the leg. But even if he does, he will never ride again. His days of fighting in the saddle are over.'

Calard shook his head, guilt weighing heavily upon him. He should not have allowed Gunthar to fight for him. Had he not, said a voice inside him, you would be dead. He pushed away the voice, and scowled up at the heavy clouds. A single black bird circled overhead.

The attack in the night had left all the knights in the camp feeling sour and uneasy, and there was little talk as the column rode through the south of Bordeleaux. There were twenty-five knights, led by the Baron Montcadas, and ten peasant outriders wearing the yellow and red of Garamont.

The baron was watching over Calard and his brother like a hawk. Whether he was concerned about a further attempt on their lives, or was merely ensuring that the brothers did nothing rash, Calard knew not.

The Forest of Chalons crouched on the hills to the east, everpresent and threatening. He could see evidence that the forest was expanding here as elsewhere. A peasant village in the distance seemed in the process of being swallowed whole, half the buildings already hidden by the trees, and Calard could see a twisted, disease-ridden oak that had somehow sprung up within one of the hovels, ripping its sodden turf roof off.

The dark shape of a modest castle loomed on a hill-top a mile away. To Calard, it seemed like a brave knight standing alone and defiant against the mon-strous forest drawing forward to besiege it. How long before the trees overran it? A week? Perhaps a month?

Something about the castle seemed oddly familiar, and he frowned at the sense of déjà vu. It was an unset-tling sensation, but he could not shake it.

A horse of purest white ran on the slopes beyond the castle, tossing its head, and Calard felt rejuvenated just watching the majestic beast. It seemed so free and full of life, running across the grass without saddle or bri-dle.

As they drew nearer, they saw that the castle was life-less, abandoned perhaps a decade earlier. A tattered flag blew in the wind from atop its highest parapet, but the design upon it was impossible to discern. Ivy had crept up the walls of the small castle, which were blackened with fire. Perhaps that had been what had forced its occupants to abandon it?

'We will stop there for half an hour to feed and water the horses,' said Baron Montcadas. The yeomen of Garamont rode ahead to prepare for the arrival of the knights. Calard watched them gallop across the grassy slopes towards the blackened castle, a slight frown on his face. He could not shake the idea that he had been here before.

They reined their warhorses in on the grassy flat before the modest gatehouse to the castle. There must have been a wooden bridge that crossed to the gate once, but it had evidently rotted and fallen onto the rocks below. The gatehouse was open, the heavy wooden doors hanging loose from their hinges.

Calard felt drawn to the abandoned, eerie castle, as if something was calling to him. Handing his reins to one of the Garamont peasants, he walked towards it, a frown on his face. He *had* been here before, he was certain of it. Perhaps as a child?

He looked down into the rocky dip that must once have served as a moat, trying to see a clear way across to the castle gate. There were patches of stagnant water there, but it would not be difficult to cross.

'Calard?' called Bertelis, but he waved him back.

Stepping carefully, steadying himself with one hand, he descended the steep slope. Avoiding the stagnant pools of water, he crossed the rocky moat, and pulled himself up the incline on the other side, wincing at the pain that flared in his side. Another wave of déjà vu washed over him as he paused at the shattered gate, gazing through to the small courtyard within the castle walls.

He shivered as a cold wind howled through the gateway. I should go back, he thought, but he walked forward, his brow furrowing in confusion. Half-remembered images flickered through his mind: running through the gateway past bemused guards, giggling, chasing his sister.

His sister…

He was drawn further into the courtyard. Stables and barracks, long abandoned, lay in disrepair along the inside of the southern walls, but it was towards the main keep that he found himself walking. He looked down at the water lilies that clogged the circular fountain in the centre of the courtyard. Water overflowed down the sides of a stone grail carved atop a pedestal in the centre of the pool. It clearly tapped into a natural spring beneath the ground, but the effect was magical nonetheless.

Climbing a set of wide stone steps, he entered the lonely, lifeless keep. He walked, like a ghost, through halls filled with cobwebs and dust. The interior had been gutted by fire, and no evidence of furniture or paintings hanging upon the walls remained. Drawn on inexorably, he climbed up a grand, spiralling staircase, to the top floor, and then he walked down a long passageway, passing countless empty, dim rooms and lifeless, cold bedchambers.

At last, he came to an archway, and there, he halted. He was sweating, though the air was chill. The door set into the archway was intact, and was drawn almost fully shut. Not knowing what to expect beyond the doorway, and his heart beating wildly, Calard pushed the door open. It creaked loudly on rusted hinges, and swung wide. Ducking his head, he entered the room.

It was dark, but he could see that the fires that had ravaged the rest of the castle had barely touched this room. Arched windows covered the north wall, wooden shutters rattling in the howling wind. A large bed was set in the middle of the room, its mattress sunken and its pillows moth-eaten and covered in mildew. A chamber pot sat in the corner of the room, and a small chest sat against the wall.

Turning around, his heart lurched as he saw movement in the shadows. His sword hissed from its scabbard, and he saw a flash of metal in the gloom.

'Who goes?' he asked, his voice sounding too loud in his ears as it broke the silence. There was no response.

The wind howled through the castle, sounding like the moaning of a tortured spirit. Stepping forward, he saw movement in the gloom once again. A bead of sweat ran down his back, and he swallowed heavily.

Did restless spirits of the dead haunt the place? He took another step forwards, and then stopped short.

Against the far wall, hidden in shadow, was a tall mirror. It had a long crack running down its surface, but it had been his own reflection that he had seen. He let a deep breath that he did not realise he had been holding. You fool, he thought.

Beneath the mirror was a vanity chest and a small, three-legged stool topped with a moth-eaten velvet cushion. Perhaps the room had belonged to a daughter of the lord of the castle.

Calard, someone whispered in his ear, making his hackles rise. He swung around, his sword raised. There was nothing there. The room was empty.

Calard, said the voice again, and he spun once more, eyes flicking around the room. The only movement came from the single loose shutter that was rattling in the wind.

There is nothing here, Calard thought. You are imagining things. He moved towards the window to close the banging shutter, for it was unnerving him. Sheathing his sword, he leant out of the window, reaching for the shutter. It caught the wind just as his fingers touched it, and whipped open out of reach, slamming noisily against the stone outer wall. He cursed and glanced down.

This is where she fell, said the voice in his mind.

A wave of vertigo washed over him, and his breath caught in his throat. He pulled himself away from the window quickly. Was he losing his mind? He shook his head, as if trying to shake it free of some enchantment. He would ride away from this place and forget it.

'Calard,' said a voice behind him, and he froze. This was no whisper of the wind, but a voice spoken from a living, human throat.

He spun around, ripping his sword from his scabbard once more.

The pale figure of a woman surrounded in shimmering white light was standing in the doorway. It is a restless spirit, he thought, reeling backwards.

'I am no spirit,' said the woman as she glided forwards into the room. The voice was hauntingly familiar, yet not. The halo of light surrounding her seemed to flicker and disappear, and he saw that she was flesh and blood. Had the halo merely been a trick of the light?

She was as delicate as a flower, little larger than a child, and wore a white flowing dress made of a material that shimmered like water. It was held tight around her petite body, billowing below her tightly corseted waist in flowing waves that trailed behind her. The sleeves of the dress were long and tapered to points that were fixed to a pair of silver rings that the woman wore, one around each of her slender index fingers.

Her face was obscured by the gloom, but he could see that her hair was long and dark, and that she wore a tiara of silver. A silver necklace in the shape of a fleur-de-lys shimmered against her skin, and Calard's breath caught in his chest.

'A damsel of the Lady,' he breathed in awe, dropping to his knees in respect. Never had he encountered one of the esteemed handmaidens of the Lady. They were priestesses and protectors, blessed by the Lady herself. Seers and augurs of great power, many of them had been granted the gift of future sight, and were among the most respected of the king's advisors. Mistresses of fey, mystical powers, they commanded the forces of nature, and were the devout protectors of the sacred places of Bretonnia.

'That window is where she fell to her death,' said the damsel, her voice fey and distant. With her long dress trailing across the flagstones of the floor, she seemed to glide forward like an apparition.

Calard could see her face now, and he stared at her in confused awe. Her face was heart-shaped and youthful, with high cheekbones and a pointed chin, and her eyes were large and striking. Her skin was smooth and pale, and make-up had been applied sparingly and artfully around her eyes. Those eyes were wide, and seemed to float around the room, as if the damsel was following the movements of things that Calard could not see.

'She stood at the window. Blood. There was so much blood,' breathed the damsel. She was looking at her hands in horror, as if she could see blood on them too, though they were pale and clean. 'She was ashamed, so ashamed. She threw herself from the window.' The damsel smiled suddenly, her face lighting up with childlike pleasure. 'For a moment, it felt like she was flying.' Then the smile dropped from her face, and she looked sad, so infinitely sad that Calard wanted to stand up and go to her, to hold her and give her comfort. 'And then… she died. Like a whisper in the wind, she was gone.'

Calard stared at her in confusion. Had she not been a damsel of the Lady, he would have assumed she was touched in the head. She was so familiar, too, that it felt like he knew her, just as he felt that he knew this place.

'Who?' he asked at last, his voice a hoarse whisper.

The damsel looked at him, and he was jolted by the sheer depths of power he saw in her grey-blue eyes.

'Our mother,' breathed his twin sister, the damsel Anara.

CHAPTER TWELVE

BERTELIS GLANCED SIDEWAYS at Anara, his eyes guarded. That she was Calard's twin was obvious, for the similarities between them were striking; they shared the same eyes and the same colouring. She was short and petite where Calard was broad and strong, but even small gestures betrayed the kinship between them: the way she unconsciously brushed a lock of hair from her eyes, and the way they seemed to mirror each other's movements.

This was *his* sister, too, he reminded himself, his half-sister, as closely related to him as Calard was. Of course he had heard his brother speak of Anara much when they were children, and though he had spoken of her less as the years passed, he knew that she had never been far from his mind. He heard him call out her name in his sleep, and though in the last few years he would not be drawn into conversation regarding his mysterious twin, he knew that Calard thought of her often, and had long dreamed of finding her.

She is not dead, he remembered Calard saying once. Anara had been missing for years, but he would fiercely rebuke anyone that suggested he let her go. I would know it if she had been claimed by Morr, Calard had said, bristling in anger. Bertelis had long believed that it was a forlorn hope that Calard clung to, to be reunited with Anara, but here she was in the flesh.

This, however, was not the carefree child that Calard had wistfully spoken of. She was clearly touched by the fey, and everything about her resonated with otherworldliness. She spoke in a soft, distant voice, and her eyes often grew unfocused. Her movements were calm and full of grace, as if time slowed in her presence.

Bertelis was certain that she was mad, but he had no doubt of her power.

She seemed to radiate an elemental strength that Bertelis found unnerving. Strangely, it reminded him of a journey he had made once as a boy, to the famed port-city of L'Anguille in the north. He had stood upon a high cliff and stared out across the endless, glittering ocean depths. There had been no wind that day, and the deep green of the sea was sublimely beautiful, calm and tranquil. The following day a storm had blown in, and the ocean had turned into a raging tyrant, destructive and awesome in its strength. Although it had been serene and comforting the day before, now it smashed against the cliffs with such power that it made Bertelis feel insignificant and small.

It had frightened him then, and this was the sense that he got from Anara. She was like the sea becalmed, serene, beautiful and peaceful, but beneath the surface, deep within, Bertelis sensed that there lay a similar power to that of the sea: destructive, dangerous, and somehow ageless.

As if sensing his eyes upon her, the damsel turned towards him. It felt as though her gaze pierced his soul, seeing every shameful act and hidden secret, and he quickly dropped his gaze, his face paling.

Clearing his throat, he moved stiffly away. That she was devoted to Bretonnia and the Lady was without doubt. She was a damsel of the Lady, and hence was one of Bretonnia's most fervent servants, but she made him feel uneasy and more than a little fearful.

A shiver ran down his spine, and he moved away from the others. In the distance, he watched, as a pair of yeoman attempted to catch the white horse they had seen earlier, running on the field beyond the castle. They were not having any success; indeed, the horse seemed to be toying with them, riding close to their ropes before darting just out of reach as they tried to throw the loops over its broad neck.

Other yeomen were laughing at them, shouting jibes and taunts towards the men who were getting increasingly frustrated. Bertelis rebuked them harshly, and they fell silent.

ANARA FELT A twinge of sadness as she recognised Bertelis's discomfort, but she repressed it instantly. She had come, as her increasingly vivid dream-visions had urged her. It had taken her three weeks to journey here, and for an hour she had paced the halls of the burnt out castle, remembering, before her twin had arrived. She had known that he would. In the scheme of things to come, the unease she caused in the others mattered not at all.

She felt the emotions and thoughts of the knights swell around her like a rising tide. She had no wish to intrude upon their privacy, and she gently allowed herself to rise above the unfocused sea of thoughts.

When this talent had first manifested in her as a child, she had been unable to control it, and had been terrified by the endless barrage of thoughts that had intruded into her mind. She had learnt things that a child should never know, having inadvertently eavesdropped on the darkest thoughts of everyone she had come into contact with. It had been maddening.

One day she had begun to cry, for she could hear the thoughts of the young maid that delivered her meal.

'I am sorry that your baby died,' Anara had said, and the maid had stared at her in horror. *Witch*, she heard the maid think, which had confused her.

Around that time, she had first begun to see glimpses of events that had not yet come to pass. They had scared and confused her.

'Don't ride the big grey horse tomorrow,' she had begged one of her father's knights at a banquet feast on the night before a tournament. 'You will fall off it and you will die.'

The knight had laughed at her fear, as had the gathered host of courtiers, but Anara would not be consoled.

'Have no fear, little one,' the knight had said, propping her on his knee and looking into her serious face. 'I have ridden Proudheart a thousand times, and he has always borne me well. I will not fall from him, I promise.'

It was not, however, a promise that he could keep. The powerful grey had been spooked by a sudden movement in the crowd, and had reared. The knight had fallen backwards and struck his head against a rock. He had died instantly. Anara's father had turned fearful eyes towards her when he learnt of the incident.

Freak.

The thought had stung her, and she had begun to cry. Calard had hugged her tight. She endured his embrace, for she knew that it gave him comfort.

Her father had been relieved when the Enchantress had come for her. She had felt the fear emanating from her father and his knights as the Enchantress strode into his hall unannounced and unchallenged, and she had secretly revelled in seeing the men cowed so.

That first meeting was forever ingrained in her mind's eye. Ethereally tall and as slender as a branch of willow, yet radiating such power that the breath was stolen from Anara's lungs, the Enchantress was at once the most beautiful and the most terrifying creature she had ever seen. She was the highest authority in all of Bretonnia, greater even than the king, for she spoke with the voice of the goddess.

Their eyes had met across the hall and in that instant the Enchantress had known her: everything that she was and everything that she could be. Anara's fear had dissipated like a fog in the rising sun. It was replaced by joy and yearning, for in those moments she realised that she was no freak and no witch, and that her powers were not a curse; far from it, they were gifts from the Lady. It seemed as though she stared into the

Enchantress's almond-shaped eyes for an eternity, sharing a silent communication, before the silence had been broken.

'I am taking the girl,' she had said, turning her ageless gaze towards the Lord of Garamont. 'From this day forth she is no longer your daughter. She is a child of the Lady. It may be that you will never see her again.'

Lutheure had nodded his head, unable to form words, as if stricken mute. Then the Enchantress had extended one graceful hand to Anara, and she had heard her voice, though her lips did not move.

Come with me, Anara. Become that which you are destined to be. You are not alone any more.

Anara heard Calard speaking to her, and she focused on him, drawing her mind back from the past. They seemed like memories that belonged to someone else, for she was no longer the same little girl she had been.

'...you doing here alone?' he was saying. She did not need to be able to read his thoughts to recognise the awe, and the fear, in his eyes as he looked upon her.

She ignored his question, eyes narrowing, as she felt... something. Her gaze drifted up into the sky, searching. Something was watching them. She could feel its rage, its need for vengeance. At last, her roving gaze focused on a single black bird that circled low above them.

CALARD STARED AT his sister blankly, and then followed her gaze. He saw the carrion bird circling overhead.

'What is it?' he asked, seeing a look of horror come over his sister's delicate features.

'The beast watches. It hungers,' she breathed, her voice fey and distant. Calard's brow creased in confusion. What was she speaking of?

'The bird?' he asked slowly, not understanding.

'It must be brought down!' she said, more urgently. Her voice was strained, and something in it made Calard feel suddenly fearful. He swung around, shouting to the yeoman nearby.

'Half a copper-crown to the man that brings down that bird!' he hollered. The men stared at him blankly for a second as his words sunk in, and then they scrambled to retrieve their bows.

'What's going on?' asked Baron Montcadas, throwing a quick glance towards the damsel Anara.

'I don't know,' said Calard. Anara was staring intently up at the carrion bird.

The first arrows sliced through the air, missing their target. The bird continued to circle, oblivious to the threat, and one peasant gave a shout as his arrow clipped the raven's wing. It dropped in the air, and black feathers began to spiral towards the ground, but it did not fall. At last, an arrow slammed into the creature's body, and it plummeted towards the ground like a stone.

Whooping and yelling, the yeoman ran to where it fell, and the bewildered knights followed after Anara, who hurried across the field in the wake of the bowman. The man's triumphant cries stopped short, and he froze as he stood over the dying bird.

The arrowhead had passed clean through the raven, which was impaled upon the shaft of the arrow. It was not dead, and was trying to right itself, flapping its wings uselessly, its cries piercing.

The bird's head was cocked to one side and dominated by a bulbous, pulsing, bloodshot eye that was far too large for its head. The pupil was like that of a cat's or a serpent's, and the flesh around the orb was blistered and bare of feathers. It was a loathsome mutated thing, and Calard felt his gorge rising. The repulsive eye flicked around, rolling in its fleshy socket, focusing on each of the figures surrounding it in turn.

'Kill it,' ordered Baron Montcadas. Nobody moved. 'Now!'

The yeoman, his face a mask of revulsion, brought his foot down heavily on the dying raven, cutting its cries off abruptly. Delicate bones crunched under his foot, leaving a bloody smear on the ground.

'What was it?' Calard breathed, horrified.

'The eye of the beast,' said Anara. 'It has been here before, long ago.'

'What?' asked Montcadas. 'The beasts of the forest?'

'It comes for us now!' said Anara, her voice suddenly urgent. 'We must away!'

'Away?' asked Montcadas. 'If the beasts come, then we shall fight them, lady.'

'Too many,' she breathed. 'It is drawn here like a moth to a flame. Hatred burns within its breast, and it has turned the full force of its herd here. They are approaching even now.'

Montcadas swore, and the knights glanced around uneasily. None doubted the word of the damsel.

The baron turned towards the yeoman, who was trying to wipe the filth of the dead bird from his foot.

'Ride for the camp,' he ordered. 'Take two of the others, and go at once. Darkness is falling, so be swift.' The Garamont yeoman looked to Calard, who nodded. 'Kegan!' called Montcadas.

'Yes, my lord,' answered a knight wearing a yellow tabard that bore a black cockatrice upon it.

'Ride with them. Ensure that the camp is ready for an attack. Allow no more patrols to leave, and send riders to gather those already out.'

'It will be as you wish, my lord.'

'May the Lady be with you, Kegan.' Then the baron swung towards Anara. 'You will honour us by riding at our side, lady?' She nodded absently, her head cocked to one side as if listening to a faint voice. 'I shall ensure there is a steed readied for you.'

'That is not necessary,' she replied. Turning, she let out a high-pitched, ululating cry. In the distance, the white mare pricked up its elongated ears and began to gallop towards her.

She was a beautiful, powerful creature. Her coat gleamed like silver, and her limbs were long and slender, though filled with vigour, speed and power. The horse nuzzled at Anara's outstretched hand, and the damsel leant forward and whispered into the animal's ear. It was tall, perhaps seventeen hands at the shoulder, and standing next to it, Anara looked like a child. Calard shook his head. Everything was happening so fast.

'Do you know how close the enemy is, sister?' asked Calard.

'I cannot see,' she said, not looking at him, focused as she was on her steed. Her voice was tense, instilling a sense of urgency in the knights. 'They are closing fast.'

Calard swore. Montcadas roared for the patrol to mount up, and a frenzy of activity erupted, as the knights made ready to leave. The trio of yeomen and the knight Kegan galloped away, thundering off to the north.

Calard licked his lips, wondering where her sister's tack and saddle was... probably in the stable at the deserted castle; the castle of his mother's family, he reminded himself. It was all too much to take in. He was about to ask her where her saddle was located, but the words died in his mouth.

The proud, pure white horse was kneeling down in the grass, lowering its massive shoulders and bowing its head. Standing on tiptoe, Anara reached up and grabbed a handful of the mare's spotless mane. With a deft leap, she threw one leg over the mare's broad back, and the horse stood upright.

An old and unenforced law within Bretonnia stated that ladies must ride side-saddle on the occasion that they ride at all, and, even had it not been the law, no noble woman would dream of riding like a man, for one who did so would be deemed a harlot. However, the damsels of the Lady existed outside traditional laws and values, and there was not a man in all of Bretonnia, not even the king, who would dare to invoke their ire by reproaching one of them.

Anara smiled down at Calard like the little girl he remembered. Her elegant dress was certainly not made for riding a horse bareback, and many of the knights averted their eyes from the exposed flesh of the damsel's toned lower leg. Calard found himself smiling back at his sister, and Montcadas gave a deep belly laugh at the unconventional sight.

The damsel's youthful smile faded, her face turning grim.

'They are here!' she wailed.

Ghastly, blaring horns sounded in the distance, and Calard ran for his mount. More horns sounded, and he hauled himself into the saddle, and accepted his lance and shield from a nervous-looking peasant.

'Get to your horse, now!' Calard ordered, nodding his thanks to the man.

The knights formed up protectively around Anara. A pair of yeomen rode ahead of them as scouts, and the remainder rode to either side of the knightly formation. Giving the signal, the baron ordered the men forward and as one they began to canter away from the castle, eyes scanning the area for any sign of the foe.

They did not have to wait long.

One of the yeomen shouted out, and Calard swung his gaze to the east, towards the forest in the distance. A group of fur-clad riders had emerged from the tree line, and was galloping across the fields towards the Bretonnians. They leapt dry-stone walls, and another piercing horn sounded.

For a moment, Calard thought they were reinforcements coming to their aid, but the riders carried no pennants or standards, and did not appear to be armoured. Peasant outriders? He dismissed the idea almost instantly, for they wore no tabards displaying the colours of their lords.

'The enemy is swift,' said Anara, and Calard squinted at the riders.

As they drew closer, he saw that they were around thirty in number, and hounds ran alongside them. Sighting the knights, the dogs erupted into a frenzy of barking and deep-throated growls that carried across the undulating hills. Then the riders split abruptly into two groups. One group continued riding directly towards the knights, while the other peeled off to the north, clearly intending to cut them off. He saw a handful, perhaps five riders, split away from this group, and they took off in the direction that Kegan and the yeomen had ridden.

Horns blared once more, and Calard glanced in concern at his twin, as Montcadas picked up the pace. His worry was unfounded, for despite lacking a saddle and stirrups, Anara rode upon the back of her white mare easily, her slight body crouched over the horse's neck.

'Lady above,' said Bertelis. 'What manner of beast are they?'

As the enemy drew nearer, Calard could see that he had been wrong. These were not riders at all. They were twisted creatures of Chaos. Their lower bodies were like those of shaggy oxen, though their legs ended in taloned claws that tore up the turf, rather than cloven hooves. Where the creatures' heads ought to have been there were instead muscled torsos, complete with thick, human-like arms, and topped by heavy, horned, bestial heads.

They were like the beastmen of the forest that Calard had fought before, but melded, somehow, with a massive quadruped to create this bastard hybrid. Long, matted braids of hair and fur streamed behind them, and they hefted crude spears and axes in their hands. One lifted a horn to its bestial mouth as it ran, blowing a long note that was echoed by a blare from the other group.

Nor were the hounds running at their side natural beasts. As large as ponies, they were slavering creatures covered in thick fur, and spines ran down their backbones. Their jaws were heavy, and filled with teeth and tusks, and their tongues lolled from their mouths as their red-rimmed eyes locked onto their prey.

The group riding directly at the Bretonnians was drawing close, and the roars and braying cries of the pack could be heard, along with the growls and barks of the massive war hounds. Up ahead, the other group was angling into their path, to block their progress to the north.

The mounted yeomen, riding alongside the knights, nocked arrows to their bows and, rising in the saddle, they began to fire into the enemy. Calard saw an arrow slam into the heavily muscled chest of one of the enemy centaur-creatures. It threw it off balance, and it stumbled. With a snarl, it snapped the arrow-shaft off, leaving the point embedded in its flesh, and continued its wild charge across the grassland. Another arrow took one of them in the throat, and it fell with a gargled scream. It struck the ground hard, and rolled, legs snapping beneath it. Its companions ignored it, trampling it into the earth in their eagerness to close with their enemy.

Two of the massive hounds, driven mad by the scent of blood in the air, leapt on the fallen creature. They tore it apart in a gory feast, clamping their vice-like jaws onto its body, and shaking their heavy heads wildly from side to side, ripping flesh and muscle.

With perfect discipline, the knights formed into a tight fighting wedge, with the Baron Montcadas at its tip. Anara rode in the middle of the lance formation, protected on all sides by the armoured bulk of knights.

When the enemy to their flank was no more than a hundred yards distance, Baron Montcadas abruptly swung to the right. The knights followed his move closely, and the formation wheeled around to face the enemy head-on. Baron Montcadas lifted his morning star high, and began to swing it above his head. The knights kicked their steeds into a charge in perfect unison.

'For Bastonne and the Lady!' roared Montcadas, and Calard and the other knights echoed the war cry.

The enemy roared and leapt forwards to meet them, unflinching, the massive war hounds running hard at their sides. They lifted crude spears up high; they did not couch them like the Bretonnians did with their lances. The lead creature hurled its spear like a javelin, the full weight of its body behind the throw. The spear lanced through the air, and a knight was ripped from the saddle as the weapon punched through his breastplate. Other spears were hurled, but they were battered aside by shields.

There was a deafening crack, as Dieter Weschler, riding within the formation, fired one of his wheel-lock pistols. A cloud of acrid smoke rose from the long barrel of the weapon, and Calard saw one of the beasts stumble and fall, the shot blasting out through the back of its head with a spray of blood.

The knights lowered their lances, and the two forces struck. The impact was immense, and the lead creature fell beneath the spiked ball of Montcadas's morning star, its skull smashed asunder. A spear thrust skidded off Calard's shield, and he plunged his lance tip into the neck of one of the beasts, using the full force of his momentum to drive it through the enemy's flesh. It sheared through the creature's body like a hot knife through a wad of butter, and the beast fell, blood spurting from the fatal wound.

War hounds snarled and growled, and jaws snapped at Gringolet's neck, but the powerful destrier trampled the beasts beneath its hooves. An axe slammed into the head of the knight at Calard's right, shearing through the metal of the man's helmet and shattering bone. The man swayed in the saddle for a moment before falling beneath the thunder of hooves.

The wedge of knights drove through the middle of the enemy, smashing them aside, and striking out with lances and swords. The bellows and roars of the enemy were deafening, but the knights fought ferociously. A serrated blade struck Calard's breastplate, and he winced from the force of the impact, though it could not penetrate his thick armour. He lashed out with the butt of his lance, smashing it into the snarling, bestial face of his attacker, before Bertelis sliced open its throat with a deft sweep of his blade.

With a roar, a massive, tusked hound with four eyes leapt, its weight dragging one of the proud Bretonnian warhorses down. The steed screamed horribly as it fell, and jaws closed around its neck. The knight borne by the destrier fell with a curse, but there was no time to aid him, as the Bretonnians thundered clear of the melee.

Ranging out on the flanks of the knights, Garamont yeomen fired their bows smoothly, sinking arrow after arrow into those beasts that had survived the knightly charge. Three arrows pierced a centaur-beast, and it collapsed to the ground, its legs giving way beneath it. A war hound dropped with a yelp as a shaft drove between its vertebrae.

The knights wheeled around sharply. They had lost five of their number, and had killed perhaps twelve of the enemy, and a half dozen or so hounds. They charged back into the reeling enemy, slaughtering the remainder.

The second group was closing on them from the north, and Montcadas shouted for order, wheeling the lance formation around towards the threat. Pain flared in Calard's wounded side, and he could feel blood running down his torso. He had clearly ripped open the assassin's wound during the fight, though at the time he had felt nothing.

He knew that the next charge would prove more costly, but he felt a fierce sense of pride within him. He would not allow anything to harm his sister now that he had found her after so many years.

'Hold,' called Anara, her voice full of authority, all hint of otherworldliness gone. 'Do not charge them.'

Obediently, the knights reined in their steeds, and the damsel pushed between them to gain a clear view of the closing enemy. They were no more than eighty paces away, and closing fast, and Calard's anxious gaze flickered between Anara and the enemy.

Apparently defying logic, Anara slipped from the back of her mare.

'Sister, what are–' began Calard, but he was silenced by a raised hand.

The knights shuffled in unease as the damsel bent down and removed the soft slippers from her feet. She wiggled her toes, and cold, wet mud oozed between them. Calard looked uneasily towards the closing enemy. They were less than forty paces away.

Anara began to chant, her voice low, moving to rhythms that were alien to the ears of the gathered knights. The warhorses of the knights, perhaps sensing the tension in their riders, began to stamp their hooves into the wet earth, and shake their heads. Calard patted Gringolet heavily on the neck, whispering calming words to the destrier, though his eyes were locked on the enemy that was so close that he could pick out individual details. He could see the jangle of bones and infernal bronze icons looped through holes in the beasts' horns, and the hellish symbols carved into their flesh and hides.

Calard licked his lips, and clenched his fist around his weapon. The enemy were closing fast, and the knights would be slaughtered if they were caught motionless.

Their charge began to falter, however. Though they fought wildly to maintain their momentum, they were slowly sinking into the water-soaked earth.

In amazement, Calard looked at Anara, who was continuing her incantation unabated. The ground around her feet had dried up, the mud hardening to a rock-like crust.

Slavering war hounds snapped and growled as they clambered over each other, frantic to escape the sinking mire. The beast-centaurs roared and bellowed in rage and frustration, thrashing frantically as they tried to free themselves from the marsh. With each violent movement, they sank further into the clinging mire. One of them roared and hurled its spear towards the knights, but it fell ten yards short.

Several of the Garamont yeomen rode in close to the edge of the swampy area, and fired into the helpless creatures. They killed several, before Montcadas ordered them to stop in order to conserve arrows. The baron stared in wonder at the diminutive damsel, who was continuing her incantation, her eyes having rolled up into the back of her head.

Her lips were turning blue, and she began to sway slightly. Calard dropped from his saddle and went to her, but was unwilling to lay hands upon her, for fear of what might happen if he interrupted her spell.

Within minutes, the creatures of Chaos had disappeared, bellowing defiance as they were swallowed by the mire.

Anara finished chanting, and swooned, falling forwards. Calard caught her in his arms.

Her eyes flicked open, blazing with sudden anger. 'Don't touch me!' she hissed, her eyes flashing with fey light. She pulled free of Calard's arms, and he gaped at her. She quickly recovered her composure, and colour began to return to her face. With an imperious glance at Calard, she mounted her white steed.

'Come, brother,' she said, her voice soft and distant once more, the sudden anger of a moment before forgotten. 'We must be away. The beast is drawing near.'

CHAPTER THIRTEEN

THE RIDE BACK to camp was like a hellish nightmare. Horns pursued the knights, and as the last of the sun's rays dropped over the horizon, they saw dark shapes emerging from the forest of Chalons. Howls and roars echoed around them, and the Bretonnians held flaming brands high to hold back the darkness that threatened to close around them like a death shroud.

Twice they were attacked, set upon by packs of beastmen that erupted from the darkness, leaping from ambush and setting about them with axes and curved swords. Five knights and a pair of yeomen were dragged from their saddles and butchered in the first attack before the knights rode free, speaking prayers to the Lady for those that had fallen.

There was no warning of the second attack, and it had been led by a monstrous creature that stood some ten feet tall, a behemoth of flesh and muscle. The massive head of a raging bull topped its powerful, hunched frame, supported by a neck thicker than the body of a horse, and its wide horns spanned almost six feet from bronze-encased tip to tip.

It pounded out of the darkness with its head lowered, and slammed into the knights, sending several of their steeds flying. It lifted a warhorse on its horns, flicking it over its shoulder as if it weighed nothing at all, sending the knight in the saddle of the horse crashing to the ground ten yards away. It wielded a massive spiked club in each hand, and rusted chains locked the weapons to its arms, so that it was unable to discard them. It smashed the skull of another horse with a blow that fell with the force of an avalanche, and roared, spittle flying from its bovine lips.

Smaller beastmen swarmed in its wake, and a frantic combat had erupted. Seven knights were killed before the massive bull-headed beastman slumped to the ground, pierced by more than a dozen swords and lances. Its lesser minions, seeing the great creature topple, took flight, and the weary Bretonnians pushed on, leaving the dead where they lay.

Sounds of pursuit dogged them, and unnatural roars and cries echoed through the darkness.

They found their path blocked by twisted branches and briars, and there were raised voices as a tense argument erupted. The yeoman scouts were accused of leading them astray, but Calard defended them, spying a small roadside shrine that he had noticed earlier that day when they had passed this way. The forest was interposing itself in their path, seeking to slow and block their passage, and Calard had been surprised to see tears glistening on Anara's cheeks.

'They are in pain,' she said mournfully, laying a slender hand upon the trunk of one contorted tree, its boughs dripping with red sap. Branches creaked and groaned alarmingly, and leafless limbs shivered and strained. Eyes filled with malice glinted in the orange light of the torches, and Calard shivered.

No man had any wish to pass beneath the twisted branches of the unnatural trees, and so they set off to the west, seeking to circumvent the disturbing woodland that blocked their way.

The ride took them hours longer than it ought to have, for they were forced far to the west by the sudden growth of the forest, though thankfully the sounds of the pursuit had faded. It was nearing midnight when they finally rode towards the camp, on the flat-topped hill of Adhalind's Seat. The night was eerily silent as peasants ran to greet them, and they slid wearily from their saddles. Looking around, Calard saw that, of the knights who had set out that day, less than half had returned. Still, for all that, he knew that they had been lucky. Had it not been for Anara's warning, he was certain that none of them would have returned.

Kegan had clearly arrived back at the camp some time earlier, and preparations for an attack were under way. Braziers had been lit around the perimeter of Adhalind's Seat, and men-at-arms and peasant bowmen stood ready. Sentries patrolled the lowlands around the flat-topped hill, wary for any sign of the enemy. The majority of the knights in the camp were fully armed and armoured, and sat in their saddles, ready for battle. The remainder were also fully armoured, and their horses were tethered nearby. It would take but a shout from a sentry for them to be ready to face the hated foe.

Calard's wounded side pained him, and he knew that his dressing needed changing, but he followed Baron Montcadas to his war tent, leading Anara gently by her arm. She seemed in no way adverse to the contact now, and Calard walked with his chin held high, hearing the awed whispers of the gathered knights as they saw the revered damsel of the Lady on his arm.

Montcadas called the senior knights of Bastonne to him, and Calard felt a flush of pride that he was included in their mix, though he knew that this was more to do with his kinship with Anara than anything else.

Calard glanced around the ostentatious tent, looking upon the faces of the powerful nobles. There were ten men gathered, all nobles of Bastonne, except for the empire envoy, Dieter Weschler, who had graciously been allowed to attend this war-meeting, and the awe-inspiring figure of the questing knight, Gundehar of Raisol, who stood leaning upon the pommel of his massive two-handed sword. Two of the knights were vassals of his father, and three were sworn to Sangasse. The remainder were vassal lords of Montcadas. With a stab of guilt, he realised that Gunthar should have been present, being one of the more respected knights in the camp.

'First, let me introduce and welcome the lady Anara of Garamont, damsel of the Lady,' said the baron. The knights bowed to her respectfully, and Calard smiled inwardly at the look the Sangasse lords shared between them. 'I give thanks to the Lady that she has come.'

Anara accepted the bows of the knights without expression. 'Of Garamont no longer,' she said. 'I am a handmaiden of the Lady, and to her alone am I tied.' Calard looked at her, aggrieved, but she ignored him.

'My apologies,' said the baron. His broad face was serious as he stared around at the gathered knights, looking at each man in turn. 'The Lady Anara has seen that a great force marches against us. Even now, it gathers in the darkness, readying to descend upon us.'

'Good!' said one man forcefully, echoing the thoughts of all the knights. 'The enemy has avoided pitched battle for too long.'

'Indeed,' boomed Montcadas. 'However, the force that marshals against us is powerful, and it is not an honourable foe. We will be heavily outnumbered, and they are certain to attack under the cover of darkness.'

'Bah!' said one knight. 'We have nothing to fear from the darkness! We are knights of Bretonnia! Each knight is more than a match for five of the enemy.' Murmurs of agreement met this statement, and Calard felt his chest swell.

'They are a cunning enemy,' said the questing knight, Gundehar. They were the first words that Calard had heard the lean, unshaven knight speak, and his voice was deep and strong. 'They are not to be underestimated.'

'With respect, lord Gundehar, are they not merely beasts?' asked one of the Sangasse knights. 'They will not attack a powerfully defended position in a pitched battle, surely?'

'If there are enough of them, and they are confident of victory, they will, Beldane,' said Gundehar, 'and we know not what they seek to achieve here.'

'Achieve?' laughed the knight, Beldane. 'They do not think like you or I. They are driven to kill and destroy, nothing deeper than that.'

'In my experience, they are not an unthinking enemy,' said Gundehar coolly. 'They are more subtle than the greenskins, who I agree, seek nothing more than bloodshed and battle. No, there is something at work here, though I am not wise enough to see what it is.'

Montcadas frowned. 'What do you mean?' he asked.

'The enemy has been attacking, apparently at random, all across the eastern edge of Bordeleaux. In doing so, they forced the duke's hand, making him split his forces to cover a wide area. Their attacks have been unfocused and chaotic. No pattern could be read in their movements, but now, their entire attention has been drawn here. For what? It seems to me that their previous attacks have not been random. It is more like they have been searching for something, and they have found it, here.'

'Searching for what?' asked Calard, speaking before he could stop himself. All eyes in the tent turned towards him, and he reddened, dropping his gaze to the floor. He felt Anara's eyes burning into him.

'I don't know,' admitted Gundehar.

'It matters not at all to me what they are doing here,' growled Montcadas. 'All that matters is that they are coming. We are faced with a deadly foe, and I have gathered you here to plan how to fight it.'

'How do we know they are massing against us?' asked Haydon, one of the Garamont knights, a broad-shouldered, balding noble. 'Could this not just be another feint?'

'The beast is watching us, even now,' said Anara suddenly, her voice vague and distant, her eyes misted. Calard felt the temperature within the tent drop sharply, and he could see his breath in the air before him. It continued to drop, and he saw beads of condensation form upon the sides of a goblet of water that sat upon the circular table that dominated the tent.

'The forest is alive with movement,' said Anara in a ghostly, unnerving voice. Ice was forming on the surface water within the goblet. 'I see children of Chaos beyond number. Their lust for violence is great, but the beast holds them in check, restraining their urges. Sacrifices are being prepared. The beast is calling more of its dark kin to its side.'

Anara blinked, as if waking from a deep slumber, and the temperature in the room began to return to normal. Her eyes came back into focus, and she looked Montcadas squarely in the eyes. 'The attack will not come this night. It will come tomorrow, at dusk.'

The silence in the tent was stifling, and the knights shuffled their feet, their faces pale.

Montcadas cleared his throat. 'Thank you, lady,' he said graciously, bowing his head to Anara.

'We know that they are many, and we know when the attack will come. All we can do is make ready for it. Kegan, what preparations have you made?'

Clearly still discomforted by Anara's display of power, the knight swallowed thickly.

'The men-at-arms and peasants of Garamont, Sangasse and Montcadas are all standing at the ready. They are posted around the perimeter of the camp, and I have ordered braziers lit. Sentries patrol the fields below Adhalind's Seat, to forewarn us of an attack, though it seems that tonight they are unnecessary,' he said, with a nod towards Anara. 'There is one patrol still out there, accompanied by the young Earl of Sangasse, Maloric. Outriders are seeking them. They are due back by midnight. I have also sent a request for aid to the duke's forces in the north: five men, riding the camp's swiftest steeds.'

'They are already dead,' said Anara. 'The message will not be received.'

'We can expect no aid in this battle, then,' said Montcadas.

'That is not quite correct,' said Anara.

'No?'

'I visited the grail knight Reolus as his body slumbered. Even now, he is leading a force to us. They will arrive before sunset tomorrow.'

'Reolus? He comes here?' asked Calard.

'He does, brother,' said Anara.

'Well, that is welcome news,' said Montcadas. He turned his broad, bearded face towards Kegan. 'You have done well. Go now, and relieve the foot soldiers from their state of readiness, and pass the word for the knights to stand down. Let them get some rest. By the sounds of it, we shall be in for a long night tomorrow.'

The knight took his leave, and Montcadas cleared the circular table in the centre of the tent. He produced a scroll of rolled, faded parchment and spread it out across the table. The gathered knights closed around it, and Calard saw that it was an intricate map. Villages, woodland and castles were painted in minute detail, and illustrations of dragons and other beasts decorated the edges of the parchment. Its colour had long since faded, but the details were mostly clear. Calard could see Adhalind's Seat marked upon it, and a small grail icon marked the position of the nearby shrine.

'The Forest of Chalons, marked here,' said Montcadas, indicating the area of faded green on the eastern edge of the map, 'is obviously now inaccurate. However, the remaining details are accurate as far as I can make out, and the scale is true.'

He turned and called for a servant. 'Bring us food and wine,' he ordered, before turning back to pore over the map.

'Now,' he said, 'we must discuss our strategy.'

CALARD YAWNED HEAVILY. The night had been long, and the discussions of strategy and tactics had raged back and forth for hours. Anara had excused herself and retired to the Baron of Montcadas's personal tent, for he had graciously given it over to her use. Much of the discussion had gone over Calard's head, and he found his thoughts drifting to his sister, and to Gunthar. Gundehar's words haunted him, and he turned them over in his mind again and again. The beasts were searching for something, the questing knight had said.

At last, a plan of action had been agreed, and the meeting concluded. Glancing up at the sky, he saw that Mannslieb was sinking towards the horizon, and he estimated that it was around two hours past midnight. He yawned again, but did not move towards his tent, though his pallet was calling to him.

Instead, he made his way through the quiet camp. Knights, unable or unwilling to sleep, nodded to him as he passed by their fires.

Word had come to the baron's war tent that Maloric and his knights had returned from their patrol, though they were bloodied and more than half their number had been lost in an ambush by the beasts of the forest. Calard was glad that the young Sangasse nobleman had not fallen. They would need every man capable of wielding a sword in the battle the next night, and besides, he would have felt cheated if Maloric had been slain.

Picking his way between the tents, Calard came to the one he sought, and slipped inside quietly.

Strong smelling herbs were burning in a small brazier in the corner of the tent, but they could not fully mask the foul scent of sickness that assailed Calard as he entered.

A single candle burned within, and it took a moment for Calard's eyes to adjust to the gloom. Moving as quietly as he was able, he moved to the bedside and looked down upon the sleeping form of Gunthar.

The weapon master had aged dramatically in the days since his injury. His face was gaunt and pale, etched with heavy wrinkles and lines, and his eyes were sunken and hollow. A sheen of sweat covered his brow, and his breathing was almost imperceptible.

Several basins of bloody water stood beside the pallet, and rags were soaking within them.

Gently, so as not to wake the injured knight, Calard lifted the blankets covering Gunthar to look at the wound, wrinkling his nose against the foul smell. Ganelon's sword had stabbed deep into his thigh, and it was clear that it was not healing well. It was open, weeping pus and blood, and the flesh around it was a bruised, angry colour. Calard placed the blankets back down gently, his heart heavy.

His own wound was healing well, but it had been far less serious than Gunthar's.

'You are a young man, strong and healthy,' the diminutive surgeon had said. 'Your body will heal quickly.' Gunthar, however, was not a young man.

Wringing out a cloth, Calard dabbed the sweat from Gunthar's forehead. The weapon master's skin felt hot and feverish to the touch. The injured knight stirred, and opened his eyes. He looked up at Calard, standing over him, and he smiled.

'Well met, Calard,' he breathed.

'How are you feeling?' asked Calard.

'Good,' replied the ageing knight, his voice weak. 'Give me a day, and I will be back in the saddle, as strong as ever.'

Calard smiled sadly, but did not refute the weapon master.

'I hear tell that you found your sister,' said Gunthar.

Calard nodded, smiling. He pulled up a chair, and turned it around before sitting himself down. 'She is a damsel of the Lady now.'

Gunthar smiled sleepily. 'Your mother would have been proud, proud of you both.'

Calard looked down. 'I do not feel proud of myself,' he said. 'You shouldn't be lying here.'

'I will be fine. I've suffered worse wounds.'

'They say that you will not... not ride again, Gunthar,' said Calard, his voice full of sadness. Gunthar scoffed at his words.

'I *will* ride again. What sort of knight would I be if I could not ride into battle for my lord? Or for my lord's son? I will be fine, Calard. You will see.'

Calard smiled at the weapon master's certainty.

'Don't be too hard on yourself,' said Gunthar. 'You are young, and all young men are eager and rash. It is their nature to act in such a manner, convinced of their own immortality. I was young too once.'

'Never!' said Calard, gently mocking. Then his face grew more serious. 'There will be a great battle tomorrow. The enemy is gathering against us.'

'So I hear,' said Gunthar, 'but the Lady is with us. We will be victorious, or we will not.' He shrugged. 'In the big scheme of things, it matters little. The mountains will still exist long after we are forgotten by history. Ah, listen to me, I am old, and getting morbid in my dotage.'

'You are not so old, Gunthar.'

The weapon master smiled. 'And you are a bad liar, for which I am pleased.'

Calard stared into the candle flame, and the silence deepened between them. 'It is strange to see Anara again,' he said at last.

'Oh? How so?'

'For almost fifteen years I have prayed to the Lady to bring her back into my life, and now that she has, I find that she has... changed. She is not the girl I remembered.'

'And you are no longer the boy that you were.'

'I know, but she is... different. There is a distance between us that I do not think can be bridged. I do not understand the powers that she wields. She... she frightens me.'

'I would call any man a liar that claimed not to be afraid of such a one.'

'She said some strange things,' said Calard after a time, staring vacantly into the candle, watching the perfect tapering flame flicker ever so slightly. He sighed and looked down, his thoughts confused and jumbled. 'I visited a castle today. I do not even know its name. I visited it once when I was a very small child. I remember it faintly now. Mother was heavy with child, though it is only now that I realise it. That was why we travelled there, I suppose, so that my mother was close to her family and in familiar surrounds when the baby's time came. Perhaps they already knew that it was going to be a difficult birth. I remember she travelled in a grand carriage, pulled by four white horses. Anara travelled in the carriage with her, and I did too for some of the way, when I was not sitting in my father's saddle, his arm around me.'

Calard gave a dry, humourless laugh. 'I think that may have been the last time my father embraced me, on that journey. I remember now, running through the castle of my mother's family, and I remember being terrified as my mother screamed in agony. "They are hurting her!" I cried, but Anara quietened me. "A baby is coming out of her," she said to me. She was so calm, and matter-of-fact. Anara! The fey child that lived in a fantasy world that only she could perceive, whom the servants were afraid of, and she was speaking to me like an adult!' He smiled wistfully at the recollection that, until today, had been lost to him, but it faded quickly.

'I never saw my mother again. I guess the babe died in the birth. You said so yourself, although I can now remember its birth screams.' He shuddered. 'They were horrific. Anara and I were ushered away by servants. We left the castle the next day. Mother was not with us, and I did not know where she was. It was only years later that I learnt she had died, in childbirth, as you had said. Today, though, Anara said some things… things I cannot explain. She said that my mother did not die in childbirth at all, but rather threw herself from a window, and was dashed upon the rocks below. I don't understand. I don't know what this all means.'

Looking up, his eyes haunted, he saw that Gunthar was asleep. He didn't know how much the weapon master had heard, and he snorted without humour. Gathering his thoughts, he stood up.

'Lady, please protect him,' he whispered, and silently left the tent.

CALARD WOKE TO the sound of tense voices. Stumbling out into the cold half-light of predawn, he saw peasants running through the camp, their faces worried and pale, and he could hear knights talking together in strained voices. Walking through the milling crowd standing on the edge of Adhalind's Seat, he gazed out over the surrounding fields to the east.

The day before, the forest of Chalons had been a distant shadow on the horizon. It had already broken its former borders, and extended far beyond its natural range. Its arms had spread out to the north and south like a crescent, arcing around Adhalind's Seat, where it had been at least five miles away at its closest point.

Now, the forest was no more than a mile in the distance.

'Lady above,' breathed Calard, his eyes wide in horror.

Calard pushed his way through the press of gawking onlookers, and ran through the camp, heading towards the other side of the table-topped hill. He dreaded what he would see there. Gaining a clear view across the fields to the west, he sighed in horror.

The forests of Chalons were only a mile away. It was the same to the north, and to the south.

The forest had completely surrounded them. They were in the belly of the beast, trapped deep within its heart of darkness, and it was surely only a matter of time before they were completely engulfed.

CHAPTER FOURTEEN

DREAD AND NERVOUS anxiety churned within Calard's stomach. Black birds, the eyes of the enemy, circled high overhead, out of bow range.

'I will be glad when night comes, just so we won't have to see those hateful things any longer,' said Bertelis.

The glare of the sun was harsh, burning an intense, blazing orange. The sky was red, fading to purple and dark blue in the east. It was less than an hour until dusk. According to Anara, the beasts would begin their onslaught an hour after sundown.

'Not long now,' said Calard. He too wished the time would pass quickly. He hated the hours before battle was met.

The day had been one of frantic activity as the camp prepared for attack. Orders were given, and men-at-arms formed into fighting echelons that were spread around the hill, facing out in all directions.

Fletchers and blacksmiths worked hard through the day, and hundreds of new arrows were made and distributed amongst the five hundred peasant archers and bow-armed yeomen of Garamont, Sangasse and Montcadas. Iron braziers were positioned around the perimeter, and peasants gathered additional firewood to ensure that none of them would burn low throughout the long night ahead.

A team of some three hundred men had marched out before dawn, under the watchful gaze of Baron Montcadas, heading towards an isolated copse of beech trees half a mile from Adhalind's Seat. Nervously eyeing the unnatural, tortured forest of Chalons, which had completely surrounded the camp in the night, the peasants set about lopping these tall, straight, grey trees. The branches and twigs were shorn from the trunks, and they were hauled back to the camp, where they were hewn into lengths around ten feet long. The tips were sharpened with axes, and hardened with fire. Over the course of the day, several thousand stakes were cut, and these were set into the ground around the base of Adhalind's Seat, forming a ring of spikes facing outwards. The overlapping lines of stakes allowed for sorties of knights to charge through them, while ensuring that an enemy trying to storm them would have to fight hard for every inch of ground they took.

The archers stood on the hillsides behind the stakes, each man with dozens of arrows stuck into the soft earth in front of him, and carrying a pair of quivers. Calard did not, of course, approve of the use of missile weapons, but he respected the tactical use of the peasants. Besides, the peasants had no concept of honour, too ignorant to understand that it was shaming to kill from a distance.

More sharpened stakes had been sunk into the earth around the sacred copse that butted up against the north-west hillside, and hundreds of archers stood behind them, supported by large blocks of men-at-arms.

The archers were under orders to fire upon the foe until they were within a hundred paces, at which point they were to pull back onto the slopes of Adhalind's Seat, joining the bulk of the archers there, and allowing the men-at-arms to step forward and hold the line. It was here that the men of Garamont were stationed, here that they would face the enemy.

Half a dozen knights, all vassals of Calard's father, had nobly volunteered to fight on foot and lead the peasant rabble. They knew that holding the line against the enemy was of paramount importance. If the line broke, and the beasts were allowed to despoil the sacred shrine, then the good name of their lord would be sullied, for it was Garamont's responsibility to see it protected. With their line bolstered by the presence of the stern knights, Calard was more confident that the men-at-arms would hold.

There were gaps in the wooden stakes, to either side of the shrine's edges, through which the Garamont knights could sally forth to attack the enemy directly, if they managed to weather the storm of arrows. Many of the nobles were confident that the unruly rabble of the enemy would not be able to advance beneath the clouds of arrows that would descend among them, but

Baron Montcadas was not convinced. Indeed, many of the nobles in the war tent on the previous evening had argued long and hard for the knights of Bastonne to ride out and meet the enemy head-on, on the flat fields around the hill, for they were unhappy with the idea of hiding behind walls of stakes and relying on peasant archers. Where was the honour in that they questioned?

Montcadas had not entertained these considerations, dismissing them too quickly in Calard's eyes, but he had held his tongue, letting the more experienced knights argue their cases.

To his surprise, Montcadas had even drawn Dieter Weschler into the discussion, asking him how an Empire army would mount a defence against this enemy. The other knights had murmured their discontent, but Montcadas had silenced them with a fiery glare.

'In my land, we would hold the high ground with our heavy infantry battalions,' started Dieter. 'We would pound the enemy with cannon and mortar, and lines of arquebuses would fire as the enemy came into range. These handguns have not the range or rate of fire of your long bows, but within two hundred yards they are devastating. We would funnel the enemy towards our strongest positions, towards the true strength of our armies, its infantry.'

Several of the gathered knights scoffed at this, laughing under their breath at the foolishness of their neighbours. Ignoring their snide remarks, Dieter had continued with dignity.

'Our knightly orders would be held back to counter-attack against enemy cavalry, or wherever the line began to falter. Regiments of halberdiers and spears would be held in reserve under the command of a senior captain, who would order them forwards into any breaches. Victory would come as the enemy broke against our infantry battalions, for there is not a more disciplined force in the Old World.' The small captain stood proudly, his chest puffed out like a cockerel's as he went into further detail about the disposition of the armies of the Empire, and their tactics. He quoted from tactical manuals that Calard had never read, and spoke of battles that he had never heard of. At last, Montcadas thanked the Empire captain, who nodded curtly in response, clearly pleased at having been given the opportunity to speak of his homeland.

'Our knights,' Montcadas had said, 'are our most potent weapon. No better knights can be found in the Old World or beyond, and they are rightly feared by all who oppose us. Given more knights, this battle would be won easily, for nothing can stand against our charge. However, as the noble damsel has foretold, we will be facing an enemy "beyond number". I fear that if we ride forth from Adhalind's Seat and engage the enemy on even ground, we will be surrounded and slaughtered to a man. Our charge will falter, and, as soon as we have lost our momentum, our advantage has been lost.'

'We will not be able to make use of our greatest advantage if we hide behind walls of stakes and peasants,' countered Kegan, spitting out the last word as if it tasted bad in his mouth.

'Quite true,' replied Montcadas. 'The enemy will break against Adhalind's Seat, and we shall charge forth and drive through the enemy where it threatens us most, before pulling back. This will *not* be the glorious battle that many of you noble knights wish it to be. It will not be the glorious battle that *I* would wish it to be. But there will be no glory if every man here is slaughtered, and I will be damned if I let such a thing come to pass under my leadership.'

At the end of the discussion, as the knights moved off to begin preparations and steal a few hours rest, Calard had seen Montcadas sit down heavily, looking tired and strained. This shocked Calard more than anything else he had seen or heard that night, for he had believed that the massive baron was utterly indefatigable, an elemental force of battle that never tired, nor ever even considered losing.

'I wish that Lord Gunthar was with us, lad,' he had said, and Calard had hung his head in shame. 'I am a leader of men, and I like to think a fine one, but I prefer to lead from the front. I am no master of strategy. I prefer to leave that to more learned men. I suppose that the Lady tests us all, and one can only hope to live up to the challenges she sets.'

'I think the strategy is sound, baron,' said Calard.

'Good,' said Montcadas with a smile. 'I've never lost a battle in my life, and I don't intend to start now.'

The tents in the camp had been mostly dismantled so that reinforcements could cross the hilltop unimpeded, and so that messages could more easily be passed with flags and banners. A few tents remained, connected by awnings of canvas, to act as a field surgery, and hundreds of pallets were laid out. Water was collected from the spring that fed the grail shrine's serene glade, and peasants were organised into small groups to transport the wounded from the main battle lines.

No peasant was spared a duty, and non-combatants were organised into teams to aid the battle, either as aides to the few surgeons in the camp, as labourers to bear arrows, water and fresh lances, or organised into lightly armoured skirmish echelons to support the men-at-arms and dispatch injured enemies with knives and cudgels.

Calard took a deep breath, trying to calm his frayed nerves. The sun was sinking ever nearer to the horizon. The attack would come at any minute. Even the knowledge that the holy paladin Reolus would fight at their side did little to curb the feeling of dread rising within him.

The grail knight had arrived at the camp hours earlier, emerging from the unnatural forest to a great cheer. Knights and peasants had stopped their work to witness the arrival of the grail knight and his entourage. The knight's self-appointed heralds ran before the resplendent knight, exhorting his exploits in loud voices, and blowing long notes on trumpets and horns.

The revered knight rode his massive midnight black stallion at the head of some fifty knights, but they seemed to pale beside him, and all eyes were locked on the renowned champion of the Lady.

He had looked like a hero of legend, plucked straight from the illuminated pages that chronicled the exploits of Gilles the Uniter. He could have been one of the companions, one of the near-mythical paladins that rode at the side of the Uniter and freed the lands of the Bretonni from darkness.

In the dull, overcast afternoon light, the holy knight seemed to glow like a beacon. The visor of

his full-faced helm was lowered, and he rode with
his head held high. Candles surrounded the silver,
heraldic unicorn atop his helmet, and the light they
created shone a halo around the knight, and
gleamed off his highly polished and ornate armour.
The lance Arandyal was held vertical in one hand,
and his shield was slung over his back. His deep
blue cloak fluttered in the breeze behind him.

To his right, a knight bore the grail knight's personal
standard: a majestic, rearing unicorn of shimmering
silver upon a field of blue. The bearer's face shone with
pride at the honoured duty.

'Hark ye, knights of Bastonne!' hollered one of the
pilgrim heralds. 'Witness the approach of Saint Reolus
the Wise, beloved of the Lady! Saint Reolus the Bold,
paladin of Quenelles! Saint Reolus the Valiant, who
slew the blood-beast of the Orcals!'

'Blessed are ye to look upon his holiness! Give
praise, for he has come to fight the beasts! Victory is
certain, for the Lady will not allow any harm to befall
her favourite, and never shall his standard fall while he
doth take breath!'

Two hundred pilgrims had marched behind the
hallowed knight, shouting of his deeds in loud
voices, and holding aloft scraps of armour, food and
clothing that had been cast off by the object of their
devotion. The ragtag bunch of peasants wore a
motley collection of armour scavenged from
battlefields, over which monkish robes were pulled.
Many wore high gorgets of stiffened leather to
protect their necks, and most had shaved the tops of
their heads as a mark of their devotion. They carried
wooden   shields,   upon   which   were   nailed

parchments and scraps of beautifully illuminated holy works, and in their rough, calloused hands they carried rusted blades, clubs and daggers.

As the holy entourage came closer, Calard noted the heraldry of the knights accompanying Reolus. They hailed from all four corners of Bretonnia, and it was obvious that they had recently seen battle. The knights' shields were chipped and battle worn, and their cloaks were bloodied and tattered. Their armour was dented, and many bore injuries. Some of the pilgrim zealots were limping, leaning heavily on wooden crutches, while others had arms in splints and were wrapped in bloodied bandages. Nevertheless, they bore their wounds proudly, not wishing to show any form of weakness in front of the grail knight.

Calard had felt the spirit among the knights of Bastonne soar as the grail knight drew near. Truly they were favoured, knights whispered. Calard almost laughed out loud. They were surrounded on all sides by a hateful, cunning and unnatural foe, but with the presence of a grail knight and a sacred damsel of the Lady, how could they possibly lose?

Black birds circled overhead, higher than an arrow could reach, and, despite the arrival of Reolus, the sense of foreboding and dread would not leave Calard.

CHLOD'S STOMACH GROWLED noisily. When had he last eaten? He couldn't remember. He had not dared to go looking for food, fearing capture. His rat companion squirmed and climbed up his arm. It nuzzled at his ear, its mangy whiskers tickling him.

'Food is coming, precious,' he whispered.

Chlod sat among the pilgrims, grinning like a simpleton and licking his lips as he watched the stale loaves being dealt out amongst them.

'Break bread with us, brother!' said one of the devout followers of the grail knight. 'You have been blessed!'

'I have,' agreed Chlod. The itinerant vagrants had embraced him into their fold, fooled by his act, and now they would feed him as one of their own. His own cleverness astounded him. He took the proffered food, gratefully, and began stuffing it into his mouth with gusto. He held a crumb to his rat, which snatched it from his fingers eagerly.

He had been hiding out for three days and two nights. He'd seen the bodies of the others, hanging from the trees, their faces purple, their eyes plucked from their sockets by carrion birds. He didn't know if any of them had spoken before they had died. They might not have known his name, but they knew his face. Were the yeoman wardens looking for him even now? Did they know that he was one of those who had tried to kill the Garamont noble?

When the order had come to dismantle the camp, he had been almost paralysed with fear. There would be nowhere to hide once all the billets and tents were pulled down, and he thought he would surely be identified when all the camp followers had been rounded up and gathered into groups.

Keeping his head down low, he had stood with a group of other bedraggled peasants, labourers all. He did not know what lord they were in the service of. He tried to make himself as inconspicuous as possible, as the yeoman assigning the various peasants to work groups stalked past. The labourers had been assigned to chop down trees, and Chlod had tried to hide among their number, moving off with them as they shuffled away.

If they thought there was anything strange about the extra number in their group, they said nothing, and a flicker of hope sparked inside him. If he moved off with them to collect lumber, then surely he would be able to slink off without anyone noticing. Then he could get as far away from the camp as possible, and he would never be incriminated in the attempt on the life of the young Garamont lord. He would travel to the west, perhaps, towards the great port city of Borde-leaux. There, he was certain that he could lose himself in the warrens around the docklands.

He had even grinned lopsidedly, thinking that per-haps the trickster god Ranald was smiling down on him.

A meaty finger had prodded him in the chest.

'Not you,' snarled a yeoman. 'Whose man are you?'

Chlod had gaped stupidly, his mind whirring.

'Who is your lord and master?' the yeoman had asked, more forcefully. There were no free men in the camp. Not even the villeins who led the ragged groups of longbow men were truly free, for they still paid taxes and dues to their noble lord. Any peasant who did not belong to a lord was an outlaw, and outlaws were hanged.

'Garamont,' Chlod had lied. The yeoman frowned and looked at him doubtfully, but did not refute his claim.

'Well, what are you doing standing over here, fool?' snapped the man, cuffing him hard over the back of his head. 'Get over there with your fellows,' he said, pointing towards a small group of men and women, who were being led to the north.

Chlod hurried towards the group of peasants, praying that none of them would say that they did not know him. He kept his head down low as he shuffled past dozens of other peasants, trying not to catch the eye of any of them, but as he moved, he felt someone staring at him, and he looked up, straight into a face that he recognised.

It was another of the would-be assassins that had somehow escaped the hanging. The man began to push through the crowd of peasants towards him, and Chlod swore under his breath. He tried to ignore the man, dropping his head and moving as quickly as his clubfoot would allow, but the man drew alongside him. Chlod saw that his face was pale, and his eyes were filled with fear.

'They are going to hang us,' hissed the man, and Chlod looked around in alarm to see if any yeoman was nearby.

'We will die like the others!' the man wailed, clutching at Chlod's clothing, and he cursed. He saw a yeoman turn in their direction, alerted by the sound.

'Be quiet!' snarled Chlod dangerously, his hand closing around the dagger concealed within his tunic. 'Get away from me, now, or we will both be dead by sunset!'

The man continued to wail, clutching at him desperately.

'You there!' called the yeoman, stalking towards them, making the peasant wail even more. Chlod swore.

'What's going on here?' demanded the yeoman.

'We are dead men, dead!' wailed the man clutching at Chlod's jerkin.

'What's he on about?' asked the yeoman suspiciously. Chlod flashed him a lopsided, idiotic grin.

'My cousin,' he said, his voice thick with feigned stupidity. 'He is afflicted.' Chlod leant forward, and spoke his next words in an over-exaggerated, conspiratorial stage whisper. 'Maybe plague.'

At the word, the yeoman stepped back, one hand flying up to cover his mouth and nose.

'Get him away!' said the yeoman, waving his hand.

Chlod grinned stupidly and nodded, leading the peasant away.

Once clear of prying eyes, Chlod stabbed the man six times in the gut, and let him fall to the ground beside a pile of grain sacks.

He had not known what to do next. There were few places to hide, and there was no way that he could escape the camp without being seen.

His salvation had come in an unexpected form.

Maybe he *was* blessed.

He had grinned from ear to ear as he saw the approach of the grail knight and his pilgrims. In the pilgrims, he saw a refuge, and an idea formed in his head. He had scrambled towards them, bustling through the press of bodies to look upon the great knight.

'My eyes!' he had screamed, falling to his knees before one of the pilgrims.

'My eyes are healed!' he had lied, yelling at the top of his lungs. 'It is a miracle! I was blind, but now I can see! Lord Reolus has healed my sight!'

He had been surrounded by the dirty pilgrims, who lifted him roughly to his feet.

'Witness the healing powers of our great lord!' bellowed one them. 'This man was blind, but now his eyes are clear! He hath looked upon the greatness of lord Reolus, and his sight has been returned to him!'

'A miracle!' shouted Chlod, and he had been embraced into the fold of the pilgrims, cloistered within their number.

One of the pilgrims leant in close to Chlod, his eyes glinting with more than a touch of madness. He carefully unravelled a cloth, his face lighting up with fanatical devotion and awe.

'Look upon this holy artefact, brother,' said the buck-toothed pilgrim. In his hands, he reverently held what looked like a rotting lamb joint, rancid flesh still clinging to the bone. 'The hallowed Reolus did eat of this bone,' said the man in a hushed voice. 'His teeth did tear at the meat, giving him sustenance, and now I am its bearer. It protects me,' he whispered, 'for the glory of the great man was imparted unto it when he did touch it with his healing hands.'

Chlod gazed at the bone in feigned awe. It stank, the rotting meat filled with squirming maggots, but he did not let his disgust show on his face.

Truly he was blessed, he thought to himself. He had food in his belly and was, for now, safe from prosecution. Life truly was grand.

THE BURNING RED orb of the sun dipped over the horizon, setting the sky on fire, and silence descended across the flat-topped hill of Adhalind's Seat.

Hundreds of knights were gathered there, and they stood in serried, concentric ranks, surrounding an open area in the centre of the circle. Every noble that would fight this night was there, to join together in prayer and receive the Lady's blessing before battle commenced.

Hundreds of yeomen and servants stood a respectful distance away from the knights, holding the destriers, lances and shields of their lords. They would not take part in the blessing, for the cult of the Lady was restricted solely to the nobility, on pain of death, and they dutifully faced away from the proceedings.

A cool wind whistled over Adhalind's Seat, and Calard shivered involuntarily. He was at the forefront of the Garamont contingent, and his brother Bertelis stood at his left.

'Where's Tanebourc?' whispered Calard, glancing sideways. Without Gunthar's reassuring presence, he had come to rely on the tall, easy-natured knight, and it was unusual for him not to be at his side.

'I don't know,' said Bertelis, glancing around. He shrugged. 'He will be here somewhere.' Calard nodded, frowning, but drew his gaze back towards the empty circle in front of him. He took a deep breath, and tried to clear his mind. Staring resolutely forward, he sought the peace that he had experienced within the serene grail shrine, but it was elusive, and thoughts kept intruding into his calm.

The gathered knights dropped to one knee as Anara walked serenely up the aisle that had been left in their ranks, her movements regal and calm, projecting purity, serenity and gentleness. She wore a dress of palest blue, and her hair was covered in a matching headdress. The sleeves of her dress were long and flowing, with streams of material hanging from the cuffs to the ground. Her silver fleur-de-lys pendant shone upon her pale neck, and a matching icon was set into the delicate silver belt that circled her slim waist. The belt had been beautifully crafted to represent entwined strands of ivy, each silver leaf perfect in every detail. A matching garland of silver ivy circled her headdress.

Anara's head was held high, and her face was emotionless. She had applied delicate make-up to her face to accentuate her beauty, and the effect was stunning. Her lips were the colour of pale rose, and delicate lines of coal surrounded her eyes.

As she held a heavy silver chalice in her slender, pale hands, she was the very image of the Lady of the Lake herself, and Calard felt the intake of breath as the knights gazed upon her.

The Baron Montcadas and the grail knight Reolus walked a step behind Anara. Their sheer size and the masculine strength they projected made Anara appear even more delicate and fragile, like a single white rose. Montcadas, almost as broad as he was tall, walked slowly, his bearded face serious. He moved like a bear, his gait rolling and powerful. Reolus, almost two heads taller than the baron, walked with the grace and languid power of a lion.

Anara stopped in the centre of the circle of knights, her gaze sweeping over the gathered warriors. She gave no flicker of recognition as her eyes passed over Calard.

The baron and the grail knight dropped to one knee respectfully before Anara, and she lifted her chalice up high before her, like an offering to the sky. Lowering the grail, she dipped the fingers of one hand into the cool water within, and stepped towards the two kneeling men.

With soft words, she flicked the water over their bowed heads, before steeping back.

Montcadas rose, and turned around on the spot to address the gathered knights.

'I am not one for speeches,' he boomed, his voice carrying easily over the gathered knights, 'so I shall keep this brief. We face a terrible foe, my brothers. They are many, and come at us with hatred and jealousy in their twisted hearts. We are like a beacon in the night, surrounded on all sides by darkness, and yet, with faith in the Lady, we shall defeat that darkness, and it will come to fear us.'

The baron prowled around the circle.

'Each man here is a knight of Bretonnia. Whether a young knight errant,' boomed the baron, giving Calard a slight smile, 'or a revered knight of the grail,' he said, bowing towards Reolus, 'you are all knights of chivalry and honour. I know that you will fight with all your heart and all your valour. I need not implore you to do so, and so I shall not. For the honour of our noble land, of the Lady, of our valiant king, of our lords, and in honour of each other, I know that each man here will give his all. I am proud to fight alongside you. I could not wish for a finer group of knights. It is humbling to have the honour of fighting alongside you, and so for that I thank you, and I thank the Lady, for she has truly blessed us by sending the damsel Anara and the noble grail paladin Reolus to us in our time of need.'

The baron slid his sword from its scabbard, and raised it high in the air before him.

Over five hundred knights stood and mirrored the action, the hiss of steel resounding across the hilltop.

'For the king, the Lady and Bretonnia!' roared the baron, and the cry was echoed by the gathered knights.

'Let us pray,' said the grail knight Reolus as the cry faded. He did not raise his voice, but it carried easily to every ear. The grail knight turned towards Anara, and dropped to one knee. His sword was held in a downward grip in his hands, its point in the soil, and he bowed his head until his brow touched the pommel of the legendary weapon.

In turn, the circular ranks of knights dropped to their knees, bowing their heads to their swords. Anara stepped to Reolus, wetting her fingers in the chalice. Speaking softly, she pressed her hand to the grail knight's crown. At a word from her, he rose to his feet and sheathed his blade. Then he took the grail from the damsel's hands, and walked behind her as she began to move along the ranks of knights, blessing each man in turn.

Calard closed his eyes, feeling the cool metal pommel upon his skin. His lips moved silently as he recited prayers and mantras long ingrained in his memory. He lost all concept of time passing, until the scent of lavender and rose filled his nostrils, and he breathed in the heady aroma.

'Lady of grace and beauty,' spoke Anara softly, 'protect this knight as he does battle in your name. Protect him from cowardly blows, and guard him from evil. Protect him, oh merciful Lady, and guide his lance and blade against your enemies.'

Her cool, wet fingers pressed lightly against his crown, and he felt warmth and calm wash through him. Now he felt no unease, and none of the dread he had felt earlier. It had been cleansed from him by the healing power of the goddess.

As he opened his eyes, blinking as if waking from a long, refreshing slumber, he saw that darkness had almost completely descended over the land.

'Go now, my brother knights,' boomed Montcadas, 'and fight well.'

CALARD SAT IN Gringolet's saddle as the sun finally dipped over the horizon. Anara was alongside him, sitting casually upon the back of her white mare. They were scanning the distant tree line, which was getting harder to see as the sun descended.

'Where will you stand?' he asked at last.

'Where I am needed,' replied Anara, her voice vague and distant.

The knights were gathering into formation, and final orders were being bellowed to the men-at-arms as they moved into position. He had to join his own formation. All the young knights errant had been drawn together into wedges of thirty men, each led by an experienced knight of the realm, whose job it was to keep the eager young knights in line.

'Will we be victorious?' he asked softly. Anara was slow to answer.

'It is… unclear.'

The black birds circling overhead erupted in a sudden cacophony of raucous cries as the last vestiges of the blazing orange sun disappeared. The cries were joined by hundreds of hunting horns that blared hatefully from within the corrupted forest encircling them. Pounding drums began to beat savagely, until the whole area resounded with the hellish sound. Roars and braying bellows echoed across the sky, and the wasted, tortured trees began to shudder and groan.

'I have to go,' said Calard, seeing the formation he was to join wheeling into position upon the hilltop, facing towards the west. He looked at his sister, his twin whom he had spent so many years seeking word of. Now that battle was to commence, he was concerned for her safety. It was a ridiculous notion, considering the power she was able to wield. He had not the words to express his feelings.

'Be safe, my sister,' he said at last. She made no reaction to his words, merely staring into the distance, her eyes clouded and vague. Calard pulled his noble destrier Gringolet around sharply, and kicked his heels into its sides, cantering towards his allocated position.

Anara shivered, feeling the malevolent hatred of the enemy wash over her like a wave.

'And so it begins,' she breathed.

CHAPTER FIFTEEN

It seemed as though the corrupted Forest of Chalons was ablaze with fire. Thousands of torches flickered between the dark forms of the trees, and dark shapes moved within the twisted woodland as the massed forces of the enemy drew nearer. The entire forest was alive with movement.

There was to be no escape. The enemy had completely encircled the Bretonnians, and they massed beyond the tree line, snarling and braying in eagerness for the coming bloodshed.

The first beasts broke from the trees, holding torches aloft, hefting spears and swords, axes and spiked clubs. Many carried foul, totemic standards of twisted wood and rusted iron, from which were hung severed heads and hands, as well as battered Bretonnian helmets. They were lean, sinewy creatures, twisted mockeries of humanity, with small horns protruding from their scalps and evil expressions upon their hateful faces.

Many of them ran forwards, snarling and waving their weapons, before turning and slinking back to the forest's edge. Thousands of the creatures moved within the concealing darkness of the trees. Horns blared and drums of taut human skin were pounded. Several of the creatures strode forward and turned their matted, furred backs towards the Bretonnians, cocking their legs to defecate and urinate. They flicked their cloven hooves backwards, kicking their foul spoor and clods of earth in the direction of the defenders, accompanied by braying barks that might have passed for laughter.

Calard tensed in the saddle, his eyes blazing with anger.

Massive war hounds prowled through the darkness, growling and snapping at each other, sniffing the air. Several of them began to howl, as the clouds parted and the green glow of the Chaos moon, Morrslieb, radiated down from the heavens.

Larger beastmen began to emerge from the trees. Massively muscled and with thick horns curling from their temples, they pushed their smaller brethren out of the way, their thick lips curling back as they snarled and spat. Many of these creatures bore evidence of sickening mutations; some had spiked ridges of bone that erupted from their spines and elbows, while others had an additional arm protruding awkwardly from their shoulders, or a single, weeping eye in the centre of their foreheads. These, it seemed to Calard, were given additional respect, and the smaller beastmen slunk around them warily.

Several herds of the centaur-like beasts emerged, roaring loudly and kicking at any of the lesser beastmen that came near them. Each of the groups held aloft a totem, upon which horrifying, skinless bodies were nailed, the muscles glistening wetly. Calard was horrified to see that not all of the men were dead, and he watched, aghast, as one skinless man writhed in agony, fighting against the iron spikes that had been driven through his hands and feet. His tongueless mouth opened in a silent scream of torment. He might well have been a knight of Bastonne, for all Calard knew, kept alive for the amusement of his tormentors. Even as he watched, he saw one of the beasts poke at the man's exposed muscles with the barbed tip of his spear, laughing uproariously as the man thrashed and struggled.

As he watched the enemy gather, Calard began to see what he took as barbaric tribal distinctions. He saw one dominant group of beasts with black-painted arms, as if they had dipped their limbs in pitch. Another group had entwined briars and branches of thorns through their horns, and they snarled at any that came near them. Another group were daubed all over with blood. Their fur had been drawn into spikes, perhaps with lime and congealed blood, giving them a daemonic appearance.

This red-furred tribe was highly aggressive, and, even as he watched, he saw them surround one smaller, isolated beastman of another grouping and smash it to the ground with blows to the head and shoulders. The pack descended on the fallen creature, ripping and tearing, fighting each other in their eagerness. Calard saw the beasts feasting on the entrails of the unfortunate creature, pulling on intestines with their teeth and claws, and fighting over the organs. When they stepped back, mere moments later, they left a trampled, bloody and mutilated corpse, and they smeared the creature's fresh blood across their chests.

There were clearly rivalries and blood feuds between the different groups of creatures, and members of the herds fronted up to each other, snarling and smashing weapons together, trying to prove their dominance over each other. Calard saw several violent clashes, as beasts slammed their horned heads together with bone-jarring force.

Most of the creatures wore little more than straps of leather across their bodies, though others wore scraps of armour that had clearly been scrounged from fallen enemies. One group wore thick plate armour that had been blackened with fire and beaten to fit their bodies. Plates of metal had been hammered into their heads, roughly hewn and cut to fit around their curling horns. These creatures bore immense, long-hafted axes and blades that they carried on their shoulders.

Even larger creatures stalked through the milling press, hulking monsters with blood-shot eyes, standing over eight feet tall, and with the heads of bulls. The smaller beasts hissed at them behind their backs, but scurried out of their paths wherever they walked.

Other nameless and formless horrors crashed through the trees, hauled into the clearing by giant chains and hooks that tore at their flesh. They were sickening, mutated mounds of fur, muscle and bone, and they screamed and howled in agony and mindless fury from mouths that opened up across their skin, and emerged from the tips of writhing tentacles. They were horrid amalgamations of torsos, heads, horns and limbs that seemed to protrude at random from their flesh, and Calard felt horrified loathing as he looked upon them.

Dozens of straining beastmen dragged one of the massive beast-spawn monstrosities forwards. Thick rings of iron pierced its flesh, and its skin was pulled taut, like canvas sails, by the black chains attached to them. It screamed and roared as it fought against its captors. Spines of bone and horn erupted from its back, and it swung its crab-like claws at any who got too close. Another of the creatures was covered in open sores that wept pus and blood, and maggots writhed beneath its skin, making it ripple like a pennant in the wind. It had a pair of conjoined horse's heads, though spines had erupted above and below their eyes, and long, barbed tongues flashed from their toothy maws.

A massive, toothed orifice gaped open in the chest of another monster, displaying thousands of inward curving teeth and an array of barbed tentacles that waved blindly. A distressingly human head emerged above this foetid, circular maw, a single blinking, red eye peering out through the crooked teeth of its slack-jawed mouth.

One of the beastmen pulling the creatures forwards stumbled and fell, and was instantly lifted up into the air by a pair of malformed flipper-like appendages. It was stuffed into a flapping mouth that was too small to contain its oversized teeth. The beastman bellowed as it was devoured. Additional mouths opened up upon the spawn's body, and slug-like tongues lapped at the blood upon its flesh.

All the while, more of the beastmen massed along the tree line, and the blare of horns and beating of drums rose to a chaotic, jumbled cacophony of tortured sounds.

Calard saw the men-at-arms below the hill shuffle and glance around at each other, their fear palpable. The knights leading the cohorts shouted encouragement to the soldiers, but their voices were tense and strained. Gringolet whinnied nervously as the scent of the beasts carried to him on the wind.

'Easy,' said Calard as he patted the destrier's neck in reassurance. The steeds of the knights around him flattened their ears against their heads, and one of them reared, hooves flailing out blindly, but the knight quickly regained control of his mount.

A tall, hellish creature stepped from the forest, surrounded by heavily armoured beastmen. It clearly commanded respect from its minions, and silence descended around the clearing. The pounding of drums stopped mid-beat, and the horns were silenced. The braying and roaring of the beasts dropped away, and even the massive war hounds slunk low to the ground, snarling, their tails between their legs, as the creature stepped forwards.

Its face was a mass of stitches, fur and skin, and three pairs of horns erupted from its head. It drew to a halt just metres from the forest edge, and stared up at the Bretonnians before it balefully. Thorns and briars flowed across the ground around it, erupting from the soil wherever the unnatural creature trod. Calard jerked as he felt the creature's eyes upon him, though that was surely impossible, for the beast was many hundreds of yards away.

It slammed its twisted, branch-like staff heavily into the ground, where it took root, bony tendrils penetrating the earth. The black birds overhead dropped like stones from the sky, swooping low over the battlefield to come to rest upon the branches of the staff, turning their malevolent, burning red eyes towards the defenders on the hill.

Lifting an arm, the creature extended a long, multi-jointed finger. It looked like the slender leg of a monstrous spider as it pointed towards the Bretonnians. To Calard, it felt as though the creature was pointing directly at him.

A mighty roar echoed across the clearing. The cacophony of noise began anew, and the beastmen began loping towards the hill in the centre of the clearing.

From every side they came, like a wolf pack moving in for the kill.

GUNTHAR JERKED AWAKE, the sound of horns filling his ears. He reached for his sword, but hands held him down. He swore, fighting against them, kicking and thrashing. He almost passed out from the pain, but struggled to maintain consciousness.

'Leave him be,' said a voice, and the bodies pressing down on top of him eased away. Breathing heavily and covered in sweat, Gunthar swung his legs over the side of the pallet, and staggered to his feet, eyes darting around. His vision swam, and he reeled, his left leg giving way beneath him. He caught himself, and stood straight once more, though his left leg was shaking and unsteady.

His feverish eyes darted around, looking at the anxious faces of the peasants that had been holding him down.

'What in the Lady's name is going on?' Gunthar managed. In the distance, he could hear the hellish sounds of the enemy. 'The camp is under attack!' he said in shock, as realisation began to sink into his feverish mind.

'You must lie back, my lord!' said a small, middle-aged man emphatically. Gunthar recognised him as Montcadas's surgeon. The ageing man had a small saw in his hand, and wore a dirty apron over his slight frame.

'Damned if I will,' snarled Gunthar. The peasants looked nervous and scared. He shouted for his arms and armour, and they jumped, but did not move to enact his order. Pain shot down his leg, and he was falling once more. He sat down heavily on the pallet. His brow was covered in sweat, and his vision blurred before him. He shook his head, and wiped a hand across his brow.

'The wound is festering, my lord!' said the surgeon.

'You were going to take my leg, damn you!' raged Gunthar, realisation dawning on him.

The little surgeon guiltily placed the saw on a small table, upon which was laid all manner of knives and other implements. They looked like the tools of a torturer. The little man wrung his hands in front of him. 'It is the only way to save your life, my lord!'

'What a life that would be! No, I will not face that dishonour.' He licked his lips. His throat felt dry and thick. 'Bring me water!' he ordered one of the men, and a wooden goblet was pressed into his shaking hands. He put it to his lips, not caring that it was a crude drinking vessel fit only for a peasant. The water was cool and soothing, and he knocked it back in one long swig.

'You would be alive,' said the surgeon softly.

'I would rather be dead than live like that,' spat Gunthar. He realised that he was dressed in nothing more than a gown over his underclothes, and he gingerly pulled back the cloth to look upon his wound. He bit his lip as the material tore away from the wound, and he tasted blood in his mouth. His vision swam once more, but he blinked quickly, trying to focus his mind.

Around three inches above his knee, the injury he had sustained was angry and red, weeping a sickly looking fluid, the flesh around it rotting and festering. He gagged at the stink of the wound, despite the honey smeared over it.

He had seen enough wounds in his time as a knight to know that if the leg was not removed the wound would kill him. He stared at it in shock for a time, and swore under his breath. He heard men shouting orders outside in the gloom, and the roar of the enemy.

Gunthar's gaze hardened, and he turned towards the surgeon's underlings. They were still standing around awkwardly, unsure what to do. 'My arms and armour, damn you!' he shouted, making them jump again. 'Go and get them now! And bring me my horse!'

The men looked to the surgeon nervously.

'What are you looking to him for? I am a knight of Bastonne, and you *will* obey me, or I shall see you hanged! Go! *Now*!'

The men fled, running to fulfil Gunthar's orders.

'You are in no state to fight, my lord!' the small man said with serious conviction.

Gunthar swung his fevered gaze back towards the diminutive surgeon, bristling in anger. The man's face was lined with concern, and he felt the anger seep from him. He was so tired. It felt like he had been kicked and trampled by a wild stallion. Everything hurt. He sighed, his shoulders sagging.

'I know,' he said finally, 'but I will not lie here while others are dying.'

'I will not lie to you, amputating a leg is not without its risks,' said the little surgeon softly. 'I have performed the procedure twenty-three times. Seven of those men died through loss of blood, and your age would count against you, but if the limb is not amputated you *will* die, no question. This I know with certainty. What good will you be to Bretonnia then?' He looked at Gunthar with weary eyes.

'You are right,' said Gunthar with resignation. 'My death might well mean nothing. Whether I fight or not will not alter the outcome of the battle.' He sighed wearily, talking more to himself than to the surgeon. 'Fighting Ganelon was humbling. Fifteen years ago, I would have bested him without breaking a sweat. That duel made me feel old.'

'You still won,' said the surgeon softly.

'Yes, and a skilful young knight of Bretonnia died,' said Gunthar. 'Who is to say what great things he may have achieved had he lived? We will never know.' Gunthar laughed softly and without humour.

'You could have many more years ahead of you, my lord. Who is to say what great things *you* may achieve?'

'Perhaps, but I have no wish to live out the remainder of my years as an invalid, an embarrassing cripple unable to fight for my lord when the call to battle is sounded. I could not live like that.'

'So you choose to die?'

'I choose to die as a knight of Bretonnia,' Gunthar said weakly. 'I will ride to battle, with my sword in my hand and with the enemy in front of me, and, if such is to be my fate, I will die.'

The surgeon sighed, looking exhausted and dejected.

'I am no warrior,' said the little man. 'I abhor violence in all its forms. I believe that life is a precious gift, and that it should not be set aside lightly. I have held the hands of hundreds of men as they died in torment from sickening wounds. I have seen countless young knights screaming in agony, tears of shame rolling down their faces as they lose control of their bodily functions. I have seen knights weep like babes as they try to hold their insides from spilling from their bellies. I see no pride in their deaths. I am not of noble birth, and as such perhaps I am incapable of understanding such things. Despite all of that, I will respect your wish, even if I disagree with it. A man should always be allowed to make his own choice of how he lives. Or dies.'

'Good. Now help me up,' said Gunthar.

A SINGLE ARROW was loosed, soaring high into the air.

'Hold, damn you!'

The arrow arced high into the air before reaching the top of its trajectory. It seemed to hang in the sky for a moment, defying the forces that were pulling it back to earth, before hurtling down into the ground, sinking into the earth several hundred yards in front of the advancing mass of bodies.

Giant hounds, mutated far beyond their natural size, pounded across the grass, their tongues lolling from slavering mouths. They streamed out in a wave before the beastmen running swiftly behind them. Like a deadly tide, they swarmed towards the Bretonnian lines.

Calard had to restrain his urge to drive his heels into Gringolet's sides, and charge out to meet them head-on. He could see that Bertelis was struggling with the same internal urges.

'I hate letting them come to us,' his half-brother said. 'The peasants will break and flee. Mark my words.'

'There is nowhere for them *to* flee,' remarked one of the knights at their side. Bertelis grunted in response.

More of the enemy were streaming from the trees on all sides, spilling out like arterial blood from a slashed vein.

'Lady above, but there are a lot of them,' said Calard.

At the base of the hill, stray arrows were being loosed by the Garamont bowmen, despite the shouted orders to hold. Calard swore, and kicked his steed forward, leaving the formation.

He thundered down the hill, and rode along the front of the lines of peasants. He swung his horse around, his face angry.

'The next man that looses an arrow before he is ordered to will be cut down, here and now!' he roared. 'You *will* wait for the order!'

He turned to face the enemy, which was racing across the field in a solid mass, and lifted his lance high in the air. The night was lit with hundreds of torches and braziers, and though the moons had not yet risen, the numberless horde of the enemy could be easily picked out.

'Hold!' he shouted, his voice carrying over the righteous din. The open ground before the archers had been paced out, and Calard had memorised the distances. The closest enemy was still almost three hundred and fifty yards away. Though an exceptionally strong bowman may be able to fire such a distance, it was too far for the shot to be effective. 'Hold!'

The enemy closed with sickening speed, far quicker than a man could run, and Calard felt a bead of sweat run down the side of his face. The slavering hounds in front began to outdistance the beastmen behind, racing over the grass with bounding leaps.

Calard blinked the sweat out of his eyes, still holding his lance aloft. The enemy leapt the low scrub bushes that roughly marked three hundred yards distance. He resisted the urge to drop his lance and order the attack. He could see more details on the creatures now: the angry brands that had been seared into the flesh of the monstrous hounds, the bronze-covered tusks that sprouted from the massive jaws of the largest beasts.

'Draw!' roared Calard, and the archers drew back their bowstrings, lifting the long weapons high.

The lead war hound, a monster of immense size with a row of horns sprouting from its head, passed a stand of low rocks that marked the two hundred and fifty yard mark.

'Now!' he roared, lowering his lance in the direction of the enemy. As one, the bowmen loosed, and hundreds of arrows hissed into the air. It looked like a dense flock of birds streaking high into the sky. Before

they reached the fullness of their flight, a second volley was loosed. The third was fired just as the first
cloud of arrows struck home.

There were roars of pain as the arrows sliced down
into the massed enemy with lethal force. Scores fell as
the arrows slammed home, driving through muscle
and flesh. The enemy was too far distant for the
archers to pick out individual targets, but it didn't matter. They were so densely packed that almost every
arrow found a mark.

The second volley struck, and Calard saw more
beasts stumble and fall as the lethal shafts slammed
into unprotected necks, heads and shoulders. A pair of
arrows had driven into the thick neck of the hound
leading the pack, but it was barely slowed.

All around Adhalind's Seat, thousands of arrows
were loosed in those first moments of battle, and
countless hundreds of the enemy were felled. Those
that did not die were trampled into the ground by
those behind them.

Still, on the enemy came, charging through the devastating volleys towards the Bretonnian lines. As the
distance closed, the bow fire became even more effective,
and innumerable foes were cut down by the relentless
storm of arrows. Beasts writhed in agony, pulling themselves forwards with their hands, desperate to be part of
the carnage that was about to erupt. The ground was littered with thousands of twitching bodies that struggled
to rise, only to be crushed by the hooves and claws of
those pressing forward behind them.

Then the first wave of the enemy struck the Bretonnian lines, and the real bloodshed began.

* * *

RADEGAR'S HEART WAS beating fiercely, his breath rapid and shallow as the twisted beasts of the forest screamed towards him. He clenched his hands around the rough-hewn shaft of his polearm, and licked his cracked lips, determined not to show his fear.

It had been a fine day when he had been chosen to join the Garamont soldiery. He didn't know how old he was, perhaps fourteen, and he had lined up alongside two hundred other young men, trying to stand tall and straight. He had been in awe as he stood beneath the shadow of the grand castle of his lord, and had gaped open-mouthed at the figure of Lord Lutheure, flanked by a dozen knights of the realm, fully garbed in their battle armour.

His heart had raced then as well.

'Don't slouch,' his father had said to him before he had left his home that morning, two hours before dawn, 'and if you are not chosen, do not return, for we cannot feed you.'

He had travelled by wagon that morning, along with the other hopefuls. Once a year, all the eligible peasants under Garamont's protection travelled to the castle in the hope of being picked to join the men-at-arms. The wagon had been filled with other boys his age, each one of them dreaming of joining the esteemed ranks of the soldiery.

He had puffed out his chest as the giant, scarred yeoman had stalked in front of the long line of hopefuls, a deep scowl upon his face. Fully half the gathered peasants he had dismissed instantly for being too small or weak from malnutrition. Others were dismissed because of their hunched backs, or because one of their limbs was wasted and useless. Others were sent home because their club-like hands were incapable of holding a weapon, and others because they were plainly simple in the head, drool dribbling from their slack lips.

Unlike his younger brother, who had passed into Morr's care the previous winter, Radegar was lucky enough to have been born with two arms and two legs, and his hands were fully functional, even though he had six fingers on his left. He was broad-shouldered, though when relaxed they tended to slump inwards, and his arms were strong from hard labour.

Every time the brutal yeoman stalked past, Radegar would pull his shoulders square and stand tall, trying to look as strong and capable as possible. Nervousness had clawed at him as the group was whittled down, and his heart had soared as he was chosen to pass through to the next round of cuts.

The remaining boys had been given wooden staves, and organised into pairs. Radegar had been paired up with a boy from his own village, who was tall for his age. In the bout that had followed, Radegar had knocked the boy senseless. He did not feel any remorse.

He had grinned like an idiot when he had been chosen to join the ranks of the men-at-arms, and he had willingly sworn his oath before the castellan with eleven others that had been deemed worthy.

He had been given five copper coins, and his hands had shook as he held them. He had never even seen such a princely sum of money, let alone held it in his hands. One of the coins was taken from him instantly, to pay for the costs of his burial should he fall in battle. Three others were used to pay for his weapon, his tabard, his leather cap and his board. He had felt seven feet tall when he had first worn the tabard, after he had scrubbed out the blood of its previous owner.

It was Castellan Lutheure's duty to provide protection for those in his service, and he had fulfilled this commitment by presenting each of the recruits with a long, rectangular shield bearing the Garamont colours and heraldry. They had seen much service already, but Radegar didn't care. Of course, if he allowed the shield to be damaged or, Shallya forbid, he lost it, he would be taxed accordingly, but Radegar had been too thrilled at receiving his post to be concerned. His final copper coin had gone to pay for training, though he had received two copper bits after his first six months of service. Proudly, he had organised one of them to be given to his family, and the other had gone towards his board.

It had been such a proud day for him, receiving his first pay. Four years had past since then, and now at around eighteen, he was regarded as a veteran. He had fought in two battles, and killed three of his lord's enemies. In the second battle, he had almost been killed but he had defied death and recovered from his wounds. But he had never had to face a foe such as he faced this day.

The big, scarred yeoman that had selected him four years earlier stood nearby, his perpetual scowl stamped on his face. The man seemed undaunted by anything, and he stood glaring at the approaching enemy, his thick-bladed sword held in his right hand. Even though the weapon was missing its tip and bore more than a hint of rust, that the yeoman was allowed to bear a sword at all was testament to the level of trust placed in him. Radegar would not allow himself to show any fear in front of the man, who he still regarded with a mixture of respect and fear.

More than the presence of this brutal yeoman, however; it was the fact that a knight of the realm stood within their ranks that made Radegar swell with pride and push his fear deep within him. The knight's helmet was high and had a miniature heraldic dragon upon its crest, and his armour gleamed in the flickering light given off by the braziers nearby. Radegar was deeply honoured to be standing alongside one of the nobility, and he swore that he would not fail in his duty. No, it would be a fate far worse than death to quake in fear in front of such a noble knight. Surely, as long as the regal knight stood against their fore, they would hold.

The enemy bore down on them, screaming and roaring, even as hundreds of flights of arrows continued to pepper their ranks from the hillside behind.

'This is it, boys,' bellowed the yeoman. 'Don't you shame me now, or I'll cut off yer ears and eat them for breakfast! For Garamont!'

Radegar braced himself. He leant his left shoulder forwards, so that his shield protected him, and the man to his left, just as the man to his right protected him. Each of the men-at-arms carried a long polearm, and the spikes of the unwieldy weapons were lowered to create a nigh on impenetrable wall of death.

The first of the gigantic hellhounds leapt between two of the heavy wooden stakes that had been driven into the ground in front of the men-at-arms. Its immense shoulders were covered in mangy, matted fur, and its eyes reflected the flames of the braziers.

It hurled itself at the dragon-helmed knight, and its massive paws slammed into his armoured chest, bowling him backwards even as his sword blade penetrated the beast's chest. With one savage bite, the knight's head, helmet and all, was ripped from his shoulders, and blood sprayed out like a fountain. The beast's thick body was impaled by polearms, but it had done its work, and Radegar felt panic begin to rise within him. It had happened so fast.

He had no time to think, as scores of the massive hounds struck the line. Radegar thrust his polearm forward, taking one of the beasts squarely in the chest. The force of the beast's momentum knocked him back a step, into the men behind him, and his feet slipped in the mud.

He saw his scowling yeoman hack his blade into the side of the head of another beast, the sword biting deep. Radegar pulled his weapon back, and with a shout he thrust again, feeling his weapon bite into flesh.

The man to his right dropped to his knees as a massive weight dragged his shield low, and in the next instant a snarling beast tore his face off with a snap of its jaws. The axe-head of a polearm slammed down onto the beast's skull, cracking it like a nut, and it died instantly, blood and brain splattering. Men were shouting in fear, panic and anger, and order began to be lost. More holes were made in the shield-wall as men died, some as their arms were savagely ripped from their sockets by the monstrous hounds and others as massive jaws ripped at their throats, spraying blood wildly.

Radegar shouted wordlessly as he struck. A heavy weight slammed against his shield, and he was pushed backwards again. In that moment, Radegar knew that the line was going to break, and that he was going to die.

A hulking, goat-legged creature appeared before him, its snarling face that of an animal's, though its eyes burned with feral intelligence. It held a curved blade in one hand, and leapt towards him. Radegar thrust his polearm desperately towards the creature. It swayed aside from the point, grabbed the haft of the polearm in one thick hand and pulled it violently towards it. Radegar was jerked forwards, stumbling off balance towards the beastman.

The beast's blade flashed, and Radegar screamed as it sliced deep into his shoulder, cleaving muscle and flesh, and striking the bone with crippling force. His weapon dropped from fingers that he could no longer feel, and he fell to the ground before the massive creature. Its stench was overpowering, like rotting meat and urine, and it loomed above him, swinging its murderous blade.

I am dead, thought Radegar. Cloven hooves pounded as the enemy drove over the top of him. He was kicked in the head, and felt one of his legs break as a heavy cloven hoof stamped down upon the limb. Moaning in agony and fear, he waited for the fatal blow to fall, praying to Shallya that it would be swift.

Rough hands gripped him around his armpits, and he cried out in pain. His eyes lolled around in their sockets, and his body was slick with blood, but, for a moment, he thought he was being rescued, carried free of the battle. A glimmer of hope flickered within him.

That hope was dashed as his eyes came into focus. He was being dragged *away* from the Bretonnian lines.

An animal groan of panic escaped his lips, and he began to fight against the stinking creature hauling him away. He kicked out and thrashed around. Hands slick with his blood slipped, and Radegar was dropped heavily to the ground. There was an angry snarl, and a hoof struck him in the side of the head. He tasted blood in his mouth, and spat out shattered teeth.

The beast grabbed him around his broken leg, and began dragging him backwards through the mud, and he screamed again. His shield, the precious shield bearing the honourable heraldry of Garamont, was still attached to his arm, and it carved a furrow in the earth behind him.

Then, blessedly, he was released from his torment as he slipped into unconsciousness.

'WHAT IN THE Lady's name are they doing?' breathed Calard in horror. Scores of men-at-arms were being hauled away from the front line by the beastmen. They were being dragged kicking and screaming back towards the distant tree line, where the monstrous tall beast stood pacing back and forth like a caged animal, surrounded by its heavily armoured guard.

He had no time to consider the grim fate of these men, however, as trumpets blared, and the order to charge was declared.

Calard slammed down the visor of his simple, unadorned helmet and kicked Gringolet into a gallop.

All around Adhalind's Seat, knights charged.

The ranks of the men-at-arms opened up before the knights errant, and they charged through the gap. They covered fifty yards in seconds, and Calard felt the thrill of battle wash over him.

Beastmen streamed into the gap created by the parting ranks of the Bretonnian infantry, and lances were
lowered. Tensing for the impact, Calard picked his target, a hulking brute with horns spiralling from its
forehead, wielding a pair of rusted cleavers.

The knights ploughed into the enemy, and Calard's
lance took his foe squarely in the chest, punching
through its ribcage. It fell to the ground, blood pumping from the wound, tearing the lance from Calard's
hands, and his sword flashed into his hand in an
instant.

Swinging the blade in a low arc, Calard carved a
bloody slash across the neck of another enemy, and it
fell with a scream, even as another lance tore through
its shoulder, smashing it to the ground.

On the knights errant charged, driving through the
enemy ranks and smashing them aside. Spears and
blades glanced off shields and armour, and dozens of
beastmen were crushed to the ground, trampled into
pulp beneath the hooves of the destriers. The ground
trembled beneath the charge of the knights. Nothing
could stand in their path.

Surging through the press, the formation swung to
the north, riding hard in front of the line of angled
stakes, tearing through the enemy pushing forward
there. Faced with enemies on two sides, the beastmen
fought desperately, many of them turning towards this
new threat only to be cut down by the men-at-arms
that, at that moment, surged forward through the
stakes, stabbing and cutting.

Hundreds more beastmen surged forwards at the
knights, screaming as they ran, covering the ground
with swift leaps and bounds. They came on in an

endless tide, and the air was filled with their braying roars.

Calard shattered the horns and skull of another beast with a downward strike, and reeled backwards in the saddle as a blade slammed into his shield, almost knocking him from the saddle. He fought for balance, his arm tingling from the impact, but remained in tight formation with the other knights. The knights errant swung around in a wide arc, cutting and killing, struggling to maintain their impetus.

A monstrous form burst through the tide of enemies, tossing beastmen aside in its eagerness to kill. Its immense, mutated form was covered in spines of bone and snapping jaws, and rents in its flesh gaped open, exposing countless mouths and tongues that writhed like serpents. It trailed lengths of chain behind it, and rampaged forwards, needing no goading now that the scent of blood was heavy in the air. A myriad of blood-shot eyes on stalks swung towards the knights, and it screamed in pain and bloodlust, the sound ripping forth from half a dozen throats. With a shout, the knights angled towards the monstrosity, cutting down the savage beastmen in their path.

A thick neck of glistening, exposed muscle burst from within the hulking mass, and snapping jaws closed around the neck of a horse, even as five lances drove home into the beast. Arms ending in bony spurs punched forward, skewering knights and tearing them from their saddles, and lashing tentacles wrapped around steeds, burrowing through flesh and eye-sockets, dragging them down.

Calard slashed with his sword, severing half a dozen eyestalks that spurted black, hissing blood as they were cut, and the remaining eyes retracted within the monstrous creature's body. More lances and swords plunged into its malformed bulk, and its lifeblood gushed forth in a torrent, spurting from a dozen wounds.

It flopped to the ground, thrashing madly in its death spasms, killing another pair of knights as it died. A spear smashed into the side of Calard's helmet, and he reeled, his ears ringing, and he saw scores of beastmen closing in around them. He kicked Gringolet forward with a shout, and the knights were then galloping clear, leaving the dying monstrosity behind them.

A horse collapsed as a swinging axe chopped its legs from beneath it, and it screamed as it fell, the knight borne upon the beast sailing into the air. The knight directly behind the fallen warhorse had no time to react, and his steed broke its front legs as it stumbled over the flailing beast. The fallen knights were set upon instantly by savage beastmen, their helmets caved in with powerful blows.

Galloping directly towards Adhalind's Seat, the massed forces of the enemy scattering before them, the knights errant urged their steeds on. The men-at-arms again parted before them, and they thundered through the gap. The ranks closed behind them, and it was only then that Calard saw how many of his comrades had fallen.

Suddenly fearful, he glanced around to see his brother. Bertelis was there, at his side, his armour splattered with blood, and he exhaled in relief. Lifting his visor, Bertelis gave him a savage grin.

Bloodied, the knights errant cantered up the hillside, and wheeled around to face the battlefield once more.

Peasants ran forward, handing fresh lances to them, and passing them flagons of water.

Hundreds of beastmen were still streaming from the trees in a relentless, never ending swarm, and Calard felt a stab of panic. He had barely survived the first charge, but it had made virtually no impact on the enemy ranks. Breathing heavily, he took a sip of water, before passing the skin back to a peasant and making ready for another charge. It was going to be a long night.

CHAPTER SIXTEEN

CHLOD SWORE AGAIN, tears of unrestrained terror running down his blotchy cheeks. He was pushed roughly from behind, and he stumbled forward. There was no way he could see that he could get out of this, and he cursed himself for a fool. He had thought he was so clever in seeking refuge amongst the pilgrims, but now he saw that he had doomed himself.

He was in the middle of the group of fervent men, being bustled and pushed from all sides. He could not have fought his way clear of them if he tried, which in fact, he had.

He had been enjoying the hospitality of the pilgrims and the sudden esteem he had gained since he had been 'healed' of his feined blindness. He had eaten better than he had done in weeks, happy to speak loudly of the miracle he had received in exchange for food and cheap wine. He had even accepted the heavy, spiked club that he had been given, thinking that, if nothing else, it could be sold or traded at a later date.

He had certainly not expected to be physically dragged into battle by the fervent pilgrims. They were madmen, he had decided; insane, deluded madmen obsessed with achieving recognition, however slight, from the object of their idolisation. They would gladly throw themselves onto the swords of the enemy if they thought that it would garner a nod from the grail knight, and indeed he had seen several individuals do just that.

The pilgrims did everything they could to be noticed by the grail knight. They cooked and cleaned for him, doted on his every word, and spit-polished his armour and boots, under the watchful eyes of his servants and squires to ensure they did not make off with anything. They threw flowers before him, and proclaimed his good deeds wherever he travelled. They immortalised him in song, and his every pronouncement, however mundane, was memorised and deemed as sacred testament.

The grail knight tolerated them at best, and did not acknowledge their presence in the slightest. So, when he had approached the pilgrims and said the words, 'Gather your weapons. We fight the enemies of Bretonnia this day,' his words were greeted with impassioned enthusiasm and fanatical devotion.

Chlod had never been in a battle before, not like this, and it terrified him. The screams of the dying and the brutal clash of weapons, the roars of the enemy and even the frenzied cries of the pilgrims, all filled him with terror.

Short even for a peasant, a fact not aided by his pronounced hump and stooped posture, he could see barely a thing, except for the back of those in front of him. Of the enemy he had seen no sign, but he could hear their savage roars and braying shouts, and he was not ashamed to feel his bladder loosen, and warmth run down his legs.

The pilgrims pushed and shoved, desperately trying to get to the front of the mayhem. Chlod tried to squirm and muscle his way further back, away from the front line, but, despite all his efforts, he was carried forwards, driven closer and closer to the terrifying sounds of slaughter.

Blood splattered into his face. The crowd surged forwards again, and Chlod could not help but trample over a fallen man, who screamed and reached out for him. Fearing that he would be dragged down under the surging crowd, Chlod knocked away the man's grabbing hands with the base of his spiked club, breaking his fingers.

Then he saw the enemy, and he thought he would die on the spot from sheer panic. Taller by far than any of the peasants, they had the heads of goats twisted into hellish, daemonic visages, sharp teeth protruding from bleating mouths.

They slashed with axes and swords, dismembering the pilgrims with savage fury. He saw one of them fall, a shattered sword stabbing into its neck, and blood drenched pilgrims fell upon it in a fury, stabbing with knives and hacking with axes.

For each of the enemy that fell, three or more of the devout, fanatical peasants were slain. The enemy was cleaving through the tightly-packed ranks of the peasants like scythes through wheat, and Chlod pushed back away from them with all his strength.

Only a few men stood between him and the foe, but try as he might, he could not pull away from them. Screaming incoherently, or bellowing the name of Reolus, the peasants surged forwards once more, and Chlod was driven closer to the enemy than ever.

An axe sang through the air and slammed into the neck of the man in front of him, and arterial blood sprayed across his uneven features. He could taste the hot blood on his lips, and could smell it in his nostrils. Then the man fell. The beastman struggled with its axe, the blade lodged between two vertebrae, and with a shout, the man next to Chlod rammed his rusted, scavenged sword into its belly. A second blade stabbed into its heavily muscled thigh, and it swung its arm around, smashing its shield into the face of one of its attackers, breaking the pilgrim's jaw and half-ripping it from his face.

A powerful shove propelled Chlod towards the beast, just as it managed to tear its axe free of the corpse on the ground. With a shout of sheer terror, he lifted his spiked club in both hands and slammed it into the creature's head. It fell to its knees, but was still alive and dangerous, and so Chlod rammed his club into its face again, knocking it backwards.

Blood covered his face, and he trembled uncontrollably. Then he was driven forwards once again by the surging crowd, and Chlod's voice joined with the chorus of manic screams.

DIETER WESCHLER, CAPTAIN within the Reikland state army and second cousin once removed from Emperor Karl Franz, had decided that he hated Bretonnia. He had an official function and duty to perform here, however, and was careful to maintain an air of civility. His duty had been given to him by the Emperor, and he would not allow his feelings and prejudices to betray him.

'A show of solidarity between neighbouring nations,' he had been told.

The nobles of this land were pompous and arrogant, and their peasants were downtrodden and lived in despicable, crushing poverty. How a nation could laud itself as being honourable while it was clearly so corrupt was beyond him. Behind the carefully constructed veneer of honourable conduct, this land was decaying and crumbling, self-centred and self-aggrandising.

What's more, he would probably die fighting alongside them. It was a galling thought.

The pistol in his hand boomed as its wheel-lock mechanism created the spark that ignited the black powder, and the back of a beastman's head exploded outwards in a spray of shattered bone and gore. Quickly holstering the precious weapon, he smoothly drew another.

Hundreds of knights were locked in battle beyond the rows of stakes in the ground, and he could see that if they were not supported, they would be surrounded and mercilessly cut down in moments. Dieter swore at the foolishness and arrogance of the knights. Could they not see that as soon as their momentum slowed, they were going to be surrounded and butchered?

Battle instincts that had been honed through years of service as an infantry sergeant, before he had been elevated to captain, reared within him.

'Sound the advance,' he ordered the peasant holding a rusted horn in his shaking hands. The man had only just taken on the role, after the head of the previous musician had been hacked from his shoulders only moments earlier. Dieter had slain the offending beast, and handed this witless peasant the instrument.

'Sound the advance,' he repeated. The man just stared at him blankly, and then lifted the horn to his mouth. His face went red with exertion, but his enthusiasm did not match the sound coming from the instrument. It sounded like a baby blowing bubbles of spit.

'Oh, for Sigmar's sake,' snapped Dieter. He lifted his sabre up high in to the air before him. 'Forward!' he roared, his voice, honed on the parade ground, easily carrying over the din of battle. He stepped forwards into the breach as the enemy gathered their strength beyond the wall of deadly stakes.

Nobody followed his move, and he cursed himself for a fool. These simple peasants could not understand Reikspiel, the language of the Empire. He repeated his order, this time bellowing it in the Bretonnian tongue.

They were the worst soldiers that he had ever led, even worse than the stubborn Middenlanders. At least the northern men could fight, even if they questioned every order he gave them. These men-at-arms were ill-disciplined and poorly equipped, and had clearly received only rudimentary training. They were not fit to be soldiers at all, in Dieter's mind, but then he was not surprised. The nobility were utterly obsessed with fighting on horseback, and gave little thought to the strategic use of infantry, no matter the fighting conditions or the foe.

'Forward, damn you!' shouted Dieter, his generally stoic manner cracking, and finally the men-at-arms began to advance.

They marched out between the angled stakes, pushing past dozens of impaled bodies. So thick had been the crush of the enemy charging at their line that scores of them had run blindly onto the fire-hardened spikes. Dieter dispatched a twitching, goat-headed creature that was trying to pull itself off a stake with a slashing cut that severed its spine.

Some fifty paces ahead, two formations of knights were locked in deadly combat as they fought vainly to ride free. They had lost all momentum, however, and were being surrounded by ever more enemy warriors, who were dragging them from their saddles and butchering them with savage, chopping blows.

'Charge them!' roared Dieter, and he ran forwards, praying to Sigmar that the men-at-arms were following.

Montcadas had clearly been uneasy when Dieter had requested to fight alongside the infantry. In truth, it was clear that the baron had not wished Dieter to fight at all, for fear of the political repercussions if he died while under Bretonnian hospitality.

'The Emperor would wish me to fight alongside his Bretonnian brothers,' Dieter had replied. 'Just as I know that if ever the Empire was in need of aid, Bretonnia would support it.'

In truth, Dieter found all the politics wearing, and he longed to return to his former, simpler life as an officer in the state army of Reikland. This was certainly a far cry from the disciplined ranks of halberdiers he had commanded, but one could not always choose one's tools.

The simple peasants had been frightened by his wheel-lock weapons, and had recoiled back from him as he had fired the handgun, crafted by the finest engineers of Nuln. The ignorant savages had thought it some form of witchcraft.

Dieter charged towards the swelling mass of unruly creatures surrounding the beleaguered knights. Levelling one of his pistols, he fired, and an enemy was sent crashing backwards, its skull pierced by the lead shot. With a shout, he reached the enemy, and slashed his sabre across the chest of one of the hulking beasts.

The men-at-arms struck then, swinging their polearms into the enemy with more desperation than skill. He saw several beasts go down, but many more turned aside the clumsy blows with swords and shields, only to tear into the peasants with brutal savagery, cutting then down in swathes.

Still, there were over a hundred peasants in the formation, and they pushed forwards relentlessly, stabbing and cutting. They took down perhaps one beast for every three of their number that fell. It was a staggeringly poor performance, but the charge was having the desired effect.

With the weight of numbers supporting them, the knights were finally able to kick their steeds free of the deadly melee, though the ground was littered with the corpses of those who had not been so lucky.

The men-at-arms were left unsupported, and Dieter knew that they would break at any moment. They were poor warriors at best, and were being slaughtered by the monstrous beasts. Dieter was walking steadily backwards, his sabre flashing left and right defensively as the enemy surged forwards.

He knew there would be no chance of an ordered retreat, and he saw the fear and panic in the eyes of the men around him. Any moment now, their resolve would be shattered. It would start with just one man turning and running, and then all semblance of order would be lost.

An axe swung at his head, and he ducked backwards, stumbling into a peasant and almost falling. A jagged spearhead thrust towards his lacquered black breast-plate, and he turned it aside with a deft parry. His blade flashed back in a lightning riposte that stabbed into the beast's groin, and blood sprayed.

Bellowing roars echoed deafeningly over the already horrendous din, and Dieter saw massive creatures of muscle and horn rampage towards the faltering line of men-at-arms.

Half again as tall as the largest of the peasants, these behemoths smashed aside their smaller kin in their lust to kill. They broke limbs and shattered bones, their giant axes and cleavers cutting through any that were too slow to get out of their way. Snorting and stamping, the minotaurs lowered their heads and charged through the press, crushing bodies under their cloven hooves, and throwing beastmen over their shoulders with dipping sweeps of their heavy heads.

The resolve of the men-at-arms was shattered, like a delicate crystal goblet beneath a hammer blow. The peasant soldiers turned and fled, scrabbling over each other in their blind rout.

Dieter was not a stupid man, and he had no intention of throwing his life away for some pointless show of bravery. While the foolish Bretonnian nobility may have seen it as a gross display of dishonour, Dieter turned and ran for his life.

Lord Reolus lowered his glowing lance and charged. He thundered over the rough ground, eyes blazing with holy fury as he focused on the phalanx of rampaging bull-headed monsters.

He aimed the tip of the sacred lance, Arandyal, at the neck of the closest of the hulking creatures as it ploughed into the infantry. It swung its lowered head sideways, impaling one man upon its bronze-tipped horns. With a flick of its head, it sent the man spiralling up into the air like a rag-doll. As the peasant came tumbling down, the minotaur's giant axe arced up to meet him. The axe cleaved through flesh and spine, hacking the man in two.

Greedily, the towering beast grabbed the upper half of the fallen man in one hand, lifting it up to its mouth to drink of the blood gushing from the terrible wound. Rivulets of hot crimson ran down the beast's neck and chest, its tongue squirming like a monstrous worm in the entrails of its prey. Engrossed in its gory feast, it saw the approach of Reolus and his knights too late.

Arandyal speared towards the minotaur's thick neck, but, with inhuman speed, it twisted, swinging its axe up to shatter the weapon. Reacting with the speed of a darting snake, Reolus rolled his wrist, and the tip of his lance flicked deftly in a tight circle, avoiding the axe and leaving a lingering arc of light in its wake.

The lance ripped the minotaur's throat out, blood boiling as it came into contact with the sacred weapon.

Arteries pumped blood from the fatal wound like geysers. It dropped to its knees, hands clutching at the wound, and Reolus smashed his sword, wielded in his left hand, through its skull.

The knights thundered on. More of the towering beasts turned to face the charge. So tall were they that they looked down upon the knights, even though they were sitting astride their massive steeds. With a roar, they leapt forwards to meet the charging knights.

With staggering power, one of them hacked its axe into the neck of a destrier, ignoring the lance that plunged deep into its thick chest. The axe-head tore through metal barding and flesh, severing the horse's spine and sending its head flying. The knight riding the brutally slain horse was thrown sideways, to be crushed by his falling, headless, steed.

Another of the beasts stood up to the charge, its massive hand closing around the neck of another steed, which it hurled to the side contemptuously. Then it was struck by a pair of lances, staggered backwards and was instantly lost beneath the thundering hooves of the charging horses.

Two more beasts died beneath Reolus's flashing weapons. Gore sprayed across his gleaming armour and tabard, but it ran off him like oil, leaving him unsullied by their foul heart-blood. One by one, the knights around him were smashed from their saddles. Arms were cleaved from shoulders, and men fell, screaming. Clubs the size of men crushed heads, and horses screamed as heavy blows cleaved deep into their flesh.

Still, no weapon came close to touching Reolus. He was like a god of war, cutting down everything in his path.

He was, however, but one man.

Oblivious or uncaring of the wooden stakes before them, consumed with bloodlust, a trio of minotaurs ploughed on after the fleeing men-at-arms. Reolus cut one of them down, his lance ripping through the tight muscles of its thigh, sending it crashing to the ground. Another of the beasts ran straight onto the wall of wooden stakes set deep in the ground, impaling itself, while the smaller and more agile humans slipped between the deadly spikes. Uncaring, the creature pushed forwards, legs pumping like pistons, and the thick stake drove deep into its gut.

The last of the beasts smashed the stakes aside with sweeps of its twin weapons and ran on, revelling in the slaughter as it continued its butchery. Beastmen streamed through the gap, whooping and roaring as they set about with abandon, chasing after terrified men and hacking them down with brutal blows to the backs of their heads.

Fighting with ferocious passion, Reolus struck down everything that drew within range of his deadly weapons. He fought like a man possessed, but the press of bodies around him was too great, even for him.

HUNDREDS OF MEN were slaughtered before order was restored. His comrades all slain and his steed dead, pierced by a dozen blades, Reolus stood alone in the breach in the Bretonnian lines, killing everything that came within range of his deadly blade.

Baron Montcadas led the counterattack against the flood of enemies that had broken through, his spiked morning star smashing foes aside desperately. He would have fallen too, his knights surrounded and outnumbered, had not Dieter Weschler rallied the panicked men-at-arms and turned upon their attackers. At last, the enemies within the camp were cut down, though the destruction they had wrought in those frantic few minutes was staggering.

With cold efficiency, the Empire captain swiftly reorganised the men-at-arms, and personally led the charge that pushed the enemy back from where they had surrounded the grail knight Reolus.

Even as order was restored, the beastmen breached the Bretonnian lines in two other places, streaming through and slaughtering the men-at-arms desperately trying to hold back the tide of enemies.

Baron Montcadas knew that the hill could not be held indefinitely. Already, they had held for far longer than could have been expected, so great were the enemy numbers. The end was not far off.

ANARA LET HER spirit soar free, and relished the familiar sensation as she left her earthly shell behind. She felt the winds of magic buffet her, but focused her mind and regained control, so that she rode the ethereal winds like a bird on the breeze.

The battlefield spread out below her like a map as she soared into the night sky. The combatants surged back and forth like tiny ants, and she watched the mesmerising patterns formed by the ebb and flow of battle.

She felt every death like a stabbing pain in her breast. Emotions flowed through her from below, and she felt keenly the exhilaration, terror, despair and savage joy of the knights as they killed and were killed.

With her spirit-eyes she could see the silvery glow of pride and faith shielding them, and she thanked the Lady for her protection. The grail knight Reolus blazed with the intensity of the sun, the power of his faith almost blinding, and the enemy fell back from him, for even in their mortal, blind states they could sense his power.

From the enemy, she felt only rage, bloodlust and deep, all-encompassing hatred. So overpowering was the hatred that it struck her like a physical blow, and her concentration wavered for an instant. Her physical eyes flickered, and she saw the battlefield through her mortal eyes for a second before she regained control and surrounded herself with the healing light of the Lady.

She wept tears of the spirit for the tortured forest that had been corrupted by the enemy, feeling its pain and its despair.

Something drew her attention, and her spirit flew low over the battlefield, dread, loathing and pity mixed within her. She came to the edge of he forest to the west, where the enemy leader stood. She flew close, looking upon him with invisible eyes that saw far more than those of flesh and blood.

Its minions were bringing men to it, dragging them forward like offerings to some brutal, primal deity. The beast lifted each of the victims to its eyes, gazing upon them intently, sniffing their scent. It seemed, however, that none of the men was what the creature sought, and it angrily stabbed its long, curving dagger into each man's neck, before tossing them aside like refuse. Already, there was a great pile of the dead and dying behind the beast, and scores more sacrifices were being dragged forward.

Darkness swirled around the creature like a living thing, fuelled by the intense hatred that the beast exuded. Anara was repulsed, and fought the urge to flee, but she peered deeper, though it caused her pain, looking past the wall of anger.

She saw self-loathing, disgust and fear there, but there was something more, something that was the true essence of this creature's power: betrayal, abandonment, and the intense, all consuming need for vengeance.

That was all it lived for, Anara realised, pitying the creature. Vengeance against the one that had done it wrong was what drove it.

There was something else too: release. It desired release.

The creature looked up suddenly, and Anara reeled backwards in shock, for the creature saw her. Its eyes blazed with blue witch-fire, and it extended its will towards her, a writhing mass of black tentacles invisible to all but those who saw with the eyes of the spirit.

One of the oily, black, invisible appendages brushed against her spirit-arm and the ethereal limb went numb. It gripped her with immense strength, and she cried out, panic rising suddenly. The mass of black, tentacles surged towards her.

Blindly, she struck out, and white light flared. The grip on her arm relaxed, and Anara fled, streaming across the battlefield towards her body, feeling the writhing black will of the creature pursuing her.

Anara gasped, and sucked in a lungful of air as she was jolted back into the physical realm, almost slipping from the back of her majestic, white mare.

'Damsel Anara, are you all right?' asked Montcadas urgently. She ignored him, and pulled up the flowing sleeve of her arm. An angry red welt was rising there upon her flawless, ivory skin, and she hissed with pain. It felt like a scalding brand had been pressed against her skin.

Numbly, she heard the baron shouting for his aides to bring water and his battle surgeon.

She knew that the beast would not rest until its vengeance was achieved, and such was its overpowering will, that it was able to dominate and control the lesser beasts of the wild woods. While it lived, the beasts would never cease their attacks against Bretonnia.

The creature was even capable of commanding the woodland, dominating it to its corrupt will. It commanded the forests in a way unlike the fey that dwelt in the holy forest of Loren. Their magic was pure and in harmony with the natural world. This creature's power was foul and brutal, filled with anger and cruelty.

The vision came to her unbidden. She saw the lands overrun with tortured forests. They were filled with sickness, like pus-filled boils, and the dead were sprawled upon the ground, rotting to feed the agonised roots. She saw castles and the great cities destroyed and smoking, covered in twisted briars and thorns, and skulls within helmets grinned at her. The land was dead, and the Lady was fading into nothingness.

At last, the vision began to fade, and she opened her eyes. All that she had seen would come to pass if the beast did not enact its vengeance. Unless…

'The beast must die,' she breathed.

* * *

DONEGAR LICKED HIS lips as he saw the telltale red and blue tabard and shield that marked his target.

'A stray arrow missing its mark in the heat of battle,' the knight had said as he handed Donegar the coin. 'It is a tragedy, but such things happen. No blame will befall you, you have my word. No one will know from which bow the arrow was fired.' The knight's face was obscured by his helmet, and he wore a tabard of plain cloth. There was nothing about the knight that gave any hint to his identity, save his voice, which muffled as it was, held a recognisably Bastonnian accent.

'Blue and red, with a white dragon,' the knight had repeated, pointing at him with one armoured finger. 'There will be another coin for you once the deed is done. Such a tragedy,' he said mockingly, 'a young knight killed by a stray arrow.'

Then the man had left, and Donegar had stared at the coin. With it, he could feed his starving children for a year.

He had half hoped that the knight with the red and blue heraldry would die in battle. He would not be able to claim the second promised coin, but he would not have to live with being a murderer. However, it had not happened thus far. Perhaps the young knight was protected by the Lady? Doubt gripped him. He had no wish to be cursed by the goddess of the nobility.

Then the thought of a second coin filled his mind. With it, he could afford to pay the wise woman to tend to his wife, who was dying of the wasting sickness.

The villein shouted his order, and the regiment lifted their bows high into the air once more, fifty arrows knocked to strings. They were the last of the shafts. Two more volleys, and they would all be expended.

Donegar pulled the string back to his cheek, the arrow knocked and ready to be loosed.

He lowered his aim, sighting on the group of knights errant that were breaking away from the battle and riding back towards the hill. He licked his lips once more, feeling sick in his stomach, but thinking only of his family.

BREATHING HEAVILY, CALARD cut his way free of the enemy and rode clear. His armour was dented and pierced in a dozen places, and he had cast off his helmet after he had sustained a ringing blow to his head that had wrenched the helm out of shape and partially obscured his vision.

Parts of his chainmail hung in loose shreds, the links having been shattered by swords and axes, and the blue and red shield that proudly bore his personal heraldry was battered and dented. Gringolet sported dozens of cuts and wounds, but none of them were deep, the destrier's plate and chain barding having taken the brunt of the damage, though the proud red and blue caparison was torn in dozens of places.

Bertelis too bore similar damage, and blood was leaking from a wound he had taken on his upper arm from a blow that had torn through his plate mail. The battle had raged for hours, and Calard had seen dozens of young men slain, never to gain their full knighthood.

No more than half a dozen knights remained in the formation of knights errant that Calard had started the battle fighting alongside, and they had been joined by the shattered remnants of other under-strength regiments. He had not known most of the knights, and one of them, curiously, bore no heraldry. His shield had been painted plain white, and he kept his helmet firmly on his head, even during the short moments of respite. Calard had recognised one of the knights, however, and he had glared hatefully as Maloric of Sangasse had joined their ranks.

The slim young knight was equally displeased, but neither of them wished to argue with their superiors. Much to Calard's irritation, Maloric had acquitted himself well, killing with cold, swift efficiency. The presence of the Sangasse noble had made Calard fight with renewed vigour, determined not to be outshone by his pale-skinned rival.

'How pleased I am to see you still alive, Garamont,' said Maloric, flicking up his visor as they broke combat, his voice thick with sarcasm.

'I thank the Lady that you were not knocked from the saddle, dear Sangasse,' snapped back Calard. He tugged on Gringolet's reins sharply, and pulled to the back of the formation, his thoughts dark. Bertelis, riding alongside him, went to drop back with him, but Calard stopped him with a curt word.

He dearly wished to lash out at the bastard Sangasse noble, and did not trust himself to remain at his side. The Baron Montcadas's orders had been strict, and he was not going to allow his hotheadedness to bring dishonour to his family by breaking his word.

He didn't see the arrow as it hissed through the air towards him. It struck him in the shoulder just above the top of his shield and he was knocked backwards out of the saddle.

He hit the ground hard, and all the air was driven from his lungs. The shaft had punched straight through his plate armour, and he groaned in pain.

Ahead, the knights errant rode on, oblivious to his fall.

THE KNIGHT BEARING no heraldry turned in the saddle and saw Calard lying motionless on the ground. A riderless grey steed was nuzzling at his body. The knight grinned.

She would be pleased. He felt suddenly aroused at the thought. Long had he desired her, and long had she teased and taunted him, maintaining a civil distance between them. Now, having done as she wished, she would be his. That had been the promise.

His grin faded as he saw the young Garamont noble push himself to his knees, one hand clamped around the arrow protruding from his shoulder. The knight cursed. It had not been a killing blow.

Pulling on his reins sharply, he peeled off from the formation and began riding towards the fallen knight. Thinking help was coming for him, Calard lifted his hand in a wave and struggled to his feet.

The knight snarled, and kicked his steed into a gallop, his fingers clenching hard around the hilt of his sword.

CALARD SAW THE knight riding towards him, and pushed to his feet. The arrow hurt like hell, and he winced.

He looked up at the knight riding towards him. The knight flourished his sword, and kicked his steed into a charge.

Thinking the enemy was closing behind him, he swung around, but there was no enemy nearby. He turned around and froze for a second, not comprehending what was happening.

The knight was not slowing down, and Calard felt a chill run down his spine. He threw a glance left and right, seeking cover, but there was none. He felt helpless, having dropped his sword when the arrow had struck. The thunder of hooves shook the ground beneath his feet.

The sword flashed down towards him, and Calard threw himself desperately to the side, wincing at the pain in his shoulder as the arrow still imbedded in his flesh scraped bone. The sword sliced through the air, an inch away from him. The knight wheeled around sharply, and kicked his steed forward for another pass. He knew he would be lucky to avoid another attack.

Calard staggered backwards, keeping his eyes locked on the treacherous knight before him. Some vassal of Sangasse, no doubt, he thought venomously.

Then a pair of knights raced past him, one on either side, galloping hard from behind him. He recognised their heraldry: Bertelis and… Gunthar!

The charging knight pulled his steed to one side, his helmet turning left and right as he sought escape. The enemy was surging forwards once more, racing across the churned up earth towards them. There was nowhere for the knight to flee.

Bertelis and Gunthar bore down on him, and he kicked his steed forwards once more, to meet them head on.

His sword arced down towards the weapon master's head, and Calard saw Gunthar's sword flash. Then

Gunthar was past the knight, who was tumbling to the ground. Calard had not even seen the blow, so fast had it been performed.

A wet nose nuzzled at Calard.

'Good horse,' he said.

Gunthar rode to Calard's side, and flicked up his visor. His face was pale and wan, but his eyes were full of concern. The enemy was no more than a hundred paces distant, and closing fast.

'Can you ride?' he asked quickly, and Calard nodded. He pulled himself painfully into the saddle.

'Bertelis!' bellowed Gunthar. 'Leave him! We have to ride, now!'

BERTELIS IGNORED THE shout, and slid from the saddle, consumed with rage. He stalked towards the fallen knight, who was scrabbling backwards, leaving a smear of blood beneath him. Gunthar's wound had been fatal, but the knight was not dead yet.

'Traitorous whoreson,' spat Bertelis. He kicked the knight's sword away from him, sending it spinning across the ground, and held the point of his blade to the knight's neck.

'Show your face before I kill you, dog,' he spat. When the knight made no move to remove his helmet, Bertelis reversed the grip on his sword and plunged it two-handed down into the knight's thigh.

The man screamed in agony, and Bertelis smiled.

As the cry faded away, he heard Gunthar call to him again. Looking up, he saw that the enemy was closing fast.

Dropping to his knees, he scrabbled at the man's helmet. If it could be proven that it was one of

Sangasse's men, then the baron must surely have to take action against Maloric.

With a wrench, he pulled the helmet free, and gasped as he stared down at the familiar face.

'Tanebourc,' he breathed in shock. He stood up and staggered back a step, confusion and horror on his face.

'Kill me, boy!' said Tanebourc desperately. 'Don't leave me to the beasts!'

Staggering backwards, his eyes haunted, Bertelis ignored the man's pleas and pulled himself into the saddle.

'Kill me!' roared Tanebourc again.

The horde of the enemies were closing fast, and with a final glance Bertelis rode away from Tanebourc. He heard the knights' tortured cries escalate as the hateful tide of Chaotic creatures swarmed over him, and rode hard after Calard and Gunthar.

A lance of knights pounded down the hill past him, charging into the packed beastman forces, but Bertelis barely registered them.

Tanebourc was his mother's favourite, there was no secret about that, and Bertelis knew that the man would do anything for her. If he had succeeded in killing Calard as he had intended, then he, Bertelis, his mother's only son, would have been the heir of Garamont.

His mind whirled. Surely his mother would never stoop so low? She could be single-minded, and had a barbed tongue, but she was no murderer. Was she?

'Who was it?' Gunthar asked him later, his voice grim.

'I didn't recognise him,' Bertelis said.

CHAPTER SEVENTEEN

MONTCADAS WAS BLOODY and weary beyond words. For three hours, the Bretonnian lines had endured constant attack, and he had no idea how many knights he had lost. More than half, certainly, and the casualty rate amongst the peasants had been even more severe.

They had exhausted their supply of arrows almost an hour earlier, and the peasant levy of bowmen was now forced to fight with knives and cudgels alongside the decimated ranks of men-at-arms.

The southern half of Adhalind's Seat had fallen, and it was only a matter of time before the hill was completely overrun, an hour at most.

His arms felt leaden, and the spiked head of his morning star was thick with concealed gore.

'Its will is driving the beasts,' Anara had said, her voice distant and vague, her eyes fey and lost. 'Kill it and the attack will falter.'

'Then we kill it,' he had replied, wearily. His orders had been passed, and every knight still fit to ride was gathered together, for one final throw of the dice. They would take the fight to the monstrous creature leading the beasts, and see it killed, or die to a man in the attempt.

'Lift the standard high,' said Montcadas. His banner bearer was as weary as him, but he nodded grimly. All the knights around him were exhausted. Only the shining, silent figure of Reolus seemed beyond such mortal concerns. Even Anara looked wan and tired, dark circles ringing her eyes.

This is it then, he thought, a desperate last charge to slay the beast leading the enemy. Montcadas snorted. It was the stuff of legends, and with a grail knight leading and a damsel of the Lady with them, it seemed like the kind of heroic charge that the bards would sing of for generations, *if* they were victorious. If they were not, then no one would remember them.

The enemy warlord was out in the darkness, at the fringe of the tortured, unnatural forest to the north-east, the damsel had said. So, it was in that direction that the knights were preparing to make the final charge. Only a skeleton defence would be left to hold against the attacks that continued unabated against the hilltop.

It would be a glorious charge, over two hundred knights arranged in a solid wedge, with he and Reolus at its tip.

Wind whipped at the heavy fabric of the banner as it was lifted high. 'Sound the horns,' said Baron Montcadas.

A single note, as clear and sharp as a freshly-forged, virgin sword blade cut through the air.

'May the Lady grant us the strength to finish this,' breathed Montcadas.

CALARD'S HEART RACED as he heard the signal. He was positioned towards the edge of the northern-most wing of the thick wedge of knights, and, though he bristled that he was not closer to the apex of the attack, just to be riding in such august company made him swell with pride.

'Be strong,' he said to his weary steed, Gringolet. 'Just one last charge.'

Had it not been nearing midnight and the battlefield swathed in darkness, the charge would have been an awesome sight, every last living knight riding forth in one final, desperate attack.

He prayed that he would make a good account of himself, and that somehow his father would hear of it.

Calard urged Gringolet forwards with a kick, the mighty grey reacting instantly to his spurs.

His weariness and the pain of his injuries were forgotten as he rode towards the enemy. Though he knew that he would almost certainly die, he felt suddenly powerful, invincible, like one of the companions of Gilles le Breton, whose deeds were recounted in ballad and song.

The arrow had been painfully drawn from his shoulder, and the wound was heavily bandaged, allowing him little freedom of movement. Thankfully, it had struck him on his left side, for if it had been his right he would have been unable to couch a lance or swing a sword. The shaft had pierced the muscle just below the shoulder joint, punching straight through his thick plate armour, and he thanked the Lady that it was not a more serious wound. It was of course impossible to determine who had shot the arrow. A fluke accident perhaps, but a niggling doubt remained. An attempt had already been made on his life, and it made sense that having failed in his first attempt, Maloric would make another.

That Gunthar was riding alongside him filled him with pride, and not a little relief. He had been astonished to see the weapon master armoured and riding to his aid, for the last he had seen of the man he had been near death, his wounds badly infected. The wounds were healing well, Gunthar said, and Calard had not seen the lie for what it was.

The fact that an unknown knight had tried to kill him mid-battle was galling. It must have been one of Sangasse's men, of that he was certain. One day soon he would have a reckoning with the treacherous worm.

The thunder of hooves was deafening, and Calard couched his lance tight under his arm as Gringolet galloped at speed across the field that had been churned to mud. The ground was littered with corpses.

He had clasped forearms with Bertelis before the charge. They didn't speak; there was no need to. Both understood that they were unlikely to survive the night.

How changed he was, Calard had thought, looking upon his half-brother's tired features. He looked older, and his eyes were haunted by the atrocities he had witnessed. Gone were the last vestiges of boyhood. All that Calard saw was a young knight, hard and tempered in battle. He wondered briefly if he too had changed so.

They had both seen so much death in the last months. The reality of war was far different from what either of them had imagined. Calard felt stupid, for though he did not really expect things to be like the tales they had listened to as wide-eyed children, he realised that he had not really known what to expect. Certainly not the stench of the battlefield.

Bertelis gave a wild whoop, and Calard grinned and tightened his grip on his lance. Not everything about his brother had changed. He was certain that if they survived this night, then they would both get incredibly drunk, and Bertelis would no doubt bed as many women as he could before he passed out. For a second, his thoughts drifted to Elisabet, and her face reared in his mind's eye. He saw her seductive, playful dark eyes. The scent of her had all but faded from the silk scarf tied around his upper arm, but its mere presence lent him strength.

Calard lowered his lance, and the wall of knights slammed into the enemy once more.

THE NEXT SACRIFICE was dragged forward, and the Gave gripped the man by the front of his tabard, pulling him close, sniffing at him and peering at him intently. Again, despite the colour of the man's livery, it was not the one it sought. With growing frustration, the Gave rammed his barbed knife into the wretch's neck, and hurled him aside, to join the scores of other bloodied corpses scattered around.

A single horn sounded across the battlefield, and the Gave rose to his full, towering height, staring out across the open ground. The enemy was surging towards him in a great wave, and he bared his teeth, hissing. Reacting instinctively, hundreds upon hundreds of the lesser beasts altered their charge towards the hill, leaping across the churned up earth towards the charging knights, but they were being scythed down like wheat. The Gave cared not.

Responding to the threat posed to their master, the heavily armoured bestigor, who had thus far not partaken in the battle, were marching forwards to interpose themselves in the path of the enemy, hefting giant axes and halberds. While the rest of the beast herd was nigh on uncontrollable, surging forth in an unruly mob, the bestigor marched in deep ranks behind icons of black iron, and the earth resounded with the stamp of their iron-shod hooves. They smoothly reordered their formation to the beating of drums, widening their ranks to form a protective barrier around the Gave.

Deep rumbling growls resonated from the darkness of the trees behind the Gave. The sound vibrated through the Gave's body, making his organs shudder, and his lips drew back in a cruel smile.

Trees were uprooted as they were pushed aside by a pair of titanic, dark shapes that rose above the canopy. With a gesture, the Gave directed them forwards.

REOLUS'S EYES BLAZED with holy fury as he cut his way through the melee at the point of the Bretonnian charge. His blade carved through the heavy armour of the foe as if it were paper, and at his side the Baron Montcadas smashed aside more of them with every sweeping blow of his spiked morning star. The questing knight,

Gundehar, rode on his other side, and he smashed the enemy away with mighty sweeps of his two-handed sword, passion and fervour giving him strength.

They were no more than a hundred yards from the tree line, and he could smell the foetid decay of the tortured trees in the air. Urging his steed forwards, feeling the malignant presence of the enemy war leader nearby, Reolus drove on, hacking his way through the heavy press of armoured beastmen.

There was an almighty crash, and his eyes flicked towards the darkness of the looming forest. Trees were being uprooted and smashed aside, and the ground began to shudder with titanic footsteps.

A pair of behemoths rose above the canopy, creatures both ancient and grown impossibly huge by the warping influence of Chaos. Like men wading through long grass, they burst from the tree line, smashing aside contorted oaks and elms, their ear-splitting roars sounding like mountains being shattered.

Each of the monsters stood some fifty feet tall, and each thunderous, loping step cleared almost twenty feet. They were malformed creatures of Chaos, their hulking shoulders covered in fur and protruding spines of bone, their monstrous gait uneven and awkward.

The ground shook beneath them, and Reolus felt the wave of panic that shuddered through the charging knights as they saw the pair of fell giants bearing down on them. He had killed such beasts before, however, and he would do so again.

It looked as though a single, monstrous creature had been sliced down the middle by a searing cut, forming two beasts from one flesh. They were perverted mirror images of each other, these Chaos giants, monstrous twins separated by foul magicks.

Each had an oversized arm and a smaller, deformed limb that was wasted and nigh on useless. One of the legs of each giant was as thick as a tree-trunk and covered with dank fur that hung to the ground like rope, while the other leg was crooked and thin.

Their heads each contained a single, weeping eye, though each orb contained a pair of pupils, and each beast had a single drooping ear pierced with human thigh bones and ribs. The other sides of their heads were a loathsome mass of red scar tissue, as if the two heads had once been one, but had been ripped apart. A single curling horn emerged from each of their heads, curved downwards from their temples. Lips flapped open to display slab-like teeth and tusks, and the creatures roared with one voice.

Each held a tree-trunk in its massive hands, and these they hefted as if they weighed nothing at all.

They loped through the press of beastmen, who came barely to their knees, smashing them aside thoughtlessly. Their monstrous cyclopean eyes were fixed on the knights, and the earth vibrated with each thunderous step,

The first of the giants struck the line of knights, sweeping its tree-trunk like a club. The makeshift weapon slammed into the front rank of Bretonnians, and half a dozen knights and their horses were lifted into the air and sent flying backwards, their bones and armour crushed. With its return swing, it sent another half dozen hurtling through the air.

The other giant came straight at Reolus, and the grail knight kicked his terrified steed directly towards it, making no attempt to move out of its way. The giant lifted its club high into the air as it pounded forwards, intending to smash him into the ground.

The heavy tree-trunk came hurtling down towards him, and he urged his steed to the side at the last moment. The tree smashed down, slamming into Gundehar, crushing him and his steed into the ground, rendering them into an unrecognisable, flattened smear of blood and armour.

With a roar, Reolus plunged his lance deep into the beast's thigh as he rode past it. It sank three feet into flesh that was as tough as wood, and the creature and its twin bellowed deafeningly in pain, as if both felt the wound.

Letting go of its club, the giant swatted at Reolus with the back of its hand, which was the size of a wagon. The blow smashed into him and his steed, sending them flying. His horse crumpled to the ground, screaming in agony, and Reolus rolled from the thrashing destrier.

Howling in savage fury, the armoured beastmen surged forwards once more.

Dazed and hurting, Reolus struggled to his feet, killing the first ones that swarmed around him.

Dozens of lances plunged into the legs of the pair of giants, and they bellowed in fury and pain. A hand clasped around the body of a horse and it was lifted high into the air, whinnying in terror before its head was bitten off. The headless corpse was hurled back down into the knights, knocking another pair to the ground, and hot blood splattered down from the monster's flapping lips.

Knights surged around the legs of the beasts, stabbing and hacking, but the charge had been all but blunted. Heavily-armoured beastmen surged into those that got past the pair of giants, smashing them from their saddles and pulling them down.

With a shout, Reolus cleaved his sword through the head of a beastman, and broke into a run towards the nearest of the two behemoths. He ducked a swinging axe and severed the leg of another beast. The closest giant swung around, sending four knights and their steeds flying through the air with a sweep of its arm, and Reolus threw himself to the ground as one horse tumbled towards him.

The knight, still in the saddle, sailed over Reolus and was crushed, his spine snapping as the weight of the horse landed on top of him. Reolus surged upright, and threw his sword with all his might.

The blade spun end over end and drove into the giant's single eye, sinking to the hilt. The beast and its twin gave a tremendous roar of agony and rage, and the wounded creature began thrashing around blindly. Black blood spurted from its eye, and more than one fallen knight was crushed beneath its staggering foot-steps. More lances plunged into its legs, and it spun around, arms flailing, killing knights and beastmen alike.

Baron Montcadas, miraculously still alive and in the saddle, smashed his ball and chain into the knee of the creature's lame leg, shattering the kneecap. As the leg gave way beneath it, the monstrous creature teetered and fell.

Its arms swung wildly as it sought vainly to maintain its balance, but its fall was inevitable. It hit the ground with a resounding boom, crushing a dozen men beneath its bulk, and making others stumble and fall as the ground shook. Unhorsed knights swarmed over it, plunging their swords like daggers into its neck and body, even as others were hacked down by beastmen.

The fallen giant's twin bellowed in pain and rage, and moved to its defence. With a violent kick, it sent three knights flying, their horses screaming as they spiralled back into their own ranks, bones crushed and armour wrenched completely out of shape.

Reolus swore. Horseless, and with the havoc unleashed by the giants, there was little chance that he would ever reach the enemy war leader. Buoyed by the appearance of the towering monstrosities, the enemy was surging forwards with renewed vigour, and, now that the charge had been stymied, the Bretonnians were being cut down in their hundreds. He prayed that those knights on the flank of the charge were continuing their attack, for, in them, lay the only chance of killing the enemy war leader.

With a growl of anger, Reolus caught the arms of a beastmen as it sought to cleave him from shoulder to sternum with a powerful axe-blow. Muscles straining to hold back the strike, he leant forwards and drove his knee into the beast's groin. Again he slammed his armoured knee into the same place, and its strength wavered. With a final blow, the beast released its grip on its weapon, and Reolus swung it around in a lethal arc that tore the beast's head from its shoulders.

The sole giant still on its feet was laying about it with destructive power, killing dozens of men with every passing moment. A score of swords and lances protruded from its legs, like bristles, and its flesh was slick with blood from the wounds, but it continued its mad rampage, apparently fuelled by the pain. Setting his sight on the towering creature, Reolus barged his way through the maelstrom of battle, the beastman's axe held tight in his hands.

CALARD SLASHED DOWN at the enemy again and again. The beastmen pushed in against the knights, surging forward in a solid mass. There was little room for grace or skill, just a need to kill quickly and efficiently.

Titanic roars echoed across the din. Their charge had swung around to the east as the point of the charge, led by the grail knight Reolus, stalled. How such a thing could have come to pass was beyond him, for he had believed that nothing in the world could stand against the knight, but halted the charge had been. Out on the wing of the attack, Calard and the knights around him had continued on, facing less resistance than the rest of the force, and they now found themselves occupying the most forward point in the attack, and still they pushed deeper into the enemy lines.

The trees were close, and they were surrounded and desperate. Calard knew instinctively that they would not last long, but he could not help feeling that they were painfully close to the beast leading the enemy forces. They just needed to keep going forwards.

He desperately parried a blow that stabbed towards his chest, and sent a riposte that sliced a bloody line across a beast's face, driving it back for a second. It was instantly replaced by another foe that roared as it thrust a spear forwards. Calard swayed to the side, and the weapon slammed into the face of another knight, punching through his skull and piercing the brain. Gringolet kicked out, flashing hooves breaking limbs.

The enemy fought with savage fury as more of them pushed against the buckling line of knights, and increasing numbers of men were being dragged down with every passing moment. Calard struck a beastman on the crown of its head, splitting the skull, and it collapsed to the ground.

All semblance of order had been lost, and the knights' charge began to falter. Each man fought as an individual now, all sense of formation gone, lost amid the chaos of the battle.

Seeing a gap open, Calard shouted and drove Gringolet on. The powerful grey reacted instantly, leaping forwards.

He didn't see his brother Bertelis knocked from the saddle behind him.

THE ENEMY CLOSED ranks, fighting with frenzied intensity, and Gunthar swore as Calard disappeared from sight. His own steed had fallen, its skull smashed, and he stood protectively over Bertelis's prone figure. Though Calard was beyond his reach, he would die before any further harm came to Lutheure's youngest son.

He ducked and lifted his shield, and a swinging axe head scraped across its surface. Lunging forwards, he stabbed his blade into the towering beast's midsection, the tip sinking deep, before stepping back once more.

Hissing against the pain in his injured leg, which threatened to collapse beneath him at any moment, he slashed his sword across the bestial, hate-filled face of another enemy.

All around him, horses kicked out with their hooves, rearing and biting as they had been trained. Gunthar stood over the fallen Garamont noble, fearing that he would be crushed beneath the hooves of the warhorses. Men shouted and screamed, and more of them were being dragged from the saddles and butchered. Blades flashed down from those still in the saddle, driving the surging enemy back, lashing out at any that came near.

A blade stabbed towards Bertelis, who was groggily struggling to rise, and Gunthar's blade flashed out, deflecting the blow. He snapped off a lightning riposte that tore out the beast's throat. It fell, blood gurgling from the wound, and Gunthar turned aside another blow that sliced towards his neck. His return blow punched through the beast's eye socket, and it fell with a roar. More creatures surged forwards to fill the gap, and Gunthar glanced behind him.

Bertelis had ripped his helmet away, and blood was streaming from his scalp. He flopped back onto the ground, and Gunthar swore. The beasts crowding around, respectful now of his skill, snarled at him, their fingers clenching and unclenching on the hafts and pommels of their weapons.

Another knight went down, his horse screaming, and the beasts leapt at Gunthar.

He smashed a spear down into the ground, and turned aside a sword thrust with his shield. His blade lashed out, scoring a deep wound across the chest of one of the beasts, and then he deftly reversed the blow, hacking his sword deep into the creature's neck. Gunthar spun away instantly, ripping his sword free, even as an axe sliced through the air where he had been standing a moment ago, and hacked his sword into the neck of another creature.

He stepped awkwardly to the side to better protect Bertelis, feeling his leg shuddering beneath him. He was breathing heavily, and his arms felt like lead weights. He was so tired.

Again the beasts came at him, and he swayed back from a wildly slashing, curved sword that passed by him, a hair's breadth from his head, and his sword sliced across the beast's arm, cutting through sinews and tendons, forcing it to drop its weapon.

A blade punched through his side, and he staggered. With a swing, he severed the beast's arm at the wrist, and stabbed the point into its chest. An axe blow smashed into his shield, breaking his arm and making him cry out. His blade slashed across the creature's leg, and it fell with a roar of pain.

Wincing against the grating pain of broken bones grinding together, his left arm hanging limply at his side, Gunthar stood over Bertelis, his heart pounding. His breath was coming in short, sharp gasps, and it felt like his lungs were on fire. The sounds around him seemed muffled and distant, as if his ears were stuffed with cloth, and he knew that his end was near.

'Gunthar,' breathed the young knight from the ground.

'I'll let no harm come to you, boy,' gasped Gunthar, eyeing the circle of beastmen closing in around them.

One of them charged, its axe swinging up from the ground in a lethal arc. Stepping to the side, Gunthar avoided the attack and slashed his blade across the creature's back as it surged by. Then he reversed the swing and plunged the point into the stomach of another beast as it surged forwards.

The flailing hooves of a knight's steed almost struck him, and he staggered back. A curved blade crashed into his shoulder, and he stumbled. His gangrenous leg finally collapsed beneath him, and he fell to one knee. Still he fought on, desperate to protect Bertelis. He hacked his blade into a beast's leg, and it fell with a roar.

A knight's sword smashed down, cleaving the head of another creature down to its teeth, and blood splattered from the terrible wound.

Gunthar's vision began to swim from loss of blood and exhaustion, and he half-crawled, half-stumbled to Bertelis's side, expecting, at any moment, to be crushed or to have the life smashed from him by the enemy. Using his sword like a crutch, he pushed to his feet once more, swaying unsteadily.

'Gunthar,' breathed Bertelis.

'I'm sorry, my lord,' gasped Gunthar in despair. 'I have failed you.'

'No,' said Bertelis, trying to lift himself up, but falling back to the ground.

A pair of beasts rushed at Gunthar. He killed the first, his blade severing its jugular, and blood sprayed out as it dropped to the ground. Desperately, he turned his blade towards the second. It slammed into him, bearing him to the ground. Its weight forced Gunthar's sword into its body, and it snarled in his face, its eyes yellow and filled with hate as it died.

The weight of the beast pinned Gunther to the ground, its heavy, muscled mass crushing him, and he felt a moment of panic at his vulnerability. With a surge of adrenaline, he heaved the stinking creature off him, rolling it to the side.

He could barely breathe, and he coughed painfully, blood flecking his lips. He was so tired. Sleep beckoned him. All he had to do was close his eyes and the pain would stop. His eyelids fluttered.

No! He would not allow himself to succumb to the enticing sleep of eternity. Not yet.

Clenching his teeth against the agony, he pushed to his feet once more, and dragged his sword from the beastman's body.

BREAKING THROUGH THE enemy's line, not knowing how many knights were with him, Calard's eyes narrowed as he saw the fell beast that was the enemy's war leader. Corpses were strewn across the ground around the creature, and, with a shock, he saw that every one of them wore the colours of Garamont. They looked like the discarded toys of a petulant infant, tossed away in disgust, bloody and broken. Dozens more men were being dragged forwards, all wearing yellow and red, fresh sacrifices to the dark gods.

The creature's head flicked around, its face rotting and covered in stitches, and its piercing eyes locked on him. Calard swayed in the saddle at the depths of hatred in its eyes.

It was a massive creature, standing perhaps seven feet tall, and, though its body was not heavy like the bull-headed creatures, its long limbs were tight with sinewy muscle. Though it was not as large or as physically loathsome as the mutated beast-spawn creatures, something about it was utterly wrong, as if such a beast should never have been born into the world. Fighting against the unfathomable horror threatening to overwhelm him, Calard kicked

Gringolet forwards, angling his charge directly at the foul creature.

It slammed its staff into the ground, and black birds filled the air with fluttering wings and raucous cries.

Beasts wearing heavy armour and hefting large, single-bladed axes snarled, and leapt forwards. Calard dimly heard Bertelis cry out, but his eyes were locked on the hateful eyes of his quarry. As if the protecting hands of the Lady were cupped around him, he rode through the enemy, unscathed, and bore down on the creature.

It crouched low to the ground, lips curled back in a feral snarl, its long limbs tensing beneath it. In that moment, it resembled some monstrous spider, making ready to spring.

Black carrion birds, each with a single, pulsing daemonic eye, swooped down at Calard, battering him with their wings and stabbing at his eyes with hook-like beaks. He flailed at them wildly, crushing wings and fragile bones with the hilt of his sword, and knocking them away with his armoured forearm.

Through the blur of feathers and wildly flapping birds, Calard saw the beast spring, leaping through the air towards him with spindly fingers outstretched. Gringolet reared, whinnying in fear, and then it struck, slamming into Calard and tearing him from the saddle. Gringolet was borne to the ground by the weight of the foul creature, legs flailing wildly, and Calard hit the ground hard, the creature above him. The wind was knocked from his lungs, and he lay on his back, gasping for breath.

Stunned by the shocking impact, Calard dimly registered Gringolet screaming in pain, and he knew, in that moment, that his faithful steed must have broken a leg in the fall.

Anger rose within him, and he struggled to stand. His vision swam, but he could see the creature crouching above him, its eyes burning with hatred, though the rest of its body was a dark silhouette. Miraculously, Calard still held his sword, and, gasping for breath, he mustered the strength to strike.

A hoof slammed down onto his forearm, pinning it to the ground.

Gringolet screamed again, and from his prone position, Calard could see the stricken horse struggling to lift itself up from the ground. Its shattered right foreleg could not bear its weight, and it buckled unnaturally beneath it, sending the horse crashing to the ground with a tortured cry that clawed at Calard's heart.

With a surge of anger, Calard smashed his shield rim into the beast's leg, and it stepped back with snarl, freeing his pinned arm. Staggering to his feet, Calard stepped towards the beast that towered above him, swinging his sword in a deadly arc towards its neck.

The monster's hand flashed out, and it caught the sword blade, halting it mid-swing. Blood began to flow down the blade, running over Calard's gauntlet, but, struggle as he might, he could not free the weapon from the creature's iron grip. With a snarl of anger, it lifted one of its powerful legs and slammed a kick into his chest, sending him flying backwards.

From the ground, he saw that the beast still held his sword by the blade, and its head cocked to one side, as if the blood dripping down the blade intrigued it. Gringolet struggled to rise again, and collapsed to the ground once more. Snapping out of its reverie, the beast surged forwards suddenly and drove the blade into Gringolet's neck. Calard cried out as his sword was pushed deep, until the hilt of his weapon rested against the grey's flesh. A torrent of blood spilled from the mortal wound, and began pooling beneath it. The steed that Calard had raised from a foal thrashed for a moment, blood bubbling from its mouth, and he cried out to see the noble creature in such pain. Then it lay still, hot blood pooling beneath it.

Grinning, the beast returned its attention to Calard, and as he tried to lift his aching body from the ground, a kick slammed him back down. The hissing creature crouched over Calard, one hoof upon his armoured chest, and one hand pulling his head back violently to expose his throat. A dagger flashed before him, the metal blackened and covered with vile runes and symbols.

The hiss escaping from the creature's lips stopped abruptly, and it drew its face close to Calard's. Its breath was hot and foetid. It sniffed at him, as if sampling his smell. He gagged, trying to pull away, but he was unable to get away from the revolting creature.

It crouched closer still, though he tried to pull away, revulsion and horror rising within him, and it licked his face, from chin to temple. His skin burned where the hot, wet tongue touched his face, and he cried out involuntarily. He saw the creature's eyes widen.

Calard cried out again as sudden pain stabbed into his mind like a hot knife, like writhing tentacles seeking something inside. It felt like worms were burrowing into his brain, and he screamed in agony, writhing beneath the monster, but powerless to pull away.

Images, memories and emotions flickered unbidden through his mind: Elisabet's heart-shaped face as she leant in close to him, the touch of her lips, and the surge of love that he felt for her; the sudden reappearance of Anara in his life, and the shock of the change that had been wrought in her over the years they had been apart; he saw again the fight between Gunthar and Ganelon, and felt again the shame of his part in Gunthar's injury; he saw him and Bertelis riding out to the outlaws on the edge of the forest, back in Bastonne, a lifetime ago.

A million images flickered maddeningly through his mind, everything he had ever experienced, and he cried out at the excruciating, writhing pain.

He saw again the battle against the greenskins, and felt the hot surge of adrenaline that he had experienced in his first foray into combat. He saw Anara as a child, and the fearful glances she received from the servants. He saw himself as a child, after his mother had died, crying himself to sleep because he believed that his father hated him. His father…

The probing tentacles dug deeper, and Calard realised that he could feel the creature's excitement rise. Images of the dying lord of Garamont reared up in an overwhelming parade: flashes of the family castle in Bastonne blurred with visions of his father from years earlier, happier memories of his father laughing, holding hands with his mother, and bouncing Calard on his knee.

He felt a surge of triumph from the beast, and he saw, for the briefest fraction of a second, memories that were not his.

He saw blood, so much blood, and horrified expressions. He felt pain and fear, and desperation... and hatred. He felt hatred like he had never felt it before, an all consuming need for vengeance, for blood, for death and for release. He saw the leering faces of daemons, and they clawed at him with talons of fire, eyes filled with the promise of power, and eternal damnation.

He watched through the Gave's eyes at it fought with tooth and nail against the other beasts of the dark forest reaches. He felt exhilaration as he stood victorious over bloody corpses that he had ripped apart with his bare hands, the sweet, hot taste of blood upon his lips. He smelt the fear that rose from the other beasts as they backed away from him, snarling. He revelled in dominating them, forcing them to his will.

He heard the keening cry of an animal in pain. He hoped he would die, prayed that he would, to escape this torment. Then the probing tentacles within his mind retracted with a suddenness that made him gasp, leaving him exhausted, and with blood dribbling from his nose and ears, and he realised that the sound of an animal in pain was coming from his own lips.

The creature above him threw its head back and roared its triumph to the heavens, and Calard succumbed to darkness.

REOLUS SLAMMED THE axe into the giant's neck as it struggled to rise from the ground, and a torrent of blood gushed from the fatal wound. Staggering back, leaving the weapon imbedded deep in the monstrous beast's flesh, and bleeding from a dozen wounds, the grail knight heard the keening roar of the beast's war leader echo over the battlefield. It was the sound of victory, and Reolus's heart sank.

CHAPTER EIGHTEEN

IT WAS LIGHT when Calard woke, blinking heavily. His head was pounding, and he winced. He heard concerned voices, and he rolled to his side, vomiting up the contents of his stomach. That seemed only to make the pain in his head worse, like stabbing needles behind his eyes, and he was sick once more, his whole body convulsing with the violence of his heaving.

When at last the nausea left him he lay back, exhausted, his body aching all over. He saw canvas above him, and felt a hand on his shoulder.

His memories of the beast came back to him in a rush, and he struggled to rise, crying out, but hands pushed him back onto the pallet. Spots of light filled his vision, and a wave of dizziness overcame him.

'…over. It's over,' said a voice that he realised was Bertelis's.

'…black tentacles, in my mind, prying, probing. Gringolet…' Calard groaned. He jerked with the remembered agony.

'…delirious,' said a different voice, one that he did not recognise. Then everything began to fade once again, and he slipped into a tortured dream. He saw daemonic faces leering at him, blood, and a dark forest canopy overhead. He saw the back of a knight riding away from him, leaving him, and he felt a stab of fear as *things* began to creep out of the darkness around him.

He cried out in his sleep, writhing beneath sweat-soaked sheets.

'WILL HE BE all right?' slurred Bertelis, looking down at his brother in concern. The ageing physician sighed wearily.

'I don't know. His physical injuries are not severe, and are healing well. The damage seems to be to his mind.' He shrugged. 'Such things are unpredictable. I am sorry, I don't know what afflicts your brother. Maybe with rest, he will come back. Now, I am sorry, but I have other men that need tending.'

Bertelis nodded numbly, and the physician shuffled away. The cries of the wounded and the dying were all around. Hundreds of men lay on pallets and blankets beneath the awning, and more were being brought in every minute. The man had probably not slept at all since battle had begun.

He heard men moaning in pain, and winced at the screams as grisly amputations were performed. He took another long draught from the wineskin in his hand.

The death toll had been high. Barely a hundred knights had survived the night of blood. Of those, perhaps another twenty would die of their wounds before the day was out, and another dozen would bear crippling injuries until their dying day.

Bertelis's head was wrapped in bandages, and his right arm was strapped and held immobile in a splint. He was told that he would not be able to wield a sword or a lance for months. He had been desperately fighting to reach his brother, and had fallen heavily as his steed had been cut from beneath him, breaking his arm as he hit the ground. As he had struggled to rise, an axe had smashed into his helmet, wrenching it out of shape and cutting deep into his scalp. He had been lucky it had been only a glancing blow, else his skull would surely have been smashed. As it was, he had been told that he had received a fracture, and he found that exerting himself in any way, even just walking for more than ten steps, made him feel nauseous and dizzy.

He had managed to pull his helmet from his head, and his face was awash with blood. He had been unable to focus his eyes, let alone stand and fight. He dimly remembered the beasts looming over him, and he had thought that, in that moment, Morr had come for him.

Then someone had killed the creatures, and stood sentinel over him: Gunthar.

With hazy, unfocused eyes he had seen the ageing weapon master kill perhaps a dozen of the beasts. With astonishing speed and displaying all his skill, Gunthar had fought furiously to defend him. At last, the knight had fallen, pierced by blades and spears, his armour covered in blood and punctured in a dozen places. Bertelis had cried out as the noble weapon master was finally felled, an axe slamming into his neck with brutal force. Gunthar had fallen facing Bertelis, and he had watched the light slip from his eyes.

He had died so that Bertelis might live, for moments later the enemy swarming around him was pushed back. The young knight swore, and took another swig of wine. The old man's death haunted him.

The end of the battle was still a confused blur. There had been a terrible sound, an exultant cry of bestial triumph that echoed across the battlefield. It had pierced his mind. Then the battle had ended.

On hearing the cry, the beasts of the forest had slunk back into the trees, abandoning the field. Those embroiled in combat fought on, and it had taken over an hour before battle had finally ceased, but the fight had been over as soon as that exultant, bestial cry had sounded.

Thousands of peasants had been killed, and the stink of the mass graves was revolting. Even in death, the peasants managed to sicken him, he thought resentfully.

He looked down at Calard's grey-tinged face. For the past twelve hours he had maintained his vigil over his brother, watching as he tossed fitfully, moaning and crying out in his sleep. Still, at least he was alive, which was more than could be said for most of the knights that had fought that night.

Garamont peasants had found Calard, lying comatose amid piles of the dead, and at first they had mourned for him. They had borne his lifeless body back to camp, convinced that he had been claimed by Morr. It was only when one of the duke's physicians had examined him that a faint, fluttering heartbeat was felt.

There had been no victory celebration, for in truth there had been no victory. They had not slain the beast leading the enemy forces, nor had they sent the creatures fleeing from the battlefield. They had just left.

What was it all for? It seemed to him that there was no point to the attack, and no point to calling it off when they had, but then, the creatures were little more than beasts, animals driven by the senseless urge to kill, like a fox in a hen house. It was folly to even try to understand their motives.

Grief and black despair gripped him, and he shouted for more wine as he drained his wineskin. He kept thinking back to Tanebourc's face, frantic with fear, as he begged for death.

He had believed, for a time, that his mother was sleeping with the man, though he spoke his thoughts to no one, not even Calard. Then, one night, his blood fired with drink, he had confronted her with the allegation. She had slapped him, hard across his cheek, her pale face flushed with anger. The blow had stung him.

'How dare you!' she had snarled, lines creasing her thick make-up.

He had believed her when she refuted his accusation, but, even if he had never consummated that lust, Tanebourc desired her, and Bertelis knew that she was manipulative. He was certain that she would be able to twist Tanebourc to perform any deed she asked of him.

Would she really try to have her husband's first son killed, though? It was with horrible reluctance that he had to admit that she might. The evidence showed that she must have been the one behind the attempts, but that knowledge was his, and his alone.

A fresh wineskin was brought to Bertelis, and he snatched it from the hands of the peasant. Breaking the seal, he gulped down the fine wine greedily, seeking oblivion.

CALARD LAY UPON the pallet for four days, tossing and turning, tormented by nightmares and daemons. He woke several times, and the peasants set to watch over him managed to force some water and food on him, but he was often delirious and confused in these moments of wakefulness. In a drunken stupor, Bertelis verbally abused the peasants and lashed out at them, ranting and stumbling, before he collapsed unconscious in a pool of his own vomit, and was carried to his tent.

When Calard finally rose from his fever, he was ravenously hungry and thirsty, and gorged himself. He felt sore all over, as if he had been trampled beneath a herd of cattle, and his head still pained him, though blessedly even that discomfort lessened as he ate and drank.

His brother came to him, looking haggard, and reeking of alcohol. He had been greatly cheered to see Bertelis, though he was disturbed by his brother's state. The young, blond-haired knight was unshaven and seemed to be fighting his own demons, though he was clearly relieved and pleased to see Calard lucid and on the way to recovery.

Calard had grieved when he learnt of Gunthar's fate, a deep sadness overwhelming him. He had wept tears for the knight, though he had hurriedly blinked them away, and it was with pride and respect that he heard of the weapon master's last moments. He had died doing his duty, but Calard wished that he had spent more time with the weapon master. He had so much yet to learn from him, and he cursed himself for not being more attentive and respectful to the knight. It was too late now, and Calard regretted it. He could not have imagined a time without Gunthar's stern presence, and now that he was gone there was a vacuum in his life that he felt would never be filled.

He mourned similarly for Gringolet. It would be impossible to replace the noble destrier.

With shock and horror, he learnt of the extent of the losses. So many men had died, the majority of whom he had got to know well over the course of the campaign.

Baron Montcadas had survived, though he had lost his left eye when a beast's jaws had closed around his head. He regaled Calard with the account of how he had killed the beast, dislocating its jaws and beating it to death with his fists. In truth, Calard had been unsure whether the baron was exaggerating or not, but he suspected not. It seemed that nothing could kill the barrel-chested bear of a man.

The baron had pursued the beasts into the forests, but had called off the hunt, fearing ambush. The beasts had melted swiftly into the trees and were gone, leaving devastation behind them.

With the departure of the beasts, the unnatural forest that encircled Adhalind's Seat had begun to decay at a heightened rate. The trees rotted away within days, collapsing under their own weight and filling the air with their putrid stench. Insects and worms writhed through the liquefying mass that blanketed the land, and birds swarmed in their thousands to pick through the rotting morass. Within a month, the existence of the vile forest would be little more than a memory, though the fields would be tainted for generations.

Driven by restlessness, Calard ignored the protests of the baron's little physician and was soon up on his feet. He moved around stiffly, flexing his tight limbs and stretching bedsore muscles. His wounds were healing well, and though it would be many weeks before his shoulder was healed, where the arrow had struck him, he had retained some movement there.

It was as he moved through some training exercises with the sword that Anara had come to him, along with the grail knight Reolus.

He had never been so close to the revered knight, and he was awed and humbled in his presence. Anara was coolly distant, not even asking how he fared, much to his disappointment, but the grail knight asked after his health with genuine concern.

Seen up close, it was impossible to gauge the grail knight's age. His face was smooth and unlined, untouched by any scar, which would have been remarkable, even if he had fought in only half the battles it was claimed he had. Indeed, if the stories were to be believed, he had once borne a horrible scar across his face, from his ear to his lips, but the scar had disappeared when he had drunk from the Lady's grail. He was not a handsome man, which had surprised Calard, his features evoking power and strength more than manly beauty. His jaw was square and thick, and his brows heavy, the nose broad and flat. It was a warrior's face, of that there was no doubt, and he wore his hair clipped short, flecks of silver at his temples.

In truth, he did not look like the romanticised hero sung about in his ballads. There were no flowing golden locks or beauty to make married women and virgins swoon, but he certainly had an awesome presence, one that demanded respect. There was something about him that Calard could not put his finger on, something that made him seem just a little larger, a little fiercer, a little more imposing than other men: something a little more… vital.

There was an off-putting, intense burning light in his eyes, a fey potency, otherworldly and dangerous. Calard found he could not hold the grail knight's gaze.

'I fought alongside your father,' the grail knight said, making Calard widen his eyes in surprise, 'a good man, strong. At Drowning Man's Moor he led a desperate countercharge against the restless dead that turned the battle.'

'That battle was more than forty years ago,' said Calard softly, his eyes large. The grail knight smiled back at him.

Calard wanted to ask a million questions, but did not wish to appear like a gawking adolescent.

'You fought the beast,' said Reolus, the smile dropping from his face.

'I… I wanted the glory of killing it,' admitted Calard. 'I thought I could best it, but I… failed,' he said, hanging his head.

'It was a brave attempt.'

'Gunthar would have said foolish.'

'Impetuous, I would say.'

'Why did it leave?' asked Calard. The question had been troubling him. 'Why did it not... finish what it started? Surely it could have won the field?'

'It could,' said Reolus, his eyes burning with witch-fire. 'Had the battle lasted another hour, there would have been no Bretonnian alive, knight or otherwise. In truth, I don't know, Calard. We were hoping that you could shed some light on it.'

'Me?' asked Calard in shock.

'It took something from you,' said Anara vaguely, staring around. Her eyes seemed to be following invisible movements through the air. It was unnerving, like the way a cat would stir and stare intently at a blank wall, as if seeing something beyond the ken of human perception. Calard shivered. What did she see? In truth, he didn't want to know. Her eyes came back into focus and she stared at Calard. 'It touched your mind. What did it see?'

Calard blanched as he felt a flash of remembered pain in his head of the insidious tentacles pushing into his mind, sifting through his memories like an open book, rummaging through his deepest desires, his hopes, his aspirations. It felt like he had been violated by the hateful creature, and he shuddered, feeling again the tainted touch of the creature inside him.

'It saw everything,' said Calard, his voice thick, his eyes haunted, 'every memory, everything I have ever experienced.'

He didn't say how for a brief moment he had felt linked to the creature, seeing its memories as if they were his. In those moments, he had experienced all that the beast felt, and he had *revelled* in the power, the destruction, the taste of blood on his lips. He had felt savage joy as he had relived the killing, the destruction that the beast had wrought. He had felt the beast's rage at all things beautiful and peaceful, felt how they mocked him, and he had yearned to see the world burn.

Were those just the beast's memories overlaid over his? Or did they reflect the dark desires that he kept hidden even from himself?

Had the beast tainted him in those brief moments when their minds had melded together? Was he now damned?

'It found what it was seeking in you,' said Anara, her eyes burning deep into his soul. Could she see the taint that he feared was lurking deep within? 'What was it? What did it find?'

'I don't know! It saw everything. Everything that I am, it saw in those moments.'

The air in the tent became icy, and the light seemed to dim. The pain in his head returned. It felt like seething maggots were burrowing through his brain, and he clenched his eyes closed tightly. Images flashed though his mind, images that the beast had seen, felt and experienced, just as he had experienced its memories. He didn't want to feel this again, didn't want to see it again, and he pushed against it.

'What did it see?' asked Anara again, her voice cold and insistent. It was she! She was doing this, making him relive those moments as he lay helpless beneath the beast.

'Stop,' moaned Calard, fighting against her, resisting.

'What did it see?' she asked icily. Unable to hold back the flood of images, Calard succumbed, and it

was like a dam bursting. He was lost adrift in a sea
of images, feelings and memories. They flicked
through his mind in a maddening parade, one after
another.

Again, he felt the hot surge of savage victory as the
beast had found what it had sought.

'Father,' murmured Calard, his vision swimming, as
he came back to himself. He was on the ground,
though he didn't remember falling, and he wiped at
the foam that flecked his lips.

'What? What was it?' asked Anara, peering down at
him, her face intense and cold, almost cruelly so. He
glared up at her. She had done this to him. She had
made him relive those painful moments. The throbbing pain in his head faded, and he pushed himself
upright, breathing heavily.

'It saw Castle Garamont. It saw our father.'

Dawning comprehension fell over Anara's face.

Reolus helped Calard to his feet, his face cold and
stern, lit with the same impassioned light that had
infected his sister.

'What does it mean?' he asked at last, looking
towards Anara. He had never felt so distant from her
than at that moment, even in all the years they had
spent apart. She seemed like someone he didn't know
at all, and she looked at him as if he was a stranger.

'I know what it is,' she said at last, 'and I know where
it has gone.'

CHLOD PULLED HIS eye away from the tear he had cut in
the fabric, and backed away from the tent. He limped
heavily through the camp, wincing at the wounds he
had suffered. In truth, he had been amazed that he

had survived. Only a handful of the pilgrims had, and he had been one of the lucky few.

He had shaved the top of his head, and had strapped a battered breastplate awkwardly to his chest. A sword, its blade broken halfway along its length, hung from his belt, alongside various artefacts of holy significance that he had stripped from the dead bodies of other pilgrims. He looked every inch the weary battle pilgrim, and he was confident that his disguise would keep him from a hanging.

He limped back to the fire of the pilgrims, and they clustered around him. A sausage was pushed into his hands, and he ate it greedily, fat dripping down his chin as the pilgrims waited on his word with bated breath. It had been easy to dominate the remaining pilgrims, and he had appointed himself their abbot. As such, he had the pick of the food they scrounged, and the least louse infested blanket to sleep beneath. He could get used to this life, he thought.

'Do you know where we go?' asked one of the devout peasants, who sported a livid, open wound upon his face. Already it was infected, and flies clustered around the cut.

'Our glorified benefactor is preparing for a journey!' announced Chlod between mouthfuls of sausage. 'And so, we must journey with him!'

ANARA WAS SPEAKING in an alien tongue, her voice soft and lilting. The sound was musical and enchanting, and it made the hair on the back of his neck stand erect. He had never heard such beautiful sounds, though something in them was vaguely unsettling, even frightening. Unbidden, the memory of a childhood rhyme said to ward off the fey spirits of the woods leapt into his mind.

His steed whinnied, and he stroked its nose to comfort it. It was a good horse, a big chestnut with a brave heart, but it was not Gringolet. At Anara's insistence, the eyes of each of the horses had been covered with cloth.

Only twenty-five knights had been chosen, though Calard still did not understand the nature of the journey. Surely they had no time for this ritual, whatever it was. The beast was the better part of a week ahead of them, and he had no idea how they were to find it, or catch up to it. It was all too confusing. He didn't understand what was occurring around him, and it made his anger rise to be kept in the dark so.

He had been surprised and honoured when he had been picked to accompany Reolus and the others, though he knew not why he had been chosen.

'It is only right. All will be made clear,' Anara had said, mysteriously. He found such vague statements infuriating, but he had not argued. He had, however, expressed his displeasure when Maloric had also been singled out to accompany them, but his words had been for nought. Reolus had chosen the young Sangasse noble, seeing in him someone destined for greatness, he claimed, though Calard found that hard to believe. Maloric had tricked him somehow, he was certain, though how he had done it was beyond him.

He wished that his brother could have joined them, but his injuries were such that it was impossible. He felt deep unease at the prospect of riding to battle without Gunthar, Bertelis or Gringolet. His brother would remain with the rest of the knights and Baron Montcadas. He prayed that he would see them again.

His sister lifted a silk kerchief before her, and delicately unwrapped it to reveal an oak leaf that gleamed of gold. She continued to speak in the beautiful, fey language and the leaf began to shine with a golden inner light.

Mist began to rise from the still pond they were arrayed before, as if summoned by Anara's lilting voice. It flowed across the top of the mirror-like pool and coiled around his legs. It billowed upwards, and, with a gasp, Calard saw a ghostly form take shape within the mist. It glided forwards like a spirit, its body transparent, and he saw that it was a woman of incredible, haunting beauty.

'The Lady,' Calard breathed in awe. Her hair flowed around her as if she was underwater, and her billowing dress rippled like the surface of a lake. Her arms were held out to either side, and she glided through the mist like an apparition. She seemed to glow from within, and yet Calard could see the trees on the far side of the sacred pool through her body.

Her lips moved, but Calard heard no sound. Anara answered her, still speaking in that otherworldly tongue, and the ethereal, graceful Lady gestured with one elegant, slender limb. She inclined her head to Reolus, who bowed deeply, and then her almond shaped eyes roved over the gathered knights. Calard felt his mouth dry up as he felt the power of those eyes turn towards him. He lowered his gaze, toying with the reins in his hands, unable to meet her stare.

After what felt like an age he felt her attention shift away from him, and he sagged, feeling drained.

Billowing mist surrounded the legs of his warhorse, as if stirred by a growing wind, though no breeze penetrated the sacred copse. He lifted his eyes once more, gazing around in wonder. Glowing orbs of light circled through the mist, like will-o-the-wisps from children's tales, and he realised that the trees around him were fading. He thought he heard high-pitched giggles from the glowing spheres of light as they swooped around his head, and he tried to focus on them, to see past their blinding light. He felt his cloak and hair being tugged as if by tiny, mischievous hands, and he almost laughed out loud in wonder.

The mist began to swirl around the clearing with more vigour, centred on the heavenly vision of womanhood, and Calard's mouth hung slack in wonder.

He heard haunting music, and a thousand achingly beautiful voices lifted in whispered song all around. Tears ran down his cheeks. In wonder he glanced towards Reolus. He realised, strangely with no sense of alarm, that he could see *through* the grail knight, as if his body was as ethereal as the mist billowing around them.

Anara too seemed as insubstantial as smoke, and, with a shock, Calard lifted his hands before his face to see that they too were transparent and ghostly, like smoke that could be carried away on the wind. His heart beat fiercely in his chest, and he found it suddenly hard to breathe. His chestnut destrier too was as insubstantial as a ghost, as were the reins in his hand.

He turned his head to the side, and saw that the other knights too were gazing in fear and wonder at their ethereal limbs, and he saw the dread in Maloric's ghostly eyes.

Montcadas lifted a hand in farewell. He alone amongst the gathered knights was not insubstantial, his body and limbs as solid as ever.

'Be calm,' said Anara's voice, sounding like a distant whisper. 'No harm shall come to you. Step forward into the mist.'

Calard saw that the vision of the Lady was fading, and he cried out to her, not wishing to be parted from her holy presence. A hint of a smile played upon her lips, and she was gone. Calard could see nothing of his surroundings now, the mist having swallowed everything. The other knights were gone, as was Anara, and he was alone, lost adrift in the mists.

'Step forward,' said Anara's whispering voice, apparently from a great distance, and Calard closed his eyes and did as she bid him, leading his chestnut warhorse.

BARON MONTCADAS STOOD motionless, watching until the knights and Anara had faded completely from sight. The ghostly mists dissipated, and he was alone in the sacred copse.

He whispered a final, parting blessing, and walked out into the sunshine. A ragtag group of grail pilgrims was clustered beyond the grail sanctuary, sitting around a small fire over which a scrawny hare was spitted. Barely a dozen of them had survived the battle, and they looked up at him expectantly, their faces brightening. Seeing that he was not their lord Reolus, their shoulders slumped, and they turned back to their fire.

Montcadas began to walk back to the camp, but paused, looking back at the wretched little band of pilgrims. Being of low birth, they would be hanged if they were discovered entering the sacred copse surrounding the grail shrine, and doubtless they would wait out here beyond its edges until Reolus emerged. He smirked, thinking that they would be waiting a long time. How long before they realised that Reolus was not going to return to them? A month? A year? Until death claimed them? That was most likely, he thought. They would wait like loyal, abandoned hounds for the return of their master, who was, even now, hundreds of miles away.

He felt a sudden pang of guilt for them. They had bled to defend Bretonnia from the beasts, just as everyone else had on the field of battle, and he felt he owed them at least the knowledge that their master was gone.

Turning around, Montcadas strode towards the pitiful group. They saw him coming and jumped to their feet, lowering their eyes and wringing their hands nervously. Nobles spoke to them infrequently, and when they did it was usually to drive them away or curse them.

Montcadas cleared his throat.

'Lord Reolus has gone,' he said. 'It is pointless for you to wait for him. He will not come back this way.'

The pilgrims traded glances, confused by his words. Montcadas nodded his head, his guilt assuaged, and turned to leave.

'My… my lord?' stammered one of the pilgrims, and the baron turned back towards them, eyebrows raised in question. The one who had spoken was a hunchbacked wretch with an uneven face. The man bowed several times, and a rat poked its head out briefly from his tunic. The pilgrim bit his thick lip, but did not speak further.

'What is it? Speak, man,' said Montcadas impatiently.

'We… we are his pilgrims, my lord, and we must follow in his footsteps wherever he leads us.'

'And?'

'We… we saw him go into the trees, my lord. He has not come out.' The man was picking his words carefully, trying not to sound antagonistic. 'Is he not, therefore, still inside?'

'I said that he has gone, and so he has. He is gone.' Montcadas turned away and began to walk away from the pilgrims, tiring of the discussion.

'Please, my lord!' cried the hunchbacked pilgrim, limping after him. 'Where has he gone?'

Montcadas gave a long sigh and paused.

'To Bastonne,' he said over his shoulder, and marched away.

IT SEEMED LIKE an age had passed before the mists began to clear and Calard began to make out shapes around him once more. Shadows of trees loomed over him, and he saw the stars overhead, glinting in between boughs and leaves. He recognised these woods, and his brow creased in confusion.

Like ghosts appearing out of the mist, he saw the others walking alongside him, each one leading his horse, and Anara, walking out in front, leading her snow-white mare. A chill wind rustled the leaves overhead, and the mists lifted away, dissipating as if they had never been. Calarc saw that his limbs were solid once more, and let out a breath of amazement.

It was night, and Mannslieb was a glowing disc of light high in the heavens overhead, though it had been the break of dawn but moments before. Anara removed the scarf covering her mare's eyes, and the other knights did likewise. In silence, they followed the damsel through the woods, gazing around in wondering incomprehension. Finally, they came to its edge, and again Calard's jaw dropped.

In the distance, out across the rolling, dark fields was his home, Castle Garamont. It was on fire.

CHAPTER NINETEEN

A MILLION QUESTIONS raced through Calard's mind as
they galloped through the darkness towards the castle.
How had they travelled so far in so short a time? Why
was Castle Garamont besieged? And by what manner
of foe? Was his father well?

He yearned to ask these questions, but An'ara's face
was cold and focused, and she chanted softly. He
dared not disturb her thoughts, and the faces of the
other knights were grim and serious, focused and set.

As they rode closer, he could hear shouts of men and
bellowing roars that were all too familiar. The beasts
had come to Garamont.

The main keep and two of the towers were ablaze,
fires roaring from windows and lighting up the night
hellishly. They galloped past rundown, peasant hovels,
whose inhabitants were standing out in the night,
wailing and staring at the distant fires in horror.

Anara's voice was getting louder, and he heard a peal of thunder roll across the heavens. Heavy droplets of rain began to fall, just a few at first, and then more, until the skies erupted in a torrential downpour.

The rain made it hard to see, and it seeped inside Calard's armour, soaking the padding beneath and weighing him down, but he pushed aside these minor concerns. On they rode, kicking their tired steeds forward. Desperation and panic was growing within Calard.

As lightning flashed, they saw a flood of black figures racing towards the castle, streaming through the shattered gatehouse into the courtyard beyond, and Calard gave a cry of despair, kicking his steed on with renewed vigour. In that split second of sudden light, he had seen countless hundreds of beastmen spilling from the forest, and racing towards the castle.

They came upon a herd of the beasts, who turned and hurled themselves into their path, and Calard's lance rammed deep into the chest of the first of them, lifting it off the ground. Reolus impaled one beast on his lance and killed another with a sweep of his sword. One knight fell, but the others continued on, smashing aside the enemy and crushing them mercilessly. Anara rode on in their centre, apparently oblivious to the engagement, as she continued to chant and the rain continued to increase in intensity.

Lightning flashed again, and Calard cried out in desperation as he saw the sheer number of the enemy. They were but a handful of knights, and he saw no hope of stemming the tide of beastmen, especially since the castle had already been breached. He rode on, regardless, determined to die defending his home if such was the Lady's will.

They got closer, overtaking scores of beastmen in the race to the castle, and Calard, having discarded his lance, swung a lethal blow into the back of the head of one of the enemy, his strike powered by desperation and rage.

They thundered onto the cobbled road leading into the castle, and two more knights fell, one with a jagged spear jutting from his neck, and another as an axe hammered into his steed's chest. Reolus kicked his massive steed into the lead, and carved a path of destruction through the beasts, hacking left and right.

They pounded across the lowered drawbridge.

The portcullis was a shattered ruin, its black iron lattice wrenched completely out of shape by some colossal force. The heavy wooden doors of Castle Garamont were twisted and contorted completely out of shape, writhing tree limbs and sap dripping roots having sprouted from the ancient planks and torn the gate apart.

They passed scores of bodies, loyal men-at-arms that had died defending the castle. Their bodies had been viciously hacked apart, their limbs thrown haphazardly across the cobbles. Galloping after Reolus, the knights thundered through the gatehouse. A beast hurled itself from an overhead balcony and tackled a knight from the saddle. The man was instantly swamped with enemies, who hacked at him with axes and swords, rending him limb from limb.

Galloping free of the gatehouse, Calard saw that the courtyard within was teeming with the enemy. They were running riot, smashing, burning and killing. Through the driving rain, he saw men-at-arms upon the battlements fighting hard against the creatures that swarmed up the stone stairways. From atop the towers, bowmen fired into the heaving mass of beasts within the courtyard, but it was like spitting into the wind. Flames licked up at another of the towers, and he saw men jump from its top, hurtling down to smash amongst the carnage below rather than be burnt alive.

There, standing among the carnage, was the beast, the Gave, revelling in the destruction being wrought. It snarled, and directed its minions towards the knights with sharp sweeps of its staff. Then it barked, animal-istic commands as it stalked up the steps towards the keep. Calard raked his spurs into the flanks of his warhorse, urging it towards the creature.

At his side, Anara released her grip on the neck of her snow-white mare and spread her arms out to either side, palms open to the heavens. She lifted her head high and cried out in a lilting tongue that Calard did not under-stand, and he felt the hairs on his arms stand up.

The dark clouds overhead boomed ominously, and then, with a barked command of power, lightning flashed down from the dark sky, stabbing into the densely packed enemy ranks like a jagged blade.

Dozens of creatures were consumed as the powerful energy coursed down from the heavens to strike raised weapons and helmets. Arcs of energy coalesced over their bodies, jumping eagerly between the beasts, con-suming scores of them instantly. They jerked spasmodically as their flesh was cooked and their blood boiled, sparks and branches of white-hot power flashing back and forth over their forms.

Another, more powerful spear of light arced down from the heavens and struck the ground in the centre of the courtyard, and the accompanying boom was deafening. Scores of beasts were slain instantly, their flesh charred and blackened, and all those within twenty yards were hurled from their feet, their fur and skin singed.

Calard struggled to remain in the saddle, clinging frantically to his steed's neck as it reared in terror. Several knights were thrown, hitting the ground hard as they fell. Calard wrenched on the reins, dragging the destrier back under control, and kicked it towards the shattered great doors leading into the keep, galloping over the burning and smoking corpses of those killed by the lightning strike.

An acrid metallic stink rose in the wake of the crackling discharge, mingling with the repulsive smell of burnt hair and flesh.

Calard slashed his sword into the charred head of an enemy as it struggled to rise, and pounded across the smoking courtyard. Other beasts were knocked aside by his warhorse's bulk, limbs broken beneath its hooves. Reolus hacked down more of the creatures, and galloped at his side, as did Maloric and Anara, and the last knights remaining in the saddle.

They rode up the great stone steps leading to the keep. The creature leading the beastmen was pushing itself to its feet, one side of its body charred and smoking, its skin blistering and blackened from the lightning strike.

Then Calard and his companions were past the creature, riding through the arched entrance, into the keep, the hooves of their steeds slipping on the smooth flagstones, echoing sharply.

The beautifully carved, heavy doors to the keep had been smashed down, and shouts and screams came from within.

The great entrance hall was wide, its walls lined with archaic suits of armour. The enemy was thick here, flooding the hall, intent on destruction and slaughter. Flames were consuming the ancient tapestries hanging on the walls. Priceless depictions of Gilles le Breton's famous twelve battles, which had taken a generation to weave, were destroyed in moments. The heat inside the keep was almost unbearable. A huge chandelier covered in candles dropped from the high ceiling, the chain clattering loudly as it ran out. It slammed into the floor with a resounding clatter, crushing a pair of beasts beneath it.

Clangs rang out as old suits of armour worn by past lords of Garamont were kicked from their pedestals, and Calard saw a servant dragged from a side door and butchered. Another man was slammed head first into a wall, his skull cracking under the impact. Sounds of fighting echoed up from stone side passages, and he could hear men and women screaming as the beasts ran rampant through the keep. The bodies of men-at-arms and knights littered the flagstones.

The knights rode up the hallway, driving the enemy out of their path, cutting them down with sword and lance. At the far end of the wide corridor, the doors to the audience hall were being forced open, the beast-men heaving a crude battering ram with all their brutish muscle against it.

'For Garamont and the king!' roared Calard.

CASTELLAN LUTHEURE OF Garamont sat tall upon his high-backed throne, the unsheathed sword of his family across his knees. His right hand was clasped weakly around the pommel of the revered weapon, while his left hand held the cold blade itself. His eyes were locked on the double doors that were the main entrance to his audience chamber.

Thick beams of wood had been hefted into position to brace the heavy doors, but they were bulging in with every shuddering impact. The battering ram slammed into the doors again and again, and timbers groaned in protest.

To Lutheure, the sound was a death knell. It may as well have been Morr knocking at his chamber door, coming at last to claim him.

A handful of loyal knights stood fanned out at the bottom of the dais on which Lutheure sat, swords in their hands, ready to step into the breach as soon as the doors were smashed asunder. It would not be long.

The side doors were similarly barred, and there was crashing against them also, though Lutheure was certain that the main doors would be broken down before they were breached.

Dozens of elderly courtiers, advisors, servants and ladies were clustered at the back of the chamber. Some of them were crying softly, while others were praying to the Lady for deliverance. They jerked violently with every crash of the battering ram. Several of them awkwardly held weapons in hands more suited to quills or refined crystal glasses.

Lady Calisse sat at the castellan's side. Her face was pale and drawn, though she showed no fear, and her head was held high and proud. Lady Elisabet of Carlemont, hovered nearby, visibly shaking, her large, doe eyes wide and tearful.

'Please, my lord,' begged Garamont's aged chamberlain, Folcard. 'The passage is hidden, and the beasts will never find it. The tunnel leads deep into the bedrock. You will be safe there until the siege is lifted.'

Lutheure turned his rheumy gaze towards the fierce old chamberlain.

'One of these days you will need to show me all the hidden passages that riddle this place,' he wheezed.

'On my word, my lord, but to see that day, you must come, now!'

'I will not,' said Lutheure softly.

'My lord, you must!'

'I will not hide from my enemies like a frightened peasant,' said the castellan forcefully. 'This is my ancestral home. I shall not be driven from it, and if the Lady decrees that my time in the world is past, then I shall die defending it to the last.'

'Then I shall stand alongside you, my lord,' said the castellan.

'Don't be a fool, man,' said Lutheure. 'You have not held a sword in your life. Go.'

'I will not,' said Folcard, his fierce eyes blazing.

Lutheure chuckled, though it descended into a painful, racking cough. He lifted a goblet from the small table at his side and took a sip of his pungent remedy. It was truly foul, and, though his health had steadily declined in the last months despite his physician's ministrations, he had continued to drink the brew rather than face his wife's wrath.

'We are as stubborn as each other,' he said when he had recovered, wiping flecks of blood from his pale lips. 'A pair of stubborn old fools.'

'Indeed so, my lord.'

Lutheure turned his gaze towards his wife, but she spoke before he could utter a word.

'My place is with you,' she said, her eyes brooking no argument. 'I am not leaving your side.'

He had never won an argument with her in his life, and he knew that he was not going to start now. Resigned, he turned back towards his chamberlain.

'Get the others out,' he said.

The chamberlain bowed low, and moved towards the rear wall. He moved with the jerky stiffness of a hunting crane. He pressed his thumb against a small innocuous stone on the wall, and it sank inwards with an audible click. Moving to another place on the wall, he pushed and there was another click, followed by the grating sound of stone on stone. A panel slid aside, revealing a dark hole. A man would have to crawl on his hands and knees to enter the hidden passage. Beckoning swiftly, the chamberlain urged the first of the courtiers to enter.

'Crawl through,' he said. 'You can stand after ten paces. Just keep following the passage. Feel your way forwards. Hurry now!'

'You too,' said Lutheure to Elisabet. Tears ran down her heart-shaped face, and she nodded numbly.

With a tremendous sound of cracking timbers, the beams barring the doors gave way, and the enemy surged in.

With shouts, the knights defending the chamber leapt forwards, killing the first of the beasts that tumbled inside.

'And so the end is here,' said Lutheure.

ELISABET WAS DUCKING down, gathering her long dress in her hand as she prepared to crawl into the hidden passage. The darkness within was complete, utterly swallowing those that had already crawled within. She was the last person to enter, and the portal would be sealed behind her. The thought was terrifying.

'Hurry, girl,' barked the chamberlain.

Steeling herself, biting her lip, Elisabet began to crawl into the darkness. The slipper of the person in front of her kicked her in the face, and she cried out, the sound echoing loudly. She could hear others further along weeping as they crawled into darkness, and some wailed in fear.

'For Garamont and the king!' came a shout from the hallway, and she stopped short.

'Calard!' she called, her voice echoing sharply around the enclosed space, and she began to push herself back the way she had came. Despite the chamberlain's protests, she squirmed backwards, back out into the audience chamber.

'Calard!' she called again as she pushed herself to her feet, oblivious to the dust and muck that coated her knees and hands. With a curse, the chamberlain tripped a switch and the hidden passageway was sealed shut.

REOLUS LED THE charge, his flashing blade, Durendyal, striking down into the back of a beast's skull, smashing it into bloody shards. The remaining knights thundered into the audience chamber.

Calard took in the scene in an instant. He saw half a dozen knights in front of him, fighting back the dark beasts of the forest, their swords bloodied. He felt a stab of outrage as he saw a wasted, skeletally thin old man sitting in his father's throne, and it took a moment for him to realise, with a shock, that it *was* his father.

Calard was filled with sudden grief. His father's muscle was all but wasted away and his skin was a sickly grey. His eyes were almost completely lost in the deep recesses of their sockets, and he was dressed in robes. He clearly did not have the strength to wear his armour, even if it had fitted his gaunt frame. That must have hurt his pride immensely, and Calard's heart was filled with sorrow.

The Lady Calisse sat at his father's side, and the vulture-like figure of Chamberlain Folcard stood behind them.

'Calard!' someone cried out, and he saw Elisabet, her face streaked with tears. He swore. What was she doing here? Still, the hope and love he saw in her eyes filled him with grim determination.

With sudden vigour, he drove the point of his sword into the unprotected back of a beastman that had just felled one of the knights. The thrust skewered the creature between the shoulder blades, and it gave out a sickeningly human squeal of pain as it dropped.

'Seal the doors!' ordered Reolus, sliding from his saddle, kicking out and sending a beastman that rushed at him sprawling as he did so. More of the braying monsters were stampeding up the corridor towards the chamber, and Calard pulled his steed around sharply before dropping from the saddle. A spear was thrust towards him, but he had no time to raise his defences. A blade knocked the blow aside, and the creature's jugular was neatly sliced open. It fell, blood bubbling from the wound. Calard's thanks died in his throat as he saw who had saved him.

'No thanks necessary,' said Maloric when it was clear that Calard was not going to offer any.

Several knights grabbed the reins of the horses and dragged them away from the main floor of the audience chamber.

Reolus stood alone in the open doorway, holding the flood of the enemy back with his flashing blade. The grail knight parried blows with consummate ease, sending flashing ripostes that killed quicker than the eye could follow. Behind the surging enemy, the Gave was stalking up the corridor, eyes ablaze with fury.

Maloric and Calard ran to the doors.

'Now!' shouted Reolus, sensing a lull in the attack. He stepped swiftly back into the audience chamber, and the two knights errant slammed the doors closed.

The thick timbers that had barred them shut were splintered and useless, and Calard frantically looked around for something, anything, that could be used to barricade the entrance. He leant his weight against them as the enemy hurled themselves against the doors from the other side, and his armoured feet began to slide across the blood-slicked flagstones.

'Help us!' he cried, and more knights ran forwards to lend their weight. Others ripped long pikes and halberds from the walls of the hall and inserted them into the heavy iron brackets to bar the doors shut, but they seemed pitifully fragile against the force battering from the outside. There was a tremendous crash, and the knights were hurled backwards a step. The beasts had clearly resumed their former tactic, and were once again using their battering ram.

'Step back, and make ready,' said Reolus, his voice calm and authoritative. 'The Lady is with us.'

As if his words were a charm, the hammering at the door ceased abruptly, and the knights looked at each

other in confusion. They backed away, hands clenching around the hilts of their weapons. The tension in
the room was thick, and Calard took the moment of
respite to wipe the sweat from his forehead. The sudden silence was eerie, and he fully expected the doors
to explode inwards at any moment.

He risked a glance up at the dais, and his eyes met
Elisabet's.

'I love you,' mouthed Elisabet to him.

His eyes shifted to his father, whose uncompromis-
ing visage frowned down at Anara, who was walking
slowly up the stairs towards him. With great effort, the
castellan pushed himself up from his throne, using the
blade of Garamont like a crutch.

THE DAMSEL ANARA climbed the stairs to stand before
the castellan. He looked like an animated skeleton, his
robes hanging loosely on his emaciated body, and
every contour of his skull pushing against his skin. She
felt rather than saw Calard following in her wake.

'Who is this?' asked the Lady Calisse as she stood up
from her throne, sensing that something was taking
place that she did not understand.

The damsel glanced in her direction, and the lady sat
back down abruptly.

'The lady Anara,' said chamberlain Folcard, with not
a little disdain in his voice.

'Your… your daughter?' asked Calisse.

'I have no daughter,' rasped Castellan Lutheure.

Anara regarded them coldly, no flicker of emotion
showing on her face. She had severed her connection
with her blood family long ago. Such was the way of
the damsels of the Lady.

Lutheure swayed suddenly, and one of his legs buckled beneath him. The sword of Garamont clattered as it struck the floor, and both the chamberlain and the Lady Calisse jerked into motion to catch the lord of Garamont, though both were too slow.

Anara stepped forward quickly and caught the castellan before he could fall. Though he towered over her, he was frail and she supported him easily in her arms.

Up close, his face a hair's breadth from her own, she could see how sallow and transparent his skin was. She saw the burst blood vessels splashed across his nose and cheeks, and the dark liver spots that marked his flesh. She looked into his yellowed eyes and saw how close he was to death.

There was something else in his face, too, some taint. There was a black sickness within him, eating away at him, that no physician would have recognised. Only one such as she would have been able to perceive it for what it truly was, for it was necrotic in nature, based on the foul tenets of those schooled in the black arts.

Even as she came to this conclusion, her eyes snapped towards the small table at the castellan's side, locking on the goblet upon its smooth surface. Lutheure was gently lowered back into his throne by his wife and chamberlain, while the Lady Elisabet hovered nervously nearby. Anara lifted the goblet to her nose, sniffing. She recoiled from the noxious, underlying taint within the liquid and cast the goblet away from her. It clattered to the floor, spilling its vile contents upon the stone.

'Who gave him that?' she asked. No one was paying her any mind, intent on the wellbeing of the castellan.

'What's going on?' asked Calard, coming up behind her. The unearthly silence beyond the doors to the audience chamber still held, as if the enemy had suddenly dissipated into thin air. Anara knew better. She could feel the foul presence of the Gave beyond the portals, gathering its strength.

'Who gave him that brew?' she asked again, this time imparting a fraction of her power into the words.

Lady Calisse stuttered as she was compelled to answer.

'It is… it is my husband's remedy,' she said, 'for his illness. His physician–'

'It is poison,' said Anara acidly.

Stunned silence greeted her proclamation. Elisabet paled. The chamberlain's face lit up in alarm. She saw Calard's eyes go cold, boring into the Lady Calisse.

'You bitch,' he said, staring venomously at his stepmother. She looked back at him without comprehension. 'Attempts on my life… Poisoning my father… And for what? So that Bertelis would become the ruler of Garamont?'

Calisse's mouth opened and closed soundlessly, and Anara probed into her mind with the powers vested in her by the Lady of the Lake, skimming her thoughts for any sign of guilt.

'I should cut you down here and now, you murderous viper!' said Calard. Covered in blood and with his sword in his hand, his eyes blazing with fury, he stepped towards the lady of Garamont. She cowered before him.

'No,' said Anara, 'it was not her.'

* * *

THE WORDS CUT through Calard's rage, and he stared down at his twin in confusion. What was she saying? It all made sense!

He looked back at his step-mother. She stared at him with murderous eyes.

Surely she was behind it all?

Wasn't she?

'Who, then?' he asked. He wanted to strike out at someone, anyone, and desperately wanted a target for his wrath. 'Who has been poisoning my father?' he asked again, more forcefully.

Anara's eyes misted over, and then settled on Elisabet. Calard's heart skipped a beat.

'No,' he whispered.

Elisabet came to Calard's side, pale and drawn, and clung to him like a child.

'Why is she looking at me like that, my love?' she asked, her voice scared.

Calard was shaking his head.

'Her,' said Anara, staring accusingly at Elisabet.

This was insane! Why in the Lady's name would his love wish to kill his father? No, Anara was wrong.

'You are mistaken, sister,' said Calard desperately.

'I am not,' she replied, her eyes glinting feyly. 'Ask her, if you wish.'

Elisabet was crying, tears running down her face, and she clung tightly to Calard, uncaring of the blood and gore splattered over his breastplate and arms.

'You cannot believe her!' Elisabet said frantically, her eyes wild. She stared up at him with imploring, desperate eyes. Her expression would haunt him forever. 'You cannot believe her!'

Calard looked deep into the eyes of the woman he loved, and saw the ugly truth that lay behind her beauty.

'Why?' he whispered in horror.

'You cannot believe her!' Elisabet cried again, but Calard stumbled away from her, tears welling in his eyes.

'Why?' he asked again.

'I did it for us!' wailed Elisabet finally, moving into him, tears running down her face. He backed further away, as if she were a plague victim, though it broke his heart to see the hurt in her eyes.

'She would have seen you disowned,' cried Elisabet, pointing an accusing finger at Lady Calisse. The smell of her perfume was intoxicating, confusing, and he stepped further away from her. 'She would have convinced your father to disown you. You know I speak the truth! He has eyes only for Bertelis! You would have been left a pauper, with nothing! *We* would have been left with nothing!'

Calard shook his head in horror at what he was hearing.

'It was for *us*,' implored Elisabet.

Calard stumbled away blindly, tears running freely down his cheeks.

'Calard,' wailed Elisabet. She went to follow him, but Folcard grabbed her by the arm.

'Haven't you done enough, girl!' the fierce chamberlain hissed.

'Calard!' she cried. 'I love you! Calard! Please forgive me. I did only what I thought best for us, for our future together! Calard!'

His world collapsing around him, Calard stumbled down to the bottom of the dais stairs and fell to his

knees, his sword dropping from his limp grasp. He
ripped the silk token of Elisabet's affection from his
arm and let it fall to the floor. He dimly heard a hard
slap, and the Lady Calisse screeching like a wildcat as
she threw herself at Elisabet.

'Stop it!' he heard Anara snap, her voice tinged with
power. 'The beast comes.'

THERE WAS STILL no sound from the hallway beyond
the double doors, but as Anara spoke they heard a new
noise. It was a groaning, creaking sigh, like a house settling in the cool of evening, or the sound a ship made
as it rolled from side to side in a heavy swell. The hairs
on Calard's body stood up, as if the air was charged
with static, and he felt an acid tingle on his tongue.

'The door,' muttered Maloric, and Calard looked up
through his grief.

The grand wooden doors were swelling and bulging
with sudden, unnatural growth. Woody tendrils were
sprouting from their surfaces, waving like blind tentacles. Thorns weeping sap pushed out, and the knots on
the surface of the doors began to seep with more of the
sticky fluid, running like blood down to the floor.

Branches burst from the wood as if it was gifted with
sudden, corrupt life. They coiled upwards, straining
against the lintel and cracking stone. Black, foul-
smelling buds unfurled, releasing bloated flies that
launched into the air. Leaves the colour of rotting vegetation sprouted, only to waste away and fall to the
floor an instant after their had appeared. Roots
erupted from the base of the doors, creeping out across
the stone slabs of the floor, probing between cracks
and digging deep into the mortar. Burrowing beneath

the stonework, they began to push the flagstones up, and spreading cracks ran out in all directions, like a spider's web.

With a tearing sound, the doors were pulled apart by the sudden growth, and there stood the Gave, eyes alight with foetid magic. The doors were wrenched further apart, and a tide of Chaotic beastmen swarmed into the audience chamber around their master.

Knights leapt forwards to meet them head-on, and Calard saw Maloric and Reolus rush into battle, their blades singing through the air. The irony of a noble of Sangasse fighting to save the lord of Garamont was not lost on Calard.

Finally facing an enemy upon which he could unleash his fury and grief, Calard swept up his dropped sword and entered the frantic combat.

He roared wordlessly as he swung the blade, all thought of protecting himself swept aside as he let his rage overcome him. He fought like one of the berserk warriors of the icy north, venting his anger in the flesh of the enemy. He hacked the arm from the first beastman that he met, shrugging off the hammer blow he received in the chest, and smashed his blade into the beast's head, cleaving through one of its horns and smashing its skull.

Calard allowed a red mist to descend over his vision, and he slashed around in his frenzy, caring not at all for his own safety. He threw himself deeper into the fray, and blows rained down upon him, but still he killed, his armour suffering the brunt of the attacks directed towards him.

'Protect the lord Garamont! Fall back!' someone cried, and Calard came to his senses. His father was still alive, and he had a duty to perform in protecting him. Throwing his life away meaninglessly would be a dishonour to his lord, and he was suddenly determined to make his father proud, at last, to protect him with his dying breath.

A meaty fist slammed into his temple, and he was sent sprawling to the ground.

Dazed, he dimly registered the towering Gave as it strode through the melee, its backwards-jointed legs giving it an awkward gait. It smashed a pair of knights aside with a sweep of its staff, and stabbed its sacrificial dagger into the throat of another. Calard cried out as it took its first step up the dais towards Lutheure.

Reolus was advancing into the roiling midst of the enemy, fighting his way to the doorway once more in an attempt to stem the flow of beastmen, while the other knights fell back to protect the castellan. The Grail knight moved with subtle grace and economy of movement, expending no more energy than was required to kill. He had retrieved a fallen sword from the floor, and was fighting with two blades, spinning them around in deadly arcs.

Calard pushed to his feet, dazed and moved towards the towering creature. A beastman threw itself into his path, its face a snarling blend of goat and man, and Calard tried to kill it quickly. His blade flashed for its neck, but it swayed back from the blow and hacked out with its axe. The blow glanced off his shield, knocking him back a step, agonisingly further away from the beast stalking up the dais steps.

A pair of loyal knights defending his father stepped forwards to slow the towering beast. It ignored them, feral eyes locked on the lord of Garamont, who was staring at it with eyes filled with horror and loathing. He had pushed himself to his feet once more, supported by his chamberlain, and once more held the blade of Garamont in his hands, its tip shaky and unsteady. His wife was cowering behind the thrones where the chamberlain had thrust her.

The two knights came at the beast simultaneously. With inhuman speed, it stepped into the attack of the knight on its right, releasing its grip on its staff, which remained upright, rooted upon the steps.

With its free hand, it caught the descending sword-arm of the knight at the wrist, wrenching the metal out of shape and pulling him violently off balance. The sacrificial knife stabbed into the knight's neck as the beast spun, punching through metal and chain, and blood gushed from the wound. Still turning, the beast slammed the knight into its other attacker, sending them sprawling down the steps.

Calard barely avoided another brutal attack from the beastman he was engaged with. The beast had put too much strength behind the blow and stumbled off balance. Calard killed it with a thrust.

Anara was still standing alongside the castellan, looking tiny and insignificant as she faced down the beast looming before her. She was muttering an incantation softly under her breath, and the creature snarled at her, baring its teeth. Then it roared, the power and fury in the deafening cry making Anara recoil back a step. It threw its arm up towards her, its long fingers splayed out.

The air blurred before its outstretched hand, like a heat haze against the horizon on a hot day, and Anara was sent tumbling backwards, as if struck by a heavy blow. She struck her head against the heavy armrest of her father's throne and fell unconscious to the floor.

Another desperate knight ran at the towering Gave, his sword held in a two-handed grip. The beast swung its staff up, and thrust it into the charging warrior. It struck the knight in the chest and root tendrils writhed over his body. His boots slipped on the smooth flagstones, and he fell heavily down the steps, the staff attached like a leech to his body. The roots of the twisted stave wriggled madly as they burrowed between gaps in the knight's armour, pushing through chain links and digging deep into muscle and flesh.

The knight screamed, his body withering as the hateful staff sucked the life from him. Dark veins pulsed as the knight's blood was drawn from his body.

It was all happening too fast. Calard surged up the stairs towards the beast, screaming in hatred and loathing. It swung towards him with inhuman speed, and backhanded him across the side of the head, sending him crashing to the bottom of the dais.

A sword sliced across its back, scoring a bloody wound. It bellowed in pain and anger, and lashed out blindly. The sacrificial dagger plunged into its attacker's helmet, sinking six inches of metal into the man's brain.

Maloric, his noble face twisted in disgust, came at the beast from the side, but it kicked one of its hooves hard into his midsection, denting the Sangasse noble's breastplate and sending him reeling, gasping for air.

A sword flashed towards the beast, and it stepped backwards quickly, its hand flashing down to grip the weapon as it lanced towards its heart. Blood welled beneath its long, spider-leg fingers as it turned the blade away, and the knight, off balance, stumbled towards it.

Releasing the sword, the beast wrapped its hands around the knight's helmet and twisted. A sickening crack sounded, and the warrior fell to the ground, his head almost completely turned around.

Nobody now stood between the Gave and the castellan.

Calard rose to his knee, his vision blurred, and staggered back up the dais stairs.

ELISABET SHOOK FREE of the chamberlain's weakening grasp and staggered backwards, half-blinded by tears. She felt cold stone behind her. There was nowhere to run.

Tears continued to run down her face, and she sobbed in terror and shame. The look of horror and revulsion that Calard had given her was imprinted in her mind. She hated herself for what she had done, but why didn't he understand that she had done it for them?

It had been an easy thing. She had given the servant, Annabelle, to the Garamont household, and the peasant girl had quickly become an integral part of the daily routine in the castle. It had taken her months to build up the courage to seek out the crone, but at last she had done so, and it was from her that she had obtained the poison.

'It is a slow acting substance,' the crone had told her. 'It will cause a death that will not arouse suspicion.'

How wrong she had been.

Annabelle had added the poison to the castellan's remedy each day, though of course the girl knew not what she did. She was paid handsomely to keep her activities secretive, and not to ask questions.

The full understanding of what she had done weighed down upon Elisabet. Though the shame and doubt had plagued her, she had overcome them, focusing only on the future that she would have with Calard. She would learn to live with the guilt. So long as they were together and happy then everything she had been forced to do, however distasteful, would have been forgotten in time.

She loved him so very much.

Barely knowing what she was doing, she fumbled against the back wall, feeling around the place where she had seen the chamberlain press. At last one of the stones clicked inwards. She quickly located the other switch, and the gaping black hole was again revealed.

What cursed twist of fate had caused Calard's twin to appear and shatter all her hopes and dreams? And why could Calard not see that everything that she had done had been for *him*?

Crying for all that could have been, and all that was now lost to her, Elisabet ducked into the crawl space, wriggling into the darkness.

Damn them all, she thought, sobbing tears of anger, bitterness and grief.

GARAMONT'S AGED CHAMBERLAIN stepped in front of his lord, his hawk-like profile defiant and completely lacking fear. He stood, unarmed, before the beast. It was half-crouching, moving like a stalking wolf, but still it towered over the man.

'Move to your right, my lord,' said the chamberlain, not taking his eyes off the creature. Lutheure, his body withered and hunched, shuffled to the right as instructed. Wise to their thinking, the beast stalked sideways, cutting off any route of escape.

'A step more,' hissed the chamberlain, and again the beast matched their movement. Its back was now to Calard, as Folcard had no doubt intended, and he stepped as softly as he was able up the steps behind it.

As if suddenly tiring of the game, the beast lurched forwards and grabbed the chamberlain by his shoulder. The elderly man was hurled to the side. He slammed into a pillar, and crumpled in a heap at its base.

Calard leapt up the stairs with a shout, hefting his sword, but the beast was too fast. It stepped forwards, its powerful legs covering the ground quickly, and swatted Lutheure's blade aside with a contemptuous sweep of its hand, the ancient sword of Garamont spinning across the stone floor.

Its hand closed around Lutheure's thin neck, and it lifted him up into the air. Knocking the thrones out of its path, almost crushing the Lady Calisse in the process, it slammed the castellan against the back wall. Calard cried out. The old lord's feet were a good foot off the ground, and he kicked weakly. The Gave bent forward and snarled, its face an inch from the castellan's.

Perhaps hearing or sensing Calard behind it, the beast swung its head around and levelled its dagger towards him, snarling in rage. Still Calard came on, and the beast bent its arm, placing the tip of the dagger against the lord of Garamont's neck. The old lord, his eyes fearful, swallowed thickly, and a bead of blood ran down his throat.

Calard froze, hatred burning within him.

Calard's stepmother was wailing from where she had fallen, tears running down her face.

'My husband!' she cried.

Calard took a cautious step towards the beast. It hissed in warning, pressing the dagger deeper into his father's flesh, and Calard froze. He risked a glance down at Anara, who was stirring at his feet, a purple bruise spreading across her temple.

Maloric, back on his feet, was circling around the flank of the beast, his body low, as if he was stalking game.

'Maloric,' hissed Calard. 'Don't.'

Ignoring him, Maloric stepped lightly up the dais stairs, intent on his prey. The beast hissed at him and pressed the dagger deeper into the castellan's neck. Calard saw blood begin to flow more freely.

'Maloric!' barked Calard. The beast, distracted by the shout, turned its head towards Calard, which was all the opening that Maloric needed.

The Sangasse nobleman leapt forwards, his slim blade stabbing deep into the beast's side. It snarled in anger and pain, and dropped Lutheure. The castellan crumpled to the floor, and Calard cried out, lurching forwards to strike the beast down.

With a downward slap of its open hand, the creature snapped Maloric's blade, leaving the tip protruding from its body. Maloric staggered back, gazing in horror at his shattered weapon.

The Gave tore the blade from its side and sent it hissing through the air. It struck Calard in the shoulder of his sword arm as he lunged forwards, shearing through his armour and sinking deep into his flesh. The force of the throw spun him to the ground, and his sword flew from his hand.

The beast turned back towards Lutheure, who was trying to drag himself away, and it stamped towards him angrily. The Garamont lord cried out weakly as the beast's hand clamped around his leg and jerked him back.

Blood was running from the wound in Calard's shoulder, and his fingers felt numb. He looked around for a weapon and saw the revered sword of Garamont lying discarded on the flagstones nearby. Shaking off his shield, he lifted the exquisite blade from the ground. He held it two-handed, forcing his numb fingers to close around the hilt.

The beast was crouching over his father, revelling in his terror. Reaching behind its heavy head with both hands, one still holding the bloody dagger in its grip, Calard heard leather ties break, and, for a moment, he could not fathom what the wretched creature was doing.

Calard stared in horror as the beast removed its own face.

It clawed at its features, and like a snake shedding its skin, the stitched, rotting flesh was ripped away. Even its horns fell away from its head, and, it was only when they dropped to the floor and he saw the leather ties and buckles, that Calard realised the beast had been wearing a mask.

The creature blinked, and its true features were exposed.

Calard's mind baulked as he found himself looking at a broad, disturbingly human face. It was like the face of a savage, its cheeks and brow heavily scarred from self-inflicted mutilations, and smeared with mud and dried blood, but it was clearly a human face. Somehow that seemed to make it even more horrific. Ice-blue human eyes darted around before fixing once more upon Lutheure.

Thick ropes of matted hair hung down to its waist, and a long goatee beard hung from its chin. If one saw just its face, and not its unnatural bestial legs and furred body, it might have passed for human, albeit one that was feral and barbaric. Its lips drew back, exposing hundreds of small, sharp teeth, and the image was shattered.

'Abomination,' breathed Lutheure in revulsion and horror.

'What is it?' Calard asked no one in particular, his voice thick with disgust.

'Our brother,' replied Anara from the floor, touching a hand gingerly to her bruised temple. Calard felt his sanity begin to fray.

'Borne by our mother before she threw herself to her death in shame,' continued Anara, 'a creature that should have been killed at birth.'

Looking past the filth that encrusted the beast's face, past the savage scars that crisscrossed its features, he saw his own face looking back at him. It was like looking in a bewitched mirror, and seeing a corrupted and distorted vision of himself looking back.

No one moved, stricken with the horror of the creature's true nature. None could dispute the familial resemblance. This beast was of the Garamont bloodline.

'Your line is cursed,' hissed Maloric. Calard wanted to strike Maloric down, but, for all that, he could not argue with his words.

The beast snarled down at Lutheure. Then, with a movement fuelled by hatred, the beast rammed its dagger into the side of Lutheure's neck. Calard screamed, yet was powerless, as the serrated blade sank through his father's flesh to the hilt. The blade was wrenched clear, and it clattered on the stone as it was dropped from long fingers.

Arterial blood pumped from the fatal wound, and Calard roared in protest and horror, running forwards. The beast lifted Lutheure to its chest, cradling the dying man almost like a mother holding a sick child to her bosom. An anguished howl ripped from its throat.

Calard swung the sword of Garamont in a powerful, two-handed arc, blinded by grief and rage. Rather than try to avoid the blow, the creature merely tilted its head back, exposing its neck. In that instant, all the bestial hatred, loathing and rage slipped from its face.

Calard slammed the sword into the Gave's neck, the blade hacking deep into its flesh. Rich blood spurted from the shocking wound, and its head tipped backwards, only loosely attached to its body by tendons and sinews. The beast fell twitching as its blood pooled beneath it, mixing with its father's blood.

Calard dropped to his knees, cradling his father's head in his hands. The life was slipping quickly from his eyes, and his mouth moved as he tried to speak.

'My son,' he gasped, blood gurgling from his neck.

'I am here, father,' Calard said, tears running down his face.

The dying man's eyes searched past Calard frantically. 'Bertelis,' he gurgled, and Calard felt a pain lance his heart as he realised it was not he that his father sought. Even in death, his father spurned him.

A deep wracking sob shook Calard's body. The Lady Calisse wailed as she threw herself over her husband's corpse.

The sounds of battle continued unabated as Reolus continued to hold the enemy at bay, but Calard did not register them.

His eyes were locked on his father's gaunt, dead face.

EPILOGUE

SPLUTTERING TORCHES MADE shadows leap like capering, daemonic figures across the roughly hewn stone walls.

The chamber had been carved from the bedrock beneath Castle Garamont centuries earlier, long before the foundations of the fortress had been laid. In ages past, chieftains of the Bretonni tribe had gathered here for meetings of great import, though this had been long forgotten by all but a handful. For centuries, the meeting place had lain dormant, forgotten and redundant, its very existence known only to the successive chamberlains of the Garamont household, and accessible only by secret passages known to few.

No one had needed to use the chamber for over five generations.

Now, seven hooded figures were gathered here, hugging themselves against the icy chill permeating from the ancient stone surrounding them. The seven sat in rough stone thrones carved into the walls.

'The Garamont line is tainted,' said one of their number, nothing more than his chin visible within the shadow of his hood, 'and one now rules whose blood-line is cursed.'

There were mutterings among the gathered figures.

'Tanebourc failed. The time for subtlety is passed. We must eradicate this stain upon the Garamont name.'

'You would have us act against the lord we have sworn fealty to?' voiced one of the hooded figures, his voice strong: a knight's voice. 'And betray our oaths of allegiance?'

'We swore an oath to protect the line of Garamont!' snapped the first speaker. 'I saw the cursed beast. It was the blood-brother of our newly appointed lord, a thing that should not have been,' he said forcefully. 'Our duty is clear. In the Lady's name, we are duty bound to stamp out this… taint, for the honour of the Garamont bloodline.'

'It should have died at birth,' he added, speaking to himself, remembering. If only Lutheure had finished it, so long ago. Who could have predicted that it would survive? He cursed himself for not seeing the creature dead.

'Then what?' asked another hooded figure. 'Does not our lord Lutheure's youngest son bear the curse in his blood?'

'It was not Lutheure's blood that was tainted,' snapped another. 'His first wife brought this curse upon the Garamont line. Bertelis is not tarred with her… unholiness.'

Several of the hooded figures rose from their seats, their voices angry. Others rose to meet the arguments, and the raised voices echoed maddeningly around the enclosed space.

The first speaker raised his hand for silence. 'Enough!' he barked, his voice authoritative and fierce. The angry din died down, and the hooded figures took their seats.

The first speaker pulled his hood from his face, and glared around, silencing the last of the mutterings.

'This is our duty,' barked Folcard, chamberlain of Garamont. 'As painful as it is, our path is clear. In the name of Garamont and of the Lady, we must cleanse the taint.'

The chamberlain's fierce gaze settled on each of the hooded figures in turn.

'Lord Calard must die.'

ABOUT THE AUTHOR

After finishing university Anthony Reynolds set sail from his homeland and ventured forth to foreign climes. He ended up settling in the UK, and managed to blag his way into Games Workshop's hallowed Design Studio. There he worked for four years as a Games Developer and two years as part of the Management team. He now resides back in his hometown of Sydney, overlooking the beach and enjoying the sun and the surf, though he finds that to capture the true darkness and horror of Warhammer and Warhammer 40,000 he has taken to writing in what could be described as a darkened cave.

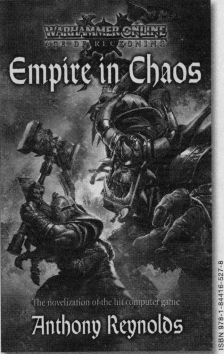